A Y

YOU WILL NEVER FIND ME

YOU WILL NEVER FIND ME

Robert Wilson

First published in Great Britain in 2014 by Orion Books,
an imprint of The Orion Publishing Group Ltd
Orion House, 5 Upper Saint Martin's Lane
London WC2H 9EA

An Hachette UK Company

1 3 5 7 9 10 8 6 4 2

A CIP catalogue record for this book
is available from the British Library.

ISBN (Hardback) 978 1 4091 4315 4
ISBN (Export Trade Paperback) 978 1 4091 4316 1
ISBN (Ebook) 978 1 4091 4317 8

Typeset by Deltatype Ltd, Birkenhead, Merseyside

Printed in Great Britain by Clays Ltd, St Ives plc

The Orion Publishing Group's policy is to use papers that are natural,
renewable and recyclable products and made from wood grown in
sustainable forests. The logging and manufacturing processes are expected
to conform to the environmental regulations of the country of origin.

www.orionbooks.co.uk

For Jane

My only Jane

1955 – 2013

1

Goodbye, room.

Shitty little prison. The only thing missing are the bars on the windows. Been locked in here a few times over the years.

She looked around the four bare walls for the last time. It had been quite an operation to gradually move out all her stuff and dump it. Every day after school, instead of going straight back to her grandmother, Esme, in Hampstead, she'd spent an hour erasing herself from her mother's Streatham home.

As she checked the room she pushed back the half-open wardrobe door to look at herself in the full-length mirror inside. Black quilted coat zipped up, red skirt, black wool tights, black biker boots. She sheafed the great swag of her dark ringlets with blonde highlights in both hands to see how she would look with it all cut off. Her light green eyes stood out from the caramel smoothness of her wide face. Feline. She didn't mind that. She let her hands fall and the hair sprang back over her shoulders. She shrugged, kicked the cupboard door closed. She unzipped her coat, took a letter out addressed to Mercy and Charles, which she tossed onto the bed. She hoisted the rucksack over her shoulder and picked up the last two packed bin liners, went downstairs, put them by the front door.

She looked in on her mother, Detective Inspector Mercy Danquah, as she liked to call her because she knew it both annoyed Mercy and hurt her.

'I'm off out for a bit,' she said. 'I'll see you at the restaurant later – what's it called?'

'Patogh,' said Mercy, looking up from the *Guardian* magazine. 'It's in Crawford Place. You've been there with us before. Best thing to do is walk up the Edgware Road from Marble Arch.'

'Through Little Beirut,' she said, closing the door. 'See ya.'

She picked up the bin liners and walked out of her old life, flicking the front door behind her with her foot so that it slammed shut, rattling the letter-box flap.

She caught a bus down to Streatham High Road, left the bin bags at the clothing bank and walked on to the police station, which was empty. The football was still on and the great British public's evening's drinking hadn't got started. She went up to the overweight desk sergeant with his grey hair and tired eyes – a family man who wasn't with his family, but wanted to be.

'What can I do you for?' he asked, smiling, hands clasped on the counter.

'My name's Amy Boxer and I'm leaving home,' she said, not even giving that old joke so much as a nod.

'I see,' said the sergeant, 'and how old—'

'Eighteen in November,' she said and slapped her driving licence on the counter.

'Got anywhere to go?' he said, taking her seriously now, checking the photo and dates.

'I won't be out on the street, if that's what you mean?' she said. 'I've got money, a bank card, a place to go.'

'You're quick off the blocks,' he said, pushing the licence back to her. 'Trouble at home?'

'You could say that,' she said, as if this was a massive understatement.

She regretted it, hadn't wanted to pique his interest, and now she could see all manner of family uglinesses coming alive in his mind.

'I just need to get away from my mother, that's all,' she said. 'We're not getting on.'

'Embarrassing, ridiculous and annoying?' asked the sergeant.

'That's not a bad summary of one of her good days, but with a little more emphasis on the annoying.'

'And Dad?' he asked, hopefully.

'He's not there. They separated a long time ago.'

2

'Why not go and stay with him?'

This was not how it was supposed to play out. He was embroiling her. She could see his daddiness coming out. Cup of tea? Take a seat. Next thing he'd be walking her back home. Job done.

'Can I trust you?' she asked, and knew she'd hooked him.

'Course you can,' he said. 'That's what I'm here for.'

'My mum's going to call when she finds out I've gone,' she said. 'And when she does I want you to open this letter and read it. But not before. Right? Her name is Mercy Danquah. You'll recognise her.'

'What do you mean, I'll recognise her?'

She didn't answer, but pushed the letter across the counter and left the station.

She caught a bus to Brixton, removed the SIM card from her mobile, which she bent and chucked. She dumped the phone in the gutter and took the Tube to Green Park and then on to Heathrow. By 4.45, she was going up in the lift to the Terminal 1 check-in. She came out onto the concourse, checked that flight BA522 to Madrid was not delayed and went straight to the ladies' toilet in Zone B.

The taxi dropped Mercy off at her home in Streatham at 10.30 p.m. She was a little drunk. She and Charlie had been celebrating the successful conclusion to a kidnap case and had polished off both bottles of red they'd brought with them to the unlicensed Iranian grill.

It was as she was hanging her coat up that she detected a certain quality to the silence in the house. For once the ambient vibe was neutral, rather than pulsing with hostile reflux emanating from the lethal brew of teenage hormones stewing inside her daughter.

She dropped her bag with renewed hopelessness, shook her head. This kid. Probably still out with her friends, having stood them up in the restaurant and failed to respond to any of her calls or texts. She stomped upstairs in a fury and, without knocking, hurled open the bedroom door, slashed on the lights and found the room much emptier than usual, echoingly empty. Mercy frowned. Nothing on the walls. Carpet hoovered. And what's this?

The white envelope on the bare bed. The two names. She picked

3

it up and, even through her drunkenness, felt the little crushes to her heart as she remembered when she'd last been called Mum. Four years ago. She tore open the seal, pinched the bridge of her nose and read the precise, rounded letters of her daughter's handwriting.

Dear Mercy and Charles,

I've had enough of this kind of life. It bores me being a child, your child. I've had it with all the expectations. School makes me sick. Literally. I vomit on arrival every morning. What's the point of it? Do the work. Pass the exams. Go to uni. Copy shit from the Internet for three years. Get a half-arsed degree in window dressing. Come out sixty grand down. Fall into the abyss of unemployment. Fuck all that. I've made my decision. I want to live my life on my own terms, which means, because you're the way you are, I'm leaving home. I will not be in any danger or at least no more than anybody else is. I will not be on the streets. I'm organised. I have money. I'm telling you all this because I don't want you to come looking for me. I don't need to be found. I want to be left alone, something you've been pretty good at most of my childhood, but not good enough. So don't go putting on your cop hats and wasting your time digging away because you'll be doing the wrong thing by me and, what's more, YOU WILL NEVER FIND ME.

Amy

Mercy read it again, went downstairs and sat on the bottom step, staring at the front door, blinking at the tears. She'd lost everything in a single night. Charlie's mind was full of his new girlfriend, the paragon that was Isabel Marks. How pathetic had Mercy been at dinner with him this evening, reaching out across the table to touch his hand, letting him know that she was still there for him if 'the Isabel thing' didn't work. Hoping that 'the Isabel thing' *wouldn't* work. Praying that it was a product of the emotional intensity of the kidnap of Isabel's daughter, which had brought them together, and now that it had been resolved, they'd have no need for each other. But, as they'd taken their separate taxis after the meal, Mercy knew that this was probably the last time they'd be having dinner together for quite some time.

And now this. Her only child walking out on her. No discussion. No question of seeking parental guidance. The Amy-style fait accompli. It took an act of will to drag her handbag to her feet, root around in it for her mobile with fat tears pockmarking the leather. She hit 'Charlie' and hugged the bannister pillar, hoping he would answer.

'Mercy?' he said.

'I ... I got back home ... after dinner. There was a letter on Amy's bed. A letter to us. I can't read it to you now. Just to say she's gone, Charlie. She's left home. The last line says, "You will never find me."'

She heard his phone clatter on the table. A woman's voice. Her. The one. Charlie repeated the line. Silence. Then Charlie again.

'I'll be with you as soon as I can,' he said. 'Report her missing to the local nick. I'm on my way.'

'She says she doesn't want to be found.'

'Just ring the police station. Tell them. It's the procedure. You don't want to be the parent who didn't report their child missing.'

'Right. Of course, you're absolutely right. I'm not thinking straight. Can't quite believe it's happened, even though it's been building for years.'

'Make the call,' he said. 'I'll be with you in half an hour. Call me again if you need to.'

She hung up, couldn't prevent his words from warming a need in her. Every time she'd tried to freeze him out of her life, dropped all feelings for him into some permafrost deep within her, he'd returned to thaw her back into womanhood.

She got a grip. Found the number of the local nick. Called.

'My name is Mercy Danquah, and I want to ... I mean, I have to ... I need to ...'

'Is this to report your daughter missing?' asked the sergeant. 'Amy Boxer?'

Mercy was stunned. Wordless.

'She was in here earlier explaining what she was going to do,' said the sergeant.

'And you didn't *stop* her?' said Mercy, incredulous.

'Well, first she wasn't under age—'

5

'And how did you know that?'

'She produced her driving licence.'

'Her *driving* licence? She doesn't have one.'

'I checked it out. She does.'

'I don't know how she could have—'

'She said I'd recognise you 'n' all,' said the sergeant. 'But I don't know any Mercy Danquahs.'

'What she meant was,' said Mercy, grunting with negative mirth, 'she calls me the cop.'

'Does that mean you're the main authority figure in her life?' said the sergeant. 'She said you were separated from your husband.'

'It means I'm a police officer,' said Mercy. 'I'm a detective inspector with the Specialist Crime Directorate 7 – the kidnap unit. And she believes I bring all the authority I've learned in my job into our mother–daughter relationship.'

'I see,' said the sergeant, finding himself considerably outranked. 'Well, your daughter was rational and calm and said she would not be on the streets. She has money and a bank card. She gave me a letter with instructions to open it only when you called. She left here at 15.47. I filed my report a couple of hours ago before the drinkers started to come in.'

'15.47?'

'I logged it—'

'This *afternoon*?' said Mercy. 'But I was in the house then. She *left* when I was in the *house*? She said goodbye, see ya, the usual ...'

'She was a cool customer, I'll give her that,' said the sergeant. 'Very together.'

'What does her letter say?'

'I don't know. I haven't opened it yet. She asked me not to till you called.'

'What the hell is going on here?'

'I think you'll find your daughter's leaving home was a well-planned and executed departure,' said the sergeant. 'She said you hadn't been getting on.'

'That's putting it mildly.'

'She said that too.'

6

'You know, Sergeant, I'm beginning to detect a certain amount of inertia coming down the phone,' said Mercy. 'Are you going to *do* anything about my daughter's disappearance?'

'Technically—'

'Just give me a yes or no.'

'I'll see how busy we are, get someone to read the letter and call you,' said the sergeant. 'Has her father been informed?'

'He's on his way here.'

She was in her hotel room getting dolled up. She liked hotel rooms, especially the sort you got in the Moderno, with a big bathroom, a power shower and a bidet with a full-length mirror in the bedroom and room service, which she didn't really need but she'd ordered anyway, hamburger and chips, because she was … free.

She was dancing in her underwear, buds in, listening to the music's fizzing beat slamming straight into her cerebral cortex. She was slugging vodka tonic from the minibar and had snorted a tiny scrap of cocaine she'd brought with her from London. She'd need more to survive the night but knew how she was going to get it.

She pulled the buds out, socked back the last of her drink and shook out the red minidress she'd bought in French Connection, slipped it on. She'd blown four hundred quid on clothes at the airport. It was like wearing nothing. So sexy, she spun around and watched the dress flare up. She looked over her shoulder to check her bum in the mirror and did a couple of rotations of her hips. Then came the shoes. No. First the little jacket. It's cold out there. She stuffed the black quilted coat, red skirt, black wool tights and biker boots into the rucksack, took a hundred euros and a few condoms and put them in a pocket in the armpit of the jacket. The passport was still in reception. She slung a small black bag over her shoulder. She'd wanted to leave it in the room safe but she needed a credit card to make it work and she didn't have one.

Now the shoes. Six-inch heels. Ankle-strap courts in black. She stepped into them and the air was suddenly thinner. She practised some of her dance moves, sure-footed as a gymnast on the beam.

This was what she loved about Spain. Coming down in the

lift and stepping out into the lobby with the whole of the reception area looking at you, appreciating you for making the effort. Nothing creepy. Nothing furtive. Not like London, where nobody looked you in the eye but stole a glance at your arse, a peek at your tits. You could walk into a bar in Hoxton looking like sex on stilts and nobody'd even talk to you. Now Spanish boys, they wouldn't even let you hang for a few seconds. Walk into a bar and they'd be roaring their approval, clamouring to buy you a drink, talk to you. It wasn't a bed thing either. Well it was, but it wasn't the main thing. What was at the forefront was: thank you for being beautiful, it's made us happy. That was why she loved the Spanish.

She went to the front desk, picked up the passport and tucked it into the small pocket in the armpit of her jacket with the money and condoms.

It was nudging midnight. She strode down the street, smiling at the guys appreciating her, even the ones with stunners on their arms. She had an address she'd been given, written it on her hand because she couldn't remember Spanish names, let alone make a cab driver understand. A Moroccan guy had given her the name of a 'brother' who knew a people trafficker who'd pay a thousand euros for a valid UK passport with an electronic chip.

Cabs were stacking up in the *plaza* and she'd joined the short queue for one when she realised a guy, late thirties, was standing next to her, looking her up and down with naked admiration. The first thing she noticed: she towered over him in her heels. He was wearing a black leather jacket, an open midnight-blue silk shirt revealing a hairy chest, but in a nice way, with a gold chain. His jeans were tight with a black belt and a metal clasp which had twin scorpions, tails meeting. He was tapping his black pointed boots with silver toe tips on the shiny pavement. He wasn't a looker, but he was built. The silk of his shirt was stretched over the muscles of his chest, his pecs stood out, nipples peaking with the cold, and she could see the rack of his abs too. The cords of his neck were like columns on either side of his protruding Adam's apple. He had black curly hair, a sardonic but sexy smile, white teeth and dark deep-set eyes whose colour she couldn't tell. Confidence radiated out of him. One look told her that this was a guy who'd never have trouble talking to women.

'*Hola, que guapa, chica. No te puedes imaginar* ...' he said and stopped. 'You don't speak Spanish? How about English?'

'I do English,' she said.

'*Mira guapa*, I'm with my friends taking a drink,' he said, speaking with a Latin American accent. 'I see you coming down the street, I say this is a girl who knows how to dress, this is a girl who knows how to have a good time, this, I bet, is a girl who knows how to *dance*. Am I right?'

And with that he did a couple of disco dance moves which showed he too knew how to dance and, despite his evident musculature, he could move fast and smooth. His two friends, one with a Latina beauty on his arm, gave him some ironic applause.

'*They* can't dance,' he said to her conspiratorially. 'That's why they're clapping. They're like cows on ice on the dance floor.'

He performed a Neanderthal two-step which suddenly went horribly awry and sent her into giggles. He came up close to her, his head at the height of her chin. He looked up, eyes penetrating right into her. The nerve of him. Ugly bugger too. She had to bring all of her London cool to bear, and he saw that he'd have to make another push.

'You know where I'm from?' he said.

She wanted to say 'the movies' but didn't want to throw herself at him. He didn't seem to be local.

'Madrid?' she said, ironic.

He came in closer.

'Col-*om*-bia.'

He saw the light come on in her face and knew what it meant.

'*Te gusta un poco de nieve*,' he said, laughing. 'You like a little snow.'

He thumped his breast pocket with the side of his fist. Smiled.

'We have enough to go skiing.'

That did it for her. No need to sell the passport. No need to haggle in the toilets. Free charlie the whole night through. He held out his arm. She took it. His friends couldn't believe it. They came over and slapped hundred-euro notes into his hand, which seemed to her like a lot of money for a bet.

They went to Le Cock and drank mojitos, snorted a couple of lines each and then moved to a nightclub called Charada, where house music was the name of the game. They danced for half an hour and then went to the toilets for another line. He kissed her. She kissed him back. He put a strong hard hand between her legs and felt the heat coming off her. The music thumped through the walls.

'What's your name?' she asked.

'*Como te llamas?*' he said. 'You ask me: *Como te llamas?*'

She tried as he sawed his hand over her crotch.

'*Me llamo Carlos,*' he said. 'But nobody calls me that.'

'What do they call you?' she asked, her stomach wrestling under the red dress with the persistence of his hand beneath.

'They call me El Osito,' he said, his eyes darkening and narrowing to blade points.

'And what's an *osito?*' she asked.

'It's a little bear,' he said, and withdrawing his massive hand from between her legs, held it up to the dim light, '*con una pata grande.*'

2

11.30 P.M., SATURDAY 17TH MARCH 2012
Mercy Danquah's house, Streatham, London

'But it's weird ... this need she has to justify her actions,' said Boxer. 'You wouldn't have thought she'd bother. "I'm out of here. Don't come looking for me. Bye." That's all it needed.'

'It's personal,' said Mercy shrewdly. 'Handwritten.'

They were in the sitting room, Amy's note on the coffee table between them.

Boxer leaned forward to reread it without touching it, looking for other levels of meaning, unable to restrain his professionalism. Both of them were used to reading and listening to notes, texts and messages sent by gangs and putting them through a special analysis, but this time there was added parental guilt, anger and denial.

'She's being rational and organised. She's getting her PR in place. She left here, went to the police station and told the desk sergeant he'd recognise me.'

'When was the last time you were at that police station?'

'Never been there in my life. She was just winding up the desk sergeant and sticking it to me at the same time. Telling him we're both coppers so we should feel right at home with each other,' said Mercy. 'Did you know she had a driving licence?'

'No. I asked her if she'd like to learn, thinking I'd pay for some lessons as a birthday present. "And what would I do with a car in London?" she said. "Who's going to buy me one? Who's going to insure it?" All in that withering, patronising way of hers. I'm not sure how much of this is to do with us,' said Boxer, irritated

11

by the defensiveness that even he could hear in his own voice. 'It's convenient to blame us: the people who'd had the temerity to bring her into this godforsaken world. And she has a go, as you'd expect … but almost as an afterthought. "It bores me being a child, your child." What's more striking to me is her despair at the way her life is unfolding. She seems to want to jolt herself out of the predictability, of knowing what's going to happen tomorrow.'

'And yet there's something in that last line that smacks of … a challenge.'

'I'm with you on that. She's definitely throwing down the gauntlet to us, the professionals, to come looking for her.'

'And she's arrogant enough to think we're not going to hack it.'

'Do you think there's part of her that wants to be found?'

'Why challenge people if you don't?' said Mercy.

'Maybe she just couldn't resist goading us. She knew, because we're the people we are, that we were going to be on her case from the moment we saw that note. This is her saying, "You haven't got a chance."'

'Do you think she's laid down some elaborate smokescreen to make us look like idiots at our own work?'

The doorbell rang. Mercy left the room and returned with two police officers and an eyebrow raised to Boxer. They were not friendly. The expected professional bond was not there, but rather the 'suspect distance'.

'I'm Detective Inspector Weaver,' said the male officer, taking in the couple in front of him: a tall slim black woman with cropped hair and almond-shaped eyes and a blond-haired man with intense green eyes who looked as if he kept himself in fighting condition.

'And I'm Detective Sergeant Jones,' said the female officer.

'We'd like to see Amy's room,' said Weaver.

'And the note,' said Jones, staring down at the coffee table.

Boxer handed it over. The note passed between the officers. They all went up to Amy's room.

'Have you established what she's taken with her?'

'Well, as you can see, there's nothing in here. She's stripped it bare.'

'Without you noticing anything?' asked Jones.

'I've been working on a very demanding case this last week and she was supposed to be staying with her grandmother up in Hampstead. But clearly she was dropping in here after school and removing all her stuff,' said Mercy. 'Tonight was her first night back home. She said she would join us at a restaurant in town but didn't show. I came back, checked her room, found the note.'

'I understand from the desk sergeant that you saw Amy when she left the house this afternoon,' said Jones.

'She had a small rucksack, that was it.'

Mercy described what Amy had been wearing. The officers didn't take notes. They asked for all details of friends and relatives, the places Amy was known to frequent, her money situation. Mercy talked them through it but omitted Amy's involvement in the previous weekend's cigarette smuggling jaunt between the Canaries and London that she'd uncovered. She wanted to investigate that little scenario herself. She told them what she knew about Amy's finances – that she had a debit card and a bank account but didn't know how much she had in it.

'We'll need some up-to-date photos,' said Weaver. 'And er ... a DNA sample would be helpful. Hair? A toothbrush?'

Mercy was momentarily frozen by this: the possibility that they might have to match DNA with a body. She gave Boxer a curious glance, which he didn't understand, and went to the corner of the room where she knew Amy dried and brushed her hair, but not a single strand of her long ringlets remained.

'I don't believe this,' said Mercy. 'She's hoovered the room.'

'Let's go back downstairs for the next bit,' said Weaver. 'And we'll check the vacuum cleaner while we're at it.'

In the kitchen Mercy gave them the vacuum cleaner but the bag had been changed. Mercy blinked at the thoroughness. She offered tea and coffee, which were politely refused. They reconvened in the living room. Boxer and Mercy sat. The policemen stood in front of the fireplace.

'What we need to talk about now is any ... er ... events that you can think of that might have been a factor in Amy wanting to leave home,' said Weaver.

'She's always been a strong, determined girl, but she was very sweet and loving until some sort of hormonal explosion at fourteen,

13

when she went up to her room as one sort of person and came down the following morning as another. That crisis has deepened over the years, to the point of continuous antipathy towards me in particular – seeing as we are the ones living together – and Charlie whenever she has the opportunity. But no, there wasn't a specific incident,' said Mercy.

Weaver and Jones turned their hard faces to Boxer.

'Look,' said Boxer, open-palmed, 'I'm not going to paint myself as totally blameless. I've been an absent father much of the time. I had a job that took me out of the country for more than half the year.'

'What job was that?'

'I was a kidnap consultant with GRM, a big private security company, running negotiations all over the world, but I'm free-lance now. Amy was becoming too much of a handful for Mercy to manage alone with the kind of job she has. I left the company nearly two years ago so that I could choose my work to fit in with spending more time with my daughter. I've developed a relation-ship with another company called Pavis Risk Management, who give me as much contract work as I want.'

'And you're in the kidnap unit with Specialist Crime Director-ate 7 under DCS Makepeace?' said Weaver, turning to Mercy.

'It's a time-consuming job with uncertain hours. I've done my best to look after Amy, and when work's got in the way I've sent her to family members living here in south London or to Charlie's mother in Hampstead.'

'Did you ever hit your daughter?'

'No,' said Boxer emphatically.

The two officers looked at Mercy, who was saying nothing.

'Ms Danquah?'

'I hit her once, yes,' said Mercy.

This was news to Boxer.

'And what were the circumstances, Ms Danquah?' asked Jones.

'Just before last Christmas, school had finished. She stayed out all night. She didn't call on Sunday morning even. Her friend Karen, who'd been with her that night, had lost sight of her in a place called Basing House in Shoreditch. She was last seen dan-cing with a black couple with bleached-blonde hair. I was worried

14

sick, calling her and texting her. I even ran down the management of Basing House, who were surprisingly understanding and told me to call the police. Then at two o'clock, Sunday afternoon, she breezes back in here as if she's been for an after-lunch stroll in the park, with that "no worries" look on her face. I was beside myself. Relieved but totally furious. And of course Amy knows how to do it to me. She saw my state and knew she was to blame so she wound me up and I blew. I slapped her once, hard, across the face, which at that point was being dangled in front of me, just daring me to do it. And she knew that where I come from, a very strict Ghanaian upbringing, my father beat us all the time, and it wasn't just slaps across the face, it was canes across the back, buttocks and legs. And that was for getting seven out of ten in a spelling test, not staying out all night in a club in Shoreditch.'

Weaver and Jones were transfixed. This was no performance. They knew London kids and the extremes they could take you to.

'And I was sorry,' said Mercy. 'I was sorry for what I'd done, because when I'd suffered at my father's hands I promised myself that I would never do the same to a child of mine. And there I was smacking her. I grovelled. I begged for forgiveness. The look I got back from her was one of total triumph. She slammed her bedroom door in my face.'

'In the letter she left at the station the reasons she gave for leaving home were "excessive discipline and harsh treatment with occasional violence",' said Weaver.

'And the word abuse cropped up a few times,' said Jones.

Mercy blurted an incredulous laugh, the emotion uncontainable.

'Abuse?' she said. 'Amy doesn't know the meaning of the word. She should see what I've seen on the estates in Stockwell and Brixton.'

Boxer put an arm around Mercy's shoulders, felt her trembling, the lava boiling in the maternal pit.

'I wanted to take Mercy out of the line of fire,' said Boxer. 'Amy's campaigns were relentless. The more she realised how much she could hurt Mercy the more inventive she became. But Amy's never lived with me. I didn't have the home or the life to offer that alternative.

'I'm sure you two have seen a few things in your time around here in south London – the teenage knifings. I was in the Gulf War before I did a few years as a homicide detective. Mercy has done twenty years in the police – beat, murder and kidnap. All that experience counts for nothing when you come up against the arrogance of youth. They think because of the marvellous connectivity of their brave new world that they miraculously know everything, even without having faced it, and that all we're doing, as their parents, is laying down unnecessary boundaries to contain their natural enthusiasm for life. They don't know what we know.'

'You're making it sound as if running away might give her some useful work experience,' said Jones.

'But we know she's not equipped for it. She can be clever and manipulative in her own world and be successful. She's experimented with Mercy as her lab rat. But put her out there in real life and she won't cut it. People will take one look and see an opportunity. For all this so-called "excessive discipline" she's actually been wrapped in cotton wool.'

'That's what you think,' said Weaver, 'but you don't seem to know too much about her. The driving licence?'

'She's secretive. We're busy,' said Boxer.

'Maybe if you'd spent more time with her?' said Weaver, which earned him a look from Jones. Weaver had kids and, even on the way here, he'd been whining about how little he saw of them.

'Since she was fourteen *she* hasn't wanted to spend even ten minutes in our company,' said Mercy. 'It's tough having breakfast with her. The disdain fills the room. I'd rather take my coffee outside.'

'You sound glad she's gone,' said Jones.

Mercy turned to her slowly as if she'd just discovered a wind-up artist in the room.

'Maybe you don't know what it's like to love a child,' said Mercy. 'There's no choice and you don't have any control over it from the moment they're born. It's not like being with a guy and thinking, look at all the grief I'm getting from this arsehole, time to move on. The child is a part of you. It would be like walking away from the best part of myself. And now she's gone I don't feel, thank God for that, at last I've got some … what's it called?

16

Me time, whatever *that* is. What I feel, Detective Sergeant Jones, is complete emptiness, as if the best love I've ever known has buggered off. And it's my fault. I'm the failure. She *loved* me.'

The tears came as a surprise to everyone in the room, including Mercy. They streaked rapidly down her face, unchecked. Jones couldn't look at her, regretted her cheap trick. Wanted to hug her.

'That's why it's so bloody difficult,' said Mercy. 'You love someone to pieces. Unconditionally. And they know it. And when they realise they have such total power over you, as a kid, with no understanding of that bond. They … they punish you with it for everything they suffer: the boredom, the inadequacy, the sexual tension, the hormonal chaos, the social ineptitude. Everything. They do it because you're responsible for bringing them into this confusing, incomprehensible world and they do it because they can do it safely, and part of me thinks they do it because they can't help it. It's nature's way of preparing you to be split up. So that the child can eventually go her own sweet way and neither of you feels too badly about it. But don't get me wrong, Detective Sergeant Jones, I want her back. She's not ready to be out there on her own. If I don't get her back, I can tell you, it will leave me with a big empty hole inside.'

A huge pendulous silence, as of the inside of a barrage balloon, filled the room. Boxer was stunned to hear Mercy speak like that. Only now did he realise what she'd had pent up inside her. It wasn't as if they hadn't talked about these things, it just had never been with such intensity.

'The first line of the letter she left in the station instructed us not to reveal the contents to you,' said Weaver. 'Apart from what I've already mentioned, I can tell you that it was written in a calm tone and rationally laid out all her reasons for leaving home. She didn't want us to consider her a missing person. She was just starting up an alternative life. The only reason we're following this up is because of the allegations she made about you.'

'That sounds as if you're not actually going to look for her,' said Boxer.

'You haven't told us that she's suffering from any mental health problems. She's over sixteen, which is the legal age for leaving home. She has money. She won't be living on the streets. It's extremely disconcerting for you, I know, but for me to allocate time to this would not impress my superiors.'

'There's a very good organisation called Missing Persons …' said Jones.

'I know,' said Boxer. 'I run a charitable foundation myself, called LOST. We find missing people, but only when the police have given up.'

Uneasy glances were exchanged.

'All this information about Amy will be posted on the Police National Computer, which means—'

'We know what it means,' said Mercy.

'Some photos,' said Jones, 'that would be useful …'

'We don't have any recent photos. She's refused to be photographed since she was fourteen,' said Mercy. 'If we find any …'

The policemen, nodded, stepped forward. Now they shook hands. Boxer walked them to the door, let them out, went back to the living room. A tap on the front door brought him back. DS Jones was there, hands deep in her coat pockets.

'The last line of her letter said, "If you do investigate my disappearance and I am found, under no circumstances are either of my parents or anyone one in my family to be informed." I'm sorry. We weren't supposed to tell you that either. I just wanted to clarify our position here. The DI's not being a bastard.'

Boxer thanked her, closed the door.

'What was all that about?' asked Mercy.

He told her and it was as if he'd jabbed her in the guts with a kitchen knife. She curled up and howled.

They went back to the dance floor, took it by storm. El Osito's shirt was drenched in seconds, his muscles stood out under the changing lights. He flicked his head back on its bull neck and the sweat sprayed in sparkling droplets.

She was standing at the bar while El Osito went hunting for his friends. The barman came over, gave her a card, nodded at the note written on it and looked down the counter to a young guy standing there, who raised his beer and melted back into the darkness. The note said in English, 'Be careful of your friend, he has a bad reputation with women.' She let the card drop to the floor.

El Osito came back, said his friends had gone. They left, went to Kapital and danced for hours, mesmerised by the music, with more coke crashing through their veins.

At five o'clock they were out in the street hailing a cab. They sat in the back and he talked non-stop to the cab driver as he slowly removed her underwear, stuffed the pants into his pocket. They arrived in some residential area about seven kilometres from the centre and El Osito asked the cabbie to pull over at the Metro station of Pan Bendito. They walked to his apartment block, which was up a rough cement pathway behind the Bar Roma. The entrance wasn't quite as luxurious as she'd been expecting for a man with so much coke on him.

Only now did it suddenly occur to her that she was breaking all the rules. She was drunk and drugged with no idea where she was, with a strange man whose rough, hard hands led her to believe that he was not unaccustomed to violence. Fear was shimmering on the outer reaches of her consciousness as he walked her past the cracked glass of the metal-framed door of the block's main entrance.

'Maybe we should go back to the Hotel Moderno,' she said.

He gripped her elbow so hard she winced and couldn't wrench her arm free.

The lift worked. The doors opened and he shoved her so hard into the filthy cubicle that she hit the far corner and had to save herself with her free arm. She tried to turn, but he was on her, rucking her dress up over her hips, reminding her of her panty-less state. She looked down at something suspect in the corner that had the tackiness of recently dried bodily fluids. Panic trembled in her throat as she felt his powerful urgency, the animal strength beneath the cold, sodden shirt. The lift door opened at the fourth floor. He backed away from her, pulled her round. She tried to push her dress back down and made a run for the door to the stairs.

'Don't do that,' he said, and leaned forward, pushing her hard so that she missed the door and hit her head against the brick wall next to it. She fell onto all fours, tried to get to her feet, remembering El Osito's impression of a cow on ice. She climbed up the rough wall, hiding her face behind her arm, not wanting to see what was going to come next.

It was the turn of *la pata grande*. He slapped her so hard that she collided with another wall, bounced off it and fell to the floor, hot buttocks on the ice-cold tiles. He grabbed her by the swag of her ringlets, shook her like a naughty pup and dragged her to the door of his apartment. He unlocked it with her still hanging from his brutal fist, threw her into the hallway, slammed the door shut behind him.

In the dark she started to scrabble away from him and he trod down on her leg to stop her as if she were some struggling animal that he still wanted to play with. The only sound was of his belt snarling and snapping through the loops as he tore it from his waist. She remembered that scorpion clasp and the thought of its sting made her whimper.

'No, please. Please don't. Please don't hurt me.'

She flinched as the black air swished above her head and the scorpions made dull hard contact with her forehead and dragged over her eye and cheek. A warm trickle followed their trail and she had the taste of salt and metal in her mouth.

'I'll do anything,' she said, 'but please don't hurt me.'

3

'We need to talk to this guy too,' said Mercy, tapping the screen. They were up early, posting Amy's details on the missing persons' websites. Mercy had remembered the photo she'd taken of Amy as she'd come into the Gatwick Airport arrivals hall after her cigarette smuggling jaunt to the Canaries the week before. Amy had met up with a good-looking black guy who'd taken the suitcase full of cigarettes off her hands. That shot was now on her computer and Mercy was looking at the two of them, lingering over the man's face, trying to work out his age.

Boxer gave her the thumbs-up. He was on the phone to Roy Chapel, the ex-policeman who ran the office of the LOST Foundation. Boxer had already sent him a cropped version of the photo Mercy was looking at. Chapel had said he'd get it out to all the street organisations as soon as.

'If she's serious,' said Chapel, 'and the picture you've painted makes me think she's worked this out very carefully, she'll cut all ties. You know how it is: the most successful runaways are the ones who transplant themselves into a new life and never go anywhere near the old one.'

Boxer said nothing. He knew this very well. That was precisely what his own father had done more than thirty years ago. He tried to breathe back down the black hole growing inside him.

'And to do that at her age,' said Roy, 'she'd need help. There's no way she could do it on her own, and that's what worries me. Who's she got holding her hand?'

Mercy wound her finger round at Boxer.

'We're building the file now, Roy. We'll get back to you as soon as it's complete,' said Boxer, glad to hang up.

'We should contact the UK Border Agency,' said Mercy.

'Bit early for that.'

'I've got a contact,' she said, holding up a business card. 'We were on a course together.'

'Still too early on a Sunday morning.'

'What's the earliest we can go round to Karen's?'

'Nine o'clock.'

'How about eight, given that it's an emergency? Karen's mum would understand. She'd be horrified if we left it till nine.'

'You might find Karen's none too sensible.'

'What did Roy have to say?'

'That he'd be on to all the street organisations first thing.'

'But what did he say that made you go all quiet?'

Boxer told her about successful runaways needing help.

She turned back to the computer, carried on inputting data into the newly opened Amy file. Everything she could think of.

'She's going to make a mistake. She's going to have to make contact somewhere,' said Mercy. 'I know you're thinking about your father here, but that was different. He was wanted for questioning about a murder. One mistake and he'd have been in jug.'

'Only if he'd done it,' said Boxer, surprised to find himself defending the man who'd abandoned him thirty-three years ago.

'Come on, Charlie, get real.'

'That look you gave me last night,' said Boxer, 'when they asked you for Amy's DNA ... what was all that about?'

'Nothing.'

'It wasn't nothing.'

'Just, you know, that they asked for it. Takes it to another level.'

He didn't believe her. Thought she was hiding something. Dropped it.

They went to work again for an hour, thrashing out everything they could think of, every conceivable contact, even down to the twenty-two-year-old boyfriend Amy had developed when she was a fifteen-year-old on a family holiday in Spain. How would they get in touch with him? Boxer went to the kitchen, made coffee, called Isabel.

'How's it's going?' said Isabel.

He read her the full text of the note, told her the extent of Amy's clearout and the lack of police interest.

'And how's Mercy taking it?'

'She's galvanised. I persuaded her to take a sleeping pill last night, but she was up at six, dying to get on with it. She's taken Amy's note as a professional challenge.'

'Mercy's going to be doubly hurt – you know that,' said Isabel. 'You're still the only man in her life. She hasn't got over you. Your attention is focused elsewhere and now the only other big emotional figure in her life has rejected her. She's going to be fragile.'

'I know,' said Boxer. 'I'm staying here with her. We're going to have to track Amy down and, at the very least, make sure she's all right even if we can't persuade her to come home. I'm sorry.'

'Don't be sorry. You have to do this,' said Isabel. 'After Alyshia's kidnap I know what you're going through. At least Amy's not in the hands of others. She's organised and in no immediate danger.'

'That's what *Amy* thinks. She's got undented self-belief so she thinks she knows what she's doing and has faith in the people helping her do it, but she's only seventeen. She reckons she's cool and clued up but, despite all her escapades, we know from the people *we* meet in our professional lives she's no match for an opportunist. That generation just hasn't had enough face-to-face experience to know when someone means you harm. So neither of us is going to be happy until we know her situation, and from the last line of her note she knows that too.'

'What do you mean?'

'I'm beginning to think this is Amy's ultimate adolescent battle – to take on her parents at their own game and win.'

El Osito came to with a low grunt. He was naked apart from his socks and lying on the bathroom floor between the toilet bowl and the wall. It was daylight. His eyes slid over the glaze of the cheap tiles to the corner and the brush in its ceramic holder for cleaning shit streaks, which he never used. There was a box of pills and a half-empty blister card with the brand name of the benzodiazepine Aneurol. Good. He'd taken a benzo to come down off the coke high. Or maybe not. His head hurt and his thick, heavily muscled body was jammed. Maybe he'd dropped the benzos and fallen, knocking his head trying to retrieve them. He squirmed his way out, hauled his head up to the basin, turned on the tap, scooped water into his dry mouth. He sat on the toilet, relieved himself copiously.

Things started to come back to him from the night before: the girl in the red dress. Dancing with her in the street in front of his freaks on a bet that he couldn't pull her. Made it look as if it was his dancing skills when it was the promise of a night of downhill skiing that had done the trick. He knew the ones that liked their blow. He wiped his wet hand down his face and his eyes came blinking out of his head as he remembered getting into a taxi, taking off her underwear in the cab, talking to the driver. He focused on his trousers, which he'd trodden out of last night, saw the girl's knickers stuffed in the pocket.

His brain flickered nervously with jolts of memory. The cab dropping them off at the Pan Bendito Metro station. He never let cabs take him to his door. The walk from there. The girl, a foreigner, not knowing where she was, the grimness of the neighbourhood. Staggering up the path behind the Bar Roma. The cracked glass, the lift, he'd sensed some fear there, had to shove her.

He shook himself and turned to the basin and for the first time saw the blood on the back of his hand, raised his head. Blood on his face and chest. He remembered his favourite scorpion belt snapping through the loops of his jeans, heard it in his head. The buckle whistling through the air.

'No, please …' a voice whimpered in his head.

He washed his hands, his face, his chest. The water swirled red down the plughole. He ran his wet hands through his hair, cooling his hot scalp, the heat building in his head.

The corridor was dark and empty. The blinds were down in the rest of the apartment, just cracks of light here and there. A smear of something down the wall. He headed towards the living room. Silence. Had she gone? *La guapita? La puta inglesa?* He checked the kitchen. The light squeezed behind the blinds made everything grey and grainy in the hard white room. No blood there. He crossed the corridor into the living room. Only one or two cracks in the blinds. He would have to turn on the light. He didn't want to turn on the light. There was a smell in the room.

El Osito lashed out at the light switch. She was lying on the floor with the red dress up around her neck, her unhooked bra twisted in it. Her legs were apart. There was something ... He didn't want to look. He slashed the lights out.

Back to the kitchen. He gripped the sink as a dark pressure took hold in the pit of his stomach.

It came to him in an instant. He knew exactly what he had to do.

'I've called Karen's mother, and she'll get her up and sensible in an hour,' said Mercy. 'Your gut telling you anything?'

'No,' Boxer lied.

It was telling him things and none of them were good. Nothing even specific or relevant. It was just an overwhelming sense that they would all be changed by what had happened. There would be no predictable unfolding, as he'd felt on seeing Isabel last night, walking into her open arms, knowing they had a future.

He called Esme, his mother, who'd been looking after Amy all last week. No answer.

Mercy drove. They parked outside the 1970s block where Karen lived. On the way up the open stairs to the second floor she called her contact at the UK Border Agency, gave him Amy's details and asked if he could help. He said he'd get back to her one way or the other.

In the living room Karen was sitting on the sofa looking stunned. Her dark hair wasn't brushed out yet and she was in her mother's dressing gown. The nail varnish on her toes and fingers was alternately dark blue and fluorescent orange and was chipped. The black tattoos snaking up the olive skin of her calves and forearms made her look more like a Brazilian hooker than a Streatham hairdresser.

'Your mum told you about Amy?' said Mercy.

'Yeah,' she said, looking at the state of her nails, anything not to have to look at Mercy, who scared her half to death.

'You got any ideas where she might have gone?'

'Like … no!' said Karen, suddenly aggressive.

'Easy up, K,' said her mother. 'They've lost their daughter.'

'She didn't tell me *nothing*,' said Karen. 'If she'd of told me, I'd tell 'em, but she didn't, so I can't.'

'Could we talk to Karen on her own for a bit?' asked Mercy, who could sense the girl's fear, too many eyes glued to her.

The panic rose in Karen's face.

'Let's just relax a bit,' said Mercy. 'Sit back and breathe. We're all in a bit of a state. Not enough sleep.'

'Speak for yourself,' said Karen. 'I don't know what Amy's up to. I swear, Mrs Danquah. You know she keeps things to herself, that one. Too many secrets.'

'So what happened in Tenerife?'

'You can't believe the grief I've had from Mum about that. How was I to know she hadn't told you? How was I to know she should've been in Lisbon with her dad? That's what I mean. She don't tell me stuff. She keeps it all in, like, tight. I mean, don't get me wrong, Mrs Danquah, she's a nice girl, Amy. I like her. But she's a hard friend to have, know what I mean?'

They did.

'Did she get on with anybody in your boyfriend's gang? I mean …'

'Get *on* with anybody?'

'Who did Amy end up in bed with?' asked Boxer.

Karen was relieved to look away from Mercy. She wasn't sure what wrath was bubbling away under that calm exterior.

'Amy might not have told you things,' said Boxer. 'But you saw things. You were all in the same party.'

Karen nodded. Less of a nod, more of a shuddering blink.

'Who did she go with?'

'Glider.'

'Who's Glider?'

'The gang leader. The boss man,' said Karen. 'He likes …'

Her eyes shifted uneasily across to Mercy and then quickly back to Boxer.

'Black girls?' asked Boxer.

Another imperceptible nod.

'Where can we find Glider?'

'North London somewhere. Dunno the address. He keeps it …'

'Does your boyfriend know where Glider lives?' asked Mercy.

She shook her head.

'How come?'

She shrugged.

Mercy found communicating with the young immensely draining.

'You're not going to get anybody into trouble,' said Boxer. 'This is only about finding Amy, making sure she's OK.'

'I know he doesn't know cos I asked him. He says Glider likes to keep it all … separate, like. Nobody knows what anybody else is doing. He says if the police break into one part of his operation it doesn't mess up the rest of the show.'

'What about the black guy who met Amy off the flight in Gatwick? The one who took the suitcase of cigarettes off her.'

'You mean, was she sleeping with him?'

'No, I didn't mean that, but … was she?'

'No. She only met him once, for five minutes, just so he'd know her face.'

'Does *he* have a name?'

'Marcus. He lives off Coldharbour Lane somewhere. I can get you *his* address, as long as you promise you won't—'

'I told you, this is about Amy. We're not interested in ciggie smuggling.'

'How much did you girls make out of the Tenerife trip?' asked Boxer.

'Four hundred quid – and a good time.'

'And at no point did Amy say anything about leaving home?' said Mercy, getting a little tougher now.

'She wasn't happy. That's all I know. She never said she was going to get out. But you know …'

'What?'

Karen's eyes cast about over the floor, looking for the right words.

'I know how you feel, Mrs Danquah.'

'Do you?' said Mercy, amazed.

'Everybody likes Amy,' she said. '*Everybody*. She had all those

27

guys eating out of her hand. Even my man. And you know how she does it? She lets you know she doesn't give a fuck about anybody. She goes to bed with Glider, but she's the one who leaves him in the morning before he wakes up. I saw him out on the balcony, smoking, looking for her up and down the beach. Wondering where she'd gone. He was hooked.'

'Tell us about Glider,' said Boxer. 'What does he look like?'

'Got to be at least thirty, maybe more. White. Shaved head. Tats all the way up both arms, but nothing on his hands. Muscles. He works out. Violent. He's got a rep for that – blows without warning.'

'And?'

'Nothing.'

'Every detail helps, Karen,' said Mercy.

'He's got a huge cock,' she blurted.

Silence.

'You see,' she said. 'Not every detail helps.'

Still naked he opened a kitchen drawer. Four knives. Two big, a medium and a small. One meat cleaver. He laid them on the counter, saw his reflection in the bright, shiny steel of the cleaver he'd bought in Toledo. His eyes gone to black.

Under the sink a roll of bin bags. He tore off six. Back into the living room. Light on. Knelt by the body, studied the mess of clothes around her neck. Her face with two cuts, one from forehead to cheek, the other down the side of her nose. He took her jacket off first, stuffed it in a bin liner. Then came the dress and bra. He put the pants he'd taken from his pocket in another bin liner, looked at her bare feet. The shoes. He checked the room, then the corridor. They were up by the door. They still had labels on the soles. He dropped them into the bin liner with the pants, retraced his steps, checking the floor. He looked under the table, lifted the sofa. Her small black handbag. He put that in with the shoes. He had a thought. Tore off another bin liner from the roll. Took his trousers, emptied the pockets, found his damp shirt, stripped off his socks, stuffed the lot in the bin liner, put it by the door. Keep it separate.

He went back to the body, squatted and lifted her dead weight in one movement without even a grunt. He put her down in the shower cubicle with her head by the drain hole.

The master bedroom had been converted into his weights room. He removed the two sets of twenty-five-kilo weights from each end of the bench press and took the bar back to the shower. He cut the hem off a sheet from his bed with a pair of scissors. He tied it around her ankles and secured them to the bar. He planted his feet either side of her legs and lifted the bar to chest height. He stepped forward and jerked the bar up above his head and rested it across the top of the cubicle. She was hanging free of the floor, just her hair making contact. He put her head into a supermarket bag, cut off all her hair and carefully tied it up in the bag. He positioned her with her head above the drain hole. He went to the kitchen for the knives and made himself a cup of coffee.

Pig killing. *La matanza*. He'd been to a few in his time. Something human trembled on the outer limits of his mind as he remembered children running around the farm while the men, having killed the pig and bled it out, scalded it and scraped off the bristles, leaving a perfectly pink corpse. This they hung up by its hocks, and, as the pig was unzipped with a blade, the women went in and hauled out the guts into massive metal bowls. The dogs came skipping around, tails wagging, heads lowering, looking for a bit of generosity. The women turned away, blood-spattered from the clean, pink corpse, as if from a freshly murdered husband.

El Osito poured himself another deep-black coffee, sipped it, relishing its tarry bitterness. He parted the edge of the blind from the wall, looked out onto the grey morning. Two young men walked towards the Metro station, hoods up, hands in pockets, no work, no money. For a moment he envied them, that they weren't standing naked in a kitchen with knives on the counter, €750,000 under the bed, a half-kilo of cocaine under the sink and a dead girl hanging by her ankles in the shower.

He let the blind fall back. He took out the coke from its hiding place and laid down two fat lines, which he chopped and shaped with the smallest knife. He took a bill from the money he'd emptied out of his pockets and snorted the lines, rubbed his gums with the remnants. He slapped his buttocks, picked up the knives and the cleaver and went to work on his own little *matanza*.

4

They were sitting in Mercy's car outside the Railton Road Off Licence opposite a line of Victorian terraced houses, waiting for Marcus Alleyne, the black guy who'd met Amy off the flight back from Tenerife with her suitcase of cigarettes that small lifetime ago. He wasn't in. The neighbour said he hadn't come back from his Saturday night out.

'Prolly wi' one his bitches,' said the teenaged black kid, trousers hanging down the backs of his legs, Knicks cap on backwards, high-top Nikes. He knew a cop when he saw one.

'Do you *have* to use that word?' asked Mercy.

'S'wat they is,' said the boy, mock puzzled, glad to be of annoyance.

'That's what they *are?*' said Mercy.

'Hunh?'

Back in the car. Mercy irritable. Everything happening so slowly. No fast-moving investigation here, with developments by the second. And she didn't want Boxer around either. He was physically close but miles off emotionally. Of course she'd wanted him there last night. She'd have even let him into her bed if he'd had the inclination. But he hadn't. He'd been affectionate with her, as he always had been, but there was a new remoteness. She wanted to be held fiercely. To have someone squeeze their strength into her. Make her feel special.

'We could be here for ever. Maybe you should do something

else. There's no point in the two of us wasting our time over the same guy.'

'What did you make of Karen?' asked Boxer as Mercy started the car and pulled away.

'Yeah, right,' said Mercy. 'You see that look on a lot of people's faces who've been in contact with Amy. She's hurt.'

'She didn't like it that her boyfriend was eating out of Amy's hand or that she was sleeping with Glider.'

'*I* didn't like it either,' said Mercy. 'Little minx.'

'Minx?'

'I'm trying to make our daughter sound a bit more playful than a slut.'

'It reduced Karen in the pecking order, that's why she didn't like it,' said Boxer. 'And every time you thought Amy was off with Karen somewhere, she wasn't. Karen was the cover. I think she's feeling a bit used.'

'Planning,' said Mercy. 'Thinking ahead. I have to hand it to Amy for that. I admire her ... for that.'

'That didn't sound like planning to me.'

'Look at us here. Look at us doing what Roy Chapel knows is a waste of time,' said Mercy. 'Talking to her friends, finding out about her nefarious contacts. Amy's a London kid. She understands a few things about this city. Just having Karen as a friend, rather than anybody from her fancy school. She knows the different strata of society. Drop out of one and into another and nobody will find you. Where are we going to look when we've exhausted the obvious? You can start in Cricklewood and I'll get going in Catford. See you in three decades.'

'And Karen feels left out.'

'Amy can inspire belief. The belief that anything is possible. People like Karen think that if they attach themselves to someone like Amy some of that possibility might rub off. And then Amy dumps them. They've served their purpose.'

'She doesn't care what people think of her,' said Boxer. 'That takes strength of character. Most people want to be liked. We admire those who don't give a damn.'

'Maybe that's what it'll take,' said Mercy. 'She won't understand until she's cared for somebody herself.'

They arrived back at Mercy's house and Boxer went over to his car. He tried to call his mother. Still no answer. Mobile off.

'I'll follow up Alleyne,' said Mercy. 'I'll call you when I've hit that dead end.'

He hugged her nicely, but not fiercely. They separated, still holding hands.

'Let's not get down,' said Boxer. 'That's the state she wants us to be in: questioning our own professionalism.'

'I'd better call the school,' said Mercy, 'even though I can't imagine ...'

'You know the rules,' said Boxer, squeezing her hand to his lips. 'Everything by the book, until you throw the book away.'

Boxer got into his car, left. Mercy found Amy's teacher's home phone number and put in a call. The teacher was shocked, especially when Mercy quoted Amy's nihilistic views on education from her note. She hadn't seen it coming. They spoke for half an hour, running through every possibility, the teacher giving her all the names of Amy's 'friends' (none of whom had ever been mentioned by Amy) and how she would interview every one of them. Mercy kept up her end but knew this was going nowhere.

She took a long bath, changed into casual clothes, jeans, a high roll-neck black jumper. She put on make-up. She knew precisely what she was doing. She finished and stared back at herself in the mirror, breathing the emotion down. She glanced at the hand where Boxer had kissed her, then back up to her own face looking for the chink that would reveal how pathetic she felt inside: the contemptible state of hopeful hopelessness where Boxer's new liaison had left her.

Downstairs, she picked up the keys, back into the car, drove to Railton Road, parked outside Alleyne's house once more. There was a light on in his flat this time. She checked her eyes in the rear-view. What was going on in her head? She'd only ever seen this guy for five minutes and he was eight, maybe ten years younger than her. She leaned forward searching for the glint of recklessness in her black pupils.

Up the steps to the front door, rang the bell, heard his feet rumbling down the stairs. Opened the door. And there he was: tall, good-looking, short dreadlocks, high cheekbones, dark brown eyes, perfect white teeth, a scar on his temple. He was wearing dark blue jeans and a white shirt open so that she could see the hard rack of his stomach, no shoes, long bare feet.

'Hey,' he said, 'I was expecting somebody else.'

'You got me,' said Mercy, holding up her warrant card. 'Police.'

'Then you'd better come in,' he said, smiling, not a flicker of nervousness.

He led her up the stairs, buttoning up his shirt, took her into the sitting room, where there was an orange three-piece suite that had seen better days and some lime-green cushions. Mounted on the wall was a home movie system with a fifty-five-inch LED screen no thicker than a slim paperback. Alleyne slipped on a pair of top-range Nikes and lay back on the sofa.

'You don't know me,' said Mercy.

'That is very true,' he said.

'But I know you.'

'You do?' he said, eyebrows raised, still smiling, enjoying the view.

'You are Marcus Alleyne and you met my daughter coming off a plane from Tenerife on Sunday 11th March. You took a large suitcase from her containing cigarettes which had been brought into this country illegally.'

She leaned forward and showed him the photo she'd taken at Gatwick on her mobile phone. Alleyne raised an eyebrow, which nearly communicated surprise.

'That's interesting,' he said, unmoved.

'Why should it be interesting rather than, say, alarming?'

'Because it doesn't look as if you're here with the full force of the law.'

'So you already know what that looks like.'

'Seen a bit of it in my time, you know, nothing heavy, no SWAT teams at dawn kind of thing. More like weary plods in the rain,' he said. 'And I can tell you none of it has been as pleasant as this little visit. So what's it all about, Inspector Danquah? Isn't that a Ghanaian name?'

She nodded. 'And you?'

'Originally?' he said. 'Trinidad. Several generations ago.'

Silence.

Mercy couldn't fathom what was going on in her chest. As if there was a thin translucent membrane stretched tight by all her loves and losses, so tight that it was about to split, and if it did she would lose all control.

Alleyne sat up, could see some sort of crisis going on in her face. He clasped his hands between his knees, shook them up and down as if he had dice in them.

'You all right, Inspector Danquah?'

'My daughter . . .' she started but couldn't continue as the membrane swelled.

'Something happened to Amy?'

'She ran away from home last night.'

'All right,' said Alleyne, relieved that this wasn't some horror for him and he wouldn't be heading for the cells on a Sunday night. 'What you need, Inspector Danquah . . . is some tea . . . maybe coffee, if you're not the tea kind. The real thing, no shit from a jar.'

'I'll take the "no shit from a jar" coffee,' said Mercy, needing him out of the room so she could get a grip. 'With milk, thanks.'

Alleyne went into the galley kitchen off the living room, shook his head at the six different espresso machines he had there, selected one, turned it on, looked for some coffee pods that would fit. He heated some milk in a steamer and under the noise of it made a call to the woman who was supposed to show up and told her not to come unless she wanted to share an evening with DI Mercy Danquah. She didn't.

'Sugar?' he asked, coming back into the sitting room, two lumps in the light palm of his hand. 'You know, Inspector Danquah—'

'Mercy. For God's sake, call me Mercy.'

'I only met your daughter for, like, a few minutes.'

'Then how did you know who to meet off the plane from Tenerife?'

'We had a coffee before. She came with her friend Karen. We introduced ourselves, clocked each other. That was it. I always get the coloured girls.'

'And apart from the Gatwick meet you never saw her again?'

Alleyne shook his head, sipped his coffee.

'Karen said she was sleeping with Glider. Do you know him?'

34

'You think she ran off with G?' he said, shaking his head at the unlikely combination.

'That's not an answer.'

'I can put my ear to the ground if you like.'

'Is that how you're still communicating in Brixton?'

'You're a funny lady, you know that?'

'Why don't you tell me where I can find G?'

'That would not win me any friends, Mercy. You hear what I'm saying?'

'I'm not interested in petty crime. I'm a mother trying to find her daughter.'

'Well, I can tell you that G, he don't like ... intrusions, even if they don't come with a blue flashing light attached,' said Alleyne. 'And if he heard that it ... emanated from me ...'

'OK, let's see if we can narrow it down,' said Mercy. 'Is he London based?'

'Sometimes.'

'North or south London?'

Alleyne demurred. Mercy got annoyed.

'All right, Marcus. I told you I wasn't interested in any of your petty crimes, but that's only until you clam up on me. Then I start calling the men in blue about this fence I know in Railton Road, etcetera, etcetera. So let's have it. We're talking about my *daughter*.'

'Has she been kidnapped?'

'No.'

'So, like you said, she ran away of her own accord. There's no need to threaten me because your daughter doesn't want to go to school any more.'

'What do you know about that?' said Mercy, mouth snapping like a dog.

'Whoa!' said Alleyne, arms up. 'Just a turn of phrase, Mercy. No need to take my hand off.'

'She's only seventeen years old,' said Mercy.

'Thinks she know everything, right?' said Alleyne.

A huge racking sob came up from Mercy's chest. The membrane had split, just when she'd taken her eye off it, loosened her grip. She coughed against it, but it was too late. The dam had burst. Alleyne went down on his haunches in front of her, held her knees. She fell forward, buried her face in his neck.

'Hey, Mercy,' he said, patting her back, amazed to find himself in this position. 'Don't worry. Everything's going to be all right.'

'Hold me tight,' she whispered. 'Tight!'

'You're on the edge, Mercy,' said Alleyne, wrapping his arms around her, drawing her up to his height, gripping her trembling ribs, holding her to him. 'Can't have you falling off.'

But she wanted to fall.

Boxer paced up and down outside Isabel Marks's house in Kensington. He hadn't called to say he was coming. He was struggling against a resistance in himself at appearing weak at the beginning of their relationship. Then again, she'd revealed everything of herself to him during the kidnap. He'd been her rock then, and she'd clung to him. But he didn't like it the other way round. Never been in this position before: needing someone.

That wasn't quite true. He'd needed someone when his father had run away, absconded from ... well, not justice – it hadn't got that far. He'd avoided a police interrogation. Disappeared. Boxer had been seven years old on the day he'd been told and it was still fresh thirty-three years later. Even now he could feel the fissure opening up in his chest.

And what had happened then? Esme had sent him away to school. There was nothing else she could do. She had a production company to run, and they'd just lost their director, the main creative attraction of the business. There were commercials to be shot all over the world. What had he done, the seven-year-old? He'd hardened up, set solid on the outside, never let anybody see inside.

Amy disappearing had brought it all back: this feeling that all he had at his centre was his own hurt. He'd noticed it more since he'd gone freelance, with less cameraderie but more time and solitude for it to pervade. And then, later, he'd been shocked to find a way of dealing with it. The first time, tracking down the Ukrainian kidnap gang member who'd abused his young Russian hostage all the way to a dacha outside Archangel, forcing the gangster out into the forest in his underpants in -22°C, watching

36

as his shivering stopped, the body stiffened, and finding himself whole again, the blackness inside down to an invisible point. Could he ever unlearn that? Or was it a part of him, in his DNA, like a black line spiralling up the middle of the double helix, a mutated gene affecting the whole?

He rang the doorbell, unsure of his reception. He sensed her on the other side looking through the peephole. What did she see? The door opened and she pulled him in, hugged him up on tiptoe, comforted him with the closeness of her body.

Isabel supplied food and drink in the effortless way she had and listened to him, gave him her full attention while he sat in the kitchen watching her, those brown eyes beneath her straight black eyebrows always on the brink of concern. It amazed him how she appeared dressed for every occasion. He couldn't imagine her slouching around in a big shirt and jeans. Even now on a Sunday evening she was in a tight-fitting dress, her bosom high, cleavage showing, make-up on. He couldn't take his eyes off that slight declivity beneath her cheekbones, the one that said kiss me, that said rest your tired face here.

He told her about his fruitless day. For all the time he was talking she held his hands across the table, but it made no difference. Something had changed in him over the long day or, perhaps, as he was standing outside her house. He was mentally slipping out of her hands, as if he was hanging from them over a cliff and she was losing her grip. He'd thought he'd be able to tell her everything. But now he knew there'd always have to be the one thing he had inside held back. He shouldn't, if he wanted to hold on to her, ever tell her that.

'Weren't we going to have a talk,' he said, 'before Mercy called about Amy?'

'A talk?'

'Didn't you say ... we needed to talk?'

She took his hand, held it to her chest and kissed him on the mouth.

'No more talk,' she said, and led him upstairs to her bedroom.

El Osito washed and scoured himself, thinking it would have been easier with a hacksaw, but he wasn't about to go out and buy one and have that traced back to him. And he didn't want anybody else involved. Nobody should know about this.

He was about to tie up each bag with its gruesome contents and put them in the shower to clean them off with water and bleach when it occurred to him that he would have to weigh them down so they didn't float in the river. He didn't want to go outside searching for rocks in the city. He went to his weights room. Everything had been bought over a year ago by one of his underlings from a big sports store, using cash, before he'd even arrived in Madrid. He selected four five-kilo weights and one ten-kilo weight for the torso, which he'd kept complete, hadn't wanted her innards all over the floor.

He weighted each bag, tied it, washed it down and then stacked them by the front door.

Outside the flat was a rubbish chute down to the huge metal bins in the garage. He took the bag of his own clothes, which he'd kept separate by the door, and threw it down to make sure there were no blockages. He heard it careen down the metal tube and land in the bin below. He propped open the chute lid and went down to the garage, got in the bin and looked up. Clear. He parked his car close to the bin, went back up. He threw down the four bags of body parts one after the other. Heard them all land safely below. The one with the torso was too tight a fit and he took that down the stairs over his shoulder. He opened the car boot, dropped in the bag and then climbed into the metal bin and lobbed the others into the boot.

Picking up and dropping off drugs had given El Osito an experience-developed talent for complicated driving procedures. He had his mobile out on the seat and satnav up on the dashboard. The car itself was nothing flashy, a Seat Cordoba from 2005 with a dent in the rear passenger door and a bit of a scrape on the driver's side.

Madrid's M40 orbital runs along the edge of Carabanchel and very early on a Monday morning is not a busy time. He was heading for the Manzanares river, which he thought the best place to dump the bags. Not all in one place, but in five different spots. The first crossing point over the river was not ideal as it was a complicated junction with too much traffic. He came off the M40

38

and joined the M45 going back towards the west. He slowed as he came to the next crossing, on the outskirts of a small village called Villaverde. No traffic. He pulled in, went to the boot and dumped the first bag over the side into the water, got back in, pulled away. Fifteen seconds.

Heading south now to the next orbital through endless industrial zones, he joined the M50. The next bag went over the side at a place called Perales del Rio. He continued east and hit the Valencia road, and just outside another industrial zone he crossed the river again. Another bag. Just two to go. He had the air con on despite the cold outside, the adrenaline making him sweat. He came off the motorway, headed south on small roads, and just outside Vallequillas Norte the road crossed the river again. He kept going south to another bridge just outside Titulcia and made the final drop. It was black out there. No light. The stars were sharp. By 6 a.m. his work was done and he was heading back to Madrid. He had his buds in, listening to music on his smartphone – Shakira: 'La Tortura'.

Boxer was lying on his back watching Isabel sleeping after making love. He'd never felt like this before. There'd always been at least a scintilla of regret as if he'd somehow misled the woman he'd been with. But Isabel had wiped out all doubt. Even the black hole left by Amy's rejection seemed to have diminished to a healed point. In this state of post-coital certainty he was excited by the possibility that Isabel's love might make him feel whole again. And just as he thought that, the darkness crept back in: the fear of what he would lose if she knew him for what he really was.

5

Ten-year-old Sasha Bobkov woke up early on Monday morning to know instantly that he was happy. He'd got through another weekend with his mother and now freedom. The prospect of some footy with his new friend. School. Mr Spencer, his new teacher, the gigantic rower who was so cool. Life was good.

He got up, made his bed, went to the bathroom with its gold taps, which had started looking brassy, took a shower and got dressed, putting on the new trainers which his dad had bought for him last month: Nike JR Mercurial Victory 111 Turf boys' football boots in orange.

Downstairs he turned the radio on super-quiet, just for some company. The tumble of voices talking about indiscernible subjects had become his family. He made himself some breakfast in the fancy Bulthaup kitchen he'd cleaned last night, just for something to do on a dead Sunday evening. Despite spending months designing it, she never came into the kitchen. It was his haven. He whisked up two eggs, dipped two slices of bread into it and fried them in some butter. He watched and counted as the egg frilled on the edges. On ninety he flipped them and started counting again. Out on the plate he spread a thin layer of Marmite over the two pieces, cut them up into soldiers and ate them standing at the table while reading through a book of chess openings his father had given him for Christmas.

On the way out he hovered at the living-room door. He didn't want to look in but felt he had to, just to make sure that she wasn't in some terrible state: on the floor, blouse off, skirt rucked up, damp patch where she'd wet herself. That had been last Friday on the way to school and it had made him late for his knockabout with Sergei. And Sergei was important to him because he didn't go to his school. He couldn't have friends from his own school for obvious reasons. They'd want to come home at some point. They'd want to have sleepovers. They'd get to see his world.

The living room was empty, just the usual bottles on almost every surface. He didn't touch this room. His mother cleared her bottles away once a week in time for the recyclers on Thursdays. The seven empty bottles around the room were evidence of her weekend's drinking. He closed the door, relieved that there wouldn't have to be a rescue operation: no helping her to stagger up the stairs, stripping her off, into the shower, towelling her down, getting her into bed. That always took him an hour but by now he was an expert.

This was great news because it meant he had a whole half-hour to himself, time to show Sergei the tricks he'd been working on at the weekend: the top head stall, Around the Moon followed by Around the World. He picked up his football on the way out and locked the front door, all the time keeping the ball in motion from foot to foot. He turned, kicked the ball high in the air, over the garden wall, ran down the path, through the gate just in time to catch the ball on his chest and let it drop to his knees. Alternating between his left and right knees he set off marching down the quiet road until exuberance took over and he kicked the ball ahead and ran after it at a fierce sprint to get to it before it reached the corner.

The ball bounced against the curved low wall and popped up beautifully for him and he did a side bicycle kick, volleying the ball, which rocketed across the street into some railings. He half-volleyed the ball back with a satisfying smack and, when it returned, let it roll up his foot. Just as it passed his nose he dropped his head and the ball came to rest on his neck. One swift flick of his head and the ball was resting on his crown. He popped it up, swirled his head Around the Moon, caught it on his crown once more. He let it drop to his right foot, gave it a little dink and whipped his right foot around the ball, then his left foot and

41

caught it on the toe of his beautiful orange Nike. All that practice had been worth it.

Applause.

Sasha looked up. Normally there was nobody in the street at this time. From between the parked cars on the other side of Netherhall Gardens came Sergei in his grey hoody, clapping and bouncing his own ball from his left to his right foot.

'How long that take you?' said Sergei in Russian.

'All weekend,' said Sasha.

'Take a look at this,' said Sergei.

He popped the ball up high and headed it even higher and then caught it dead on his neck, rolled it down his extended right arm and then across his back to his extended left arm and then back to his neck.

'Yeah?' said Sasha.

Sergei let the ball drop down his back to his heel and, looking over his right shoulder, he did Around the World with his right foot and then, looking over his other shoulder, did the same with his left foot. Then he back-heeled it high above his head and as it came down he dropped onto his hands, flicked his legs up and rocketed the ball into the railings.

Sasha gaped in awe. Sergei was fourteen years old to his ten, but he knew that some of the pros would have trouble with a trick like that. Around the World behind your back!

They walked down Netherhall Gardens towards Sasha's school, keeping their balls on the move, swapping them every now and again until Sergei darted down a side street taking both balls with him. He snaked around some bollards at the bottom and sent a ball up high, which Sasha took on his chest. The second ball he swept up and over Sasha's head. Sasha turned to chase and ran straight into the arms of a man in a thick wool coat, who threw him onto the back seat of a black Mercedes, where another man pressed his face hard into a rag in his gloved hand. The door slammed after him. Sasha didn't hear it. Sergei retrieved both balls as the Mercedes came out of its parking spot. He got in next to the driver, pulled the door to. The Mercedes took off with a sharp squeal from its front tyres.

*

Mercy came awake, stretched, eyes closed, languorous as a cat. She was warm and relaxed under the duvet, still with the thrill of last night in her sex.

That fierce hug had turned into a long kiss and urgent sex on the sofa and then a much longer session in bed, followed by a strange, careless sleep to be woken by Alleyne with a plate of cheese on toast and a glass of white wine, which they'd gulped down in bed. This was followed by a joint, from which, in the spirit of recklessness, she took two tiny tokes. There was a lot of giggling and then more sex and a longer sleep from which she'd had to struggle to come round.

She ran her hands over her head and face, stretched them up into the air trying to recall if there'd ever been a time when she'd woken up caring so little about the world roaring beyond the bedroom window.

She rolled her head, knew what she would see. His back. She was just reaching out to touch him when she noticed a piece of paper curling away from the ceiling with the damp and only then did the full horror of yesterday kick back in to her mind.

What a fool am I?

Sliding out from under the duvet, she gathered her clothes, went to the bathroom. She swilled some odd taste out of her mouth with water from a tap encrusted with limescale and refused to look at herself in the demanding mirror. She had a quick basin wash just to feel bearable and had to dry herself off with toilet paper as the only available towel was of the rough and slightly damp sort found in a car mechanic's toilet. She dressed. Had to look at herself to put on lipstick, hoped the make-up would drive out some of the self-pity from her face.

Her cop instincts, as Amy would call them, meant that she was unable to resist opening the one door in the flat she hadn't seen behind. The room was bigger than the bedroom they'd been sleeping in and was full from floor to ceiling with cartons of cigarettes, high-end trainers, state-of-the-art headphones, Bose iPod docks and Samsung, LG and Panasonic LED flat-screen TVs. She shook her head. Fucking with a fence, she said under her breath, determined to be hard on herself.

'Now I'm going to have to kill you,' said a voice with so little

43

threat in it she turned very slowly to see Marcus Alleyne standing naked in the doorway, running his hand up and down his washboard stomach. For a fleeting moment she thought about going back to bed with him, taking a break from the ugly world in which she operated, but then DI Danquah reasserted herself.

'Just tell me where I can find Glider, Marcus.'

'He not going to love me for sending you to his door.'

'You said that last night.'

'Did I? Must be all that weed making me forgetful.'

Yes, that figured, thought Mercy. The taste of it still in her mouth. The smell of it still heavy in the flat like a morning mist in the tropics.

'I'm only interested in Amy,' said Mercy, rolling her finger over in a repeat, 'and Glider doesn't have to know how we got to his door.'

'He's not a fool, G,' said Alleyne. 'He'll work out the info chain. And then where my balls going to be?'

'Just tell me, Marcus, or I'll get the plods round here to take a look at this lot,' she said, nodding into the room.

He gave her an address near the Caledonian Road in north London.

'Is that why you slept with me, Mercy?' he said, smiling. 'Break me down?'

'It seemed to work.'

'You're cruel, lady, you know that? You're very cruel,' he said. 'Not to me. No, sister. You're cruel on yourself. You need to take your foot off that pedal driving you into the dark.'

Is it that obvious? she thought, looking at him, questioning.

'Thanks,' she said, and brushed past him.

'You going to call me?' he asked, amused at this odd reversal for him.

'Why?'

'I like you. When you're nice and smoothed out you're a very likeable woman.'

'Goodbye, Marcus,' she said, smiling. 'The cheese on toast was memorable.'

She turned her phone back on and left.

In the car, messages: Charlie, Charlie, Charlie.

'Where are you?' she asked before he could start.

'I thought I'd go and see Esme.'

'Ask her what rank ideas she stuck in Amy's head?'

'I won't put it like that,' said Boxer. 'You?'

'Work. Talk to DCS Makepeace, see if I can get some flexibility on time. Chase the UK Border Agency. Go and see Amy's teachers and the headmistress at Streatham and Clapham High. And I've got an address for Glider.'

'How did you get that?'

'I slept around; people told me things.'

Boxer wasn't sure how to take that – not funny enough for a joke, too ugly for the truth.

'I got to Marcus Alleyne, broke him down,' she said to end the silence, and gave him Glider's address. 'It would be better if *you* went round to see Glider. Alleyne doesn't want the responsibility for sending the cops to his door and … he's violent.'

Boxer called his mother, said he was coming to see her. She didn't sound overjoyed, but then again she was someone who, if she'd felt joy, would be disinclined to show it.

Esme Boxer lived in an expensive development in Hampstead. The old Consumption Hospital in Mount Vernon. From the outside it looked like the set of a Victorian horror movie with a pointed turret on the corner, from which someone could be hurled onto the sharp railings below. Esme had a two-bedroomed apartment on the first floor. They sat in the kitchen, where she made coffee for one. Esme smoked Marlboro full strength, despising anyone who ate, drank, smoked or even spelled anything 'Lite', and poured Grey Goose vodka direct from a bottle she kept in the freezer into a small shot glass. She sipped, smacked her lips, took long, luxurious drags from her cigarette, which she inhaled down to her heels, and listened to what had happened to her granddaughter.

'Well, it's in her genes,' she said. 'You ran away twice and you helped Mercy run away too. What can you expect?'

'Amy didn't know anything about that.'

'Yes, she did. I told her.'

'And why would you do a thing like that?'

'She wanted to know something about her parents. The two of you were a mystery to her. That's why we got on. We just used to sit at this table and talk. She'd ask about my life. I'd ask about hers. And, thinking about it, quite a lot of the time we were talking about you and Mercy. A couple of dark horses if ever there were.'

'You ran away from home too,' said Boxer. 'And you never went back ... not even for your father's funeral.'

'It's a long way to go to see a bastard stuck in the ground.'

'And I suppose you covered the subject of my father, your husband's ... disappearance.'

'You mean, seeing as we're talking about bastards,' said Esme, her accent drifting back towards Parramatta, the vodka loosening her throat.

'That doesn't sound like you gave him—'

'A fair press?' said Esme, cutting in mercilessly. 'It was one thing to leave me, but quite another to walk out on you. I told Amy the truth with no slant: that he was wanted for questioning in connection with a murder and he absconded. Clothes and passport found on a beach in Crete. Heard of no more.'

'When did you tell her that?'

'She wasn't a minor. She was over sixteen. Able to hold her liquor. If that's what's worrying you. She'd asked me a couple of years earlier and I'd been vague. Then she mounted one of her campaigns and I cracked.'

'Everything?' said Boxer. 'As in, who he was accused of murdering?'

'He never got as far as being *accused*,' said Esme. 'But yes, I told her it was my business partner and director.'

Esme's hand trembled slightly as she reached for the shot glass. She sipped, took a crackling drag from her cigarette, held it in, let it trickle from her nose.

'It's just history,' said Esme, 'and you told me that was the very reason you didn't want to be a homicide detective any more. It was all past tense. It wasn't going to bring anybody back. And it won't bring Amy back. You might be able to winkle out some cockeyed reasoning as to why—'

'I'm angry,' said Boxer.

'With me?' asked Esme, astonished. 'You think I put this idea into her head? Don't be bloody ridiculous. This has been building for years.'

'I'm not angry at you,' said Boxer. 'I'm angry at myself.'

'Welcome to the club,' said Esme. 'We're all platinum card members here.'

'So what have you got to be angry about?' asked Boxer.

Esme didn't answer but looked out of the kitchen window, and Boxer saw what looked like some colossal hurt worming its way across her face as if she too had a stack of unanswerable questions, which for a moment had seen the light of day.

'I suppose that's what humans do when left to their own devices,' said Boxer. 'Rake things over. Part the shit in the hope that there will be some revelatory nugget to explain it all.'

'In my experience,' said Esme, taking another thumping drag deep into her lungs, 'parting shit will only reveal more shit underneath. The best thing to do, and also the most impossible, is to bury it. Forget about it. Move on with your life. Remember, nobody ever learned anything from history.'

Silence while Boxer wrestled with her penetratingly cynical insight.

'Did Amy leave a note?' asked Esme.

Boxer produced a copy. Esme read it and was visibly struck by something.

'Kids,' she said, shaking her head and scratching around in a kitchen drawer. 'Nosy little buggers.'

She found a key. He followed her through the living room to the second bedroom, which doubled as Esme's office. There was a large wooden desk with a leather inlaid top and drawers down either side of a footwell. The key opened the bottom drawer and she sorted through some papers.

'This is where Amy slept when she came to stay,' said Esme.

'You think she went through your stuff?'

'She's that kind of girl. I was the same. Incurably curious. Had to know everything,' said Esme. 'I'd go out for dinner and come back to find Amy waiting for me with a bunch of questions which could only have come from nosing around.'

She pulled out a small sheet of paper ripped from a notepad, handed it to him.

The note was short and written in his father's handwriting but an extremely erratic version of it, as if he was hurried and stressed. *'I've had to leave. Don't come looking for me, Esme, because you will never find me.'*

6

Mercy dropped her bag on her desk in the offices of Specialist Crime Directorate 7, Kidnap and Special Investigations Team, and went straight into see her boss, DCS Peter Makepeace, who was in his early fifties but looked ten years younger even with his almost white hair cut en brosse. He glanced up from the documents on his desk, fixed her with his grey eyes.

'I've heard about Amy,' said Makepeace before she could get a word out. He nodded her into a chair. 'I'm sorry, Mercy.'

Her eyes dropped from his face to the papers on his desk, not used to this kind of emotional interaction. She knew he was an understanding man from her colleagues who'd been in to see him after difficult cases. She wondered how he'd react if she told him of the strange state of intent that had developed in her when she'd looked at the photo of Marcus Alleyne with her daughter and found herself incomprehensibly attracted to the much younger man. How she'd gone round there, burst into tears, ended up on his sofa, in his bed, smoking a joint, eating cheese on toast and gulping down wine and then walking away from the towering evidence of his illegal trade.

'Don't be hard on yourself, Mercy.'

'Sorry, sir?' she said, crossing her legs at the thought of Alleyne's young, hard body.

'I can see it. You're working yourself over. It's the most natural thing in the world to blame yourself. Don't. It won't help you to think clearly, and that's what you've got to try and do now. How do you think I know about Amy?'

She wiped last night from her mind and blinked her way through the possibilities until she focused once more.

'The UK Border Agency.'

'That's right. We've just heard back from them this morning. Amy left on a flight to Madrid from Terminal 1 at Heathrow last night. Her arrival at Barajas Airport passport control has been confirmed. The police in Madrid have been informed.'

'What you want?' asked the guy, hood up, hands in pockets around his flat stomach, knackered jeans, trainers. He was leaning against the handrail halfway up the stairway in Perth House on the Bemerton Estate, a spit from the Cally Road. He was looking at Boxer in his knee-length black wool coat, jeans and brown leather boots and knew just from the man's haircut and health that he wasn't from the estate.

'I've come to see Glider,' said Boxer, breathing in some calm, which he ordinarily had to do after his visits to Esme. He started up the steps.

The guy pushed himself off the handrail and barred Boxer's way, hands still in pockets.

'You police or what?

'No.'

'You look like police.'

'Well, I'm not,' said Boxer. 'I just want to talk to Glider.'

'What about?'

'He knows my daughter.'

'He's not in. Gone away,' said the guy, confident now.

'So you know him,' said Boxer. 'Why don't you take me to his flat so I can see for myself.'

'You don't believe me?' said the guy, his face gone dead, eyes threatening.

Boxer grabbed the handrail on either side of him, hopped up and flicked his boot out and caught the guy on the inside of the knee. He went down with a shout, slipped down some steps, holding on to his leg.

'Fa-a-a-ck!'

'Which floor's he on?'

Boxer tore back the guy's hood, twisted it so that the neck tightened around his throat and banged the guy's head, first into the wall and then onto the step as if he was no more than a rag doll. An eyebrow split, blood trickled down his face.

'Tell me,' said Boxer. 'I'm not feeling very patient.'

'Up the stairs, third floor, flat 306.'

'Introduce me,' said Boxer, pulling the guy to his feet by his hood, throwing him up the stairs.

The guy hobbled up the dark stairs on all fours like a chimp, with Boxer following him at a measured pace. They reached the third floor and went down the covered walkway to Glider's flat. The guy knocked on the door, Boxer stood back. The door opened and he pushed the hoody forward, charged in behind him.

'What the fuck?'

Boxer bundled the two guys down the short hallway and they came out in a heated living room with dark blue walls and red furniture that looked better than the rest of the flat. A thickset brutal-looking shaven-headed thug sat on the sofa in a white vest, jeans, no shoes, with his hand resting on the bare thigh of a young black girl in tight black shorts. His nose looked as if it had been broken a few times and his eyes were set wide apart over its shattered bridge. This was Glider, Boxer could tell from the heavily muscled arms, which were black, blue, green and red with tattoos, while his hands didn't have a mark on them. It made him look incongruously gloved. Boxer's imagination failed him as he tried to picture Glider with his daughter.

'Says he's not police … just wants to talk to you about his daughter,' said the hoody, leaning against the wall rubbing his knee, while the other guy, arms held out, biceps tensed, pecs twitching, was looking for a way in to Boxer.

'Don't bleed on the fucking carpet,' said Glider, pointing a vicious finger. 'Fuck off back downstairs, both o' you. Useless wankers.'

He flicked a thumb at the girl, who got up and took her shorts, straining over her large behind, into another room. The hoody and his friend limped out; a door closed elsewhere in the flat. Glider supported himself with his hands on the sofa arms as if he might split them away from the seat. There was a large glass ashtray filled with butts on the seat next to him and, on the coffee table in front, a carton of Marlboros and a Zippo.

'You don't look like the kind of bloke whose daughter I'd know,' he said.

'You went to Tenerife ten days ago with a bunch of girls to bring back cigarettes.'

'How do you know it was me?'

'Your name came up as the gang leader.'

'None of those girls knows where I live.'

'It didn't take me long.'

'Ten days?' said Glider, smirking.

Boxer dead-eyed him. Glider frowned, trying to work out what this was about: an angry father, that was clear, but about what and why now?

'Let's start with your daughter's name,' he said.

'Amy.'

'Oh yeah,' he said, holding eye contact. 'The coloured girl.'

'I can see you've got a taste for them,' said Boxer.

'You and me both, I'd say.'

Glider's hand slipped off the arm of the sofa and came to rest on the glass ashtray. Boxer didn't miss a thing, kept his eyes on Glider's.

'As I remember, there were four girls, all friends of Karen's,' said Glider. 'We met up in Tenerife. Had ourselves a nice weekend.'

'Smuggling cigarettes.'

'Right,' said Glider. 'Just covering our costs. They knew what they were doing and they were up for it. Nobody got hurt and they all got paid.'

'You slept with my daughter,' said Boxer, matter-of-fact, not injured by it.

'She's twenty-one.'

'Seventeen.'

'Well, there you go. Not what she told me. And not a criminal offence neither,' said Glider, getting riled now. 'If every dad came hunting for every bloke their daughters had slept with of a weekend this city'd grind to a halt.'

'Where is she now, Glider?'

Silence while the import of that question elbowed along Glider's synapses.

'So, she done a runner,' said Glider. 'Not to me, she hasn't. None of those girls knows where I lives … remember?'

Boxer was on him in a flash. One foot treading on the hand around the ashtray, the other foot in his crotch, knee on his chest. He reached for the ashtray, emptied it in Glider's face, who spat out the butts and ash.

'You want to take a bite of this?' asked Boxer, ashtray high above his head.

Glider rested his head on the back of the sofa, showed he wasn't fighting. He'd seen the speed with which Boxer had moved, and the expertise had made him realise that this was no ordinary unhappy dad.

'No need for that,' he said. 'We're just talking.'

Boxer was surprised at how wound up he was. He wanted to ram the ashtray into Glider's teeth, and he'd have done it if the brute had given him the slightest cause. He stepped back off the sofa, turned and hurled the ashtray into the open-plan kitchen, where it smashed against the wall. Shards cascaded down onto the dirty plates and glasses on the counter.

Glider eyed him as he would an unpredictable animal, one prone to tail-wagging and seconds later taking chunks out of legs. He didn't move.

'You're going to do two things for me,' said Boxer. 'You're going to put all your feelers out to everybody you know and find out if they've heard anything from Amy. And you're going to be very cool about it. You don't want to spook her. When you find out something you call me, right?'

Boxer flipped Glider a card, which landed on his chest. He didn't reach for it.

'And give me your number,' said Boxer, punching it into his mobile.

The mobile buzzed in his hand. Mercy. She told him about the UK Border Agency, said that Security at Heathrow Airport was going to put together some CCTV footage of the person they believed to be Amy and would send it to her at SCD 7. The Spanish police were already on to it. Boxer hung up.

If there was any change in Boxer's demeanour, Glider didn't see it.

'You do that for me?'

Glider nodded.

Boxer trotted downstairs, nodded at the two hoodies in the stairwell on the way.

'Amy,' said Mercy, riveted to the screen as she stood watching at her desk, fists planted, checking the clothes her daughter was wearing, the same ones as when she'd left the house, dropped in to say goodbye.

There were no passport checks on leaving the UK, but the Border Agency had summoned a passport photo of Amy Boxer and sent it to the terminal manager at Heathrow. One of the computer operators in Security, as a favour, had put together footage of the girl they believed to be Amy Boxer arriving at Terminal 1, visiting the ladies' toilet before heading through security and the departure lounge.

Once Mercy had seen that clear shot of Amy, arriving at the terminal and heading for the lifts wearing those clothes, despair settled in her stomach. She unplanted her fists, stretched out her hands and sat back in her chair, watching vaguely as the footage jumped to different cameras and angles tracking Amy over the concourse, through security, in and out of shops.

Mercy stared at the screen, her mind flitting between strange vignettes: an indistinct image of Madrid, a city she'd never been to, her daughter somewhere in the Spanish cliché Mercy's mind was inventing and the rather more uncomfortable memory of her own shameful liaison with Marcus Alleyne because she'd first seen him with Amy in an airport.

Her concentration slipped away from the CCTV images as she tried to remember whether she'd felt any attraction to Alleyne on seeing him meet Amy at Gatwick just over a week ago. Then she was vividly reliving last night, with Alleyne's hard body on top of her, his face staring down from above, his arms outstretched as he rammed into her, while her heels came up to the sides of his buttocks and spurred him on. He'd whispered her name, Mercy, Mercy, Mercy with each thrust as if begging for clemency. She sighed as the phone rang. The guilt kicked in once more as DCS Makepeace said he was ready to see her again.

'Do you want some time off, Mercy?' he asked.

'Not at the moment,' she said. 'Now that we've established she's gone to Madrid we'll have to wait for the Spanish to give us some kind of lead.'

'Does she know anybody in Spain?'

'She had a Spanish boyfriend a couple of years ago, a holiday romance, but out on the coast. She's never been to Madrid.'

'So she's probably in a hotel at least for the first night,' said Makepeace. 'Everybody who stays in a hotel in Spain has to give their passport details when they check in, but that information reaching any sort of data centre takes time.'

'Well, I don't speak Spanish. So I'm not going to be much use out there.'

'Do you or Charles have any contacts who could speed up the process?' said Makepeace. 'What about that old friend of his from the army days? The one who works in MI6?'

'Simon Deacon?' said Mercy. 'Well, first of all, he's on the Asia desk so Europe's not really his area, and second, I don't know, that seems like a big gun to pull on a tiny little bird.'

'But he'd have some kind of link into Spanish intelligence, who could make it happen now rather than it taking days, during which time Amy moves on and you lose the trail.'

Mercy was nodding at him but with no show of engaging the gears.

'Mercy?' he asked.

'I'm just thinking,' she said, 'how well she's planned this. She's been meticulous. Far more meticulous that I was when I ran away.'

'And?'

'I'm just thinking out loud, sir. She hasn't torn off into the night after some huge family row, which is the ultimate vulnerable and dangerous state to be in. She's rationally and logically executed her plan to leave home.'

'It's been difficult for you over these last three years, I know.'

Mercy grunted at the understatement.

'Part of me is thinking ... let her go,' she said and waited for the shocked intake of breath, not just from Makepeace, who had two children, but from the whole of child-centric Britain.

'What's the other part of you thinking?' said Makepeace, shrewd, used to seeing people operating under stressful circumstances.

'Oh, that's the usual mess of love, anger, rejection, inadequacy, guilt,' she said, stumbling on, 'you know, the whole gamut of emotions of the failed mother.'

'Isn't the one influencing the other?'

'What would happen if we got her back or rather brought her back?' said Mercy. 'Or maybe *dragged* her back is the word I'm looking for?'

'I suppose you'd go into some kind of family therapy where there was a forum for you all to express your ... anger, disappointment and frustration,' said Makepeace, thinking he didn't like the sound of that much either.

'Or she could go out into the big wide world and see if she could make a go of it,' said Mercy. 'Like I did.'

'Your father never spoke to you again.'

'A blessing,' said Mercy. 'And I would never cut Amy off. She can come back any time, talk to me whenever she likes.'

Makepeace frowned, couldn't imagine having these thoughts about his own children.

'And her education?'

'She wouldn't get A levels but she doesn't want them. She doesn't want to go to university. She's not interested. She's bored by it all. She wants a life,' said Mercy. 'But she doesn't want anything to do with the old life. Karen, her girlfriend, told us that she's terminated her Facebook and Twitter accounts.'

'Is Karen in on this?'

'The one thing I can tell you from looking in my mirror every day is when someone is hurt,' said Mercy. 'Karen is hurt and Amy's the one who's done it. She's walked out on everybody, not just Charlie and me. Her friends, family, even her grandmother, although ...'

'What?'

'I'm suspicious of Esme, but that's because I don't like her and the feeling is mutual.'

'Do you think …?'

'What I'm thinking my way around,' said Mercy, waving away the notion, 'is whether it's better just to let her go or to hunt her down and force her back to a life that she's so consciously rejected?'

'But she's only a kid,' said Makepeace, getting bewildered now. 'What does she know?'

'I can tell you that she thinks she knows it all and that she doesn't need any further parental instruction.'

'But in Spain?'

'All the CCTV footage from Security at Heathrow has now been sent to Barajas Airport. With any luck they'll find her on their network and we'll see if she was met or … what happened.'

'You're taking this better than I thought you would.'

'I'm not. I'm just showing you my calm, reasonable, rational-thinking kidnap consultant side,' said Mercy. 'I think you'd prefer that to the messy side. That way you won't have to hose down the walls when I've left.'

Boxer was with Roy Chapel at the LOST Foundation's offices. Chapel's twenty-four-year-old-son Tony, who'd lost his job the previous week, was helping him pack up to make the move to the new office in Jacob's Well Mews off Marylebone High Street. This new office would normally have come out of the foundation's budget, but it had been gifted to Boxer by a Brazilian friend for an unmentionable favour he'd done for him in Lisbon less than ten days ago.

LOST only covered missing persons in the UK so he'd already told Chapel to stand down on the Amy investigation, but the ex-policeman was reluctant to let it go too early.

'Wait until you get the final confirmation from the Spanish and then I'll stand down,' said Chapel. 'You never know.'

It was late afternoon when Mercy called with her request. Boxer phoned Simon Deacon from Roy's already empty office, explained the situation with Amy and asked him for the favour. Gave him Amy's passport details.

Deacon was appalled, hadn't seen Amy in years, still had an image of her as very young and innocent.

'Do you think she's been groomed by some creep on the Internet?' he asked.

'She's a bit old for that, Simon,' said Boxer. 'And way too sassy.'

'Well, as it happens I do know someone with good connections to the CNI, the Spanish intelligence agency,' said Deacon.

'Look, I realise it isn't exactly a question of national security,' said Boxer, 'and I'm certainly not expecting—'

'I know what you want,' said Deacon. 'Just a bit of friendly pressure put on the hotel department of the Cuerpo Nacional de Policía to find out where Amy stayed on Saturday night and whether she's moved on to somewhere else in Spain, Europe or … Africa.'

'Try not to scare the crap out of me, Simon.'

'What I meant was, that I'll make sure that my guy has them looking out for her in Tarifa and Algeciras so she doesn't get that far.'

'Right. Thanks. Sorry.'

'Leave it with me. These guys know how everything works,' said Deacon. 'How's Mercy?'

'Could be better.'

'I don't like the thought of you on your own,' said Boxer.

'This is how I am almost all the time,' said Mercy. 'I'm OK. I'm fine.'

He knew she was lying. She knew he knew.

'I'm coming over,' he said, which Mercy translated as, 'I want to go to Isabel's.'

'Just leave me alone,' she said and hung up.

Mercy hated this, couldn't stand not having a case to work on. Just paperwork or watching TV for the rest of the evening. Flicking through the mediocre crap. Nothing on … ever. She was walking around her newly emptied house, which strangely reminded her of father's place after he'd died. She was searching for something. A vestige. A remnant of family life. In the kitchen she surveyed the clean walls, the white fridge door with not even a magnet on it ready for a photo or a list. She drifted back to the living room, blinking, determined not to allow the tears to well.

A thought occurred to her, a task. She would trace that boyfriend

Amy had taken up with in Spain when she was fifteen, lost her virginity. He was seven years older than her. Was that a clue? This Glider, Alleyne had told her, was nearly thirty – thirteen years older. Did she like them mature? Was this her striving for adulthood?

Upstairs was one of those half-rooms that so many London houses specialised in, too small for a bedroom, too big for storage. She used it as a study.

Mercy unlocked the column of metal drawers in the second-hand desk and worked her way through stuff she hadn't looked at in years. There must be something in here. She remembered a discarded letter she'd seen in Amy's wastepaper basket: the end of the unsustainable affair. She'd rescued it, found the sentiments in the Spanish boy's poor English rather sweet. Had there been an address? Would she have gone back to him? Maybe he was in Madrid now. She turned on her computer with the intention of looking through the photos. He was in there somewhere. What was his name?

Flicking through the papers, she was conscious of not finding anything she expected to. She went through all the papers in her desk, even the ones where she never kept Amy-related stuff. Nothing. Everything had gone. Even the childish drawings and paintings of Amy's before she went to school had been removed. She clicked on her photo library and saw that this too had been tampered with. None of the old shots were there. Not even the baby shots. Even the holiday snaps in which Amy featured had been either deleted or cruelly cropped. Mercy sat back in her squeaky swivel chair, surrounded by her stupid police paperwork and paraphernalia, a fingerprint kit from some course she'd attended way back in the homicide days. All that was left. Then the tears did come. In rivulets. Streaming to the corners of her mouth, where their saltine sweetness leaked onto her lips.

And then her mobile phone rang.

Sasha Bobkov came round into a world of complete and impenetrable darkness. The fear leaped from his stomach and fluttered into his chest. He could feel his heart ticking in his neck. His eyelashes brushed against some sort of mask which was stretched over his head and the top part of his face, but left his nose exposed. A strip of material passed over his top lip but nothing covered his mouth. Everything was pulled tight by some sort of clasp at the back of his head. He was panting. His mouth was dry, couldn't find a bead of mositure in it. If he shook his head he thought his tongue might rattle.

His hands were tied behind his back and he was lying on some wooden slats. He could feel the gaps with his fingers. He reached out a foot and found the edge was about half a metre away. He reached his hands back and felt the wall. It was panelled wood, unpainted, unvarnished.

He lifted his head, felt dizzy, thought he was going to be sick. He lay back down again and tried to call out, but produced nothing but a dry cough.

A minute later the door opened and someone came into the room, bringing no sense of the outside world with him, as if this room and beyond were well insulated. A male voice spoke in accented English.

'You awake?'

Sasha didn't answer, couldn't. His fear had closed up his throat.

'I heard you cough,' said the voice.

Sasha opened his mouth but no sound came out.

He felt a spout pushed between his lips, liquid trickled over his parched tongue. He licked his lips.

'How you feel?' asked the man in a voice that didn't care, that was angry even.

'Is my mum all right?' asked Sasha in a whisper. 'She'll be ... she'll be worried, you know.'

Silence. Nothing. Sasha felt the man's eyes measuring him.

'You scared?' asked the man.

Sasha nodded.

A finger poked him hard in the chest. He felt its point between his ribs.

'You stay that way,' said the voice. 'Then you don't get hurt.'

Mercy flickered into consciousness, her eye drawn to the corner of the ceiling where the lining paper had come adrift. She was back here again. Not in her own bed. The black muscular back of

Marcus Alleyne was lying next to her. How was it that the obvious mistakes she was making were becoming so irresistible?

He'd called her at a moment of particular vulnerability, asked her over. She'd known with absolute clarity that this was not an invitation she should accept. *He* had called *her*. How had he got her number? He was working on her. She knew it. And before she could say 'No spliff this time' she was out the door and in the car on the way to Brixton. She recognised everything. All her pathetic motivation revolved in her mind as she headed down Coldharbour Lane, which, to her, had always sounded like a place of last resort.

Then she was drinking a Cuba libre and trying to refuse a joint, which within two puffs was making her giggle uncontrollably.

Miraculously she found herself naked, her throat so clogged with lust she had to loosen it with more Cuba libre from the bedside table. She'd never been noisy during sex, but now something had been released from deep within her, something that had come up from her viscera and raked across her vocal cords so that she'd had to sink her teeth into Alleyne's hard, smooth shoulder to muffle her shouts.

Mercy put a closed fist to her forehead. This was going to have to stop. This crazy reinvention of herself was no way for the mother of a runaway child to behave.

'I can hear you thinking,' said Alleyne without turning. 'I can hear you blinking, Mercy, you know that?'

'That's because I'm screaming at myself for being such an idiot and I've got loud eyelids,' said Mercy, getting out of bed, needing to wash and leave.

'I told you something really important last night,' said Alleyne, rolling over.

'Really important?' she said doubtfully.

'You've got to rela-a-x, Mercy,' said Alleyne. 'You know you can do it. You're just fighting something that's in your head. I don't think I've ever met a woman that's so ... What's the word? *Conflicted*, that's it. You ask me, what you're going through now hasn't got anything to do with Amy. She's gone, Mercy. She's out of your hair.'

'You know nothing,' said Mercy, quick and vicious.

'Calm down, for Christ's sake.'

'Stop telling me to calm down. And what did Amy say to you about me, about running away, about whatever it is she ... ?'

'You're still right on the edge, Mercy. All it takes is one little word out of place and all that guilt comes rushing to the surface.'

'Tell me what she's said to you.'

'Nothing. No-thing. I've met her once, then again at the airport. Five minutes both times. She's a cool kid. I liked her. You got nothing to worry about with that one. She's going to be fine.'

'But she's spoken to you about me. All that "conflict" shit.'

'Yeah, the "conflict shit". That's good. Good description of the bind,' said Alleyne, as if tying something up tight. 'Know what I mean?'

'No.'

'I've seen the conflict shit for myself,' said Alleyne. 'I don't need anybody to tell me about it. I can feel it inside you. It's like you want to come but you don't think you should, it's not ladylike or something, but then it gets too powerful for you so you drop your barriers and it all comes pouring out. That's what you've got to do, Mercy. Stop interfering. Just—'

'Just relax. Yeah, I know. Get stuffed, Marcus,' said Mercy brutally. 'Some of us have to stay focused. I relax and people die. What do you want out of this?'

'What I'm getting,' said Alleyne, hands open. 'I like you, Mercy. I don't know why, but if I start poking around in that too much I might end up *not* liking you. And that would be a sad day.'

Mercy stormed off to the bathroom.

'Take a real shower,' Alleyne shouted after her. 'A nice hot shower. No need for any of that bird-bath shit you did the last time you were here.'

She looked at herself in the mirror. Naked. Taut. Looked closer. Was there the worm of something dangerous in her eyes? She smiled at the 'bird-bath shit', shook her head.

The shower was good. She could feel it tenderising her. All the tension flowing away down her back, pouring off her hamstrings. She dried herself with a big towel he'd put out for her, went back to the bedroom, got dressed.

'Amy went to Spain,' said Mercy. 'Madrid.'

'How did you find that out?'

'The UK Border Agency.'

'You got some connections.'

'What about yours?'

'I gave you Glider. Did you go see him?'

'I sent somebody else.'

'Like who?' asked Alleyne, looking nervous. 'Just so I know.'

'Amy's father.'

'Oh shit. The heavy dude.'

'"The heavy dude"? I thought Amy didn't tell you anything.'

'She told me you were a cop and her dad ...'

'What?'

'I'm struggling to find the right word for him, Mercy. Don't want you getting the wrong idea again.'

'Try using Amy's words.'

'Dangerous,' said Alleyne. 'No, she didn't say that. I *thought* that. She said he's secretive. That's the word she used. He hides things. He looks like Mr Straight, like he was in the army and a detective ...'

'That's right he was.'

'But up here,' said Alleyne, tapping his temple, 'he's different. He likes gambling. High stakes. She told me when she came back from Tenerife that the reason she didn't want to go to Lisbon with him was that he'd play cards all night.'

'He likes poker. It's not a crime.'

'He keeps a gun under the floorboards in his flat. How about that?'

'What?'

'I'm just telling you what Amy told me.'

'I think she was probably just showing off, Marcus.'

'Maybe you're right, Mercy. Let's hope so. We don't want to find Mr G with a bullet out the back of his head, do we?'

Mercy returned home and went straight into cop mode, as Amy would have it. She picked up the fingerprint kit and a torch from her study and stood in the doorway of Amy's room and inspected the smooth surfaces. She turned off the light, flicked on the torch and walked around the room, angling the torch light across the bedside table, dressing table and chest of drawers looking for patent prints. She was astonished to find that all the surfaces had been carefully wiped down. She double-checked by dusting one for latents. Nothing. She dusted the handles. Again nothing. This girl had learned too much.

She inspected the windows and their handles, the sills. Not even a partial print. She went to the built-in wardrobes and all these had been wiped too. She looked inside to check the shoe racks and drawers. Nothing. She sat back on her heels and looked up at the full-length mirror on the inside of the wardrobe, and it was in the angled light of her torch that she at last found a complete set of Amy's fingerprints on the glass where she'd pushed open the door.

She stood on a chair, applied the dark powder, laid the cellophane tape over the top and then stuck it onto a white card. As she wrote Amy's name and date of birth she remembered why she had the kit at home: to show Amy how to dust for fingerprints when she was small. That was when they did things together. She put the card in her inside coat pocket satisfied that she'd captured this faint but identifying vestige of her daughter.

Her mobile rang. It was the assistant to the terminal manager at Heathrow, who had heard back from Barajas Airport. Amy Boxer had arrived there and had not taken an onward flight. They'd checked CCTV cameras in the arrivals hall and identified her going down into the Metro housed within the Terminal 2 building. It seemed likely that she'd gone into the city. She called Boxer, gave him the news.

'That squares with what I've just heard from Simon,' said Boxer. 'His guy from Spanish intelligence has confirmed that she checked into the Hotel Moderno near the Puerta del Sol. I've just booked a flight. I'll be on my way to Heathrow in an hour.'

7

11.30 A.M., TUESDAY 20TH MARCH 2012
Rented apartment, Calle Mayor, Madrid

Dennis Chilcott and his son Darren had flown in on easyJet and taken the Metro into the city centre. They were in a fourth-floor apartment a hundred metres down Calle Mayor from Puerta del Sol, in a building which did not have an operational lift. Darren, being young and strong with none of the blood-pressure problems of his father, had lugged the cases up eight flights of stairs and he hadn't been too happy about it. He was even less happy when he saw the spiral staircase up to the bedrooms.

Darren knew from his tyrannical management of their London dealer network that his father's crack/cocaine business was turning over a minimum of £20 million a year and felt that a little Club Class with swanky lounge facilities wouldn't have dented their profit margin in any noticeable way. Dennis Chilcott had been fifteen years in this business and had never even had a visit from the police, apart from when he'd called them in himself after one of his hardware stores had been broken into in the run-up to Christmas last year.

'You look like me,' he said by way of explanation, 'and anybody would know I don't belong in Club Class. The boys in SOCA know that. You don't think they're not looking at everybody going in and out of Heathrow and Gatwick Club Class lounges? Course they are. You got to look like nobody; that way you stay nobody.'

So for his first business trip to Spain Darren was travelling as he'd always travelled, and he wasn't convinced it was his dad playing safe. He reckoned he was just being a tight old bastard.

'So who is this guy L. Osito?' asked Darren, now sitting, huge and slumped, at the kitchen counter, eating fried eggs and chips with ketchup, drinking beer.

'He's a Colombian,' said Dennis from the sofa, lighting up his first cigar of the day. 'His real name is Carlos Alzate ... if that helps.'

'I thought his *real* name was L. Osito,' said Darren, who didn't speak a word of any foreign language, not even *cerveza*. 'Like Larry Osito or something.'

'Larry?'

'L for Larry or, maybe Lee or Leonardo seeing as he's South American.'

Christ, thought Dennis. This could be long day.

'El Osito is his nickname. *El* means 'the' in Spanish. They all have nicknames these guys, like Joaquin Guzman is called El Chapo, which means Shorty, cos—'

'He's six foot eight?'

'No, because you'd never dare in a million years to call him Shorty or he'd have a blowtorch to your balls before you could say boo to a goose.'

Darren stared into his plate, frowned. His father quite often chose the wrong saying for the occasion and nobody ever put him right.

'I thought you said *El* meant "the", so why does El Chapo mean Shorty?'

'That's how the English say it. The real translation would be the Short One.'

'So what does El Osito mean? And do we call him that?' asked Darren, scratching his shaved head with one hand while the other was daintily poised with chip between thumb and forefinger. 'I don't want to balls it up and end up with my tackle under the grill.'

'It means Little Bear – like Teddy Bear.'

'So, like old Shorty, he's a nice cuddly teddy?'

'No,' said Dennis firmly. 'I'm told he *is* short, but he's built like a brick shithouse. Pumps iron. There's something funny about that name of his that I don't get. So it's best we just call him Carlos. All right? Remember to shake hands. That's what they all do every time they meet in this country.'

'What happened to the Mexicans? Didn't you used to deal with Mexicans?'

'The Mexicans are still here: the brothers Jaime and Jesús. But the big boss, Vicente, told me they've moved their cartel guy back to Cuidad Juarez and they're letting this Colombian run the Spanish end of things for a while. Nothing changes. This is a get-to-know-you meeting.'

'And what do we know about El Osito?'

'Not a lot,' said Dennis, thinking: enough and I'd rather steer clear. 'It's just that the Mexicans have done a supply deal with his Colombian clan, which means they give them a share of the demand end in return.'

'And what does that mean?' asked Darren, not that interested but knowing he had to ask questions.

'The Colombians used to sell to the Mexicans for $2,000 a kilo. The Mexicans sold that to wholesalers in the States for $10,000, who sold it to dealers for $30,000, who cut it and split it and sold it for $100,000. Now the idea is to split it a bit more evenly so that everybody in the chain makes decent money and you don't get resentments building up. It's also means that their rival, El Chapo, doesn't have quite such a big percentage of the European market as before. Vicente's got his toe in the door; now he's trying to get his foot in.'

Darren zoned out when his father talked about business, concentrated on sticking his chips into the egg yolk. Dennis kept an eye on him, thinking: is this going to work? He could do violence, could Darren. He was bloody enormous. And he could do numbers if it was to spend money on himself or his girlfriend, but business, logistics, man management, meeting the foreign suppliers? He should have sent him to college ... then again, he'd got chucked out of school for half-killing some kid in the play-ground.

The intercom phone buzzed.

'I'll take it,' said Dennis, who knew some Spanish.

He ran a hand over his head, which like his son's was shaved, but in his case to disguise his baldness. It took him a couple of goes to get to his feet and answer the phone.

'*Buenos dias*,' he said and listened without understanding

everything that was said back to him, but let them in from the street anyway and managed to add, 'No hay ascensor.'

He waited with the door open, heard them pounding up the marble-clad stairs. El Osito arrived first, not even out of breath. The two Mexican brothers arrived panting. Dennis started up in his crap Spanish. El Osito stopped him with his hand.

'It's OK, we can do this in English,' he said. 'I am Carlos. You know Jaime and Jesús.'

Dennis introduced himself and his son. They shook hands. Dennis offered coffee, which was accepted. They sat around the small table in the living room while Darren made the coffees with capsules in a machine.

'This a nice place,' said El Osito, looking around at the rented duplex apartment. 'Better than a hotel.'

'We prefer it,' said Dennis. 'Less public, know what I mean?'

The coffees arrived in what looked like doll's house cups in Darren's massive hands. El Osito disdained sugar and sipped his coffee with one hand resting on his vast thigh, the muscles of his forearm standing out thick as hawsers. The two Mexican brothers emptied two sachets of sugar each into their coffees, which they stirred meditatively. Jaime was early forties, heavily built with thick, black, unmovable hair, very dark eyebrows, a moustache and a permanent shadow on his cheeks. Jesús was thirty, more slightly built, and wore his hair long but tied back into a ponytail to show his smooth, unblemished, good-looking features.

'Vicente says we going to continue to send you two hundred kilos a month,' said El Osito. 'He also want you to know that he sees the UK as a growth market, especially London. They want to start moving much more product this year.'

'Like how much?'

'Five hundred kilos a month by the end of the year.'

'That's a big jump,' said Dennis.

'You know, with the crisis here in Spain they don't have the money to spend on blow. The market going down. We need to expand in other places. Everybody going to London. A lot of money going out of the euro and into the pound. Twenty billion euros a month leaving Spain. Most of it to London. That's where the market is. Italians, Greeks all putting their money over there and let's not talk about the Russians. You sitting on a big market expansion if you want. If you don't want … ?'

El Osito opened his hands as if Dennis was giving it all away.

'I want,' said Dennis, conscious of imitating El Osito's speech patterns. 'It's just that I've got to expand my end of things. It takes time to develop a dealer network. A safe one, properly vetted so you don't get infiltrators.'

Dennis could see he was losing him.

'This the problem here in Spain,' said El Osito. 'The *costas* are dead. Property going down. The buildings empty. The *puti* clubs are closing. The local government is cutting everything. No money in the economy and Spain gone from being the biggest consumer to almost nothing. We suffering, Dennis. So we looking to the outside. We move our operations away from the *costas* now. We just keeping a team in Algeciras to take the deliveries, but we all here now. Madrid is the transportation centre for the rest of Europe. Now we looking to send containers direct to Liverpool, forget Algeciras. We looking for markets for like a thousand kilos a month.'

'I reckon we could manage three hundred a month easy, don't you, Dad?'

Darren's first words, and they might as well have come out his arse for all he knew, thought Dennis. Didn't have the first idea.

'That's what I like to hear,' said El Osito. 'Positive thinking. Three hundred a month it is.'

'Maybe we should just analyse thi—' started Dennis.

'You a big strong boy,' said El Osito to Darren, pulling his chair up to the table, putting his elbow on the surface, opening his hand. 'You like to arm-wrestle?'

Jaime and Jesús sat dead-eyed on the other side of the table as if they had to put up with this kind of thing all the time. Making a quick comparison between his vast but slightly overweight son and El Osito's evidently powered-up musculature, Dennis thought, at least I don't have to worry about Darren winning.

They engaged hands, Darren's not easily swallowed by El Osito's monstrous grip. The Colombian stared into the Londoner's blue eyes and with a grunt their shoulders popped and they started. After two minutes they hadn't moved. The cords stood out in their necks. Jaime's eyes started shifting in his head. This never happened. El Osito always won inside ten seconds. Dennis was trying not to feel too proud. Slowly the Colombian began to ease Darren down, but no sooner had he dropped him a couple of inches than Darren put him back to upright. A vein stood out in El Osito's forehead. It throbbed with extra blood. His eyes had gone black with concentration.

Slowly Darren eased El Osito's wrist back, one inch, two inches, three inches. Jaime was thinking, don't do this or none of us will get out of here alive. Only when El Osito's knuckles were just off the surface of the table did Darren relent. The Colombian took advantage and slammed him back down.

El Osito smiled, which was the good news.

'I *thought* you a big strong boy,' he said.

'Right!' said Mercy, meaning business. 'I need to work. I'm no good at this limbo ... My life is falling apart.'

She was back in Makepeace's office and had just managed to stop herself saying 'limbo shit', Alleyne style.

'What happens if you start something over here and then there are, let's say, developments with Amy in Spain?' asked Makepeace.

'I'll stick to the job. Charlie's more than capable of dealing with anything that comes up. He speaks the lingo for a start, after all those jobs he did in Mexico, Colombia and the Philippines. He's not far off fluent.

'I spoke to him as soon as I heard from the Spanish, told him that Amy had been seen on CCTV arriving in Barajas Airport and taking the Metro into the city. He'd already spoken to his friend at MI6, who asked Spanish intelligence if they'd help find out where she stayed on Saturday night, and he's got a hotel name. If anything comes from that, Charlie will deal with it. If I don't go back to work I'm going to go nuts. You know what I'm like, sir. Need a job to keep me focused.'

'You're in an emotional state, Mercy, and that's no way to be for a kidnap consultancy job.'

'I *was* in an emotional state. I've come to terms with what's happened now. I've rationalised it. Amy told the police officer she had money and wasn't going to be on the streets. She's not in any danger.'

'Look, I don't want to distress you unnecessarily but I have to ask you these questions,' said Makepeace. 'What if you get bad news about Amy?'

'No, that's fair. You're right. I would not be in a strong mental state.'

'You'd be devastated.'

'That's true,' said Mercy, changing tack. 'And for that reason I would not ask you to put me on any consulting job where negotiations could be jeopardised. I'd be quite happy with a role on a special investigation team. Just as I did on the D'Cruz case when Charlie was the lead consultant.'

'You're happy with that?'

'Anything that takes me outside my head. I need process, sir, more than anything else. Logical process to counteract emotional turmoil.'

'Are you happy working with George Papadopoulos again? He said he learned a lot from you.'

'Did he?' said Mercy. 'OK, I'll take him under my wing again, sir.'

'This is an extremely sensitive job,' said Makepeace. 'I got a call from a Home Office official yesterday morning telling me that he needed someone from my department to consult on negotiations for the release of a ten-year-old boy. His name is Alexander 'Sasha' Bobkov. He was kidnapped on his way to school in Hampstead at around eight thirty yesterday morning.'

'I assume we're talking Russian.'

'Mixed. His father, Andrei Bobkov, was married and is now separated from Tracey Anne Dunsdon. The boy lives with his mother in Netherhall Gardens and attends Northwest International School, which is down the end of the street.

'It's only just come to light that for the last few years the boy has been getting himself up and out of bed every morning, dressing himself, making his bed and his own breakfast and going to school on his own. I know it's only down the end of the road but you know what parents are like these days.'

'So what's wrong with the mother?'

'Alcoholic.'

71

'And the kid's been hiding that from the world?' said Mercy. 'Where's the father in all this?'

'Until yesterday he didn't know how far gone she was. When the boy didn't show for school they called the mother. Tracey was incomprehensible. Someone from the school went to the house, couldn't gain entry. The father was called. He had keys. They went in. Tracey was in her nightie on the living-room floor, surrounded by bottles, with the telly going. Her bed had been slept in so they think the call woke her and she'd gone straight back to the booze. The living room and bedroom were a tip. The rest of the house is unused except the boy's room, which was described as "heartbreakingly neat and tidy". Bobkov senior was stunned to find this state of affairs, but because he is who he is he reckons his son's disappearance has nothing to do with the chaos at home.'

'So who is he?'

'We're getting to that. The school told him to call the police and report the boy missing, but Bobkov can go one better than that. He has a special number which puts him in touch with all sorts of people – the intelligence services, the Home and Foreign Offices – you name it. The police are round there in fifteen minutes treating it like an ordinary disappearance to start with. A bit later on a "close friend" of Bobkov's turns up. An English guy, businessman, speaks fluent Russian and is Bobkov's chess partner in London. His name is James Kidd.'

'And what's he? A spook, or something like it?' said Mercy.

'It's not meant to be quite that obvious, and we don't know, but we assume. What we do know about Andrei Bobkov is that he's an old friend of Alexander Tereshchenko, and we're talking proper close friend. Bobkov named his son after him.'

'Are we talking about the same Alexander Tereshchenko who fled Moscow, came to London, made all sorts of uncomfortable revelations about the Russian government's involvement in the Moscow apartment bombings, the Beslan school hostage debacle, the Russian mafia and the assassination of crusading journalists. And who then had a tea party in the Millennium Hotel where two of his old FSB mates stirred in something a lot more radioactive than two sugars?'

'Yes, *that* Alexander Tereshchenko. Bobkov and Tereshchenko were in the FSB together. Bobkov left the security service before it got really ugly while Tereshchenko did some time in prison for giving an unauthorised press conference about FSB activities. On his release in 2000 Tereshchenko came to London with his wife and son and has lived here ever since. Meanwhile Bobkov got a job in the Russian oil and gas company Gazprom, before moving out in 2001 and setting up his own business. He now trades in chemical gases from an office in London. In 2002 Bobkov married Tracey and their son was born later that same year. Tereshchenko was at the christening. In 2006 Bobkov was graveside in Highgate cemetery when they lowered Tereshchenko's sealed coffin into the ground.'

'So Bobkov and Tereshchenko are very close,' said Mercy.

'It's believed that after the funeral Bobkov made a promise to Tereshchenko's widow that he would find out who had poisoned her husband with the polonium 210 and who ordered it.'

'I thought they already knew that. Wasn't it this guy Lubashev and his sidekick under orders from the president?'

'Whatever you do, Mercy, don't do a press conference on this without speaking to me.'

'I thought I was quoting the CPS, sir.'

'What you've just said is not what the Russian government want to hear, nor their henchmen in the FSB. They really are the last people you want on your back,' said Makepeace. 'What *is* our business is that we have to make this look like a perfectly kosher kidnap and rescue operation.'

'Did I miss something, sir?'

'There was a phone call before the police arrived. Bobkov took it. An electronically manipulated voice asked to speak to Tracey. There was a lot of background noise as if it was from a call centre. At first Bobkov thought it was a sales call. He said she wasn't able to come to the phone, which was true. An ambulance had been called. She was confused, undernourished, dehydrated ... whatever. The voice insisted it was very important and would only speak to Tracey Anne Dunsdon. Bobkov reiterated that she was incapable and on her way to hospital. The voice asked him who he was and he replied. There was a short silence. The phone was muffled by hand. The voice came back and made a demand for five million euros in used notes in denominations no greater than fifty. The money was to be ready for delivery by 17.00 today. Instructions were to follow.'

'Is Bobkov worth anything like that or is that just a mad first demand?'

'He's not at the Premiership-football-club-owning level, but he's very well off. He gave that house in Netherhall Gardens to his ex-wife. And that's got to be a few millions' worth.'

'So how did Bobkov react to the demand?'

'Possibly because of his long-standing friendship with Tereshchnko, he'd been expecting something like this, or maybe it was just his old FSB training kicking in, but he had the presence of mind to ask for some kind of proof of capture. The voice asked him for a question to put to the boy. Standing in the living room, surrounded by bottles, he asked them what Tracey's favourite drink was. The caller said he would come back to him and hung up. Within minutes he was back with the answer: Harvey's Bristol Cream.'

'God almighty,' said Mercy.

'Can you imagine? She had cases delivered by Tesco.'

'It's not a conclusive proof-of-capture question,' said Mercy. 'If somebody had been watching the house they could have known that.'

'It was the best he could come up with at the time.'

'Is anybody jumping to conclusions yet?'

'No. They're open-minded so far, but wary. Despite this spook dimension we're going to run it as a completely normal kidnap and rescue operation by the SCD 7 Kidnap and Special Investigations Team. Bobkov's friend James Kidd is staying with him, as is his lawyer, Howard Butler. They're the Crisis Management Committee.'

'Who's been appointed the consultant?'

'Chris Sexton,' said Makepeace, naming a colleague.

'This is his first case flying solo, isn't it?'

'He's proved himself,' said Makepeace, 'and it will be good for him to have you and George in support. Doing your usual brilliant investigative work around the boy's disappearance. Door-to-door, school, teachers, pupils, parents. You know what to do. While you do the routine stuff MI5 will try to find out whether this has got anything to do with his … interference in the Tereshchenko affair.'

'If this gang are straight criminals and have nothing to do with Tereshchenko, you don't want them to think they've bitten off more than they can chew and get frightened into some sort of drastic action.'

'Everybody's aware of the situation.'

'Has Bobkov made any recent breakthroughs in his Tereshchenko research and, now that the Russian prime minister has been re-elected president, has that—?'

'Don't even think about it, Mercy. Leave that to MI5. You and George just do your work. Don't tell George the bigger picture just yet; get him concentrated on the detail.'

8

'We're still in shock,' said the principal. 'I've taught in schools all over the world and never in my career has a child been kidnapped. And Sasha, such a lovely boy. Do you know what time he was … taken?'

'We've got a problem with that,' said Mercy. 'The boy's mother, Tracey Dunsdon, was in no fit state to speak to us.'

'I can imagine.'

'What I mean is she's an alcoholic. Has been for a while. So we're having to work back from when Sasha's teacher first called her to find out where her son was. That was at 08.55.'

'Sasha's mother is an *alcoholic*?' said the principal, aghast. 'There's nothing in his file about that.'

'I'll be interested to hear what his teacher's got to say about it.'

'Mr Spencer will join us in a minute,' said the principal. 'He's only been with us since last September. A young chap. Cambridge. English degree. Goldie. It's not easy to find male teachers at primary-school level so we grab the well-qualified ones when we can.'

'Goldie?' asked Mercy, who could tell the principal had a soft spot for Mr Spencer.

'The Cambridge University second crew … in the Boat Race,' she said, stunned at the ignorance.

A knock at the door and Jeremy Spencer, a colossus, came in. He was the sort that made ordinary folk lean back, as if looking up at a tall building, to talk to him. Introductions made, they sat down. His trouser material strained over his massive quadriceps. Solemnity sat awkwardly on what would normally have been a cheerful demeanour. He sat very still as if one false move and he would crack.

'Detective Inspector Danquah tells me that Tracey Dunsdon is an alcoholic,' said the principal.

'Maybe it would be better if I spoke to Mr Spencer alone,' said Mercy. 'I think we want different things from the same interview. It could be confusing.'

'As you wish,' said the principal, swishing out of the room in her crisp trouser suit.

'You're in shock,' said Mercy.

'Doubly so,' he said. 'Sasha's been kidnapped *and* Tracey's an alcoholic.'

'Is that what you called her – Tracey?'

'I started with Mrs Bobkov, but she didn't want that. She insisted on Tracey,' said Spencer, gnawing on his thumbnail, staring into the floor between them. 'She came to every parent–teacher evening. She listened. She was attentive. She even asked questions. I can't say she looked that great. Heavy bags under the eyes. Thin hair. People told me that she'd taken the bust-up with her husband very badly. I thought she was probably depressed. And she struck me as lonely.'

'I understand from the principal that she was friendly with one of the other mothers, whose son has since moved to the Westminster school of Northwest International. A Russian woman. Irina Demidova. Perhaps they—'

'Before my time,' said Spencer quickly. 'The school secretary will more than likely know about that.'

'Tell me about Sasha,' said Mercy. 'Let's start with his routine. Was he ever late for school?'

'No, no, the opposite. Registration is at 8.45 every morning, but the school is open by eight o'clock. Sasha was always the first here at eight or eight fifteen,' said Spencer, slowed down by his thoughts. 'Now that I think about it, with your new information, he was probably desperate to get out of the house. You know, not easy for a kid to be around that sort of thing. I still can't believe it of Tracey. She must have really pulled herself together to be able to handle those parent–teacher meetings. They're not easy. I mean, I know when someone is drunk, and she was never … '

'When you know you're going to lose your kid if there's the slightest suspicion that you're incapable you make sure you present a perfect image to the outside world,' said Mercy. 'Don't blame yourself. Alcoholics are very practised at that kind of thing. And Sasha was protecting her too. I doubt the state she was in this morning was that unusual. When they went into the house all the washing-up had been done for dinner and breakfast. One setting for each.'

'Jesus. The poor kid.'

'You don't have to be underprivileged to be neglected,' said Mercy from personal experience. 'What else about him?'

'He's bright. Not a genius, but you never know at his age. I would say more orientated to maths than the arts, but I saw some interesting paintings he'd done. He's good at chess. He's an unusual boy. What I like about him is that all these kids are from very privileged backgrounds. They come with a thick artery of entitlement running through them. Some of them are little buggers, you know, really think they're the business. It's what they've been led to believe from year zero. Sasha isn't like that. He always stands up for other kids and especially the more unfortunate ones, the socially awkward ones. I suppose his mother being in that state, he probably did a lot of caring for her. Must be in his nature.'

'Is he popular?'

'He kind of disdains popularity. Some kids set out to become popular. They have an innate understanding of PR. Sasha isn't like that. He's never short of other kids wanting to sit next to him, but he never courts the big personalities. He's just himself and, yeah, he's crazy about football. Thinking about it now, he must spend a lot of time on his own because he's the best trick footballer I've ever seen. He can do amazing things with a ball. He can stand there talking to you and just keeping it going on his foot and pop it up onto his head, roll it down his back and arms. Like Beckham. Other kids like that kind of thing. It impresses them. But Sasha never showed off. He could have brought the playground to a standstill but he didn't. It was a private thing. Something he could lose himself in maybe.'

'Sounds like a really great kid,' said Mercy, dismayed to find her own parental ache intruding on her professional life. Should she be in Madrid with Charlie? 'What about the father? Did you meet Mr Bobkov?'

'Yes, but only once a term. He never came to the parent–teacher evenings. That was Tracey on her own. He travels a lot. He and I have had a couple of good talks about Sasha. He's an impressive guy. I know he's a businessman – he has his own trading outfit in the West End – but he didn't strike me as one.'

'What do you mean?'

'Businessmen are all about surface. My father's one, and all my father's friends are like that. They know *how* to get on with you. I'm always aware of technique. It's why I didn't want to go into that world myself. My father was furious when I stayed on at Cambridge to do a PGCE. And primary school teaching? He just shook his head. He's the CEO of something in the City and even I don't understand what they do.'

'And Mr Bobkov?'

'Yes, sorry. He was different. He had no artifice … at least not with me. From the moment we started talking about his son he just opened up. I can't quite put my finger on it, but you knew you were talking to the real person and not some carefully fashioned image. When I talk to the other fathers, the only real thing they show me is a little bit of condescension, not so much that you'd want to hit them, but just enough to let you know they're unim-pressed.'

'Mr Bobkov and Sasha, were they close?'

'I'd say so. Even though I don't think they saw that much of each other. If he was in London they'd always go to a game. They were big Arsenal supporters. Yeah …'

'You're nodding to yourself, Mr Spencer?'

'What? Yeah, I know. You only really start to think about people when something like this happens, or maybe it's that the things you thought subconsciously come to the surface. I always felt about Mr Bobkov that he was operating in a whole other mys-terious and unknowable world and that his son was the only true person in his life. Why? I have no idea.'

*

'Yes, I remember her,' said the male receptionist at the Hotel Moderno. 'She's a very pretty girl. Red minidress and a little jacket, black, over her shoulders. It was cold. High heels, black too. Bare legs, I think. I remember shaking my head. Oh yes, and a small black leather bag over her shoulder.'

'And you didn't see her again?' asked Boxer, thinking, guy, late forties, hair thinning. He probably noticed all the pretty girls, every detail.

'I go off at midnight. The night shift comes on until eight in the morning.'

'We've spoken to everybody in the hotel at the time,' said the manageress. 'We're absolutely certain she didn't come back. I'm afraid it's not unusual in this city.'

'So what do you do when people don't come back to their rooms – with their belongings, I mean? The bill?'

'She paid the bill in cash on arrival. Two nights. One hundred and eighty-six euros.'

'So how did she make the booking?'

'Online.'

'With a credit card?'

'Of course. That's how we take the booking from the website she used and then they pay however they want to on arrival or when they leave.'

'In whose name was the credit card?'

The manageress scrolled through the computer.

'Mercy Danquah.'

'That's her mother,' said Boxer. 'What about her things?'

'She paid for two nights, so we just cleaned the room on Sunday morning. We didn't need the room on Monday, but today we have a conference so we put her things into storage and changed the room.'

'Was there anything in the safe? Her passport?'

'I don't know; I'll call housekeeping,' said the manageress.

'The passport,' said the receptionist. 'I remember now. She picked it up from the front desk on her way out. It was a busy time when she arrived so she left it with us so that we could take the photocopy and fill in the registration details. When she came down she signed the registration document and picked up the passport. I remember she put it in a little pocket on the inside of her jacket. It had a small button. She had to fiddle with it. You know the jacket? It was very short. It only came to here.'

The receptionist chopped himself on the ribs not far below his armpits.

'A bolero jacket?' said Boxer. He didn't know the jacket, had never seen it.

'Yes, like the horsemen wear in the *feria* in Sevilla,' said the receptionist. 'It's just that I would have expected her to put the passport in her handbag.'

'Maybe it felt safer to have it close to her in her jacket.'

'She was going dancing,' said the receptionist. 'You don't wear a jacket for very long when you go dancing.'

'If I'd been her I'd have left it in reception,' said the manageress.

'How do you know she was going dancing?'

'She asked the concierge for some good places to go.'

'Is the same concierge on duty now?'

'Until midnight.'

'Can I have a look at her things?'

Boxer shook hands with the manageress. The receptionist took him to the storage room behind the reception area, which he unlocked.

'Everything in the room we put in her rucksack,' he said, pulling it down from a shelf. 'Apart from that jacket hanging there.'

'Can I take a look at her stuff in here?'

'Sure. I'll be on the front desk if you need anything. Let me know when you've finished and I'll lock up.'

Boxer started with the jacket, checked all the pockets. He knew this coat – she'd had it since last winter, more than a year. In the inside pocket was a note to Amy from her class tutor at Streatham and Clapham High School. It was a nothing note about a change of time for a rehearsal, but it somehow made Amy's presence in the city come alive. He smelled the coat's lining and his eyeballs pricked and he had to blink back the emotion.

He opened the rucksack: jeans, pants, T-shirts, tights, a jumper and her favourite Converse trainers. Nothing unusual. He checked the jean pockets and found a bill from French Connection at Terminal 1 Heathrow for a Calling Apollo Dress £150, a mini

Adventurers jacket £92, and Tiarella ankle-strap courts £120. Nearly four hundred quid on clothes, paid in cash. This was a new side to Amy – maybe just an expression of freedom. She didn't have to ask for anything any more.

The rucksack sagged, his daughter's life reduced to this. He checked the side pockets, found a bikini he recognised from last summer. A pair of cheap earrings he'd bought for her in Brazil and been surprised that she liked so much. On the other side was a book. The *Footprint Handbook to Morocco*. He flicked through it. Places had been marked and there were scribbles in Amy's hand-writing. A slight weakness entered his arms. The book felt heavy. He dropped it, pushed his hands through his hair. Something *had* gone wrong. He'd tried to ignore it up to this point, but this book with its determination for onward travel confirmed it to him. Something had stopped her in Madrid. He breathed in, trying to keep positive, she could have just fallen in with some people.

A knock at the door: the manageress. Housekeeping had con-firmed that the safe had not been used. She offered him a room for the night, no charge. He thanked her, asked if there were CCTV cameras in reception or outside. She shook her head. You hate it in the UK, all that constant surveillance, he thought, and then, when you really need it, it's not there.

'I'm sorry for what you're going through,' she said. 'I have a daughter, fourteen years old.'

'Is the room that Amy used available?' he asked.

'I can arrange it.'

He picked up his cabin bag from behind reception, took it up to the room with Amy's rucksack. He walked around the bed, looked in the mirror, tried to imagine her in those clothes, getting ready to go out. He called Mercy.

'I'm at the hotel,' he said, 'in the same room that Amy had.'

'What's the news?'

'She was definitely here. I've got her rucksack and clothes. Her passport details are in reception. She used your credit card to book the room and paid in cash.'

'That was big of her.'

'She bought some clothes at Heathrow. Going-out, partying clothes. If I give you the details and product numbers of what she bought could you Photoshop her into them and send me the image? I'll make up a flyer, push it around the bars and discos, see if I can get a lead or at least a sighting.'

Boxer talked her through the bill while she looked the items up online.

'Have you seen the state of this dress?' said Mercy.

'Calling Apollo … ?'

'More like Screaming Sex,' said Mercy. 'This is what I'd expect Karen to flooze around in if she had better legs.'

'I thought they all dressed like that nowadays.'

'Hooker chic,' said Mercy. 'And light on the chic.'

He could sense Mercy trying to keep it all at bay with her savage humour, making light of it so she didn't drop down the worry hole. He wasn't going to tell her about the Moroccan guidebook.

'You all right?'

'I'm working,' she said, 'which is better than not.'

'I could have had him, you know,' said Darren. 'El O-fucking-sito. All strength, you see. No technique, Dad. Know what I mean?'

'I'm glad you didn't,' said Dennis. 'I had the feeling if you'd dumped him the guns would have come out. I had no idea you were—'

'I came third in the British Novice Championships hundred-kilo-plus class in November last year,' said Darren, refilling their glasses from a litre bottle of Mahou beer.

'Not bad,' said Dennis. 'And next time, Darren, just stick to the arm-wrestling, don't volunteer to take on another hundred kilos when you haven't got the first bloody idea whether we can shift it.'

'We can shift it,' he said, chiding his old dad. 'I know guys who want to open another five crack labs in Brixton and Stockwell alone. I know there's been a bit of a lull in the City since the credit crunch, but now they're back to screaming for it.'

'That may be the case,' said Dennis, puffing his cigar back to life. 'You might have *heard* that, but you don't *know* it. We haven't done the research on it. Do you know how much we have to come up with for an extra hundred kilos?'

'Go on, then.'

'Two million quid.'

'Shit.'

'That's two million a month. And if we can shift it, we end up with six million more we have to send to the laundry and that has to be set up. It doesn't happen like that,' said Dennis, snapping his fingers. 'And if you can't shift it, where do you put it? The longer you store gear the more likely it is to be found. The risk levels go up. That's why you don't make commitments to people like El Osito unless you know you can keep to them. Otherwise you'll be flushing gear down the crapper just so you don't end up with half a ton of inventory.'

'So now what?'

'We're going to have to talk him round. Talk him back down. We're going to have to persuade him that we want to take on the extra gradually.'

'He's talking about us taking on five hundred kilos a month by the end of the year.'

'So we have to say we'll take twenty-five kilos more a month for four months and then see how it goes before we agree anything more.'

'He doesn't look like a gradual kind of bloke to me, Dad.'

'The good thing is he likes you. You didn't show him up in front of the Mexicans and that's important. He'll remember that. You must never mention it, mind. But that's what you've got between you, right? Are you with me?'

'So you want me to talk to him about it when we go out tonight.'

'We'll be going drinking in bars and clubs. We won't talk about it then. I'll leave early. I'm too old for all that crap. You've got to find the right moment, in private, to talk to him about it. Like if you go back to his flat, or the Mexicans' place. Somewhere like that. Not in public. All right?'

'It'll have to be, won't it?'

Boxer was in the square at Puerta del Sol with a handful of flyers, which he was handing out to anybody who would take one. He saw a young guy, no more than twenty-four years old, who had his arm around a girl so pretty that people behaved strangely around her. The couple were huddled under an umbrella with two broken spokes in the throng of people on the square. He felt drawn to them, gave them each a flyer.

'Who is this?' asked the young guy.

'She's my daughter,'said Boxer. 'Seventeen years old.'

'What happened?' he asked, holding the paper Boxer had given him up to the light.

'She flew in from London on Saturday and disappeared on the same night, never went back to her hotel room for the two nights she'd booked, hasn't been seen or heard from since.'

'She looks very dark,' said the guy. 'For someone English.'

'Her mother's from Africa,' said Boxer.

The pretty girl squeezed his arm in sympathy, said she was sorry.

'Is this what she looked like when she disappeared?'

Boxer told him about the clothes she'd bought and how he'd got Mercy to Photoshop them onto her photo.

'That's cool,' said the girl.

'You know, with paper isn't the way to do it. These people,' said the guy, sweeping his arm around, 'don't look at paper. Paper gets dropped. Paper gets wet. Paper gets cleared away. Paper gets ignored. You stick this up in a bar or club, nobody will see it. You have to get it onto one of these.'

He produced a smartphone. The girl nodded. Encouraging.

'That would be great if I actually knew anybody here,' said Boxer. 'I'm English.'

'You don't, but I do,' said the guy. 'You got a Twitter account?'

'No,' he said, thinking how many times he'd been told to open one.

'Juan has fifteen thousand followers on Twitter,' said the girl.

'Are you a pop star or something?'

'He tweets cool things,' said the girl, birdlike under his arm, 'about art and music.'

'I thought Twitter was just words and not many of them at a time,' said Boxer.

'That's true, but you can also upload photos and add a message,' said Juan. 'You got the photo on your phone?'

Juan opened a Twitter account for Boxer which they called @ SeekingAmy and uploaded the photo through Twitpic. He added

85

a message with the number of the Spanish mobile that Boxer had bought at the airport so as not to incur massive roaming charges. Juan re-tweeted the photo and message to his followers.

'I can pretty much guarantee that everybody in this area will see that tweet in the next hour. The same people hang out here most nights. They're the regulars. If they've seen your daughter they're more likely to tweet you than call the number so keep looking at the tweets. You can follow mine too, see if they come to me.'

'You'll find her,' said the girl. 'She's here somewhere. Don't worry.'

Boxer went to the Taberna Galacie on Calle del Carmen and ordered a beer, sat with the Spanish mobile and his smartphone in front of him. The last line of Amy's note, the exact opposite of what the pretty girl had said, reverberated through his mind. He'd offered the couple a drink, but they had places to go, fifteen thousand followers to see or shake off. He'd handed out a few more of the flyers, gone back to the hotel and left some on reception and with the concierge. Already, as he was leaving the hotel, he'd seen the young with their smartphones and a girl with a red dress on their screens and some of his flyers stuck to the wet pavement, trodden in.

He'd left GRM before they started the Twitter and Facebook tutorials. All he'd picked up was bits and pieces from friends who didn't understand it too well. Amy had actively discouraged him from using it when he'd asked her about it. Said it wasn't for him. Too banal, she'd said. Now he wondered whether it was because she didn't want him seeing her tweets. Of course, he and Mercy had been barred from her Facebook page since its inception.

The tweets started coming in during the second half of the first beer. Most of them said, *Lo siento*. Sorry. But they'd re-tweeted. He suddenly realised how Juan's fifteen thousand disciples could turn into a complete religion whose sole aim was to find the girl in the red Calling Apollo minidress who didn't want to be found. And that, of course, was a problem. He'd started this process because his gut was telling him that something had gone wrong. His nose for catastrophe had rarely let him down. He felt it was how he'd survived the 1991 Gulf War intact: knowing a booby-trapped place just by the look of its huddled explosive intent, reading through the innocence that scarfed acute danger in a man's face. But part of him also believed that he might just be alerting Amy to his imminence, scaring her off. Or was that just hope, batting away his rising fear that he was already too late?

His Spanish mobile rang, startling him. A number he didn't recognise. A male voice.

9

6.00 P.M., TUESDAY 20TH MARCH 2012
Netherhall Gardens, Hampstead, London

'The key to the abduction was Sasha's craze for trick football,' said Mercy.

'That's all he does all day,' said Andrei Bobkov, flicking up his feet in imitation. 'He has a football on his toes every minute of the day, but I tell him it's not everything. He has to understand the game. That's why we play chess. I teach him tactics and strategy. Position and play.'

Bobkov was a dark, good-looking man, whose hair had gone to salt and pepper but who retained black eybrows and dark lashes. He'd once been a man in peak physical condition, which was visible from the power in his shoulders and arms, but his jowls and waistline had since seen too many business lunches and dinners. Mercy also saw what Sasha's teacher, Spencer, had perceived: that Bobkov carried a sense of other things of importance in his life, apart from his business and what he showed of himself. One of those things was, without doubt, his son.

Mercy let him have his say. She could see his emotional involvement with the boy and his desire to express it. Nobody was going to take that away from him.

They were in the living room of his ex-wife's house. The mess of bottles had been cleared away and the Crisis Management Committee had gathered around a half-full cafetière on the table surrounded by small cups with coffee dregs.

Chris Sexton, the kidnap consultant, who at thirty-five years old was a thickset, square-headed bruiser who'd recently had to give up his positon as tight head prop forward for Saracens in order to pursue his career, had given his introductory speech about how he envisaged the negotiations playing out.

'The gang's first contact with Mr Bobkov was, to my mind, tentative. They were hoping to get Tracey Dunsdon on the line and were unprepared for what happened. They conceded pretty quickly, which indicates that they probably already knew her likely state. Their lack of proof of capture or life might mean they're inexperienced or they were just probing to see if there was any organisation at this end. Our aim is to keep Mr Bobkov away from direct talks with the gang to minimise emotional leverage. The Crisis Management Committee will engage as extensively as possible whenever they call. We want to develop relationships with these people, to give ourselves the opportunity through our tracking system to find out where the gang are holding Sasha and to effect his release. The crucial thing is to maintain communication for as long as possible, to be firm without being aggressive and never to show weakness, even in the face of threats.'

Butler, Bobkov's lawyer, late forties, bald with blond hair streaking across his pate and massively contained by some Savile Row suiting that did its best to supply structure, had sat nodding affirmatively throughout the pep talk in an armchair to Sexton's right. On the sofa next to Bobkov was James Kidd, the suspected spook from MI5, late thirties, smooth, urbane but with no feature that would help you pick him out in a crowd: brown hair, brown eyes, bland-looking and an occasional tic that meant he winked at disconcerting moments. He offered no visible reaction to Sexton's vision as if, as far as he was concerned, everything at this stage was conjecture and only the eventual reality was worth considering.

Mercy and the swarthy, dark-haired, Detective Sergeant George Papadopoulos sat on dining chairs, notebooks open.

'Sasha leaves the house at around seven fifteen every morning,' said Mercy. 'He spends the time before school registration practising his latest tricks.'

'You can't believe what that boy can do,' said Bobkov with irrepressible pride.

'His teacher, Jeremy Spencer, told me that Sasha was normally in school by eight fifteen just after the doors open,' said Mercy.

'Except for these last two weeks, when he's been turning up close to registration time at eight forty-five. The school caretaker told me this so I asked George to build it in to his door-to-door interviews.'

'Once I knew about the football tricks I started to get a lot more hits from people who remembered seeing Sasha with his ball at that time in the morning,' said Papadopoulos. 'Once you're round the corner from this house in Netherhall Gardens the houses on the right aren't set back but are actually on the street. A lot of people saw him and they mentioned another kid who'd been getting involved recently. They all say he's a bit older than Sasha, slightly taller and broader with short blond hair. We're talking twelve to fourteen years old. The other boy was always wearing a black Adidas tracksuit, white lines down the arms and legs. Black Adidas trainers. Sometimes he had a hood up from under the tracksuit. To start with he didn't bring his own football and just involved himself with Sasha's games. By all accounts he was pretty useful with the ball too.'

'So where did this other boy come from?' asked Bobkov.

'I can't trace him,' said Papadopoulos. 'He's too old to be at the same school, which finishes at eleven years old when they progress to the Westminster school. Further down the road is South Hampstead High, but for girls only. The only other sighting I've had so far is from someone who lives on Netherhall Gardens and cuts through Netherhall Way to get to the Finchley Road. She does it every morning at the same time, seven forty, and she's seen Sasha and this other kid playing for the last ten days or so. She gave me the clothes and physical description. Last Friday this same woman had to go to work early and she found herself down Netherhall Way half an hour earlier, at seven ten. She saw the other boy, Sasha's footballing partner, get out of a black Mercedes parked by the hedge in front of a block of 1970s flats on the corner.'

'So this other boy was being positioned as bait,' said Butler.

'That's what it looks like to us,' said Mercy.

'Has anyone heard Sasha talking to this boy?' asked Bobkov. 'Are they speaking in Russian or English? Sasha speaks both, although his Russian is elementary it's still good enough to play soccer.'

'Not so far,' said Papadopoulos. 'I've got to find more people who use that cut-through at that time in the morning and anybody who saw him on the morning he was taken. Nobody's property overlooks Netherhall Way. On one side is the brick wall of a house and opposite is a block of flats behind a hedge. There's no CCTV either.'

'So, a carefully chosen place,' said Bobkov.

'I have the name of a woman who was friendly with your ex-wife. She had a child at Sasha's school who's since moved on to Westminster. Her name is Irina Demidova. I was given an address for her in Cannon Place, but she seems to have moved. Does that name mean anything to you?'

Bobkov shook his head. James Kidd took in the name, processed it.

'The school was stunned to hear about your ex-wife's alcoholism,' said Mercy. 'Were you aware of it?'

'I hadn't realised it was so out of control,' said Bobkov. 'Tracey was always up for a good time, but she started drinking more around the time we split up, which I put down to the stress of the situation. I didn't dispute her custody of Sasha. She was in a much better position to look after him than I was, given my work life, and I knew how important Sasha would be to her at this difficult time. I offered her the house. I hoped that her drinking would sort itself out once I was out of her life and she took full responsibility for the boy.'

'Does that mean once you left this house you never came back?'

'I was the focal point of all Tracey's problems,' said Bobkov. 'In my experience of relationships it's better to remove yourself entirely from the other person's life, so that they can start again without any distraction from false hope, past pain or residual anger – all those things that mark the end of what had been a good relationship.'

'You broke it off?' asked Mercy, entranced by Bobkov's sincerity.

'I had to,' he said. 'I didn't want to, but she had become so jealous I couldn't move, I couldn't look, I couldn't speak. If the accusation wasn't on her lips it was incessantly in her mind. We tried marriage counselling, but too many of the meetings ended up focused on her problems and she couldn't take it.'

'How did you communicate with her about Sasha once you'd left?'

'By text and occasionally we'd talk on the phone. Bare bones. Nothing more.'

'And Sasha never talked about her problems?'

'I can't believe how he's been living, but it doesn't surprise me that he's coped. He's that kind of boy. I've always taught him to look out for others less fortunate than himself. It was in his nature anyway. It was only when I got in here and saw Tracey's state and the bottles that I realised how hard he'd been working to maintain the façade. He's never said a word against her. Only positive things.'

'If you don't mind my saying,' said Butler, 'these are strangely angled questions.'

'We're just building a picture,' said Mercy. 'My next question is whether there would be anybody else who could possibly know about her vulnerability – apart from the Tesco manager who's been supplying the cases of sherry.'

Butler nodded his approval. Bobkov stared into the floor, thinking.

'Somebody's studied this situation very carefully,' said Mercy. 'There's nothing spontaneous about it as far as I can see ... except, maybe, not having a proof of life sorted out before the initial phone call. But then they were expecting to talk to your ex-wife. I noticed they caved in pretty quickly when you said she was incapacitated. Normally a kidnap gang would fight harder to keep the mother in the frame as she's their best chance of emotional leverage. They gave up quickly, as if they knew about Tracey's state already.'

'The only people who would know the answer to that are Tracey and Sasha,' said Kidd. 'Andrei's too removed from the situation to be of any help.'

'So nobody else comes into this house. Not even a cleaner? Not even once a week?' asked Mercy. 'We'll have to do some digging on that.'

The phone rang. Sexton nodded his big square head, blue eyes concentrating. He'd given everybody some preliminary training before Mercy and Papadopoulos had arrived. Kidd pressed the

speaker button. The recording equipment connected to the tracking equipment back in South Lambeth Road kicked in.

'Hello,' said Kidd.

'Who is this?' asked a voice.

'My name is James.'

'Where is Bobkov?'

'He's out trying to arrange the money. The last time you called
you said you would come back to us with instructions, but you
didn't give us a time.'

'He has until six o'clock tomorrow evening.'

'We're going to need longer than that. He's just called to say
that so far he's managed to put together one hundred thousand
euros.'

'Don't fool around with us. We know perfectly well that Mr
Bobkov has the capacity to pay. You tell him: if he's only got one
hundred thousand then that's how much he'll get of Sasha. A
hand, or maybe one of those magic feet.'

The line went dead.

'Are you the guy looking for the girl in the red dress,' said the
voice in English, music thumping in the background.

'That's right, her name's Amy,' said Boxer.

'I saw her. I didn't speak to her. I didn't know her name. I just
saw her with some people she shouldn't have been with,' said the
voice. 'One guy in particular. I wrote her a note and asked the
barman to give it to her. She read it and dropped it on the floor.'

'Was the note in Spanish?'

'No. I could see she was foreign so I wrote it in English.'

'What did the note say?'

'Something like, "The guy you are with means you harm."'

'Your English is good.'

'I lived in London for three years.'

'What's your name?'

'David Álvarez. I'm a musician and DJ. I saw your daughter
in a club called Charada on Calle de la Bola on Saturday night.'

'That was one of the clubs the concierge at the Hotel Moderno
mentioned to her as a good place to go.'

'I work there. I do a two-hour slot for them on Friday and

93

Saturday nights. I always go a bit early to see what sort of a crowd they've got, see whether the music's working for them, ask around and see what I can change to make it better. I saw this girl in a red dress. She looked very beautiful and very young and I wasn't sure she knew what she was getting herself into.'

'Can we meet?'

'Sure, but I'm just about to start a set at Joy.'

'I can go there,' said Boxer.

'OK, it's in the Calle Arenal, close to the Hotel Moderno. It's a big place so I'll get the doorman to let you in and arrange for you to be brought up to my zone.'

'Your zone?'

'It's an old theatre. El Teatro Eslava. You'll see what I mean when you get here.'

It was a short walk from the bar. Even in recession-hit Spain there was a queue in the rain. He walked past the crowd. There was nobody over twenty-five. Two girls in silver shorts, silver boots, black tights and silver hair went through their moves under their raincoats, cigarettes in the corner of their mouths. Boxer veered into the entrance. The doorman, very wide, hair cut en brosse, black coat, black polo neck, put a hand on his chest, lightly. Boxer said his piece. The doorman spoke into his cheek mike, nodded, told him to wait by the door for a girl to come and take him up.

The girl arrived, dressed head to toe in black, her hair cut in a bob that was so black and shiny it looked mineral. She had bee-stung blood-red lips and told him that house rules demanded that everybody bought a ticket but that it came with a free drink. He paid the money, followed her into the club. The music entered the structure of his body, fizzed in his joints. He followed her swaying hips, past people in varying states of undress by the cloakroom. They burst into the old auditorium of the theatre with three gold tiers ranged above them: dress circle, upper circle and balcony. The girl ordered a drink at the bar, which she handed to him with words he did not hear. It was slightly cloudy with ice and greenery in it. They went through a door at the side of the bar and got into a service lift, which took them up to the first floor. The girl stared ahead with a smile on her face as if amused at something going on in her head. Out of the lift onto an empty floor, none of the old

94

theatre seating. They walked around the balcony to the middle, where the DJ was operating on a raised platform above the dancers. The girl waved him through and left him. Boxer sipped his drink. Mojito.

The DJ standing in front of his electronics and turntables was almost as active as the people on the dance floor. The scene below was like the devil's vision of paradise. Girls with massively enhanced tasselled breasts danced on podiums in string knickers and thigh-high boots. Two bodybuilders, one black the other white, in tiny trunks struck poses on the stage behind. In between them on a walkway a masked woman in a black rubber bodice and red cape lashed at the two men with what looked like a carriage whip. Dancing around the podiums was the disco crowd, a fluid mass of arms, shoulders and heads that rippled in different colours as the overhead lights changed from blue to yellow to red. It was fantastic, a lurid dream sequence of thwarted communication but ever-rising emotional pitch.

A pair of headphones was put in his hands. He slipped them on and the music was muffled to a dull ache.

'I'm David,' said the voice that appeared in his head. 'Can you hear me?'

Boxer nodded. They shook hands, during which Álverez switched the shake to a hand clasp. Boxer was glad it didn't get any more complicated than that.

'She's going to be OK,' said Álvarez.

'I'd like to believe you,' said Boxer, uneasy with this constant reassurance. 'What you told me was not encouraging. Who is this guy you were warning her about?'

'He's a Colombian.'

'Does he have a name?'

'I don't know his real name, only his nickname, which is El Osito.'

'The Little Bear?'

'Yeah, it's pretty creepy that. It's what a girl would call her boyfriend if she was being really cutesy – *mi osito*. But it also describes him physically. He's short, very broad, muscular and mean. The opposite of *mi osito*. *Tiene muy mala leche.*'

'Nasty enough to turn milk off?'

'More like his mother's milk being bad,' said Álvarez. 'It's made him evil.'

'How do you know him?'

'He's been a regular at all the places where I DJ for the last year or so. For an *osito* he's a really good dancer. Very light on his feet and fast. Endless stamina … but that's probably because of the coke.'

'Does that mean he's a Colombian who's in the business?'

'We're not supposed to know this – we're not supposed to even talk about it – but a lot of people here are users. That's how they keep going. We know he's a big man in a gang, but we don't know which gang. He's not a dealer. He doesn't work on the ground. He's the guy who runs things. That's why nobody talks about what he does. Total respect. I've heard people say that he purposely lives a bit of a low-life existence so as not to attract any attention. They say he lives in a cheap block in a *barrio* called Pan Bendito, which tells you quite a lot … if you know Madrid.'

'I don't.'

'Don't go there if you don't have to.'

'I can understand you warning my daughter not to get involved just because he had some kind of criminal background, but you said he meant her harm. What's that about?'

'I could see she was on her own and foreign. Her type is one of his prime targets. Young. Vulnerable. Out for a good time. He's a charmer. Everything is great until it turns bad. Maybe it's something to do with the coke. It's turned him a bit psycho. He's beaten up girls I know in the clubs where I work.'

'And they're too scared to tell the police?'

'You've got to be kidding. He's the sort who'd have them killed.'

'Did you see Amy leaving with this guy?'

'No, I didn't. I was working later. I saw them on the dance floor while I was doing my set, but they were gone by the time I finished.'

'What state was she in when you asked the barman to pass her the note?'

'She was pretty far gone. I'd say drunk and coked up … Sorry.'

'I need to know these things.'

'Not many parents *want* to know these things about their kids. Mine wouldn't.'

'So where can I find El Osito?'

Álvarez turned, took a good long look at Boxer, sized him up.

'I can tell you're not an idiot,' he said. 'You look like you've had some training. A friend of mine from school was in a special operations unit in the navy and you have that look. So you know he's not the sort of guy you walk up to and say, "Do you know where my daughter is?" He has his freaks around him for a start. Mexicans. You know what I mean. Cuidad-Juarez-type Mexicans. I think they're brothers but they don't look it. The older one is heavy, lots of dark hair, moustache, while the younger one is slimmer, has long hair in a ponytail, smooth skin, nearly effeminate but always with a girl.'

'But where would I find *him*, El Osito? Just to take a look.'

Álvarez checked the time on his phone.

'I've only just started here. I've still got a couple of hours to go. I'll see you out front at two thirty. I'll point him out to you on one condition.'

'What's that?'

'That you don't try anything with him,' said Álvarez. 'You want to talk to him, you've got to come up with a strategy.'

'You hungry?' asked the voice, different to the first one but male with a Russian accent.

'Yes,' said Sasha. 'You haven't given me anything to eat.'

'The drugs can make you sick. We had to wait.'

'What have you got?' asked Sasha, who was sitting up, hands still tied behind his back, the weird blindfold over the top of his face. He leaned against the wall, knees up, heels dug into the wooden slats.

'Spaghetti Bolognese.'

'I can make that.'

'This will be better.'

'How do you know?'

'It's been cooking for three hours.'

The man left the room and came back minutes later with a plate of food that smelled fantastic. He set the plate down on the bench.

'Are you going to untie me?'

'Just wait.'

Sasha heard a sound and flinched as he felt something cold come to rest on his cheek.

'Know what that is?'

Sasha shook his head.

'Open your mouth.'

Sasha opened his mouth a little bit.

'Wide,' said the voice.

Something large, intrusive and metallic was pushed between his lips, grated against his teeth. His tongue made contact with the hole in the end. Unmistakable.

'Know what that is?'

Sasha, too terrified to even nod, unable to speak with his small mouth full of the massive weapon, managed a squeak at the back of his throat.

The gun came out of his mouth, taking a string of saliva with it.

'Now I'm going to untie you so you can eat your food,' said the voice. 'I just wanted you to know what's pointing at you. You touch your mask, I'll hit you over the head with it. You try anything, I'll shoot you dead.'

Boxer went back to the Hotel Moderno, managed to sleep for a couple of hours and was back outside Joy for two thirty. David Álvarez came out still wired from the music. They didn't talk but headed back to the main square and then on to a club called El Sol. Boxer waited outside. It was easier for Álvarez to go in on his own. A lot of the doormen knew El Osito, and if they didn't the barmen did. Most of the time it was a matter of asking a question and getting out. He wasn't and hadn't been in El Sol. They went up Gran Via to Ohm and then on to Reina Bruja. No luck. They caught a cab when it started raining and stopped outside a club called Mondo. Álvarez was back in five with the news that El Osito had been there with his freaks, no girls. They tried the Charada, where Álvarez had first seen Amy, and finally asked the taxi driver to go down to the bottom of Calle de Atocha to Kapital, where Boxer paid him off.

'If he's not in here we'll have to try again tomorrow night,' said Álvarez. 'You've got my number now.'

'Is there any way we can get El Osito's number?' asked Boxer. 'Of all these people you know there must be someone who wants to buy some coke. Someone must have his mobile number.'

'Like I told you, he's not on the ground. He has dealers doing that. He's running the operation.'

'How about if you wanted a kilo?'

'A kilo?'

'The dealers are doing grams, right?'

Álvarez studied him again. Thinking.

'Who the hell *are* you?' he asked.

'I'm an angry father.'

'Right, but you're not an ordinary angry father. You're very cool for an angry man. You're thinking clearly,' said Álvarez. 'Clearly, but dangerously. I said there was something trained about you. You're not a special cop of some sort, are you?'

'I'm used to working in very stressful situations,' said Boxer. 'And I know Colombians. I've worked there. You know FARC?'

'Shit. You've been in there?'

'I'm a kidnap consultant.'

'That's more useful than a marketing consultant for the work *you've* got in mind,' said Álvarez.

They heard male laughter. An exchange of obscenities. More laughter.

'There he is,' said Álvarez, looking up. 'El Osito. Coming out of the door now.'

They stood back as the group of four men walked past. El Osito was unmissable. He was smaller than the rest of the group but there was no doubt who was in charge. The overworked quadriceps of his thighs gave him a particular gait, like a weightlifter approaching the bar. There was an arrogance in the strut. His colourful shirt was open to the waist despite the cold and rain and strained over his biceps. His chest and stomach had no spare fat. El Osito beckoned and pointed to his back, and one of his freaks put a coat over his shoulders. Two of the guys peeled away and hailed a cab. Boxer was sure one of them was English. El Osito and the coat carrier headed for the Metro station. It was now after six in the morning and it had just opened.

'I'll see you tomorrow, David. Thanks.'

'Where are you going?'

'I'm going to follow him, find out where he lives.'

'Be careful and not just of him, Pan Bendito is not the best place to be in the dark.'

'Just try and get his number for me,' said Boxer. 'And it'll be dawn soon.'

He headed into the Metro, bought a ticket. There were a few other people on the platform, but not enough. He stood behind the Colombian and his friend, who looked Mexican, and followed them into the train. They sat in the empty carriage. No glances were exchanged. They got out at Pacifico and transferred to Line 6. There were more people around now and it was easier to get lost in the pockets of the crowd. This time he boarded a different carriage and kept an eye on them through the door.

They were the only people to get out at Plaza Eliptica and they were the only people on the Line 11 platform. He got into the carriage behind them and, when the train arrived in Pan Bendito, he waited until the last possible moment before getting out. El Osito was almost off the platform. Boxer let him get away before following.

Outside the Metro he saw the two men had turned left and were heading towards a park, where they parted. The bigger man crossed the road and walked by the park while El Osito took a path behind a Mahou beer sign over a place called Bar Roma, which seemed like a long way from Rome. The Colombian disappeared into a run-down eleven-storey block of flats. The glass in the door had recently been broken and shards were still scattered all over the floor. El Osito's shoes crunched over them to the elevator.

The lift doors closed and Boxer sprinted up the stairs, listening for the moment when the machinery stopped. Each floor had a door with a square glass panel through which the lift doors were visible. At the fourth floor the lift stopped. El Osito got out, turned to his right. Boxer opened the door a crack, enough to see the flat into which the Colombian disappeared.

Back down the stairs, crunching over the glass and out into the dark. Coming up to the Bar Roma Boxer saw the darkness waver and a guy appeared in front of him, head buried in a hood. No words, just the sound of a mechanism, and Boxer looked down at a steel blade pointing at his abdomen.

Still no words. A gesture. Hand it all over.

Boxer made no move. The hooded head came up. Their eyes connected. The ones under the hood realised they'd just made a very big mistake.

10

'You're doing that loud blinking shit again,' said Alleyne sleepily.

'Leave me alone,' said Mercy, her eyes stuck on the curl of lining paper in the corner of the room, which was lit by the orange street lamp coming through the slatted blinds.

She was here again. Couldn't leave Marcus Alleyne alone. She was telling herself it was naked desire, that this would run its course, and sooner or later she would no longer feel that thrill. It was new, this feeling of being in lust with someone. There'd been lust with Charlie, but it had never been this pure. It had been cut with emotional baggage, or 'head shit', as Alleyne would have it.

He made her laugh. He was freeing up her mind, relieving her of some strange feeling of restraint she never knew she had. Having this mysterious, unknown fantasy life gave her power. It was so unlike the real Mercy, but then again she wasn't sure who that was any more.

Now she was going through the morning routine of beating herself up over it, but lightly, not bare fists but kid gloves. What was worrying her more was the call she'd had from Boxer. He'd told her how he'd used the photo and struck lucky with the DJ, but he'd also added that his famous nose was playing up. He was sensing that something had gone wrong, but not where it was on the scale of catastrophe. This had sent Mercy into a mental spin and she'd called Alleyne almost immediately and asked herself round to his flat. Rum. Sex. Guilt. Self-loathing. A natural progression from the shock of hearing Boxer's words on a bad line from Madrid. At least she'd held back from the spliff this time.

'What are you doing now?' asked Alleyne.

'I'm getting up, Marcus. What does it look like?'

'It's four thirty in the morning, Mercy. We've only been in bed a few hours.'

'I've got things to do.'

'What? Like a paper round?' he said, rolling over. 'Make ends meet?'

'A paper round would be a fine thing,' she said. 'Beautifully mindless.'

She showered, trying to be thorough with her nether regions in a pathetic attempt at post-coital prophylaxis. She really had to get a morning-after pill. What *was* she playing at? She didn't know this guy. She wasn't taking precautions. She tried to think when she'd had her last period, wouldn't admit the other thing into her brain. She got dressed. Cuffed Alleyne on the shoulder.

'Are you sleeping in?' she asked.

'Trying to,' he said. 'People keep batting me around.'

'I'll call you.'

Alleyne rolled onto his back, put his hand behind his head, smiled.

'You're just using me like your toy boy.'

'Bigger than a toy, older than a boy.'

'Stop with the clever shit, Mercy. You just hiding behind that stuff.'

'At least I haven't become one of your bitches yet,' she said.

Alleyne blinked, not quite sure how to handle her.

'When I first came round here your neighbour said you were out with one of your—'

'Right, well that's just the way the kid speaks. It's not the way I *am*, Mercy.'

She nodded, conceding nothing, and shoved herself away from the door jamb.

'You can push me away, Mercy,' he called out after her. 'Then you'll be out there all on your own.'

She put the battery she'd had on charge overnight in the camera she'd brought with her. She went back into the bedroom, knelt on the bed, Alleyne put his hands up in mock protection of himself. She kissed him and smiled her enjoyment at him. He smiled back but was puzzled by her.

Brixton was almost silent as she drove through it to Clapham. The Common struck her as dark and threatening, its emptiness defended by high, swaying trees that clacked in the wind above her head. She thought, as she made her way towards pursuing her hunch, that she was on the brink of something terrible but was unsure of where the horror was going to come from. She was playing a rash game, as if outside a railing on a high building, leaning back and letting go and then snatching back at it. There was only one possible end to this kind of recklessness and it was a long way down.

The Wandsworth one-way system hadn't had the chance to develop its usual mortar-grinding slowness, and she flashed through it and drove alongside the park with some early-morning dog walkers. In the blackness beyond was the turbid Thames and the point of her hunch. She parked near Putney Bridge outside the Star and Garter pub, got her camera ready.

The grey river was materialising out of the first light, flowing rapidly and relentlessly towards the bridge. The traffic was beginning to tighten, headlights no longer flashing over the bridge but moving spasmodically. And now the first cyclists appeared in front of her, freewheeling down the ramp and onto the embankment. She got two decent shots of the blond-haired Jeremy Spencer as he leaned round the bend and came out of his saddle for the final sprint to the London Rowing Club boathouse, his black rucksack bobbing on his shoulders.

It was almost an hour before the boat returned to shore. Clearly the crew had jobs to go to because they had the boat out of the water and stowed with their oars and were all cycling away before seven o'clock. Mercy drove up the ramp behind Spencer and they joined the rush-hour traffic heading across the bridge. The queues weren't too bad, but Spencer was making much better headway on his bike. Mercy was dodging and ducking, trying to keep an eye on his massive shoulders, the rucksack in between. He went down the New King's Road and after about a mile swung right and stopped outside a large Edwardian house on Ryecroft Street.

He lifted the bike up the steps and let it hang from his arm as he rang the bell.

Mercy's next shot was of the woman she suspected was Irina Demidova in her dressing gown, blonde hair brushed, make-up in place, opening the door to Spencer. The woman backed down the hallway as he brought in his bike and leaned it against the wall. They kissed in a way that no one could describe as chaste. Mercy took two more shots. They came apart. Spencer stripped off his rucksack and dropped it next to his bike. Irina Demidova went back down the hallway and closed the door to the street.

The camera shutter clicked for the last time and Mercy sat back in that curious cop state of elation and sadness. Elation that she'd been right about Spencer's nervous reaction when she'd asked if he might have known Tracey Dunsdon's old friend, and sadness at having to root around in other people's dirty secrets, the necessary confrontation and the inevitable denial. Or maybe not. Perhaps the spook, James Kidd, would have other news about Demidova's pedigree.

Irina Demidova had kissed some ugly frogs in her time so Jeremy Spencer was a welcome change. He had a body that she found genuinely exciting and she could see from the bulge in his training tights that the feeling was mutual.

Pulling out his waistband, looking into his eyes, she closed her small, cool hand around his hot tumescent cock. He pushed his hands down the front of her dressing gown and grabbed her breasts, caught her nipples between his fingers.

She wanted this to happen in the bedoom so she started to lead him up the stairs, but Spencer had more urgent needs and ran his hands up her legs to her buttocks and tried to bring her down to her knees to take her from behind on the staircase.

This really had to happen upstairs, so she broke free and ran up to the top where she looked back at him and let the dressing gown fall away to reveal no bra and a ridiculously small pair of knickers. He leaped up the stairs three at a time. She ran to the bedroom at the front of the house and threw herself on the bed. He came after her, stripping off his top. She sat up on the edge of the bed and beckoned him to her.

She wrestled his training tights down to his knees and ran her fingers up his bare thighs and took him into her mouth. She could sense his urgency, that he wasn't in the mood for foreplay, but she needed to slow him down, create as much time as possible. Spencer had other plans. He pulled away, rolled her over, stripped down her pants and drove into her, gripping her hips. Within a few maddened thrusts he was finished and fell forward, crushing her beneath his colossal frame, moaning into the duvet. She squeezed out from underneath him.

'Sorry,' he said, panting, face down on the bed. 'Bit quick. Bloody desperate.'

She rolled over on top of him, fitting her breasts in between the wings of his shoulder blades.

'You could always make it up to me,' she said, whispering over his shoulder into his ear.

A noise came from downstairs. Spencer looked at her over his shoulder.

'What was that?' he said.

'I didn't hear anything.'

'Christ,' said Spencer, rolling over so that she slid off his back. 'Valery's not here, is he?'

'No, no,' said Irina. 'He's staying with a friend.'

Spencer slumped back.

'So what was that noise?'

'I don't know what you're talking about,' said Irina, taking hold of his limp cock, trying to renew his interest. 'It was probably just the writer guy next door. He's always knocking around the place, tearing his hair out.'

She bent her head down over him, but he pulled her back up, held her in the crook of his arm.

'I told you,' he said. 'This is going to have to stop. After that detective came to school yesterday. I can't ...'

'What?'

'I told you,' said Spencer. 'The Bobkov boy was kidnapped. There's going to be a lot of poking around. They're going to find things out and I'm a hopeless liar.'

She'd read him just right. It was, after all, like looking in the

106

mirror. She knew he felt guilty, manipulated too. His cock wasn't responding.

'So why did you come here?' she asked.

Silence.

'To say goodbye,' he said, which he knew wasn't quite the truth of it, but it would have to do in the absence of any willingness on his part to face up.

She rolled away from him, could feel his eyes on her back, but no hand reached out to draw her back in. He stood and pulled up his training tights, slipped his top back on. She sat up, drew her heel up onto the bed and rested her chin on her knee.

'You know it really is best you say nothing if you want to keep your job,' she said. 'Because you won't get another one if you talk … ever.'

'I know,' he said, 'but you should see this detective. She has a way of looking at me, listening to what I'm saying. Not believing me.'

She got up, walked straight past him and retrieved her dressing gown from the top of the stairs, wrapped herself in it. She could see that his rucksack had been moved. They went downstairs. Spencer didn't notice a thing, too involved in himself. He shrugged into the rucksack, picked up his bike.

'It's been good,' he said and kissed her on the cheek, let himself out, shut the door behind him.

She shook her head sadly and went downstairs to the basement. Valery was sitting in front of a computer with three-dimensional shots of Spencer's house keys on the screen.

'Everything OK?' she asked.

'I've just sent them through,' said Valery.

'He heard you,' said Irina. 'I told you to be quiet.'

'I heard you too.'

Mercy drove to the school in Hampstead wondering where Demidova's son might be during these trysts, and waited in her car for the teacher. She had no chance of following him through town in traffic. He arrived at 8.35 and weaved his way between the Range Rover Evoques, Porsche Cayennes and BMW X5s. He was still dressed for rowing with his rucksack on his back. She waited five minutes and went in to see the caretaker. She showed him the last shot of Irina Demidova closing the door. He confirmed it was her.

On the way up Netherhall Gardens she saw George Papadopoulos on the pavement and pulled over, told him about Spencer and Demidova.

'Interesting,' said Papadopoulos. 'Have we got a shot of Demidova's son?'

'That might be pushing it a bit, to have him as the bait,' said Mercy. 'Too risky, don't you think?'

'Worth a try.'

'I haven't checked to see if the boy enrolled at the Westminster school,' said Mercy. 'If he did, he might find it tough getting all the way from Hampstead to Westminster in time for registration in the mornings.'

'There's also the fact that Sasha would know him, which is a good and a bad thing,' said Papadopoulos. 'As a kidnapper you would never release Sasha if you knew he could identify the Demidova boy.'

'Something ugly for us to think about,' said Mercy.

'I'll see you up at the house,' said Papadopoulos.

Bobkov and Kidd were playing chess, sipping small cups of tarry coffee, leaning forward, elbows on knees, the tension between their shoulder blades palpable. There'd been no further calls from the kidnappers. They broke off to listen to Mercy's report. No sign of Butler, the lawyer. Sexton listened in.

'I've checked out Jeremy Spencer and he's clean,' said Kidd. 'Demidova's a bit more complicated.'

'Is she legal?'

'Oh yes, she's legal. She has a son called Valery. She was married but split up with her husband before she came to the UK.'

'Why did she come to London?'

'She answered one of those Russian girl ads, you know – sad, lonely guy in London seeks gorgeous blonde, totally out of his league, to be a part of his fascinating life in Lewisham,' said Kidd. 'She got here, enrolled in a language school and after a year got a job. Then she rented a flat in Cannon Place and brought her son over.'

'That must be some job,' said Mercy. 'Thousand pounds a week rental, boy at an international school. I mean the place I've just seen in Ryecroft Street down in Fulham has got to be a couple of grand a week. What does she do?'

'That's where it gets complicated. Originally she was self-employed and paid by several different Russian companies as a freelance consultant.'

'That sounds entirely above board,' said Mercy, easing her foot off the irony brake.

'I'd appreciate it if you didn't bring her in for questioning just yet. We've got people working on the Russian end of things,' said Kidd. 'As far as the UK is concerned, her self-employed status finished last June and HMRC haven't been able to track her down since.'

'So she might have become a consultant kidnapper or reverted to being a member of the FSB,' said Mercy.

'Or both,' said Bobkov.

'I don't expect you to tell me anything specific about your investigation into your friend Tereshchenko's poisoning, but could you indicate whether your enquiries had started annoying powerful people?'

'That's not any easy question to answer,' said Bobkov. 'Let's put it this way. I haven't been walking around Moscow asking my old FSB pals openly about what they know, but I have been working with people and we've been talking to sympathetic scientists to try to find the provenance of the polonium 210. We know, from the contamination of BA flights, that it came in from Moscow. What we're trying to prove is that it came from a specific nuclear facility to which only certain people have access and from which, we imagine, very few people have the right or power to remove something as deadly as polonium 210.'

'And have people started to feel ... uncomfortable?'

'We've had no luck, yet.'

'Has there been a change of approach as a result?'

'Yes.'

'Has that involved more open talk?'

'Not by me. I'm too obvious. But I have carefully selected people working in Russia, making visits to nuclear facilities.'

'You heard who won the presidential election on March 4th?' said Kidd.

'Plenty of people were unhappy with the way the vote was … manipulated, if that's the right word,' said Mercy.

'And here we are two weeks later,' said Bobkov, taking a call on his mobile.

They watched unmoving as he listened. Sexton got to his feet. Bobkov held up a hand.

'Tracey had a stroke,' he said, closing down the call. 'They've moved her into intensive care.'

At 7.30 a.m. Juan Martín, still unemployed and now twenty-one, was walking his parents' dog by the River Manzanares on the outskirts of Madrid not far from Perales del Río, close to his parents' flat. He was just going under the bridge of the M50 orbital motorway when the dog scrambled down the bank to the river's edge to inspect a black plastic bin liner. As Martín drew near he coughed against the horrific stench of bodily putrefaction. He shouted at the dog, who became more frantic in his scratchings. As he slid down the bank trying to control his gagging reflex, Martín saw a swollen human foot sticking out of the bag. He grabbed the dog's collar, hauled him back up onto the path and connected the lead. The dog lunged and barked. Martín dragged him away back to the motorway bridge. He tried to call his parents. No signal. He walked back to the flat.

At 8.00 a.m. Juan Martín's father called the police, told them what his son had seen and gave his address. As it was the most exciting thing the local police had heard of in the last five years they turned up in their Citroën Picasso within minutes. Juan got into the car and directed them over the railway and under the M50 to Perales del Río, where they parked and walked down to the river.

As soon as they saw the human foot one stayed with Martín at the site while the other went back to the car to radio it in. Ten minutes later the cop was back with rods and tape and they cordoned off the area.

Over the next hour a team of forensics turned up, a homicide team led by Inspector Jefe Luís Zorrita, a prosecutor and a team

110

of four divers. Zorrita interviewed Martín with the prosecutor and one of the forensics listening in. By 9.15 a.m. Martín had been sent home and the forensics were suited up and the divers had walked upstream as far as the railway line and eased themselves into the water.

At 9.20 the photographs had been taken of the crime scene and the bin liner had been moved to a tent set up under the M50 motorway. From the bag the forensics extracted a lower leg, cut at the knee, foot attached. Balled up and sodden at the bottom of the bin bag was some clothing which did not appear to be stained with anything darker than the river water in which it had been found. From this ball they unfolded a minidress which originally had been red in colour and a black jacket.

At 9.35 one of the forensics called the *inspector jefe* into the tent. On the table was a red European Union passport with a British cover.

'It was found buttoned up in the inside pocket of the jacket,' said the forensic.

Wearing latex gloves the *inspector jefe* opened the pages to reveal a photo of a mixed-race girl with long, thick dark ringlets and the name Amy Akuba Boxer. He took a note of the passport details and handed them over to his sub-inspector to take to the next stage. He walked down to the bank where the diving team were working. Two divers' heads came up out of the green river. He held up a questioning hand. They signalled back. Nothing.

Boxer was having toast with olive oil, tomato and *jamón* in a bar with the unambiguous name of Casa de las Tostas, which was not far from his hotel. He'd already had a *café con leche* with his toast and had just ordered a *café solo* when David Álvarez called.

'I have El Osito's number,' he said. 'But look, I'm told by the guy who gave it to me that he won't talk to you and he certainly won't meet you. He has to know you. You have to be vouched for, vetted or whatever, if you want direct talks. He also said a kilo won't be enough. To talk to El Osito directly you have to be interested in at least two hundred kilos a month, which means you're already a player before you've even met and he'll know more about you than you do yourself. All he did say was that the

Spanish market was now dead and they're looking to expand into northern Europe.'

'At least I come from the right area,' said Boxer.

'London is a place he particularly has in mind for expansion.'

'OK. Just give me the number. I'll work out an approach.'

'My friend knows an intermediary who can make contact for you, but you'd have to be in the business.'

'That won't be necessary,' said Boxer. 'The important thing now is that you forget you ever met me. You wipe my name and number from your phone.'

Silence.

'Did you hear me, David?'

'I can't tell you how dangerous this guy is ...'

'You don't do his line of work without being dangerous,' said Boxer. 'You've been a great help, David. I can't thank you enough.'

'Hey, look, *hombre*, it was nothing. I'm just sorry I wasn't able to stop her from getting involved in the first place.'

'You did the best you could and more than most people would have done. She's young, headstrong and, by the sound of it, high.'

He entered El Osito's number in his Spanish mobile, sat back with his beer.

Another call. The Hotel Moderno.

'We have an Inspector Jefe Luís Zorrita here. He would like to talk to you.'

'It's very important that Irina Demidova does not know anything about this enquiry into the activities of her son Valery,' said Mercy.

The headmaster of the Westminster branch of Northwest International School, Piers Campbell, a grey man in his late forties who didn't seem to be getting enough sunlight, nodded his agreement. The woman was making him nervous with her pacing. He wished she would just sit down and tell him what it was all about.

Mercy looked out of Campbell's office window across Portland Place to the Institute of Physics on the other side of the road. On the way up it had been unsettling to see apparently balanced sixteen- and seventeen-year-olds piling in and out of their class-rooms like normal children while her own had lost herself in

112

Madrid. She asked her questions, keen to get out of there.

Campbell said he hadn't been told of any late registrations, that the boy Valery was a conscientious student who was doing well in his studies, especially the sciences and maths. He showed Mercy a photograph of a bespectacled boy with narrow shoulders and a crumpled mouth which couldn't quite decide on laughter or tears. His blond hair and blue eyes were the only positives as far as Sasha's footballing friend was concerned.

'Does he have any football skills?' asked Mercy hopefully.

'If he does he hasn't revealed them to us,' said Campbell. 'He's definitely on the studious rather than sportif side.'

'And his mother? Does his mother have any friends here, among the other parents or the teachers?'

'I've seen her at PTA meetings, but she's not a great one for picking Valery up and all the school-gate socialising that goes with it. I think she works in an office not far from here, which I believe is where Valery goes after school.'

'Would you say she's close to any of Valery's teachers?'

'Close?'

'I mean intimate ... sleeping with.'

'Good God, we wouldn't allow anything like that here.'

'What about in the Hampstead school?'

'Of course not,' said Campbell. 'Are you implying—'

'Forget it,' said Mercy, not quite sure where she was going with this line of questioning. 'What about that photo? Would you mind if I took a snap of that? We need to check some things out.'

'I'd really prefer to know what this was all about,' said Campbell.

'I don't like being this mysterious myself,' said Mercy, 'but there's a very delicate situation involving the safety of another boy from the Hampstead school.'

'That wouldn't be the Bobkov boy, Sasha, would it?' asked the headmaster.

'Why do you ask?'

'Now he *is* a good footballer, so I'm told,' said Campbell. 'And a good chess player. I run a chess club here, and when Valery and Sasha were at the Hampstead school they were very advanced players, far ahead of the other children, so Mrs Demidova would bring them here.'

'And now?'

'Since Mrs Demidova has moved from where she used to live in Hampstead I don't think the arrangement is so convenient.'

'What time does school finish for Valery?'

'Four thirty except Wednesdays, when it's two thirty.'

Mercy took a photo with her mobile phone, sent it through to Papadopoulos with an explanatory text.

She waited outside the school for Valery Demidova to come out and followed him for five minutes to an address in Welbeck Street. Mercy watched which bell he rang, waited a few minutes after he'd entered and took a closer look. The company name on the card was DLT Consultants Ltd.

'There's no easy way of saying this, so I'm just going to lay the facts out as we know them,' said the translator.

There were three of them in the office: Luís Zorrita, Boxer and the translator. Zorrita looked directly at Boxer as he talked in Spanish, and although the translator spoke good English, Boxer only looked at Zorrita. The *inspector jefe* had been relieved to discover that Boxer was not completely a civilian. On the way to the Jefatura Boxer had revealed the rites of passage he'd been through to become a kidnap consultant. It was a way for both of them to avoid what was coming.

It was never easy to tell anyone that someone close to them had died. The level of impossibility to comprehend and accept was always raised with violence involved. On the two occasions in his career when Zorrita had had to explain the offensively macabre details of a body dismemberment he'd been met by total blankness on the part of the relatives. This facial blankness was just a manifestation of what was going on inside their heads: complete denial.

It was clear from their conversation in the car that Boxer spoke passable Spanish and could understand everything, but Zorrita understood the stress of these situations, which was why he had the translator present. He didn't want there to be any chink of doubt into which the human mind could dive and cut itself off from reality.

Zorrita pushed the evidence bag, which contained the passport

114

they'd found in the inside pocket of the jacket, across the table towards Boxer.

'Is this your daughter's passport?'

'She probably lost it,' said Boxer. 'Or it was stolen.'

Zorrita nodded, pulled the bag back towards him, laid it to one side. They went through the facts as they knew them, starting with Juan Martín's discovery of the black plastic bin liner. Boxer was aware of himself trying to slow things down, not wanting inevitability to gain momentum.

'What actually alerted Juan Martín to this black plastic bag?'

'The excitement of the dog and the very bad smell.'

'There must have been something else for him to notice something suspicious.'

'A human foot was protruding from it.'

Silence.

'That would do it,' said Boxer.

The translator didn't know quite what to make of it. He knew English, but not English people so well. Zorrita ploughed on, relentless, with interruptions about time and detail from Boxer, which he patiently supplied. Occasionally he glanced at the photo on his desk of his wife and children, who were a constant presence, not just in his office but in his mind as well. His stomach winced at what was coming.

'... from their experience the forensics believe that this female had been dead for between seventy-two and eighty-four hours. The leg had been bled and had not been—'

'The leg had been what?' asked Boxer.

'The blood had been drained from the leg, probably from the whole body, prior to dismemberment,' said Zorrita, watching the ugliness of the crime sinking into the man's consciousness. 'There were no bloodstains on any of the clothing within the bag.'

Boxer nodded him on.

'They think this lower leg had been in the river for around forty-eight hours.'

'You didn't mention any divers,' said Boxer. 'Have you sent any in there?'

'The divers arrived at the scene after the forensics.'

'And what did they find?'

'As yet, nothing. They've searched a one-kilometre stretch of the river. We're assuming that the bag was dumped into the river from the M50 motorway bridge at night. The river flows from north-east to south-east so they've searched three hundred metres upstream and seven hundred metres downstream.'

Boxer asked about the width of the river just to maintain a barrage of questions, hold back the flow of fate. He ran out of steam. Zorrita moved on to the clothing. As he walked over to the plastic sheaths hanging on a rail, he described the colour and material of the dress and jacket. He held it out for Boxer to see.

'Both came from the shop French Connection. We've checked the product codes with the company and they inform us that these items were bought from their store in Terminal 1 at Heathrow Airport on Saturday evening.'

'With a card?' asked Boxer desperately.

'No, with cash,' said Zorrita, letting fall the sheaths. 'In the inside pocket of the jacket the forensics discovered one hundred euros, a fifty, two twenties and a ten along with that British passport in the—'

In a couple of strides Boxer was at the rail. The translator flinched at the suddenness of the movement. Boxer held up the dress as if imagining it on a person.

'This dress,' he said, 'is just not the sort of thing she would ever wear. I've seen her in short skirts, but in a dress like this and a jacket – never. I've never seen her in anything like it. Never.'

'I understand you were in the Puerta del Sol last night, distributing this leaflet,' said Zorrita, holding out a piece of paper. 'You left some at the reception and with the concierge. It shows—'

'I know ...' said Boxer. 'I know. I'm just saying ... that was something put together by her mother from receipts I found.'

'What receipts?' asked Zorrita.

'I found receipts in the jeans she left in her rucksack in the Hotel Moderno. They were for clothes and a pair of shoes.'

'Where did those receipts come from?'

'French Connection,' said Boxer, defeated by himself. 'Terminal 1, Heathrow Airport.'

The translator was so fascinated by the intensity of the human drama he forgot to translate, but Zorrita, who had almost no English, grasped it all the same.

'The passport found in the jacket belongs to Amy Akuba Boxer,' said Zorrita, looking down on his desk.

The plastic sheath fell from Boxer's hands. He stormed over to the desk, stared down at the passport again, open at the ID page inside its plastic evidence bag.

Amy's unsmiling face looked back at him.

'Is that your daughter's passport?' asked Zorrita.

11

'Do you have something of your daughter's from which we could extract a DNA sample to confirm the identity of the body?' asked Zorrita.

No response. Boxer stood, hands splayed on either side of his daughter's passport, his head hanging down as if its weight had become a terrible burden. Zorrita pitied him, couldn't help but despise himself as he went on: 'In order to release the body we're going to require a DNA—'

Zorrita stopped as his huge desk was shunted forward about an inch by the intensity of the sob that racked Boxer's frame. Zorrita was about to reach out a hand and take hold of the Englishman, but stopped himself as he realised that this was a man who was used to keeping his emotions under control, used to suppressing all personal feelings, who had now come across something too big to contain. What stopped Zorrita was that he'd never been with the pain on the inside. He still had his parents, siblings, wife and children. He was a homicide detective who was a personal tragedy virgin and something told him this man wasn't. Boxer's shoulders heaved another brutal sob that once more inched the desk towards him.

Had Zorrita been able to look inside Boxer at that moment he would have been mystified by the colossal Gothic darkness within. He would have expected a wincing rawness, a laceration of all that was good, but not a bottomless black chasm. Surely that would come later, with the realisation of loss, the terrible emptiness, the endless longing for that unattainable fullness. The unfillable gaps of empty shoes, limp dresses, a hollow in a mattress.

He moved around the desk, lifted Boxer away from the table and got him onto a chair, which the translator, snapping out of his paralysis, held steady. They studied him as if he was a drugged tiger, fascinated but wary. His face was strangely still and dry of any tears while his body seemed to be under tremendous strain, as if trying to withstand some terrible G force.

'Are you feeling all right?' asked the translator, unused to these emotional crises in his work.

'No, I'm afraid I don't,' said Boxer, his body smoothing out as if suddenly weightless.

The translator and Zorrita exchanged looks.

'You don't what?' the policeman asked.

'I don't have any sample from which you might be able to extract my daughter's DNA.'

'What about her mother?' asked Zorrita. 'Are you living together or ...'

'We're separated. Amy lives with her mother but ...' Boxer struggled to find words, ransacked his mind for correct terms. 'Amy left home,' he said, 'and her leaving was extremely thorough.'

'I'm not sure what that means,' said the translator.

'It means she was punishing us,' said Boxer. 'She removed all traces of herself. She took everything out of the house – old toys, clothes, drawings, the lot. She vacuumed everything up in her room, every hair from her head, the whole house.'

'Then we'll establish her identity with a sample from you.'

'I think I'd better speak to her mother before anything else happens.'

'Of course,' said Zorrita. 'We'll leave you to do that. Use the phone on my desk. We'll wait outside.'

Boxer pulled himself up to the desk and wondered how he was going to do this impossible thing: tell Mercy. His mind was flying off on tangents, remembering when he'd been told something that had inspired intense grief thirty-seven years ago. He pulled himself back to the task. He had to find Mercy first. He decided on Makepeace. Get her back to the office, tell her there. Then call Mercy's Aunt Grace and ask her to look after her.

119

Makepeace came on the line. They knew each other.

'How's it going, Charles?'

'It's not good, Peter.'

'Oh Christ.'

'Do you know where Mercy is?'

'I can find out.'

'I don't want to tell her ... tell her this thing when she's on her own out in the street somewhere. I want her to be with people.'

'I'll bring her back to my office.'

'I'll get someone from her family to be there with her.'

'When you know, give me a name and I'll alert security.'

'What I'm going to tell her is very hard, Peter,' said Boxer. 'It looks like Amy's been murdered.'

'What do you mean by "looks like"?'

'A body has been cut up and disposed of in a river.'

'My God.'

'What's been found is a leg, the clothes she was wearing and her passport.'

'I'm sorry, Charles. I'm so sorry.'

'They're searching the river now, looking ... looking for ...'

'Yes, I understand,' said Makepeace, who knew how impossible it would be for any parent to have to say 'the rest of her'.

'Call me when Mercy's with you and I'll speak to her.'

Boxer put the phone down and went out into the corridor. Zorrita was up by the stairs on his mobile.

'They're calling her mother back to her office and I'll speak to her then,' he said.

Zorrita turned, hung up. They went back into his office.

'That was the head of the diving team,' said Zorrita. 'They've been searching near the bridge further upstream where another motorway crosses the river. They've found a second bag, identical, which had partly split open. The forensics are looking at it now.'

'I want to go to the toilet,' said Sasha, who'd worked out that there was a microphone in the room and they could hear him remotely.

After a minute the door opened and he was handed a cardboard bottle.

120

'What's all this about?' said the voice. 'You just been … less than an hour ago.'

'I want to go number twos,' said Sasha.

'What's that?' said the voice.

'Er, a shit,' said Sasha, thinking that was more their language.

'OK,' said the voice. 'I'll take you for a shit.'

The man hauled him off the bench, shoved him towards the door, opened it for him. They shuffled into a room where the walls were also wood-panelled. The man reached over his head, pushed another door open and Sasha felt cool air on his face. He was shunted sideways into a second room only a few metres across and through yet another doorway where he ran into something like a washing machine.

'Go to your left. The toilet's at the end.'

Sasha put his hands out, trailed them along the wall on his left and other electrical goods on his right. His knee hit the toilet. He put the seat down and turned.

'Don't watch, or I'll never go,' said Sasha.

He heard the door shut. He leaped to his feet and started feeling the wall behind the toilet, hoping for a window. There was nothing, just a blank wall.

'You're underground,' said the voice.

Sasha spun round, realising that the man was still in the room. He flinched as he heard feet lunge towards him. The first slap across the face knocked him onto his backside by the toilet. The man grabbed him by the scruff and hit him again with the back of his hand, and then again with the palm. Blood came into his mouth from his torn cheek.

'No more games,' said the voice, dragging him, feet trailing, out of the room.

Mercy was in the sitting room with Bobkov and Kidd, who'd long given up trying to play chess. Bobkov didn't have the concentration for it. Still no call from the kidnappers. Nearly twenty-four hours of silence. The front doorbell rang. Bobkov stiffened. Sexton, who was in the kitchen making tea, took it.

'George for you,' he said, sticking his head in the sitting room, nodding at Mercy.

She went out to the hall. George was looking wary.

'What's the story?' he asked.

'No story,' said Mercy. 'No contact. Let's go to the kitchen.'

They passed Sexton coming out with a mug of tea.

'I've got as much as I'm going to get on the football wizard kid,' said Papadopoulos, sitting at the table, 'so now I've started working on the car that turned up every morning and which I'm pretty sure brought the bait to manoeuvre Sasha into the trapping zone.'

'So no takers on the photo of Valery I sent you?'

'Definitely not the kid in question.'

'Tell me about the car.'

'It's a black Mercedes, which was all I knew until this morning. Now I've got a bit closer in and established that it's a four-door saloon,' said Papadopoulos. 'I went to the Mercedes dealership at Fortune Green and they showed me all the different models it could possibly be. I took the brochure round to my witnesses and I've got lucky because the C, E and S classes are kind of the same to look at, but the CLS is a very different beast. The kidnappers' car was a CLS.'

'Did any of the witnesses see inside the car?'

'Tinted windows.'

'Registration number?'

'Not yet, not in full. They all agree that it started with an L, so it's London, and either LC or LG. The number they're pretty sure is 61, so the end of last year. That's as far as I've got.'

'Irina Demidova works for some people called DLT Consultants Ltd on Welbeck Street. The letters stand for Dudko, Luski and Tipalov. They find clients and investors for Russian businesses and offer investment advice to Russians looking to buy in the UK and Europe,' said Mercy. 'You might want to see if the company or any of its people, including Demidova, owns a Mercedes CLS with corresponding plates.'

Her phone went. Makepeace calling her back to the office.

'Is that really necessary, sir?'

'It is, Mercy. It's very important. Soon as possible in my office.'

'Have the phone trackers found where they're holding Sasha?'

'No, it's something else entirely.'

He hung up. Mercy shrugged, left the house, got into her car.

122

Boxer called Mercy's Aunt Grace. No response from her mobile. He called her Ghanaian restaurant in Peckham. A young man answered and explained that Aunt Grace was away in Ghana for the funeral of Uncle David. Boxer remembered now why they'd had to send Amy to his mother's while he and Mercy had worked the Alyshia D'Cruz case. The whole of Mercy's Ghanaian family had left the country. Funerals were huge occasions in Ghana and everybody in the family would attend. The ceremony lasted three or four days, but it would be a reason for them all to stay for weeks. He put the phone down, walked around the room, thinking.

'Problem?' asked Zorrita.

'I need someone to look after Amy's mother once I've told her this news and her whole family's gone away.'

He stopped by the clothes rail where Amy's dress and jacket hung. On the floor inside a plastic bag was a blue circular weight with 5kg written in white on it.

'What's this?'

'It's what the killer used to weigh down the bag so that it sank in the river,' said Zorrita. 'We're lucky that the bridge is wide and the river narrow at that point so the bag landed partly in the water, partly on the bank. Otherwise we'd never have found her.'

'Fingerprints?'

'None,' said Zorrita. 'These weights are sold in a large sports department store called Decathlon, of which there are five in and around Madrid.'

While Boxer picked up and handled the weight, the translator and Zorrita spoke to each other briefly in Spanish.

'What about you?' asked Zorrita. 'Do you have anybody you can stay with in Madrid?'

Boxer shook his head.

'You must come and stay with my family,' said Zorrita. 'I don't think you should be on your own in an hotel.'

'I'll be all right,' said Boxer, whose mind as he held the weight was already filling with what he wanted to achieve tonight.

'I insist,' said Zorrita. 'No man should be alone with what you've discovered today. It could be ... dangerous. You know, the mind can play games with you.'

123

Boxer assured him that he would be fine and in the same moment had an idea. He asked them to leave the room again. He called Isabel Marks. He told her the terrible facts as Zorrita had just told him to a phone so absorbingly dead that he had to ask her several times whether she was still there.

'I can't believe you're telling me this,' said Isabel.

'The only reason I can believe it myself is that I've seen her clothes, her passport.'

'No, I mean, I don't know how *you*, Amy's father, can say these things ... these terrible, terrible things.'

'To be honest with you, Isabel, it's because I'm not quite on the inside of it yet myself,' said Boxer. 'My brain has taken it in, but it hasn't gone anywhere else, and that's because the rest of me is thinking and feeling for Mercy. It's going to be devastating for her. I've no idea how she will react.'

'You haven't *told* her yet?' she said, astonished.

'They're trying to find her, bring her back to the office in Vauxhall so I can speak to her,' said Boxer. 'But her whole family is in Ghana at the moment and I need someone to look after her until I can get there tomorrow.'

'Do you think *I'm* the right person for that job?' asked Isabel, as it dawned on her what he was asking. 'This is family. Someone who knows Amy should be with her. Maybe your mother is the right person for this.'

'Mercy can't stand my mother and Esme finds Mercy very difficult.'

'These are special circumstances, Charlie.'

'Remember how it was between you and Frank during Alyshia's kidnap? You think people should be able to make exceptions under stressful circumstances, but invariably they can't. Especially when there's history.'

'OK, Charlie. Mercy and I might not have any history, but we met at a major historical moment. You're Amy's father. Mercy is still in love with you. And we've just started a relationship.'

'There's nobody else I can trust on an emotional level to take care of her. My mother can't do it. Her colleagues don't know her. She liked you on sight, I could tell.'

'Of course I'll do it,' said Isabel. 'I'll do it to help you at this terrible time and for Mercy if she'll let me. But you'd better make out that you haven't told me first. She wouldn't like that. This is between the two of you. It's . . .'

'It's what?'

'Nothing.'

She couldn't say to him what she'd thought many times on seeing her ex-husband during her daughter's kidnap, preparing herself to accept those awful words: the end of our creation.

Mercy parked in the underground car park and went up to Makepeace's office. He was on the phone but beckoned her in, showed her a seat. He finished his call in seconds. Mercy sat down in the fake-leather armchair against the wall.

'I've had a call from Charles in Madrid,' said Makepeace, dialling the number. 'He wants to talk to you.'

'What?' said Mercy, suddenly afraid. 'No.'

'Hello, Charles, I've got Mercy here.'

He handed her the phone. She wouldn't take it.

'No,' she said, eyes wide with panic. 'There's no need for this. He knows my number.'

'Take the phone, Mercy. Just talk to him. I'll wait outside.'

'No,' she said, taking the phone.

'I'll be right outside. Just here,' he said, closing the door.

She looked dumbly at the phone in her hand, could hear Boxer's tinny voice calling for her. She fitted the phone tentatively to her ear.

'It's me,' she said in a voice that even to her sounded very far off. 'What's all this about?'

'It's about Amy.'

'Have you . . . have you found her?' said Mercy. 'She said we'd never find her, but you've found her. I knew you would.'

'I'm going to tell you everything,' he said tenderly. 'It'll take some time, so you'd better sit down.'

She kicked off her shoes, drew her knees up to her chest, jammed herself in tight between the arms of the chair. She stared into the floor with the phone to her ear.

'Go on,' she said.

Boxer started and didn't stop until he'd got to the end of Inspector Jefe Luís Zorrita's terrible facts.

Mercy said nothing. She didn't feel anything. She didn't think anything. All she knew was that something big had cracked inside her as she listened to his words. Her structure looked the same, but she knew it could collapse at any moment.

The news left her at a strange distance from the world. Was this what people called an out-of-body experience? She couldn't react emotionally or proceed intellectually. She was stuck with this persistent feeling of difference. She'd witnessed this state from the outside when she'd worked in homicide and gone into people's front rooms and told them their world's most damaging news. Being on the inside of it was odd. Painless and yet horribly new, like coming to in a familiar place where everything was lit to a terrifying brightness.

'Mercy?'

'I'm still here,' she said. 'Sort of.'

'You shouldn't be on your own tonight.'

'I'll be OK.'

'No, you won't,' said Boxer. 'You're going to have to tell your family and none of them are in London. I checked.'

'They're all in Ghana. Uncle David ... he died,' said Mercy. 'But he was very old, you know.'

'I'm going to ask Isabel to look after you for tonight ... until I get back to London tomorrow.'

'Isabel?'

'You and I worked together on the kidnap of her daughter.'

'Oh, you mean, *your* Isabel.'

'You liked her ... and she likes you.'

'Yes,' she said, half statement, half question.

'I'm going to call her, get her to come to the office and pick you up.'

'No, it's all right, really. Don't worry.'

'I want you to be with someone who can help you do the things you have to do.'

'I won't be on my own.'

'Who are you going to stay with?'

'When do they think it happened?' asked Mercy. 'The … the killing.'

'Sunday morning.'

'She was so convinced of herself,' said Mercy, 'and she didn't even last twenty-four hours on her own.'

'She was in Madrid. If she'd been in London maybe she'd have been able to read the signs better.'

'The signs?' asked Mercy.

'The people signs. The way people behave. Spain's a different culture. She couldn't read people so well.'

'Sorry, I'm being a bit stupid,' said Mercy. 'Are you going to call your mother?'

'I'll call Esme soon.'

'I don't want to speak to her,' said Mercy. 'I don't want to even see her. She's got some responsibility for this. She's poisoned Amy's mind. It's no accident this happened after Amy had been staying with her for that week.'

'I'll talk to Esme.'

'Why don't you come home now?'

'I have to help the police with their enquiries for a little longer,' said Boxer. 'They haven't interviewed me yet. I want to see if the divers find anything more.'

'That could take weeks,' said Mercy. 'Searching every bridge across every river in the area of Madrid.'

'And I have to give a blood sample so that they can extract my DNA and confirm—'

'No.'

'No?'

'What's there to confirm? They've found her passport, the clothes she bought and some body parts,' said Mercy, suddenly furious. 'What more do they want?'

'It's a procedure for positive identification so that they can release the body.'

'It's ridiculous. And if they're going to use anybody's DNA to identify *my* daughter, it's going to be *mine*.'

Silence. This was vintage Mercy: fine on the face of it, fully in control, capable of speech and action, but inside was turmoil with violent storms of emotion, irrationality and insecurity.

'They can use samples from both of us.'

'No,' said Mercy, vehemently. 'I'm her *mother*.'

'And I'm her father,' said Boxer. 'Ideally they'd like a sample of Amy from your house, but I've explained the situation there. So, you send a cheek swab down, I'll supply them with my sample here and we'll get the necessary confirmation.'

'No.'

'Without it we won't be able to bring her back.'

'I want Amy to be identified from *me* and me alone,' said Mercy, bursting into tears. Chunky sobs blattered down the line to Madrid.

'OK,' said Boxer. 'Then that's what we'll do.'

'The point being,' said Mercy, the emotion clearing as rapidly as it had come on, 'that I already have my DNA. There's no need for them to derive it from a sample. We all have ours on file here in the office. I can email it to you.'

'Then that's how we'll do it,' said Boxer. 'Send it to my email address. That's fine. And in return will you do this one thing for me? Let Isabel look after you. At least for this first night.'

'OK.'

12

'Esme, this is Charlie.'

'Oh, hello, what do you want?'

'I don't want anything, Esme.'

'Sorry,' said Esme, detecting a tone. 'What I meant was, why did you call?'

'It's about Amy.'

'You've found her? Already?' said Esme. 'My God, she didn't last long.'

'Where are you?' asked Boxer. 'You sound as if you're out walking.'

'I'm just letting myself into the flat. I've been shopping.'

'OK, I'll wait until you're settled.'

He heard her working the locks, the door opening and closing.

For some reason, this time, with Esme, he felt the horror of being the bearer of such news. Going about her everyday life in her retirement, not a happy woman, she'd never been a happy woman. How could she be with that battering father, her business partner and ex-lover murdered and her husband disappeared? No, Esme could never be described as remotely happy, but she did 'apparent contentment' very well. And if anything punctured that contentment she always had alcohol to fall back on. Having said that, there was never anything pathetic about her drinking. There was no weeping and wailing or imposing of herself on others. It was just something she did to maintain some equilibrium.

'You're not talking to me,' she said.

'I'm waiting until you're ready,' said Boxer.

'I'm going to put you down while I take my things off.'

Strange that he hadn't been so conscious of this terrible feeling with Mercy, to whom he had been bringing the very worst possible news. He supposed that this was because they were in it together, that it was equally devastating. Also he suspected that somewhere in Mercy's mind she was prepared for the worst. Her profession had prepared her. She knew this hell could and did happen every day.

'OK, I'm ready. Tell me where you found her and what she had to say for herself.'

'I want to make sure you're sitting down, Esme,' he said, and that silenced her.

He told her, and when his words had finally stopped tumbling into the unresponsive phone there was a monumental silence, as if not just one human being had been struck dumb, but an entire city. After it had gone on for too long he said something that he might have expected her to say to him: 'I'm sorry, Esme.'

Grief is essentially a selfish emotion. It's inspired by the loss of others, but it's private and deeply personal. No one but the individual experiencing it can understand its power, which is why, thought Boxer, couples who've lost a child often don't last long together. Their grief makes them too self-centred. As he thought this he realised that he had no idea how Esme would take this news. His mother's emotional state was a mystery to him. He knew she liked Amy. He knew they had a relationship. He also knew, from recent conversations, how Esme worked the relationship. No expectations. She liked Amy when she was nice and disliked her when she was being objectionable. He'd assumed that there was a closeness but with a respectful distance. He was not prepared for what Esme now revealed to him.

The deathly silence was broken by a shuddering, guttural sob and the phone clattered onto the table. Hissing intakes of breath came down the line as if she was being cut again and again and each cut was introducing another horrific slash of newly angled pain. He was shocked to hear his mother crying and knew that these were no ordinary tears but a retching up from the absolute bottom, as if she was vomiting up her soul to get free of her terrible body.

He'd seen this before in his professional life when a kidnap he'd been working had gone badly wrong – a child murdered by a drug gang – but the mother was already mentally prepared and surrounded by family. Here, now, with his own mother fifteen hundred miles away, he was appalled by what he'd unleashed: helpless, even panic-struck by her reaction. He'd never imagined such emotional depth in her because she'd never shown any; she'd always insisted on a determined anti-sentimentalism.

'Esme!' he roared. 'Esme. Pick up the phone.'

There was a desperate inhalation as of someone coming up from the depths or seizing a moment during an uncontrollable vomit.

'Mum!' he roared. 'Pick up the phone, Mum!'

The reply was a clattering and smashing to silence. Phone dead. Nothing.

He redialled. Nothing. Again. Again. Again. He tried her land line. No answer. It rang to death every time. In a panic, which was an emotion he had rarely been aware of, he called Makepeace. He didn't want to burden Mercy.

The words poured out of him and Makepeace had to slow him down, get him to repeat. He got it out in sound bites.

'She's taken it very badly. Had an immediate and total break-down. I need someone to go round there. I know this isn't your business.'

Makepeace told Boxer to leave it with him. He'd have someone round there in minutes.

'Just call me as soon as someone gets to her,' he said.

Boxer paced Zorrita's office, couldn't think of anybody he could call. He didn't know any of his mother's friends; in fact, he wasn't entirely sure she had any. Although there was ... what was her name? It shocked him how far removed he was from his mother's life. He slumped in the chair, gripping the arms with an even greater emptiness expanding in his chest. Now he had this sense of the permanent, the one person he'd known his whole life, spinning out of control.

George Papadopoulos was glad to get away from the Netherhall Gardens house. Twenty-four hours had passed with no contact.

The strain was telling on Bobkov's face, his body starting to sag under unseen weights.

It was past 19.00 by the time Papadopoulos reached the redeveloped old Consumption Hospital in Mount Vernon. The sun had gone down and it was on its way to becoming dark. He pressed Esme Boxer's bell. No answer. He called the porter, showed his warrant card to the camera and explained his business. The porter brought him into his office. He was in his sixties with brilliantined white hair and a white moustache that had yellowed where he smoked. He was a Londoner and, from his bearing, looked as if he'd been in the military.

'She's gone out,' said the porter.

'Like when?'

'I passed her in the corridor outside her flat about ten minutes ago. I said good evening but, you know, she's a funny one that. Sometimes says hello, sometimes you're lucky to get a nod.'

'Can you describe her? What she was wearing?'

'Long dark blue coat, trousers, big black handbag over her shoulder.'

'Could you tell what state she was in?'

'State?'

'I mean, did she look distressed?'

'Not particularly. Like I said, sometimes she'll give you the time of day, other times she'll look straight through you. Quite a few of them are like that in here.'

'Have you got a key to her flat?'

'Yes, but you'll need a warrant for that.'

'I need a photo of her. I have to find her but I don't know what she looks like. All I've been told is that she's had some bad news and is very upset.'

'Bad news?'

Papadopoulos sized him up, knew he was going to have to give out if he was going to get anything back.

'Her granddaughter was murdered in Madrid at the weekend.'

'You mean, Amy?' said the porter, his face coming apart in shock.

'That's right.'

'Oh, dear God,' said the porter. 'I can't believe it. Such a lovely

132

girl. Murdered? Who'd do a thing like that to a sweetheart like Amy?'

Papadopoulos had heard a few things about Amy from Mercy and none of them had featured the words 'lovely' or 'sweetheart'. But he could see the porter was genuinely broken up, had slumped back onto his desk, arms folded, head dropped and shaking.

'Now Amy, she *did* have time for you,' he said, looking up. 'She'd come in here, have a little chat and a cup of tea, a bit of a laugh. Tell you what was going on. My God. Murdered? No wonder Mrs Boxer's upset.'

'Were they close?'

'I never saw it. She wasn't the sort, Mrs Boxer, to show anything like that. Amy told me. Said her grandma was the only person in the world she really loved.'

'And the parents?'

'She was having terrible trouble with them. Especially her mother. I told her it was just a phase but ...'

'Did you ever see her mother?'

'Mercy? Yes, but not much. She and Mrs Boxer ...'

The porter winced on one side of his face.

'Families,' he said. 'Funny old game.'

They went up to Esme's flat. The porter limping because he'd sprained his ankle on the Heath walking the dog. Papadopoulos phoned Makepeace, who was stunned to hear of the successful relationship between Amy and her grandmother.

'Get a good photo of her,' said Makepeace. 'I'll check with the Hampstead force, see if they can spare some manpower.'

The porter opened the flat. They went through the living room and bedroom. No photos. Not one family shot. In the kitchen they found the shattered mobile on the floor, the fridge door open.

'I need photos,' said Papadopoulos.

'Try the desk in the spare bedroom. That's her office.'

There was a camera on a tripod leaning in the corner. On the desk a closed Macbook Pro. In the central drawer were a number of black and white photos of an attractive woman knocking on seventy with a mixed-race girl. Both of them had eyes which, even in monochrome, were piercing.

'You can see where Amy gets those eyes from,' said the porter.

Papadopoulos flipped through the shots. They were taken using a self-timer. Sometimes Amy hadn't been able to get back quick enough and there were shots of the two of them collapsed back on the bed laughing. The most gripping shot was of Esme looking straight to camera while Amy stared into the side of her face with what could only be described as pure joy.

'They're bloody crazy about each other,' Papadopoulos muttered to himself.

The porter nodded. It hadn't occurred to him before. He'd been caught up in his own friendship with the girl.

Papadopoulos opened the laptop, booted it up, isolated the best shot he could find of Esme Boxer and sent it through to the Central Communications Command in Lambeth with an explanatory text. He took a shot with his own phone.

Also in the drawer was an old Filofax stuffed with papers, business and restaurant cards. There were names and addresses, some crossed out with new addresses reinstated elsewhere.

'Did Mrs Boxer have any friends?'

'Only one woman came regularly. Sounded Australian but said she was South African and had lived in Perth. Betty Kirkwood. They were in the same line of work – making TV adverts.'

Papadopoulos found numbers for her and put them into his phone. He went back to the kitchen, looked in the fridge. He'd rarely seen one with so little food in it. Just ranks of white wine, some beer and plenty of tonics.

'She liked a drink?'

'Oh yes,' said the porter. 'Ten in the morning she'd have alcohol on her breath. Mind you, never saw her the worse for wear. She was trained up for it.'

'Alcoholic.'

'Not the only one in this building,' said the porter. 'She toned it down when Amy came. Didn't need it so much. Had the company.'

'Reckon she had a bottle in that handbag she had over her shoulder?'

'It'd fit.'

'Where's the bathroom?'

Papadopoulos followed the porter's directions and opened the

134

door to find packets of pills for high blood pressure, paracetamol, small tubes of creams all over the floor. Above the towel rail the medicine cabinet was empty.

'Shit,' he said. 'Looks like she's taken a bottle of booze and some pills and gone somewhere to make sure she's not found.'

'The Heath,' said the porter. 'Get lost up in the woods. Nobody'd find her. Only the joggers and dog walkers are out and they stick to the paths.'

'Where on the Heath?'

'The East Heath is heavily wooded right up to the Kenwood Estate, but at least the estate will be closed by now. Parliament Hill Fields is open land so I doubt she'd go there,' said the porter. 'You're going to need some people if you want to cover East Heath and Springett's Wood.'

Papadopoulos put another call through to Makepeace, gave him the update and the porter's information.

'The Hampstead police are up against it after all the cuts,' said Makepeace.

'So a chopper's out of the question?' said Papadopoulos. 'Because that's what I'm going to need to cover this kind of ground.'

'I can't put in a chopper request for this.'

'Any chance of some dogs?'

'I'll work on some handlers. See what I can do.'

'I've got some fitness fanatic friends with big followings on Twitter. I'll see if they can steer a moonlight triathlon in this direction,' said Papadopoulos.

They hung up. The porter was on his mobile. They left the flat, went back to his office. The porter had a scarf and a hat he'd taken from Esme's coat rack.

'You'll need these for the dogs,' he said. 'I've just put out word to some of my dog-walking friends. Some of them belong to ramblers' clubs. They should be able to turn out some people between them.'

'We'll take a cab back to my place,' said Isabel.

'No,' said Mercy before she remembered who she was with. 'It's OK.'

They were heading for the lift outside Makepeace's office. Mercy had been surprised how glad she was to see Isabel. They'd fallen into each other's arms.

'I didn't bring a car,' said Isabel, 'and I'm not taking you back on the Tube.'

'No.'

Why did she keep saying no? Was this just a manifestation of denial? Negate everything. And yet she wasn't in denial. She'd faced what had happened to Amy, taken it in. Maybe she hadn't dealt with it, but she hadn't blocked it out.

They stood by the lift, looked at each other. Mercy saw the woman's kindness. This was probably the last place she wanted to be: looking after her new man's ex. She reached out for Isabel's hand.

'I'm sorry. I've got my car here. I'd like to drive, you know, do something that'll occupy my ... my crazy mind. Don't worry, I'll take it easy. No blue flashing lights.'

Isabel squeezed her hand. They went down to the car.

'Is it OK if we go back to your place?' said Mercy. 'I don't think I can face my own house, just yet.'

Mercy drove over Vauxhall Bridge and took a left down the Embankment. She gave herself over to the occupational therapy of driving, the demand for concentration, which blocked out the horror thoughts.

'What do you think of me?' she asked, the question appearing in her brain and coming out, uncontrolled. 'As a person? I'd be interested to know what somebody who doesn't know me very well thinks.'

Isabel looked at her in the strange intimacy of the half-lit dark of the car. An odd question, and she wasn't sure how much truth was being asked for. Or whether Mercy was looking for reassurance?

'Even if it's something ... bad, I still want you to tell me,' said Mercy. 'I ... I'm ... I don't know what I am right now. Maybe you can help?'

'Something bad?' said Isabel, astonished. 'You're not a bad person, Mercy. I know bad people. I spent a lot of time with people who didn't care, who didn't give a damn about anything human.

That could never be said of you. Charlie told me how relentless you were in tracking down the people holding Alyshia. He said that without your intervention she wouldn't have survived. The only possible motivation people like you have for doing that kind of work is that you care. So stop thinking you're bad.'

'I find it easier to care about people professionally,' said Mercy. 'I imagine people's relationships as perfect examples of what, say, a mother and daughter's love should be like. So I imagined you and Alyshia together. That motivates me. But in real life my own relationships are hopeless.'

'So are mine. So are everybody's,' said Isabel. 'It's a messy business being human.'

'At least you can show people close to you what you feel about them,' said Mercy. 'I can't ... unless I hate them. Like Esme. I hate her.'

'You can't hate without being able to do the opposite,' said Isabel. 'Why do you hate Esme?'

There were all sorts of reasons. She could enumerate them. But if she started to trot them out they'd seem piffling, unworthy of such a powerful emotion as hate. And yet she did hate Esme. She hated the influence she had over Amy.

'I'm thinking about that, you see,' said Mercy. 'And I'm already lying to myself. My mind is telling me I loathe Esme because she has a bad influence over Amy. But the reality is that I hate her because I envy her relationship with my daughter.'

'Grandparents are always more successful with their grand-children than they ever were with their own. The pressure of bringing them up properly is off.'

'Esme and Amy have a connection. I see it every time they're together. It drives me crazy.'

'Because almost every teenage girl has a problem with her mother?'

'No, because when I look at Esme I see myself. I see a woman incapable of showing her feelings for another human being,' said Mercy. 'You can't believe what she was like with Charlie. The life he had as a kid, his father disappearing, and yet she gave him nothing. And now she has this meeting of minds with *my* daughter. It makes me sick. Now don't tell me that isn't bad.'

'It's completely understandable,' said Isabel. 'And not many people have that sort of insight.'

'It seems ugly to me, which is why I've never told anybody about it before. I should be happy that at least they have a relationship with each other even if they can't with their ... own.'

'Remember, you have no real idea what's happened to Esme in her past, the experiences that shaped her. You only ever know about yourself, and most people don't know that much, and it's in a constantly shifting state, rarely still for long enough to be analysed.'

'I'm glad you're here,' said Mercy. 'I didn't really want it to be you and I think you know why.'

'I saw it from the beginning,' said Isabel. 'You're still in love with Charlie.'

Mercy shook her head as they crawled in traffic up Warwick Road.

'I don't know whether I *am* still in love with him,' said Mercy. 'All I know is that there's never been anybody else who's come close.'

'He was there at a crucial moment in your life,' said Isabel. 'He helped you escape from your father, installed you in England and you had a child together. That's a deeply connecting history. You don't extricate yourself from that very easily. In the same way it took me the rest of my life to get away from my ex, Chico.'

They finally got through the lights and headed up to the Cromwell Road.

'Don't think I've forgotten that you haven't said what you think of me,' said Mercy. 'I'm a cop. We've got a memory for dialogue.'

'Back in your office you seemed scared, which was a bit confusing,' said Isabel. 'I'd have expected you to be scared or worried if you *didn't* know what had happened to Amy. But in finding out, however terrible it is, at least the fear of the unknown is over. There's all sorts of other emotions going on, but not fear. As soon as I knew Alyshia was safe, the fear finished. My terror had no limits and then it was gone. Yours was still there. Was it me? Could I fill you with such dread because I might take Charlie away from you?'

'No, it wasn't you,' said Mercy. 'As always, it was me. The fear of being found out.'

13

The Pryors were a couple of very large Edwardian mansion blocks built in the first decade of the twentieth century on the edge of Hampstead Heath. They were flanked on one side by the open space of Pryor's Field, and on the other by the tree-lined Lime Avenue and the woodland beyond. Someone answering the description of Esme Boxer had been seen by a group of smokers outside the Well's Tavern making her way towards the Heath. Papadopoulos had taken the initiative of setting up a command post in the Pryors car park from where volunteers were dispatched to help in the search for the missing woman.

Thirty people had responded to Papadopoulos's Twitter call and twenty of the porter's dog-walking rambler friends had turned up. They had been dispersed mostly through the dense woodland between the Pryors and Kenwood House. At around half past eight police dog handlers arrived with a couple of German shepherds. Papadopoulos produced the scarf and hat taken from Esme Boxer's flat for the dogs to get the scent.

The female handler, Kirsty, took Esme's hat and went up the path towards the Vale of Health. Reg, the other handler took the scarf. Papadopoulos joined him going down Lime Avenue. The volunteers' torches flickered in the blackness of the Heath. They moved forward in a vague line, the dry leaves rustling under their feet. There were other, untrained, dogs – golden retrievers, Labradors, various terriers, spaniels and a rather haughty standard poodle which seemed wary of leaving the main path to pursue this possibly dangerous work in the dark. Voices called out for Esme amid the barking of dogs and the distant thunder of overhead jets banking south to follow the Thames and land at Heathrow.

It was a clear, cold night and, with no rain for a couple of weeks, hard underfoot and good going for the volunteers. This made the task of finding a lone woman, dressed in black, in a large, heavily wooded, undulating area full of ditches and streams and the occasional lake only marginally easier.

Once beyond Pryor's Field the volunteers split into two groups, the larger heading north while the smaller group went south in the direction of Hampstead Ponds. Papadopoulos and Reg stayed with the larger group with the German shepherd roaming the woodland.

'This is a business,' said Reg. 'When they've made up their mind they don't make it easy, do they? You related?'

Papadopoulos explained the relationships and the murder in Madrid.

'Vicki!' roared Reg. 'You there?'

Two barks came back from the woods.

'That means yes,' said Reg. 'You getting anything, Vicki?'

One bark.

'That means no.'

'You're kidding.'

'Yeah, I am. I like to think dogs can talk and understand, but they can't – I mean, not really. But I know what her bark means. I've been with her longer than my last girlfriend – and I didn't understand a word she said and she was English and of the same species. At least, I think she was.'

'Did she react badly to being brought to heel?'

Reg laughed.

'She couldn't cope with the fact that I spent up to ten hours a day with a complete bitch and loved every minute of it,' said Reg. 'Then I'd get home and she wouldn't do what I told her to *and* she was bloody useless at catching biscuits.'

'I thought dogs were supposed to be a great intro to women.'

'Not police German shepherds, mate,' said Reg. 'That's why I've got my eye on that Kirsty, but then she's only got eyes for Dougal. We're a lost cause, us dog handlers.'

They were crossing Bird Bridge on the way up to the Hampstead Gate when Vicki crossed their path and stayed on it for forty metres before heading off into the woodland on the left with three sharp barks.

'She's on to something,' said Reg.

They plunged into the woodland after the dog. Reg kept calling out and the dog would respond, sometimes trotting back to make sure she was being followed. After fifteen minutes they came into a clearing where, on the far side, there was a carved wooden seat that looked like a miniature whale.

Vicki was up on this carving looking down the other side and barking repeatedly. From the left side of the clearing came the other police dog, Dougal, travelling at full speed, followed by Kirsty. They met at the seat. The dogs piped down. Esme was lying on her back in the grass, wrapped in her coat, the contents of her handbag all around and an empty bottle of Grey Goose vodka which looked as if it had been flung from the bench.

Papadopoulos put a call through to Central to send for an ambulance. Reg felt for a neck pulse. Kirsty searched for any pills that might have been taken. Other volunteers came into the clearing.

'We've got a pulse, but her breathing is shallow,' said Reg.

'Temazepam,' said Kirsty. 'There's two empty twenty-mil bottles here.'

'That's bad news with the Grey Goose,' said Papadopoulos. 'I'll get the volunteers organised to direct the ambulance here from Spaniards Road.'

Reg and Kirsty moved Esme into the recovery position while Papadopoulos jogged back to the radio mast leaving a string of torch bearers behind him. The ambulance whooped up the hill and ten minutes later Esme was under oxygen and on her way to the Royal Free Hospital, with Papadopoulos by her side holding the empty Grey Goose and the temazepam bottles.

The paramedics took her straight into A & E, where a team was waiting. Papadopoulos gave them a probable ingestion time of somewhere between 19.15 and 19.30. The team glanced at the clock, which showed it was close to 21.00, said nothing and went into action.

*

'So what were you afraid of?' asked Isabel.

Mercy didn't answer. She needed more time, more trust. This wasn't something to tell another person lightly, especially if that other person was going to be deeply involved with Charles Boxer.

'Amazingly enough, the one thing I was never afraid of was Amy getting ...'

She stalled, couldn't get the word out.

'You know how it is these days. The media whips us up into a frenzy of panic about the imminence of all sorts of horrors. Not ... not murder, strangely enough, unless you're a fifteen-year-old black kid in a gang or ... not,' said Mercy, things spilling out as they came into her head. 'Terrible how ruthless children can be, isn't it? Only life can teach them how to behave, and yet they feel this great need to overtake it. To have an experience before they're ready.'

'Charlie said he'd always been worried about Amy getting ahead of herself.'

'Which isn't a bad thing – being independent, I mean, given that some kids like to hang around at home until they're thirty or more,' said Mercy, running out of steam, knowing that there'd have been no chance of Amy doing that.

'Somehow they've got to learn to make choices and understand consequences,' said Isabel. 'You can't be with them all the time. I thought the difficulty with Alyshia would be to get her to understand failure. I thought she'd never known it. It was only during the kidnap that I realised how much she'd shielded me from her disappointments and failures.'

'It's only after her ... her death that we're finding out how removed Amy had become,' said Mercy. 'And ... cruel too. The punishment she's meted out ... to me especially. Why are kids so cruel?'

'They don't know what it's like to have a person's love, hope and expectations wrapped up in another human being.'

'The more I sought it, the more I wanted it, the more I demanded it ... the crueller she became.'

'I was the same with Alyshia when she came back from Mumbai,' said Isabel. 'She was living with me and I thought I deserved some intimacy. She didn't want to talk because, well ...

142

it was too complicated. The more I wanted something from her, the nastier she got.'

But even as Mercy was talking and listening, she didn't quite believe it – not of all kids. She thought about Sasha, the kidnapped boy: the way he'd looked after his mother, protected her from the world, which would have taken him away from her. He must have known he was everything to her and built the ideal fiction around her so the worst wouldn't happen. His case had gripped Mercy and she needed to go back to it precisely because of what had happened to Amy. Sasha must not go down on her watch.

'You're thinking.'

Mercy told her about Sasha, not his case, just his life. Isabel stared out of the fogging window as they arrived at her house in Aubrey Walk.

Isabel installed Mercy in a bedroom, gave her some pyjamas. Mercy took a shower, let the water pummel her shoulders while she stared, mesmerised, at the vortex in the plughole. She hung on to the glass walls and wept with her head jammed into the corner and wondered if she'd ever be able to stop because it had just hit her with a terrible force that this was not finite. This was for ever. They were never going to able to repair the complex damage done between them because Amy was never coming back.

Esme Boxer was not in good shape. Her breathing was fast, her heart rate rapid, pulse thready and her blood pressure low. The doctors and nurses working on her knew that time was against them. The drug and alcohol were already in her system. They were battling against coma and death.

They administered large volumes of intravenous fluids in the hope of stabilising her condition. They intubated her using a ventilator to maintain her breathing. Finally they gave her kidney dialysis to remove substances already absorbed into her system. During these procedures her heart stopped beating twice. The crash team stepped in to revive her.

Papadopoulos saw nothing of this. He paced the waiting room taking calls from Boxer, who'd been given his number by Makepeace, every five minutes.

143

'Still nothing,' said Papadopoulos. 'No news is good news at this stage.'

'But she was definitely alive when the ambulance brought her in?'

'I was with her. She was breathing. The paramedics handed her over in that state. I'll call you as soon as there's news.'

And five minutes later Boxer would call again.

'I'm bored,' said Sasha tentatively.

'Shut up,' said the voice, a third one. They were taking it in turns to be with him after the business in the toilet.

'Why won't you talk to me? I could practise my Russian.'

No answer. Sasha heard the pages of a magazine turning.

'What are you reading?'

Still no answer.

'Can I have a football? You won't have to talk to me and I won't be bored.'

'No,' said the voice. 'Shut up.'

'You play chess?'

A sigh from the corner of the room.

'I play chess. I'm good. I could beat you,' said Sasha.

'I doubt it.'

'Why?'

'You're a kid. I've been playing chess longer than you've been alive,' said the voice. 'And anyway, you can't see.'

'I play from memory. I do that with my dad all the time. You make the moves, and I'll still beat you.'

Silence and he knew he'd got to him.

'Wait.'

The man cuffed Sasha's wrists and left the room, came back minutes later with a chessboard, set out the pieces. Sasha played white. The man quickly realised that Sasha was no novice, found himself in trouble.

'My bishop takes your knight,' said the man.

'I don't think so,' said Sasha.

'What do you mean?'

'You've only got one bishop and it's on white; both my knights are on black squares.'

'You're not thinking straight.'

'I am,' said Sasha. 'You've seen that you're checkmate in two moves and now you're trying to cheat.'

The man hit him hard on the side of the head, knocking him off the wooden slatted bench.

Mercy was sitting on the sofa in a white towelling dressing gown and slippers. She stared into space and sipped sweet tea while Isabel made some mushroom risotto in the kitchen. The phone rang several times. Her own mobile was upstairs. She didn't want to talk to anybody, couldn't face calling her family in Ghana. Uncle David's funeral was starting tomorrow and news of another death would be too dreadful. At least, that was how she rationalised it to herself.

Isabel called her in for supper. She wasn't hungry but knew she had to eat. They drank red wine from Portugal. Mercy had to hold herself back, tamp down that real need to get blotto.

'The phone's been going,' said Mercy.

'The first time it was Alyshia from Paris. The other times it was Charlie making sure you're all right. He wants to talk to you. I told him to wait.'

'I just don't know what to say,' said Mercy. 'I've never been any good at translating feelings into words. Nothing seems … adequate.'

'It doesn't matter. Nobody is expecting anything. People just want to hear your voice. It places you in their world.'

'I'll talk to him if he calls again.'

'What about your family?'

'They're in Africa. They forget the UK when they're there. There's no time. The days fill, especially with a funeral. It's more important to lay someone to rest than it is to get married. That's when you become an ancestor.'

'Did they all know Amy?'

'They all looked after her at one time or another when I was working and Charlie was away,' said Mercy. 'But, you know, I'm not quite trusted.'

'Why not?'

'I ran away. They all knew what my father was like and what

it was like for us to be in his house. The darkness. The fear. But you never run away from your family. That is suspect behaviour.'

'Is that why you're not there?'

'I use work as an excuse. I know I should go, especially for this particular man, who is very important. I just don't want to get involved. I was the eldest daughter. My mother died so I was mother to the others. And I ran away. When I go over there people can hardly bear to look at me, although it's got better since my father died.'

'Did you go into the police force to ... make amends with your father?'

She'd never thought of it like that.

'That's probably true,' she said. 'Although I'm not sure how I'd disentangle that from the family mess inside me. The awful truth is that I'm very like my father. I'm strict, demanding, thorough, self-disciplined ... In a word, I'm hard. Being here in the UK I've learned to cover it up. I make jokes. But my colleagues know what I'm like underneath.'

'You're not *hard*, Mercy,' said Isabel. 'I've been with someone very hard. My ex-husband wasn't an actor when I met him – at least, I didn't think so. Then I realised he'd been one all the time. He understood what people wanted to see. You're just using humour to soften your edges. My ex pretended so that nobody could see the real horror underneath. When you say you have trouble putting feelings in to words, to me that means you're not sentimental, which is what we've all become now. You're not hard, Mercy. You're admirable.'

'Amy didn't think so,' said Mercy and she started crying.

The leader of the A & E team treating Esme Boxer came into the waiting room in greens, a mask hanging off one ear. He looked weary, as if he was coming to the end of a long shift. The doctor beckoned to Papadopoulos and they went into an office behind the reception area.

'Are you next of kin?'

'No. I brought her in but I can get her son on the phone for you. He's in Madrid,' said Papadopoulos. 'She's OK, isn't she?'

146

The doctor cocked his head from side to side as if there was something sixty–forty about it and the wrong way.

Boxer was sitting on the edge of the bed back in the same room that Amy had booked in the Hotel Moderno. It had taken him time to extricate himself from the care of Inspector Jefe Luís Zorrita, who was determined that he should not spend the night alone. The Spaniard had given him a cheek swab for DNA purposes and confirmed that Mercy's DNA details had arrived by email. Zorrita assured him that his home was open to him any time, day or night. They'd hugged, a manly Spanish hug which didn't mind cheek-to-cheek contact. It felt like a small betrayal to Boxer as he left the detective in the Jefatura and got into the police car Zorrita had arranged for him.

The only state Boxer wanted to be in now was alone. He had plans forming rapidly in his mind and they included acts that were best executed some distance from the eyes of a homicide detective.

The call came through from the Royal Free and Boxer listened to the doctor's description of his mother's condition and her treatment.

'The good news is that she's stable and her pupils are still reacting to light. What we don't know yet is the real extent of the brain activity. I'm still concerned she may lapse into deep coma and become effectively brain dead while we artificially maintain vital signs.'

It was not a terminal conversation but the prognosis was not great. The doctor did not hold back on how serious it was to mix benzodiazepines with alcohol, even if the litre bottle of Grey Goose had not been full. It was, he said, the most common combination for successful suicides. Boxer told him he would be on the first flight out of Madrid in the morning. The doctor hoped there would be no change in her condition for the next twelve hours. They hung up.

Boxer lay down with the mobile on his chest and stared at the ceiling. At least he hadn't lost both mother and daughter on the same day. It didn't make him feel any better. It wasn't cold in the room, but he felt chilled to the bone, his fingers as stiff as porcelain. A wind was whistling past the window, rattling

147

something against the side of the building. It was no different to what was going on inside his chest except somehow smaller. The vast, cratering blackness under his ribcage felt as terminal as a collapsing star. All vestiges of light were being consumed by it. He couldn't ever imagine being refilled or lit in any way.

He reached for the phone, called room service, ordered a hamburger and chips. He booked a flight out of Madrid in the morning. He waited for room service to arrive and called reception to say he wanted no calls or visitors, that he was going to sleep. He put the food into the wastepaper basket's bin liner and tucked it into his jacket. He put the plate outside his room and took the stairs down to the garage, where he threw the hamburger into the rubbish. He located all the CCTV cameras and worked his way along the walls and up the access ramp and out into the cold Madrid night.

14

'I don't talk to anyone now,' said Isabel.

'What do you mean?'

'I don't have intimate talk, revealing talk, interesting talk with anyone any more,' said Isabel. 'My closest friend lives in Brazil. My daughter has her own life and keeps me at arm's length. I have my colleagues at the publishing house, but I don't tell them anything important.'

They were in the sitting room. Mercy was back drinking tea. The second glass of wine had set off an inner trembling, as if there was a lot more in the sub-cranial murk of her mind that wanted to surface. She needed to be in control if she was going to talk to Isabel, whose intuition and clarity of mind was attractive but unnerving. She'd spoken to Charlie briefly, just to say she was all right. Hearing his voice had given her some solidity and made her more wary of Isabel. There'd been a change in Mercy's body language. At the table they'd been close and open. Now Mercy was leaning away, heels up, while Isabel was lying on the sofa, head propped on hand, wine glass on the floor, unaware of this other Mercy now watching her.

'I thought you and Alyshia were close, especially since the kidnap.'

'I learned more about her during the kidnap than I wanted to. I'd built an idea of her, but now I know there was a lot missing from it. That's all gone. She's still my daughter and I love her, but I don't know her any more. I *wanted* to know her, which was probably my mistake because it made her secretive. It's a difficult thing to learn that your child is ... another person. And Alyshia is more like her father, which means I'll probably never know her. It's strange that all the things I found romantic and sexy in Chico, like the dark side, the mystery, his secrets, his ambition, I find I can't abide in Alyshia. Things might change now. She's been more loving since the kidnap was over but ... There I go again. Ever hopeful.'

'And Charlie?'

'We haven't had much of a chance,' said Isabel, taking a huge glug of wine. 'But you know, Mercy, that's not how I am in love. I say that as if I'm an expert, and yet there hasn't been anyone since Chico. But on that form I would say that I'm not looking for total intimacy from a partner. Chico was never that intimate – we never revealed things to each other – which was probably why we lasted so long. If I'd known more I'd have run screaming.'

'So what was it?'

'He was beautiful and unknowable. I'm a sucker for both. I'm not destined for happiness.'

'You must have *talked* about something.'

'We talked about everything except the thing that was always just out of reach.'

'And you wanted to find out what that was,' said Mercy. 'And when you did ... was that the end of it?'

Isabel slumped back and stared at the ceiling.

'I suppose that was it,' said Isabel. 'What made him tick was his ruthlessness. Nobody mattered more than him. Everybody was dispensable, including me. So I got to the bottom of him and found there was nothing there.'

'Is it the same with Charlie? Mystery and good looks?'

'It sounds pathetically romantic, doesn't it?' said Isabel. 'I wouldn't buy it in a book, but it's different on the inside. I know I'm not attracted to the light. I want to be intrigued. On the other hand, I don't want to find myself lying next to someone dark and empty ... or evil.'

'You think your ex was evil?' said Mercy. 'You'd go that far?'

'Hard to admit, but yes, I would.'

'I've come across evil people. Serial killers. Most of them are

150

boringly normal until you find yourself in their basement.'

'Chico wasn't that,' said Isabel. 'Nor is Charlie, but there's a dark side to him. He's secretive. There's definitely something ...'

'Charlie isn't *bad*,' said Mercy adamantly; 'he's as straight as an arrow. He's the good guy. He'd do anything to bring a hostage back safely. And he'll do anything to provide for and protect his family ... even if we are all over the place.'

And as she was saying it Alleyne flashed through her mind, telling her Charlie had a gun under the floorboards.

'Then again,' said Mercy, 'you can never tell.'

In one of those strange developments of the global village Chinese people now had shops in almost every urban centre on the Iberian Peninsula. They sold beer at a price cheaper than the breweries made it, which brought the Spanish through the door, then they sold them anything they could think of, from crisps to hardware. Boxer went into a Chinese shop on Calle de Alcalá and bought a length of thick electrical wire, a roll of gaffer tape, some latex gloves and an adjustable spanner, all of which he stashed in the inside pockets of his jacket. He went back out into the cold wind-blown night.

There were always young people gathered in the square at Puerta del Sol at night, drinking and talking. Boxer circulated among them, finding himself drawn to groups of teenage girls, watching them show each other their smartphones or pass a litre bottle of Mahou beer between them. He expected this to make him feel sad, but it didn't. He felt nothing now. There was no room for any emotion as the black hole inside had expanded to maximum capacity.

Boxer stared at a mime artist dressed as a cowboy, who stood stock-still with face, hands and outfit painted a tarnished silver. There was no reaction until, just as Boxer was about to leave, the cowboy drew his gun and blew him away before mechanically reholstering and reforming into a statue once more.

He went to a bar and ordered a *caña* of beer, saw himself in the mirror behind the young woman who served him. He seemed normal. The girl smiled at him as she handed him the beer, asked him if he wanted a *tapa*. He smiled back, shook his head. She gave him a sweet shrug. He found a dark corner, stood at a high table, sipped his beer, looked at his fellow humans.

Two guys, one in his forties, the other thirty, came in, ordered beers and walked through the crowded bar to the empty space around him, asked if he minded if they put their beers on his table. They knew from his face he was foreign. They talked to each other in a Spanish that even Boxer recognised as South or Central American rather than *castellano*. Boxer went to the bar, ordered another beer. He returned to the table to find that a woman with long black hair perched on very high heels had joined the two men who did not involve her in their conversation but kept glancing at the entrance to the bar.

Boxer had one of his untraceable mobile phones with him on which he prepared a message to send to El Osito. He was so concentrated on his task that he didn't notice the door to the bar swing open and the two guys beckoning and calling out to the person who'd just walked in. The newcomer worked his way through the scrum of people and embraced the two men. Boxer looked up, couldn't take his eyes off the newcomer. It was El Osito. After extricating himself from the manly hugs and ignoring the woman he looked over the high table to Boxer.

'*Quién es?*' he asked. Who is he?

The two guys glanced over and quickly explained. They asked El Osito what he wanted to drink.

'We're leaving,' he said, turning and shouldering his way through the crowd.

The two guys exchanged glances. The younger one grabbed the girl around the waist, pushed her forward, and they followed El Osito out of the bar. They stood outside in the street, lit cigarettes, had a discussion with their backs to the door and moved off, blowing plumes of smoke over their shoulders.

'You don't know anything about anybody until you live with them,' said Mercy. 'The mask can stay in place for quite a while, but not for 24/7.'

'The risks you take,' said Isabel, shaking her head, 'when you're young.'

'You make assumptions,' said Mercy. 'Anybody looking at

my father would only ever see a chief of police, an upstanding member of society, a man who didn't tolerate corruption in his force, which in Africa is a major achievement. But if you lived in his house you'd see the real man, how cold and cruel he was. Incapable of love. Capable only of delivering pain.'

'So what was Charlie like to live with?'

'It didn't last that long, and it was seventeen years ago so I'm not sure it's relevant,' said Mercy.

'Everything's relevant.'

Yes, thought Mercy, when you're crazy about him.

'So what was being married to him like?' said Isabel, pushing.

'That was the worst time,' said Mercy. 'He was in the role of a husband and father he didn't want to be in. I was feeling guilty for putting him there, even though I'd wanted it. But, of course, what I wanted was the real thing, not this hideous scenario that we were playing at. It was a relief when it ended and we could go back to being how we always were.'

'How was he as a father?'

'He was good with Amy as a baby. He was at home a lot, studying to get into the police force. I used to tease him that he liked her better when she couldn't talk back. That was the only decent length of time he had with her. Once he went into the police and then kidnap consultancy he hardly saw her. In fact we both saw less and less of him. So much so that when he came back, Amy wasn't that happy to be left alone with him. He was a stranger to her but oddly loving and fatherly. She couldn't work it out.'

'And how were you in all this?'

'I was all right. My family started to come over from Ghana so I was able to help set them up, and they gave me support. Amy got to know them all; they all loved her and she thought they were great. It worked fine ...'

'Until she became a teenager.'

'It was extreme, an overnight phenomenon. She went to bed sweet and came down in the morning a real pain in the arse. I stopped being Mum and became the beast she loved to bait. I sucked it up for a year before I took her to a psychologist. Amy played her brilliantly. We were interviewed separately at first. She was obviously charm itself whereas I was Mrs Uncontrollable

Anger. In the joint interview she behaved so perfectly I ended up trying to bait *her* into being the real Amy. It was a disaster. The psychologist had more concerns about me, probably wanted to report me to social services, but I was a detective sergeant by then, which must have counted in my favour.

'I can nearly laugh about it now. Nearly, but not quite.'

It had been fate: El Osito coming to him. Boxer couldn't help but believe that. There'd been some sort of recognition too. It was as if El Osito intuited something from their brief contact. Boxer assumed it was his profession, or military past, which had given him the authoritative look of a drug enforcement agent or an Interpol cop. What he now had was power. Boxer knew his enemy, had looked him in the eye and felt no fear.

There was no need to follow El Osito and his friends, which would have been awkward after their chance meeting. The mobile number that David Álvarez had given him, which he'd entered into his phone tracker app, meant that he could follow the Colombian from a distance or wait for him in bars.

At first he was with his friends and the perpetually ignored lone girl. Then the other guy picked up a girl. Some time after one o'clock in the morning El Osito came out of the club Joy with a young girl in her early twenties. She had expensively curled long black hair and a dark complexion. She wasn't that steady on her feet and he held her up with a big hand around her waist, as if he already owned her. They hailed a cab in Puerta del Sol and he took her to Kapital on Calle de Atocha.

This looked like a modus operandi: cut the girl away from any herd she might belong to, lose his own friends, show her a great time. Then take her away, move in for the kill. Boxer felt a sudden urge to talk to El Osito. He had to know this man, get an insight into his particular darkness. He would have to find out from the *inspector jefe* whether any other dark-skinned girls with long ringletted hair had gone missing. Where did El Osito's obsession come from; what were the motors that drove his grotesque needs?

'So what was going on with Charlie when he left the army? Was he damaged by that experience in Iraq?' asked Isabel, back on the sofa with her wine and levering at her own little obsession. 'I mean did he suffer any post-traumatic stress disorder? I'm surprised he came back and wanted to break up with you. I'd have thought he'd be looking for stability rather than ... chaos.'

'It was a time when everything changed. He left the army and was trying to get into the police. I think there was another woman too. So, you know how it is, I just became a part of that change. We agreed to split up and then I complicated it all by getting pregnant.'

Her voice wavered over that word. Even Mercy heard it falter. Hardly surprising after all the talk they'd been through.

They looked at each other. This was, after all, the ultimate aim of the confessional, thought Mercy, to bring oneself to the point where you can tell someone everything. She said nothing until Isabel caught the look in her eye.

'Oh Christ. You can't be certain that Charlie's the father?'

Silence.

'I hadn't been seeing much of Charlie in the run-up to our split. I was lonely. I had no family in London. I was a runaway. I was emotionally needy. I was having an affair with another police-man. A dark, brooding Irishman. Not my type really, but he did have green eyes, which reminded me of Charlie's. We had sex. Charlie reappeared. I had sex with him too. Eight weeks later I was pregnant and ... I decided it was Charlie's.'

Boxer was in Kapital. It was massive, arranged over seven floors with music ranging from house to trance to R & B. He walked into the noise, was sucked into the sound, became part of it.

Once he'd spotted El Osito he watched him from different vantage points on the various balconies. He and his girl disappeared frequently and came back with their energy revived to do some more frenetic dancing. They left some time after four in the morning. As they stumbled out into the night, it was clear the girl's limbs were barely coordinated. She must have been a model: her balance mechanism so hard-wired that she tottered and teetered but never tripped and fell. El Osito bundled her into a taxi. Boxer shuddered as he watched him folding her legs in after her, as if he were dealing with mannequin parts.

Boxer got into a cab and offered the driver a twenty-euro tip if he could get him to Pan Bendito in twenty minutes. The driver went at the task as if he'd been waiting for this role all his life. They were there inside seventeen minutes, the rain steaming off the bonnet, smoking away from the wheels. Boxer gave him thirty euros. The cab screeched away.

The Bar Roma was long shut – if it ever opened in these crisis-torn times. The temperature had dropped and the wind was cutting. Boxer, wearing latex gloves, waited in the dark until he heard the unsteady *tickety-tockety-tack* of the girl's crazy heels on the uneven pavement. El Osito yanked at the metal-framed door of the apartment, which screeched over the tiled floor. Still no replacement glass, but someone had cleared up the shattered fragments.

El Osito jabbed at the lift button. The girl tried to rest her head on his shoulder, but he was too short and the angle impossible for her to sustain. In the poor automatic light of the foyer Boxer could see a pair of lacy pants hanging from El Osito's pocket.

The lift arrived, doors opened. El Osito shoved the girl in, his big hand in the small of her back. She fell against the wall, slid down a little, caught hold of the rail. The doors closed behind them.

Boxer sprinted up the stairs as the lift ground its way up the shaft.

15

As Boxer started on the last flight of stairs to El Osito's floor, the window in the door to the stairwell darkened with a thud. There was a shocked cry of pain as the girl fell away and the light returned.

'*Qué haces tío?*' said the girl. What are you playing at, man?

There was no reply from El Osito, who was in action mode now, driven by motors fuelled from a concentrated source. Boxer reached the door, looked through the window at an angle, the side of his face pressed against the cool gloss surface. He drew out the disposable mobile phone with its prepared message as El Osito's big hand came back above his right ear. Boxer sent the message.

'*No, no, no ... por favor, no,*' said the girl, imploring, shocked at the way things were careering out of control.

A terrible sound. A mixture of a smack and thump as the girl's face absorbed some unseen punishment and the back of her head made contact with the hard tiled floor. Boxer weighed the warmed shaft of the heavy-headed adjustable spanner in his hand. The girl was gurgling and spitting, coughing tears.

The electronic signal of the message arriving sounded loud in the echo of the building's hard walls. It was enough to draw El Osito's attention. He reached into his pocket for his phone, opened the message and his head jerked back.

Boxer shoved through the door, right hand holding the spanner, arm across his body. Two steps, and with a backhand drive he smacked the head of the spanner into an area behind El Osito's

157

left ear. The Colombian went down hard, his face hitting the floor with an audible crack. His feet slid out behind him, his arms lifeless at his sides, palms up. The mobile phone spun on the tiles close to the floundering girl. She propped herself up on an elbow. Her left eye was already closing. She touched her face with her fingertips, spat blood onto the tiles.

Boxer straddled the unconscious El Osito, rolled him over, unzipped his jacket and unbuttoned his shirt. He let him fall back and stripped both bits of clothing from his insensate body. He secured El Osito's wrists behind his back with the gaffer tape. A police siren came up in the night and receded into the distance. He pulled the girl's knickers from El Osito's trouser pocket and the apartment's keys came with them, which he pocketed. The girl put her arm up in defence, turned her face away as Boxer stepped towards her. He picked up El Osito's phone, the screen showing Amy with her long ringletted hair wearing the red minidress. He put it in his pocket, went down on his haunches.

'Don't be afraid,' he said in Spanish. 'I'm not going to hurt you.'

He put a hand out to her shoulder, touched her gently. She was crying hard now, blurting snot, blood and tears. He cradled her, put her on her feet, took her to the lift, which was still there. The doors opened. He walked her in, got her leaned up against the wall of the lift.

'Go now,' he said. 'Run for your life. You understand?'

He held the doors for a moment while he checked her, made sure she was going to make it.

'Can you hear me?' he asked.

She nodded. He put her pants into her hand. She looked at them, uncomprehending.

'You've been very lucky tonight,' he said.

She nodded again.

'Now forget everything. Only remember that tonight you could have been killed.'

'*Gracias*,' she said without looking at him.

He gave her twenty euros, told her to take a taxi and let the doors close. The building swallowed the lift.

El Osito started to come round, blood seeping from the wound at the back of his head.

Boxer opened the apartment, slapped on the light, grabbed El Osito by his ankles, turned him through a hundred and eighty degrees and hauled him all the way into the living room. The blinds were already down. Probably always down. He went back and shut the door, pulled a chair out from under the table. El Osito was groggy as Boxer pulled off his boots and yanked off his trousers to reveal the man wore no underpants. He put his hands under El Osito's arms and lifted him up onto the chair.

A mistake. El Osito wasn't quite as groggy as he appeared to be. His knee came up between Boxer's legs, not with any force but enough to propel him forward. They toppled back, El Osito's face in Boxer's stomach. El Osito's head hit the tiled floor first with Boxer's weight on top of him. It was enough to knock him back into unconsciousness. Boxer rolled away. The girl wasn't the only lucky one tonight.

Isabel had given Mercy a sleeping pill, which she'd only taken because it was called Halcion, and she knew she'd need something to stop the nose-to-tail circulation of the horrors churning in her mind. It had worked like a club to the head for four hours.

On surfacing she had a fraction of a second's grace before consciousness engaged, Amy entered her mind, her heart contracted and her stomach plummeted into the dark. She lay alone in the silent house, her hands involuntarily clasping, as if wanting to hold on to something. She tried reaching for the good memories, but her mind was too relentless. Perhaps her own sense of guilt was making her do this. She hadn't been there to protect, hadn't been there to prevent some unprovoked violence. She forced herself to confront her daughter's final terror. It unleashed a bout of crying so intense she had to bury her face in the pillow to suffocate the pain. She rolled onto her back, gasping for air. She had nothing inside but a deep, hollow emptiness.

And it came to her more forcefully than before that there was somebody she could fight for, the Russian boy Sasha. And she decided there was only one thing for it: to get back to work. There was no chance of sleep now. She got dressed, left a note for Isabel in the kitchen and left.

Driving through the quickening city but still in the woolliness

159

of her drugged mind, she attempted to dissect last night with a blunt knife. Her feelings about Isabel were ambivalent. When she'd first met her, during the initial hours of Alyshia's kidnap, she'd liked her immediately and had felt it reciprocated. Then, as Isabel's involvement with Charlie became apparent, some jealousy set in. Last night that ambivalence was even more pronounced and she knew why. Isabel's kindness had led Mercy to entrust her with her deepest fear. Mercy was guilty of omission rather than outright deceit. She'd never mentioned the affair with the green-eyed sergeant because the lifelong connection she craved was with Charlie and not the other guy. Now that it was out, or rather there was the potential for him to find out from another quarter, and with her daughter gone, she might have condemned herself to a Boxerless future.

So why had she told her? It took a while for her to come clean to herself. What she'd done was bind herself to Isabel by telling her that secret. It had created loyalty, put them in league. By giving Isabel something she would find impossible to tell Charlie, Mercy had made herself a presence in their relationship.

The traffic was beginning to stretch its legs as she drove south to Streatham. She turned her mobile on, flipped through the missed calls and messages. A few of them were from Marcus Alleyne. At some point she was going to have to work out why the hell she was going to bed with a petty thief and fence from Brixton.

At home she showered and changed. Within half an hour she was out on the road again, doing the only thing she believed she was good at: working.

It was too early for the rowers. She was quite often early for stake-outs. She liked to see the world preparing itself for the scenario she wanted to observe. The river was barely visible, only the occasional shouldering current picked up a glint of light from the shore and bridge. She went off on foot trying to find somewhere selling coffee and something to eat. Nothing was open.

Back down on the river she had to take a firm grip of the ice-cold railing to curb that desire to throw herself in, even though she knew she wasn't the suicidal type. Makepeace had described her as one of life's terriers. She knew she'd clamped her teeth on

160

the rope of life a long time ago, and no amount of shaking would persuade her to let go.

This strange mental turmoil made her think of her father's four-day funeral. In her own selfish way she'd expected no one to turn up, even though he was what the locals would call a Big Man. The turnout had, in fact, been enormous. The number of people who came up to her and told her how much they admired her father was absurd. Her brother had arranged for some tiered seating to be built around the dance floor because there were always traditional performances at a Ghanaian funeral. It was packed every day. She was stunned to find how much love there was for this man who'd had so little to give his own children and wife. Towards the end she'd met an old boyhood friend of her father's, a man in his late eighties, who was permanently bent over, holding on to a staff in his black funeral robe.

He'd told her a story about her father when he was a boy: how happy he was, how popular, how he was going to marry the prettiest girl in the village. Then there was a dispute over land between different tribes in the area, and before the British could step in to arbitrate there was a night of violence. Men went through the village with machetes. The prettiest girl did not survive the attack, nor did a number of older people. Mercy's father was never the same. He went into the police force so that there would never again be a night of violence, not on his watch.

The old man left; company was tiring for him. Mercy sat with his story in her lap, unable to associate it with the man in the coffin. She mentioned the story to others who'd known her father. Nobody knew about the night that had made her father unknowable. She'd filed the story away in her mind as if it were an old photo album featuring unrecognisable people, over which fingers hovered and moved on. Then she'd dust it off and bring it out on a night like this, when somebody in the world had taken the life of another and ruined somebody else's corner of it for good.

The cold made her tear up. She went back to the car and waited for the rowers.

Boxer taped El Osito's ankles to the chair legs and righted it. He arranged the man's arms around the sides of the chair and taped his elbows to the struts. He pulled El Osito's head back by his hair and looked into his eyes with a pen torch from his pocket. The pupils reacted. His breathing was regular. He let the head drop back and went to check the other rooms in the apartment.

The master bedroom had been changed into a weights room. A floor-to-ceiling mirror occupied the central third of one wall: pumping iron the spectator sport for an adoring audience of one. There were a hundred and seventy-five kilos on the bench press bar and a two hundred and fifty kilos on the higher squat bar. Beyond it was a rack of dumb-bells and another rack of blue bar-bell discs with their kilo weights written in white. There seemed to be a number of weights missing from the five-kilo section. He unthreaded one from the rack, went back to the living room and confirmed his taping was secure. He didn't want this monster suddenly on the loose.

The bed, with its duvet humped in the middle, was in a smaller room. A wall-mounted TV was connected to a cable channel box on top of a DVD player. DVDs were spread over the floor, un-named recordings. Boxer used the remote and found the TV was on the Mexican bullfight channel before it switched to a DVD showing tattooed gangsters indulging in violent porn. Blood sports and hard core for El Osito to sleep on, or maybe to brighten his day when he woke up in the afternoons. He turned it off.

The wardrobes were full of neatly arranged clothes in plastic dry-cleaning sheaths. One cupboard held a metal rack of highly polished boots, some intricately tooled with pointed silver tips. In the chest of drawers under the socks was a handgun. Boxer knew the make, a Star Firestar M-43 with eight rounds, a weighty piece. He took it with him in case El Osito got free. In the bottom drawer was a tangle of women's underwear, possibly as many as fifty or sixty pairs. The collector's haul. It made him think this was obviously a regular activity, but he couldn't have killed them all. There would have been a manhunt for a serial killer by now.

The third bedroom contained three empty suitcases, a video camera mounted on a tripod and some baseball bats leaned up in the corner. Baseball was not, as far as Boxer knew, a Spanish sport. The bats looked new and undented by contact with any ball. Several were painted white with NEW YORK YANKEES emblazoned

162

in blue. One in natural wood had a brown stain. Old blood. Punishment bats for slow or non-paying customers? He took one back to the living room.

El Osito came round to find, in his blurred vision, a man sitting in front of him, head propped up on an elbow. As his vision sharpened he realised that he'd seen this man before but couldn't quite remember where. He saw his own handgun on the table. Nausea slewed in his head and the pounding between his temples made him narrow his eyes to cope with it.

'*Hablas ingles?*' asked Boxer quietly.

No answer. Pure hatred from slit-dark eyes.

'I think you do, El Osito, because my daughter barely has a word of Spanish.'

El Osito blinked once.

'Do you remember my daughter?' asked Boxer, holding up El Osito's mobile phone with the photo of Amy in the red dress.

El Osito shook his head slowly, not taking his eyes off Boxer, still trying to work out where he'd seen him.

'Last Saturday, 17th March, you spent the night with her. She was staying at the Hotel Moderno, but I doubt you met her there.'

Boxer saw that the Hotel Moderno triggered some sort of memory in El Osito's brain. The narrowed eyes widened a millimetre.

'Remember anything more than that?'

'You were in the bar,' said El Osito. 'Standing at the table *con mis amigos.*'

'A coincidence,' said Boxer. 'Happens to me all the time when I get a nose for people.'

Nothing from El Osito, just a long hard look, as if he was sculpting him into his mind.

'Tell me what this is all about,' said Boxer calmly. 'I've seen the drawer in the bedroom full of underwear. Then there was the girl tonight, the one that got away. She looked similar to my daughter, don't you think? A bit older maybe. My daughter wasn't as lucky as she was tonight. No guardian angel for her. So what's going on in there, Osito?'

He leaned forward and tapped him on the forehead. El Osito jerked his head away, winced at the pain.

'What was it? A miserable childhood? Bad mother? Abusive aunt? Nasty sister? Lost love? Did you fall for the girl who didn't like you, thought you were below her? It looks like a pattern. Young, dark-skinned, long hair in ringlets, pretty, innocent face, nice legs. So what is it about this kind of girl that ... makes you so angry?'

Still nothing from El Osito. The rock-hard stare. The eyes gone to black, no whites visible, two chinks of diamond light in the pupils.

'You'll remember my daughter,' said Boxer, sealed in, detached. 'She was probably the last girl you killed. You won't have killed them all. The media would be full of it. And it's hard to get away with killing so many. So what happened? Did you hit her too hard? Did she bang her head? Fall badly on the tiled floor? You can tell me if it was an accident. I'll listen. I won't believe you because of what I saw you do to that girl tonight. But I'll listen. Because I want to know what you did to my daughter and why you had to cut her up and throw bits of her off motorway bridges around Madrid.'

The glint in El Osito's basilisk stare changed a little, but he kept his mouth shut.

'Things coming back to you now?' asked Boxer. 'Do you want to put them into words for me?'

Silence.

'Let's talk about what was found. Maybe that will help you to remember what you did. A young man walking his dog saw a black bag under a motorway bridge that hadn't quite made it into the river. Inside was a girl's lower leg, some clothes and in the jacket, a passport. That was my daughter's passport. Now the police are trying to find the rest of her. So where did you kill her, Osito? In here? How did it happen? Her body had been bled so I suppose you did that and the cutting up in the shower.'

Still nothing.

'Talk to me, Osito. I know you can speak English, so that's not the problem. I know you're remembering things – I can see it from your face. So, now I'm going to have to get rough with you.'

Boxer tore off a piece of gaffer tape and smoothed it over El Osito's mouth. He laid the chair down on its back, which, given

164

the position of the Colombian's arms, was not comfortable. Boxer took the baseball bat and showed it to him. El Osito was wide-eyed with the horror of it. Tried to speak.

'Too late,' said Boxer.

He'd never played baseball so he swung the bat along the more formal but accurate line of a cricket shot, a sweep to square leg, which hit El Osito on the point of the ankle. He delivered a matching blow to the other side. There were muffled screams and two streams of snot shot out of El Osito's nostrils onto his chest. His face screwed in agony. Boxer righted the chair, waited for a minute while the Colombian got himself back under control and stripped the tape off his mouth. El Osito still wouldn't speak, but this time it was the agony preventing him. He ducked his chin onto his chest, determined to give Boxer the minimum of satisfaction.

'Now let's have it,' said Boxer. 'No more hard-man stares. I can carry this on all night.'

'You don't know it was me killed your daughter,' said El Osito. 'You know it was me, you go to the police.'

'I *do* know it was you,' said Boxer. 'I've got witnesses. You've got a reputation for beating up women. You were seen leaving Kapital with my daughter. And when they found her leg, clothes and passport they found one of these weighing down the bag so it would sink in the river.'

Boxer hefted the five-kilo weight, brought it down hard on El Osito's toes. The Colombian gasped and growled with the pain, clenched his teeth.

'I saw you tonight in Kapital with another girl. I followed you here. By the time I arrived you were already beating her up. I had to step in. Maybe you'd have killed her too, by accident. Now tell me what you did to my daughter. What did she say that made you want to kill her? Or didn't she have to say anything at all?'

'This not for you, *mi amigo*,' said El Osito. 'You get the police. I talk to the police.'

Another piece of tape across the mouth. The chair once again laid on its back. This time it was the knees. An off drive on one side and an on drive to the other followed by two less stylish shots: hammer blows to both kneecaps.

Boxer sat him back up. The Colombian's head twisted and turned with the agony from his shattered joints. It concerned Boxer that El Osito could have avoided this brutal retribution just by being a bit more talkative. He wondered if he might see this as some necessary punishment for all the wrongs he'd committed in his life. They were deeply Catholic, these Colombian gangsters. They had to be, with what they had coming in the afterlife. Boxer could find no pity for the man. He'd seen the terror in the eyes of the girl he'd rescued that night and had imagined that same terror in Amy's eyes when the monster had turned on her at the end of her first night of freedom.

'I think you've realised that this is not a case for the police, El Osito,' said Boxer. 'This is between you and me. Now tell me what you did to my daughter.'

He stripped the tape off El Osito's mouth. The Colombian gulped in air trying to cope with the pain.

'I don't know what happen to her,' he said finally. 'I woke up in the bathroom. I came in here. She dead on the floor. We taking a lot of blow and drinking. Maybe she not used to it. Maybe her heart not strong enough. My cocaine very pure. That's it. That's all I can tell you, *mi amigo*.'

'All right. One more thing,' said Boxer, getting up close, looking into the eyes, which had lost some of their hardness now. 'What's this all about? This obsession with hurting girls? Tell me that and I'll finish it quick.'

El Osito looked at him out of the corner of his head, eyes, puzzled.

'What's it to you, *hombre*?'

'You don't question why you do it?'

'You know, when I see you that first time in the bar I know you kill people. I see that look before.'

'Is that why you left?'

'No, no, I see that look in the mirror every morning,' said El Osito. 'I leave because I don't like the *way* you look, something like a cop or maybe a judge. But now I see you in the revenge business and I'm asking myself, why you doing that? You look like police and acting like a gangster.'

'I just don't like people getting away with murder.'

'Yeah, most people are like that but they don't go killing people, taking revenge. How you get into that business? You tell me yours, I tell you mine.'

They looked at each other for some time.

'You recognise yourself now?' said El Osito. 'You don't know the answer any better than me. We just doing what we *have* to do, *mi amigo.*'

'I am not your *amigo*,' said Boxer.

'OK, how about *compañero*?'

Boxer stood up, took the baseball bat in both hands, reached out and touched the fat heavy end to El Osito's ear. He eased the bat back slowly and gave the Colombian's ear another light touch in a slow measured practice swing.

The front doorbell rang.

'JAIME!' roared El Osito.

There was a splitting crack as the front door was shouldered open.

16

The rowers started turning up at 6.00 a.m. Even to Mercy's in-expert eye she could see the tide was going out and it would be low water by eight thirty. She counted off the crew as they arrived. Seven men plus the cox and the coach, but no Jeremy Spencer. The crew brought the boat out and set it on the river while the cox hopped onto his bike, swung back up the ramp and pedalled crazily down the Lower Richmond Road. Mercy followed him.

The cox veered left into Roskel Road, stopped near the top, threw the bike against a low wall and went up to the front door of a Victorian semi-detached house. He thumbed the bell hard. Mercy pulled up by the open gate, lowered her window, watched. The cox stood back, went to the front bay window and peered through the curtains, knocked on the window. He kicked the front door with his plimsolled foot and was about to turn away when the door eased open. Mercy got out of the car. The cox was halfway up the hall, where a bike was leaning against the wall.

'Just wait a sec,' she said and showed him her warrant card.

The door to the house had been on the latch. The flat's front door was by the bottom of the stairs, which went up to the two flats above. She pushed it with a gloved finger. It too opened.

'Just wait outside while I take a look at this,' she said to the cox.

She put on latex gloves, turned on the torchlight of her mobile phone and went into a narrow hallway with four closed doors. She started with the door to the front room, which was set out as a living room, with a wall-mounted TV over the fireplace. The next door opened into the bedroom with a window looking out onto a small garden. The double bed had a T-shirt cast over the duvet and jeans and a jumper hung over a chair in the corner. She backed out, walked past the most suspicious door in the flat and took a cursory look at the empty kitchen.

Back to the bathroom. The sweat came up on her hands inside the latex gloves. She pushed the door but it only opened a few inches, as it butted up against some wet towels on the floor. She pushed harder, stuck her head around the door. Jeremy Spencer was lying in a full bath, one leg over the side, the other bent awkwardly into the corner. His head and torso were underwater. She crammed herself around the door. The water was stone cold, the window was open, all the towels underfoot were sodden and Jeremy Spencer was long dead.

'What's going on?' asked the cox from the doorway to the flat.

'I'm afraid Jeremy's dead,' said Mercy. 'There's going to be an investigation. Somebody's going to need to speak to all of you. Give me your mobile number and then you can go back to your crew and tell them they won't be going out on the river this morning.'

'What do I say?' asked the cox, looking overwhelmed.

'You tell them Jeremy's dead and the police are dealing with it. At this point we know nothing. It could be an accident, suicide or murder.'

'But what about you? What were you doing here?'

'Don't let it get complicated in your head,' said Mercy. 'Stick to what you know.'

'Jesus Christ.'

Mercy called DCS Makepeace. The cox turned his bike and pedalled off.

'What are you up to, Mercy?' asked Makepeace.

'I'm working, sir,' said Mercy. 'I'm working the Sasha Bobkov case.'

'You're off that case,' said Makepeace. 'You're not on duty. I've given you indefinite leave.'

'I don't want it, sir. I can't do it. I can't sit alone in my house knowing Amy's gone. I *have* to work,' she said. 'I went down to the river this morning.'

'The river?'

'The Thames.'

'I guessed that.'

'I was following up on Sasha's teacher, Jeremy Spencer,' said Mercy. 'He didn't show for rowing practice and I've just found him dead in his bath.'

'Oh shit,' said Makepeace, the day gone to hell before he'd even got away from the breakfast table. 'Let's hear it.'

She gave him the details. Makepeace made the call, came back to her.

'I'd like to go after Irina Demidova now,' said Mercy. 'Did George get anywhere with the Mercedes?'

'He hasn't filled in the rest of the numberplate, but he's established that one of the cars owned by DLT Consultants is a black Mercedes CLS with an LG 61 plate.'

'Do we have any opinion on Messrs Dudko, Luski and Tipalov?'

'They've been established here for some time, since the mid-1990s. They've filed accounts at Companies House and paid their taxes,' said Makepeace. 'As for the individuals, none of them has any record, and George ran their names through our organised crime database and didn't come up with any matches.'

'So, I'll talk to Demidova, and if I'm out of luck there I'll move on to DLT Consultants, if that's all right with you.'

'Do you really think this is the best thing for you to be doing right now, Mercy? This is more than likely a murder. It'll raise the Bobkov case to a new level.'

'I want to be involved. Amy got away from me and I couldn't save her. But this boy, Sasha, sounds like a really great kid,' she said, her voice cracking. 'It would help me if I could do something for him. It would give me a chance to make something right in a world that's gone badly wrong for me. I'm not in the front line. I'm not under the same pressure as the consultant in the case. I'm just investigative. I'm good at it. I'll work with George. If I'm too unstable, he'll tell you and you can take me off the case.'

Mercy hung up, waited for the homicide team to show. One of the occupiers of the upstairs flats came down the stairs, slowed at the open front door, looked around. Mercy showed him her warrant card, told him there was an investigation going on to do with his downstairs neighbour.

'Are you alone up there?'

'Last night I was. My girlfriend only stays over at the weekends.'

'Are you first floor or top?'

'First. The top-floor guy is away on business in the States. Won't be back until next week.'

'Were you here last night?'

'From around one thirty onwards,' he said. 'I was out on business with some Norwegian ship owners. We went to a club afterwards. It was a heavy night – always is when the Norwegians come to town.'

'What happened when you got in?'

'Stripped off, face down, out for the count.'

'I meant, how did you get through the front door? Was it locked?'

'Jesus, I'm not sure. That's why I was a bit freaked when I saw the door open. Did I leave it like that?'

'I'm asking *you*. Did you unlock it, put it on the latch for any reason? Or did you put the key in and find it was already open?'

There followed a long thought process during which he checked his watch.

'It's important this. I know it doesn't sound like it, but it'll help us establish some things. A chain of events.'

'How did *you* get in?' he asked.

'The door was on the latch.'

'Shit. I was so bladdered last night I could have done anything.'

'How did you get home?'

'Cab.'

'From where?'

'Marylebone High Street.'

'Where were you?'

'Sophisticats on Marylebone Lane,' he said. 'You don't believe me?'

'Just checking. You told me you were legless.'

'We always end up in Sophisticats with the Norwegians.'

He whipped round suddenly and stared up the hallway.

'Thank fuck for that,' he said. 'At least his bike's still there.'

'This happened before?'

'Last year before Christmas, got home late one night, fell through

171

the door, landed on the floor, woke up a few hours later, crawled to bed, left the door open. Jeremy's bike got stolen. I had to buy him a new one,' he said, looking at his watch again. 'Got to go.'

'Homicide are going to want to talk to you.'

'Homicide?' he said, giving her his card.

'Jeremy's dead.'

'Because *I* might have left the door open?'

Boxer swung the bat. He was going to make sure he took out the man who'd murdered and dismembered his child. He missed. El Osito tipped himself backwards, clipping the table with his foot. Boxer's bat flashed overhead, wheeling him round in the process. The bat smashed into a panel of glass between the living room and the kitchen, shattering it. His swing had been so violent that the bat smacked into the wooden frame, jolting it out of his hands. He was in two minds about going for the gun on the table or the bat on the floor, but saw that the gun had been knocked off. He scrabbled after the bat. Got hold of it again. There was no time now. No time to take another swing at El Osito, no time to search for the gun, no time to get out.

Bodies and feet thundered down the corridor. Boxer lunged forward and swung the baseball bat through the narrow doorway. The end made contact with something and there was a grunt of pain. A man went down, a flash of chrome in his hand and a clattering of metal on the ceramic tiles and fragments of glass.

El Osito shouted something from behind him.

Boxer knew that his only chance to get out was in the chaos and adrenaline surge of the first rush or get cornered in the room with two armed men. He followed the trajectory of the bat into the corridor, kicking out and stamping on the flailing legs of the first man. He kept low. There was no chance of swinging the bat so he thrust it forward, fat point first. El Osito shouted again, something he couldn't decipher, but it sounded like an order.

The bat rammed into an oncoming body. Another grunt and an exhalation of air. The man fell back and Boxer felt the bat wrenched out of his hands. He stumbled over the fallen man, felt his ankle grabbed at and, as he wrenched that away, his trouser leg. He went down, lashing out madly with his free foot, his head thudding into something hard. Another shout from El Osito. A definite command.

Boxer rolled, launched himself forward and came out of the apartment barely off the ground. He scrambled across the floor, hands trailing and flailing for purchase. He bounced off the lift doors. The bat shot past him at knee height and clattered against the far wall. He fell through the stairwell door and down the first flight, grabbing at the handrail. He righted himself, thumped against the wall on the first landing, took the next flight in two leaps. He careered down the six flights of stairs and crashed out into the foyer, ricocheted through the metal-framed door, which was stuck ajar, and out into the cold night. He sprinted diagonally to his left, past the entrance to the Bar Roma, ducked down between parked cars, crossed the *avenida* and let the darkness of the park engulf him, suck him away from the garish street lighting.

He ran without looking back. He ran until his lungs burned and his legs screamed. He ran in a swerving arc as he saw the green light of a taxi flashing between the trees on the wide Avenida de los Poblados. He came out into the ghastly glow of the street lights arm raised. The taxi screeched to a halt and he threw himself across the back seat, told the driver to take him to Puerta del Sol. He lay in the back, staring at the roof pulsing in his vision, heart thumping in his throat, blood crashing between his ears, trying to calculate, with no access to numbers large enough, the extent of the trouble he was now in.

Mercy was outside Irina Demidova's house in Ryecroft Street having briefed the homicide squad on Jeremy Spencer's death. She'd rung the doorbell six times and there'd been no answer. On the seventh ring the neighbour's door opened and a furious guy in his fifties, bald, grey and red-faced, came out.

'Look, she's not there, for Christ's sake,' he said. 'How many times are you going to ring the bell before you believe it?'

'I was thinking of taking it to the full rounded ten,' said Mercy, showing him her warrant card. 'DI Mercy Danquah.'

'I'm sorry, officer. I'm trying to work. I've got a book to write and I could do without the bell,' he said. 'The pressure's enough without the bloody bell.'

'Do you know your neighbour?'

'I wouldn't say I know her exactly. I know her name's Irina. I say hello to her and her son, Valery. She's asked me to take deliveries for her once or twice. That's about it.'

'When did you last speak to her?'

'Yesterday evening she came round and I gave her a box that had been delivered in the morning.'

'Who delivered it?'

'Some guy in a Mercedes.'

'What colour was the car?'

'Black.'

Mercy tapped away at her phone and brought up a Mercedes CLS.

'Was this the model?'

He nodded.

'Registration number?'

'Give me a break.'

'I had to ask,' said Mercy. 'What sort of books do you write?'

'Crime novels.'

'Would I know you?'

'I doubt it. Nobody else seems to.'

'Maybe you should brush up on your observation skills,' said Mercy.

'Thanks for the tip.'

'Glad to be of service. Tell me about the box that was delivered.'

'It was the size of two reams of A4 and about as heavy.'

'You're improving already,' said Mercy. 'And you haven't seen her or her son since?'

'Not strictly true. Yesterday was the last time I *spoke* to her. The last time I saw her was a bit later. She came out of the house with her son and got into a minicab. I didn't get the registration number of that one either.'

'Time?'

'Seven thirty-ish.'

'Luggage?'

'None.'

'Did she come back?'

'Could have done. I'm in bed by ten.'

'Did you see her leave for work this morning?'

'That's true, I didn't. Nor her son.'

'Can I have your number?'

'Only if you give me yours and let me call you and ask you technical questions.'

'It's a deal,' she said. 'You've been a big help.

'It didn't sound like it.'

Boxer lay spreadeagled on the hotel bed trying to think. The one thing he knew with absolute certainty was that El Osito would never forget his face. The way the Colombian had stared at him was like an artist clearing away the onion layers of the persona to get down to the real and memorable man. He'd looked at him as if he might learn something about himself from such a face. He knew El Osito would take his visage to the grave with him, would remember him so well that he'd be able to come looking for him in another life. And he wouldn't have to wait that long. Boxer had been stupid. He should have just done what he set out to do. Taken his revenge. Killed him for murdering his child. He had no idea why he'd started questioning him or what he'd hoped to gain from such a ridiculous interrogation.

That was when he got his first glimmer. It shunted him up and off the bed and in front of the full-length mirror. Staring at his reflection, he realised he hadn't been looking for an insight into El Osito's bizarre brain, but hoping to see inside his own. He stood, hands on either side of the mirror, as if he had to steady himself to confront his own presence. What was going on in there?

Nothing came back at him. He pushed against the wall, willing the monster inside to come clean. He shoved himself away.

It was impossible now to stay in this room, the last place in which he knew his daughter had been alive, the place where he'd got uncomfortably close to himself, the place where El Osito knew to come looking. He packed his bag, went down to reception and checked out.

The receptionist gave him a package, which had been personally delivered by Inspector Jefe Luís Zorrita late last night. He had expressly asked for Señor Boxer not to be disturbed and had

175

written an explanatory note. Boxer asked them to call a cab to take him to the airport and read Zorrita's note.

Because of the recent cuts, the police forensic laboratory would not be able to derive DNA from the tissue taken from Amy's body for another three weeks. There was a backlog of DNA samples that stretched to November 2011 and there was nothing Zorrita could do. He knew how important it was for parents to bring their child's body home, but in this particular case, because of lack of facial ID, the authorities would not allow repatriation unless there were matching DNA samples. Zorrita had been able to persuade the lab to prepare tissue slides taken from the leg, which he enclosed in the box attached. He had also persuaded the Spanish authorities to accept a UK lab's analysis of the tissue samples matched to the mother and father's DNA to allow the release of the body.

The cab arrived to take him to Barajas Airport. He sat in the back and tapped out a message to Mercy, asking if the police forensic lab could get a DNA match done in less than three weeks. Then he remembered their last conversation on that issue and saved it as a draft, didn't send it.

He sent a text to Zorrita, thanking him for the attention he'd give to Amy's case. As they headed through the northern outskirts of the city he couldn't help but find the *inspector jefe*'s total integrity admirable. He wondered how many murderers Zorrita brought to justice every year. Real justice. A justice that the victims might equate with the terror they'd suffered and whose families could weigh against the grief they'd endured. As he performed this ridiculous balancing act he realised what he was doing. Assuaging his guilt. He'd just caught sight of himself on the integral scale between good and evil, where Zorrita was at one end and El Osito at the other, and he was closer to El Osito's end than he was to Zorrita's.

The cab dropped him off at departures. He went through the tedium of check-in and security and only started thinking last night through more carefully when he had a cup of coffee in front of him in the departure lounge.

What had gone wrong at El Osito's apartment last night? Why had his 'freaks' turned up? El Osito had split away with the girl.

If he'd wanted the others involved he'd have stuck with them. So how did they get to be there? He must have had a way of alerting them, but Boxer had picked up the Colombian's mobile outside his apartment and had taped his hands behind his back as well.

Was there a panic button somewhere in the flat? If El Osito had product there and money it wasn't such a far-fetched idea. He'd been unconscious when Boxer had dragged him in. Then he remembered El Osito kneeing him in the crotch as he'd lifted him onto the chair. It hadn't been a brutal blow that caused any damage and he'd put that down to the Colombian being groggy. Maybe rather than trying to inflict pain he'd been kicking out at a button under the table.

And what had he shouted out? What was the command he roared to his freaks? The first word had been '*No*'. He remembered that, and the second had three syllables. He replayed the scene in his head. The swing and the miss. The shattered glass. The bat on the floor. Recovering it. The men bundling down the corridor. Driving the baseball bat through the doorway. The grunt of pain. The flash of chrome. A gun clattering across the floor. El Osito, on his back by then, must have seen it all.

Boxer connected to the Internet and went to a free translation site. On a hunch he entered, 'Don't shoot,' and asked for the translation in South American Spanish. The answer came back: '*No disparar.*' That was it. El Osito was telling them not to shoot, and he hadn't done that through fear of bringing the police to his door.

El Osito wanted him for himself.

17

8.30 A.M., THURSDAY 22ND MARCH 2012
Clinica Privada Iberica de Madrid

'Your left ankle was broken into a number of pieces, which we have pinned together. Your right ankle was undamaged, but you have sustained a fracture to the lower part of the fibula,' said the surgeon. 'Your knees? Well, both patellae have been broken: the left in two pieces, the right into four. The end of the femur and fibula on both sides sustained cracks but luckily nothing has broken off. The medial ligaments on both sides have been torn—'

El Osito, lying in a hospital bed, held up his large left hand. He didn't need to hear anything more about the damage.

'When will I be able to start walking again?'

'Two to three months if everything—'

'Two *months*?'

'Possibly three,' said the surgeon. 'Look, you've refused to tell me what happened to you, but I can tell that these four joints have sustained severe, directed blows from something hard. This was done to you with the specific aim of causing you maximum pain and making sure that, if you did walk again, it would always be with difficulty and discomfort. You've been lucky that some of the blows weren't as accurate as others. Had they been, you'd probably have had to be in knee braces for the rest of your life and your ankles would have required multiple operations.'

El Osito's big left hand came up again.

'Two months it is,' he said. 'Send in *mis compañeros*.'

The surgeon was used to being dismissed like this, especially by private clients who didn't have any insurance and wanted to

178

pay in cash. He left the room, glad to get out. He nodded at the two men sitting in the corridor. He'd just treated the one with the ponytail for cracked ribs. He knew, by the look of them, the types he was dealing with, which was why he hadn't bothered offering to send the police to the victim's bedside to take a statement. They went into the room without acknowledging him.

This was the first time they'd spoken to El Osito since they'd cut him free from the chair and, in total agony, he'd ordered them to take him down in the lift and put him in the back seat of the BMW they'd arrived in. Jesús knew better than to make any fuss about this or to whinge about his own cracked ribs. He could tell from the sweat standing out on El Osito's forehead in the cold night air that this was a man in serious pain. Jesús had elected to stand guard over the apartment until someone else came to relieve him. Jaime drove El Osito to the clinic.

They stood at the end of the bed, one on either side, faces arranged to mask both dismay and concern that their boss was in such a state. They were glad to see he was no longer in pain and hoped that the self-administered morphine would take the edge off his rage.

'So, who was he?' asked Jaime. 'We've got everybody on full alert here, including up in Galicia and down on the *costas*. Was he Russian?'

'The Russians haven't forgiven us,' said Jesús. 'They still think we tipped off the police before Operation Scorpion.'

'He was English.'

'English?'

'He was the guy in the bar.'

'What guy?'

'When I came into that bar where we first met last night, there was a foreigner standing at your table, drinking a beer,' said El Osito. 'Him.'

Jesús and Jaime looked at each other as if they might have been in some way responsible for this.

'The man thinks I killed his daughter, cut her up and threw her pieces into the River Manzanares.'

Silence. Jesús and Jaime barely dared to breathe. They knew this was distinctly possible. Their boss, Vicente, had warned them about El Osito and his odd habits before the Colombian had arrived in Madrid. He liked to live in downbeat neighbourhoods, he lifted superhuman weights, he used his own product and he didn't like black girls or *mulatas*, liked to beat them up.

'You mean this English guy is some crazy person,' said Jesús, remembering that they shouldn't show too much knowledge about El Osito's foibles. They also knew about guys who used too much of their own product and its tendency to short the wiring in their paranoid brains, resulting in blowouts of uncontrollable rage.

'You're going to do two things for me and you're going to do them fast,' said El Osito, calm with the morphine in his system. 'You're going to talk to our friends in the police and you're going to find out the name of the girl who was killed last Saturday, or maybe Sunday, and whose body was found cut up in bags in the river. I want as much information as possible. He said the police found her passport, so I want a photocopy of that passport. If it costs money, you pay. That investigative journalist you spoke to, giving him the dirt on the Russians in Marbella, what was his name?'

'Raul Brito.'

'Tell him you want the favour returned. You want to know the inside story about this girl. Everything. You understand?'

'Is that it?'

'I said there were two things.'

'The police and the journalist,' said Jesús.

'That's two people but about the same thing,' said El Osito. 'You're going to find out *why* the Englishman thought it was me who killed his daughter.'

'How do we do that?' asked Jesús.

'You have to use your head. *No*, Jesús, sorry, my mistake; you have to use the brain inside your head,' said El Osito. 'The other thing the Englishman told me was that his daughter stayed in the Hotel Moderno and that she was seen leaving Kapital with me. There was a photo of her wearing a red dress. He sent it to my phone.'

'Where's your phone?'

'I don't know. Maybe the Englishman took it. Use the tracker software, see if you can find it. If you find it, you might find the Englishman. Why d'you need me to tell you these things?'

'I don't ...' started Jesús.

'Start using your brain, Jesús, or you'll end up with more than a few cracked ribs. You understand me?'

'We know the people on the door at Kapital,' said Jaime, saving his brother from El Osito's attention.

'Maybe it was the people on the door who *told* the Englishman ...'

'No, no, no. They don't talk to anybody. They know you're connected to us. They wouldn't tell anybody you left with any girl. They need their blow as much as the people inside.'

'And the Charada,' said El Osito. 'You ask around there too. Maybe Joy. You know the clubs. Somebody's got to have seen something.'

'And if we find the guy—' started Jesús.

'Not if. *When* you find the guy you take him to La Escuela and I will go down there and do the talking. You know what I mean, Jesús?'

They knew what La Escuela was: an old warehouse in the middle of the country, distant from any villages. The walls were still standing and about half the roof. It was called the School because it was where they took people to learn hard lessons about money, debt and interest payments, and in the event that they found these lessons too difficult to take in, they were given the hardest lesson of all.

'I'm very sorry about Amy,' said Papadopoulos, brown eyes concerned under his heavy black eyebrows. 'I couldn't believe it when the DCS told me. You must be devastated, Mercy. I mean ... are you really OK to deal with this sort of crap? Wouldn't you rather—'

'Sit at home?' said Mercy. 'No thanks.'

She was glad that Papadopoulos wasn't one of the touchy-feely coppers who'd become more prevalent in the force in the age of New Sentimentalism. He didn't try to put an arm around her shoulder when he was somebody who'd normally salute her. He kept a respectful distance, said his piece, maintained eye contact

181

but was still slightly awkward. Technically they were partners, but she was his superior and he the understudy, which meant that they were not equals and he shouldn't seek to comfort too much. Mercy didn't want any of that from her colleagues. She'd never liked the enfolding kind, the ones she suspected used the tragedy of others as an excuse to find out what it was like to hold someone in their arms.

'But thanks anyway, George,' she said. 'I'm all right. The DCS told you to report me if you thought I wasn't up to the task.'

Papadopoulos nodded.

'As long as you don't do that we're going to be fine,' said Mercy. 'What's going on here?'

They both looked at the door to the office building they were standing outside.

'No answer,' said George, who was now certain that Mercy didn't know what he'd been involved with last night and wasn't sure how he should play it.

'Still early,' said Mercy. 'What's the matter with you, George? You're looking ... stricken. I don't need you to look like that. No kid gloves, OK? Just act normal, or as normal as you can.'

'I checked with Chris Sexton to see if they'd heard anything from the gang,' said Papadopoulos. 'You could smell the sweat coming down the line. Thirty-six hours and still nothing.'

'That wasn't it.'

'What?'

'That look,' said Mercy. 'Don't ever hide stuff from me, George.'

'I was on Hampstead Heath last night, looking for Charles Boxer's mother,' he said, looking across the traffic. 'We found her unconscious with the best part of a bottle of vodka inside her and plenty of temazepam. I got her to the Royal Free as fast as I could. She's on life support.'

Mercy stared into the gutter. He was surprised to see her frowning, her lips tight over her teeth, muttering, 'Fucking typical.'

A young blonde woman fiddling with a set of keys passed between them. She opened the door to the DLT Consultants building. She was in a grey pencil skirt and very high black patent-leather heels.

'You with DLT?' asked Papadopoulos.

'What's it to you?' she asked, checking him out head to toe, unimpressed.

'We're police,' said Mercy.

They flipped out their warrant cards. The blonde shifted her blue eyes to Mercy, parted her chilli-red lips. Mercy was still furious. Typical of Esme to make a scene, for it to be all about herself, and irritating as well to be outdone on the emotional stakes. There was more to this. Esme had to have been involved in Amy's plans and now felt responsible.

The blonde turned back to Papadopoulos, who was more restful to the eye.

'We'd like to talk to Messrs Dudko, Luski and Tipalov and Irina Demidova,' said Mercy, putting away her card.

The blonde shouldered through the door, didn't hold it for Papadopoulos, who had to lunge forward to stop it closing. She picked up the post, dropping to her haunches while Papadopoulos held the door.

'Mr Luski is in Tashkent, Mr Tipalov is in Siberia.'

'Then it looks like we'll have to settle for Mr Dudko,' said Papadopoulos.

The blonde gave him a 'think you're clever' look as she slowly came back up to his height.

'He'll be here soon.'

'And Irina Demidova?'

'Now there we have a problem,' said the blonde. 'I don't have the first idea who you're talking about.'

'You don't?' said Mercy, producing a photo of Demidova. 'We're talking about this woman?'

'Then you'll be referring to Zlata Yankov,' said the blonde.

'Will we?' said Mercy, intrigued now.

'Yep, and Ms Yankov is a law unto herself.'

'What does that mean?'

'It means I don't always know where she is or what she's doing.'

'Why's that?'

'Ask Mr Dudko when he gets here. He hired her.'

They followed her upstairs, Papadopoulos behind the swinging hips, the taut material of the pencil skirt practically creaking under the strain of containment. She took it slowly as if she might

183

be enjoying the induced mesmerisation behind her.

She unlocked the office, keyed in the alarm code, turned on her computer and the Nespresso machine. She put on a headset and listened to the messages. As she listened she took notes and sent emails. After five minutes she tore off the headset.

'Coffee?' she said. 'We don't do Greek, I'm afraid.'

'Espresso?' said Papadopoulos.

'With milk for me,' said Mercy.

'Strong,' they said in unison.

'Quite a double act,' said the blonde, assembling the coffees. 'Apparently Ms Yankov won't be coming in today. She left a message last night saying, "Gone to Moscow."'

'For ever?'

'That would make my life a lot easier,' said the blonde. 'Sugar?'

She handed out the coffees. Papadopoulos poured two full sachets of sugar into his cup and stirred it slowly while he thought up his next question.

'DLT Consultants own a Mercedes CLS registration LG 61 FKR,' he said.

'Is that you showing me your homework?' said the blonde, crossing her legs, managing not to split a seam. 'You get five out of ten for being half right. We've also got a BMW 5 series, LG 61 PRK. Fucker and Prick we call them. They're pool cars. Whoever's in town can use them. There's a booking system which nobody bothers with because, as you've just realised, they're hardly ever in town at the same time.'

'Do you know who was using the Mercedes CLS on the morning of Tuesday 20th March ... early?'

She turned to the computer, opened up a file.

'Nobody, according to the booking system, but, as I said, that doesn't mean anything.'

'Can we assume it would either have been Mr Dudko or Ms Demidova, or rather Yankov?' asked Mercy. 'Or was somebody else in town on Tuesday?'

'I think you can assume that ... if it was being used, that is,' said the blonde. 'What's with the Demidova business, by the way?'

'It's her more commonly used name,' said Mercy. 'Do you know her son, Valery?'

'Yes, he comes here after school sometimes.'

'Well, his present school and the one he went to before know his mother as Irina Demidova.'

'No shit?' said the blonde, delighted by this revelation.

'Do the cars have drivers?' asked Papadopoulos.

'What?' said the blonde, irritated by the distraction from the scandal. 'They can come with or without. If we're picking up a client from the airport we'll send a driver. If Mr Dudko is going home for the weekend he'll drive himself.'

'Who is the driver for the CLS?'

'We'd normally use Big Mal,' said the blonde. 'Malcolm Lavender. A surprisingly fragrant name for a man of his size.'

She gave him a mobile number.

'Where do you keep the cars?'

'What's with the cars?'

'We need to know, that's all.'

'The underground car park in Cavendish Square. Bays seventy-four and -five.'

A dark-haired man in his mid-forties wearing a navy-blue wool coat and carrying a briefcase came in. He spoke Russian to the blonde, whom he called Olga and who replied in kind. He hung up his coat. She talked him through his messages and other business. Olga introduced Mercy and Papadopoulos, using their ranks and full names, which she'd memorised from glancing at their warrant cards. Mr Dudko shook hands, asked for a few minutes and disappeared into his office.

'Your Russian is pretty good, Olga,' said Papadopoulos.

'That's because I *am* Russian. How many non-Russian Olgas do you know?'

'None,' said Papadopoulos, looking up into his head. 'Then your English is excellent.'

'I went to school here,' she said, 'and university.'

'I thought you must have married someone English to speak it that well,' said Papadopoulos.

'I didn't mean to come across as *quite* so argumentative,' said Olga.

Papadopoulos laughed. Mercy gave him a slow look, eyelids at half-mast. Mr Dudko called Olga to send them in.

'*Try* to keep it in your trousers,' said Mercy in his ear as he opened the door for her.

Mr Dudko walked around his sizeable desk on the verge of breaking into a trot. They shook hands. He settled them in some low chairs, jogged back and collapsed into his own jacked-up black leather chair. He looked fit, a careful eater and not much of a vodka socker, if Mercy read him right. She suspected he had a weekly manicure.

'How can I help you?' he asked in thickly accented English.

'We would have liked to have spoken to the woman we know as Irina Demidova and you know as Zlata Yankov,' said Mercy, 'but we understand they're both in Moscow.'

Dudko blinked and his mouth fell open as he took in that complicated sentence.

'You say Zlata has another name?' asked Dudko.

'She calls herself Irina Demidova at the school where her son is currently studying. She is also known by that name at his previous school and by the teacher who taught her son, with whom she is having a relationship.'

'This is all news to me.'

'This teacher is also a rower and had rowing practice early this morning but didn't show. He was later found dead in his flat, drowned in his bath. We're waiting for the autopsy and the forensics, but the circumstances indicate that he'd been murdered.'

'So this is a murder investigation?' asked Dudko, looking shaken.

'Not exactly. We work for a special investigations unit in the Metropolitan Police,' said Mercy, preferring to keep it vague. 'Where were you early in the morning on Tuesday 20th March?'

'I was driving up from my house in Godalming. I must have left about six and arrived here about seven, seven fifteen.'

'Which car were you using?'

'The BMW. The Mercedes was in use on Friday when I wanted to leave for the country.'

'Who was using it?'

'I imagine it was Zlata as nobody else was in London at the time.'

'And what was she doing with it?'

'I have no idea.'

'How did Zlata Yankov come to be employed by you, Mr Dudko?'

'She was recommended.'

'By whom?'

'Her name came up in a number of different ways. Somebody on a Russian trade delegation, a couple of our old clients – you know how it is?'

'Not really,' said Papadopoulos. 'We're in the police. We undergo constant assessment before any advancement.'

'Well, here we have very specific requirements. Any employee has to be bilingual in Russian and English. They have to have a good understanding of finance, the raising of finance, Russian business practices and most importantly Russian networking, which includes both the private sector and government. So, you see, with those very specific demands we don't go into the open market. If we need someone we ask around and candidates are put forward.'

'How many?' asked Mercy.

'In this case we just saw Zlata. We all liked her and thought her capable. So, rather than waste our time interviewing ten people, we agreed to give her the job.'

'So you all approved her appointment?'

'Not all of us were here at the time,' said Dudko, 'which was one of the reasons we needed to employ someone.'

'Does that mean *you* effectively gave her the job?' asked Mercy. He writhed a little at that, but nodded.

'She moved from an expensive flat in Hampstead to an even more expensive house in Parson's Green,' said Mercy.

'We own residential property in London. We let it at very advantageous rates to our employees on the understanding that if we want to sell they have to move out immediately. Olga is currently living in a very nice flat overlooking Regent's Park, for instance.'

'And was Zlata well remunerated?'

'Her base salary was low at around forty thousand, but with bonuses she'd earn in excess of a hundred and fifty thousand.'

'What was it about Zlata's profile that you particularly liked?'

Silence while Dudko frowned and steepled his shiny nails.

187

'The Irina Demidova *we* know came over here in answer to a Russian-girls-meet-English-guys advertisement and enrolled in a language school. Her business credentials weren't that clear on the CV I saw,' said Mercy.

'Olga says she's a law unto herself,' said Papadopoulos. 'She never knew where she was or what she was doing.'

Dudko launched a flash of annoyance in the direction of the door.

'Clearly you're having difficulty articulating Zlata's capabilities,' said Mercy. 'Can I ask you whether it was specifically her Russian government contacts that attracted you?'

'Look, I'll be honest with you,' said Dudko. 'She's not been all we hoped for. We've begun to realise that perhaps her greatest talent is for personal PR. She's done an excellent job of talking herself up.'

'Do you think she could have been employed by the Russian government? Their security forces?' asked Mercy. 'The FSB?'

Dudko stared wide-eyed into his desk.

'Were you approached and "asked" to employ Zlata Yankov by a Russian government official?'

'No,' he said emphatically, searching his brain, looking for a way out. 'But there was … something.'

18

'What have we here?' asked Dr Perkins, white coat, white shirt, blue tie, glasses, a man used to resolving paternity cases.

'These slides are tissue samples taken from my daughter by the forensic lab of the Madrid police,' said Boxer.

'Tissue samples … forensic?' said Perkins, alarmed. 'Madrid police?'

'She was murdered in Madrid last weekend. The police are unable to process her DNA for another three weeks and we want to repatriate her body, or what's …'

'I'm very sorry for your loss,' said Perkins. 'Does this mean she was unidentifiable?'

'This was taken from a body part found with her clothes and passport.'

'My God,' said Perkins, looking at the man across the desk from him, stunned by his professional detachment. 'You must be … Are you all right? This is … I've never come across anything like this before. It's … it's a tragedy.'

'It is for me,' said Boxer, suppressing the emotional surge. 'I want to bring her body back to the UK, and to do that I have to have positive identification. I need you to match my DNA to this tissue sample's DNA and document it.'

'And what's on the pen drive?'

'That's my ex-wife's DNA. She's the girl's mother and a police officer. Her DNA was already on file. That was taken from an

189

email attachement she sent to the Madrid police before we realised they couldn't complete the task for another three weeks.'

'It would be cheaper and quicker to match your ex-wife's DNA to the sample's.'

'I know, but I want you to do both.'

'Does that mean there's a question mark about paternity?'

'I didn't think there was,' said Boxer, recalling Mercy's outburst yesterday. 'But there might be.'

Perkins looked at his watch, made a call down to the lab.

'That's OK,' he said. 'We can still get your samples into this morning's PCR slot, which means we could have the results for you by close of business today. We're going to have to shift other tests into the following day, but under these tragic circumstances I think it's the least we can do for you.'

Papadopoulos was driving Mercy's car. They were on their way to the Northwest International School in Portland Place. Mercy was on the phone, giving the details of the passports belonging to Irina Demidova aka Zlata Yankov, a photocopy of the latter having been supplied by Olga. They'd already been to the underground car park in Cavendish Square to establish that the Mercedes CLS owned by DLT Consultants had been taken out on Friday and still not been returned.

'Need I ask, but how do you feel about "engaging" with Olga?' asked Mercy.

'Christ, Mercy, I'm not sure I'm in her league,' said Papadopoulos. 'And my girlfriend wouldn't be too happy about it either. Mind you, the way these cases are going and the four-in-the-morning phone calls ... that might not last for very much longer.'

'Welcome to Specialist Crime Directorate 7,' said Mercy. 'It's not easy fitting relationships into the little time slots before you both crash out, is it?'

'Tell me about it,' said George, thinking of last night on the Heath and in the Royal Free Hospital.

'And I didn't mean get her into bed, George, although I must say you didn't look as if you'd have minded me giving you that kind of order,' said Mercy.

'That wasn't part of my training,' said Papadopoulos. 'You?'

'Don't be cheeky,' said Mercy. 'So how about Olga? Fancy giving her a call and ... I was going to say pumping her for information but I don't want you to misconstrue the directive.'

'Is this copper to civilian or something else?'

'Bit of both. You seemed to get on, right league or not,' said Mercy. 'Let's call it a friendly between Panathinaikos and CSKA Moscow.'

'Sassy, sophisticated Russian graduate seeks Greek plod with sideburns?'

'You need some talking-up classes from Demidova,' said Mercy. 'You're a detective sergeant in an elite department in the Met. You know a whole load of interesting stuff that she hasn't got the first idea about. You even have the same alphabet ... more or less.'

'You've just talked me into it,' said Papadopoulos, perking up as he parked outside the school. 'What are we doing here?'

'You're staying in the car and calling the DLT Consultants' driver, Big Mal, to see if we can find that Mercedes CLS,' said Mercy. 'I'm going up to see the headmaster with the cattle prod this time.'

'The old colonoscopy treatment?' said Papadopoulos, wincing.

Mercy went up to Piers Campbell's office, barged her way in.

'Did Valery turn up for school today?' asked Mercy.

Campbell slowly put down the file he was reading, weighed something in his head and decided against a demonstration of headmasterly authority. He checked his computer, made a phone call, put the phone down slowly.

'When there's a no-show you're supposed to phone the mother. Is that it?'

'Yes, and it went straight to answerphone.'

'Did you call Irina Demidova after my visit here yesterday afternoon?'

Silence. Campbell went for a hard, direct look, trying to assert himself. Unfortunately for him Mercy was used to a lot worse than that from rapists, kidnappers and murderers.

'Did you?' she asked, eyebrows raised.

'Yes.'

'When I'd expressly asked you not to,' said Mercy. 'It was very important for my investigation that she was unaware of my enquiries.'

'I did not talk to her about the activities of her son, Valery,' said Campbell. 'I respected that. We did *not* talk ab—'

'So what *did* you have to talk about, if it wasn't Valery?'

Unable to take any more of the inexorable Mercy, he stood up, went to the window, looked down into Portland Place and wished himself elsewhere.

'Are you married, Mr Campbell?'

The headmaster nodded, hands folded behind his back, shoulders braced.

'Were you having an affair with Irina Demidova?'

He nodded again.

'Did you discuss her intimacy with a young male member of staff at the Hampstead school?'

Campbell's gaze fell to the window sill, where it alighted on an innocent ornament, some piece of glass or porcelain. He picked it up and, with the sudden animation of a cricketer going for a run-out, dashed it against the wall. Fragments showered down onto the floor, snicked against the window glass.

'I'll take that as a yes,' said Mercy. 'Did you find out who she'd been intimate with before you spoke to her?'

'Jeremy Spencer,' he said icily.

'So when I asked you if there'd been any intimacy between Ms Demidova and a member of staff you made the assumption of the jealous lover,' said Mercy. 'How did you find out it was Mr Spencer?'

'The caretaker,' said Campbell. 'Caretakers always know what's going on.'

'Is that why Ms Demidova never came to the school gates here?'

'I'm not a fool,' said Campbell. 'Well, not all the time.'

'Jeremy Spencer is dead,' said Mercy. 'Drowned in his bath. We think it's murder.'

Campbell staggered to his chair, fell into it as if his legs had stopped operating. The chair rolled slowly to the wall, where it stopped.

'Holy fuck,' he said, as the last element of his professional headmasterly façade collapsed. 'Holy ... fuck.'

'Any theories?'

'Hunh!' said Campbell, wild-eyed, panic-stricken. He drew himself up to his desk, rested his hands on either side of some documents and stared down at his disappearing life: marriage, children, job … the lot.

'Any theories apart from the obvious one, which the homicide squad are going to leap on because they love a good strong motive like jealousy.'

'You think *I* did it?'

'*I* think you have some responsibility for it,' said Mercy. '*They* will see you as the only clearly motivated suspect, now that Irina's gone.'

'Gone?'

'She vamoosed with Valery. The UK Border Agency are on to it now.'

He formed two fists and dropped his head onto them.

'Any theories before homicide come knocking would be helpful,' said Mercy.

'You mean, that's not you?' he said.

'No. My interest is in Sasha Bobkov's kidnap, remember?'

'And you think Irina was involved in that?'

'I'm sure she was involved in the set-up. Anything you can tell me would be very helpful,' said Mercy. 'I've just come from her place of work, where she was known by another name.'

'Another *name*?'

'Yes. They're not as pleased with her now as they were when they took her on. She's a con artist, as I'm sure you're now aware. So, seeing as the only other person who knew her intimately is dead, I was hoping for some insightful pillow talk.'

Campbell's eyes roved the desk for inspiration. He squeezed his hands white.

'How did it come about, your affair with Irina?' asked Mercy. 'What did you do for her?'

'Why would you think that I—' He stopped as he saw the flat of Mercy's hand put up to his face.

'Don't kid yourself,' said Mercy. 'What are you? Late forties to her thirty-six?'

'Valery earned a scholarship,' he said finally.

193

'You mean he was awarded one,' said Mercy, 'and you became a regular at her flat in Cannon Place?'

'Yes.'

'Did you hear anything unusual while you were in her company? Any odd phone calls or strange visitors?'

'The phone calls were always in Russian,' said Campbell. 'There was one visitor while I was there. We were in bed. The doorbell rang. She checked her watch, dressed quickly, told me to go into the spare bedroom and keep quiet. I looked through a crack in the door. I had to see who it was. He was a big guy. Russian. She was nervous. He grabbed her by the hair and said things into her face while she squeaked with pain. He punched her in the side and she dropped to her knees. He left. I went to help her. She puked up with the pain, told me to leave and crawled into bed, fully clothed.'

'And you asked her who he was?'

'Of course, but I didn't get an answer.'

Boxer had tried calling Mercy but her phone was shunting him straight to voicemail. She did this when she was working, couldn't stand having her interviews interrupted by calls. Why was she working? He couldn't understand it, called Makepeace.

'I'm not happy about it either,' said Makepeace, 'but I have an agreement with her. If it gets too much she's to stop and George is reporting to me on her.'

'She'll never stop and she controls George.'

'Sometimes I think … no, not sometimes, I *do* think she has a split personality,' said Makepeace. 'She has this professional mode … no, it's more than a mode, it's even more than a role. It's like I said, a different personality. One that she escapes to when her life has become too chaotic or upsetting. She seems able to bring her twenty years of experience to bear on a case while leaving her twenty years of emotional history behind.'

'I know it,' said Boxer. 'When Amy's campaign was at its worst she would just go to work. Her police partners over the years told me she was always calm, focused and had a line for every situation: funny, tough, insightful, unrelenting, whatever was demanded. What worries me now is that this isn't a normal level of turmoil.

We're in uncharted territory. I know you can't discuss it openly, but what is this case?'

'The case is the point,' said Makepeace. 'She said it would help her deal with the ... the loss. A young boy's been kidnapped. A kid who's been hiding his mother's alcoholism from the world and going to school as if nothing's wrong. It's given her something to hold on to. She couldn't save Amy but she can save this boy. Her words, not mine.'

Boxer swallowed hard, trying to keep his own mind at bay. All he could see was El Osito's black stare beyond the fat end of the baseball bat in his hands. He changed the subject, told Makepeace about the Madrid lab's processing problems. Boxer asked if he was able to deliver Amy's tissue samples to the Met Police's forensic lab in Southwark could Makepeace get it fast-tracked?

'I'll pave the way at Southwark,' said Makepeace, 'but they work a system, and the best I'll be able to do is to get it introduced into tomorrow's processing run.'

They hung up. Boxer dropped off the samples, took a cab to the Royal Free Hospital and found his mother in ICU. She was still on a ventilator, wired up to machines, entubated and catheterised. It was a sobering sight to see his mother reduced to such incapacity when her default setting was 'utterly capable'.

He held her hand, which was cold, lifeless and wrapped in tape. The ventilator hissed and sucked. He'd never seen her so helpless. It occurred to him that he'd never actively thought whether he loved his mother. She was not the loving type herself and, once his father had disappeared and she'd sent him away to school, an even greater distance had developed. He'd retreated and she'd got on with her life assuming that everybody was like her and work stood still for no man. Then his own life took off and he was immersed in the army, homicide and kidnap consultancy.

And now here they were at a strange haitus. Maybe that was one of the purposes of death or life-threatening moments, to put everything on temporary hold so that thoughts could be gathered. Mercy had never liked his mother. She had reciprocated with a lack of enthusiasm for Mercy. Boxer himself didn't much like his mother. She didn't make herself likeable. She needled him when they were together as if he represented something too complicated for her to deal with. Too much communication and interaction were required for them to reach a point where they overlapped. So they clashed rather than merged. They air-kissed, bumping cheekbones, and never hugged. He'd read somewhere about the narcissistic mother and decided that Esme fitted that bill almost exactly.

The registrar came in. She was in a hurry. She told him the first brain scan post-admission had shown decent activity. They were proceeding with the detox, which would finish later that day. As long as brain activity continued to develop they would try taking her off the ventilator tomorrow. She was optimistic. She left and the ICU nurse came in carrying his mother's effects in two plastic bags. She told Boxer to talk to Esme out loud. It helped this sort of patient to hear the voices of those close to them – it started things up in the brain. Boxer wondered what those 'things' might be in his mother's head: 'Oh God, not Charlie again. I think I'll stay in the coma world if there's only him to look forward to.'

Boxer took a closer look at Esme. Her skin had that ancient parchment look, the smoker's lines around the lips, paper-thin eyelids. He was struck by how little he knew her and yet how he'd never quite extricated himself from her bond. And with that thought her finger twitched against his and was still again.

'Irina Demidova was working for DLT Consultants under the name of Zlata Yankov,' said Mercy, in the sitting room of the Netherhall Gardens house.

The effect of those words was instantaneous. Bobkov and Kidd came off the sofa, phones in hand, punching in numbers. They left the room, yabbering into the mouthpieces, and went into the study, where they'd set up a computer and communications station.

'What did I say?' said Mercy.

Sexton looked at her imploring. The lawyer wasn't there.

'I can tell you're not happy, Chris.'

'I've never been on a case like it,' he said. 'Never had so little communication with the kidnappers. I don't know what to do with myself. They just don't call. It's been nearly forty-eight hours without a word. Have you ever been sweated like this?'

'What's the DCS make of it?'

'What can he say? There's nothing to comment on. I'm the pork chipolata at the Jewish wedding.'

'Ease up on yourself,' said Mercy. 'You can only work with what comes your way. If they won't communicate there's nothing you can do about it.'

'It's as if they know the game,' said Sexton.

'They might well do,' said Mercy. 'Let's hear what those two have to say once they've moved the threat levels up to critical.'

Bobkov and Kidd returned after fifteen minutes, took their seats with Mercy watching them, expectant. She got nothing.

'It's just been confirmed by the UK Border Agency that Irina Demidova left the country, under the name Zlata Yankov, with her son on the Eurostar with tickets to Paris,' said Mercy. 'We're now waiting to hear from the French whether she boarded a flight or took other transport out of the city. Interpol have been alerted.'

She talked them through Jeremy Spencer's alleged murder and Demidova's affair with the headmaster and the assault she sustained in his presence in her flat at Cannon Place.

'When did that take place?'

'Late June last year. By September she was working for DLT Consultants and had moved to Parson's Green,' said Mercy. 'It's not the sort of treatment you'd expect to be handed out to a spy, is it?'

'It depends,' said Kidd, 'how you want things to look to the outside world.'

'Where the Russian state is concerned you can't leap to any conclusions,' said Bobkov. 'The FSB, which the president used to run, operates in all strata of society. He understands perfectly not only the nature of control, but also the strange blend of business and the criminal, the government and business and therefore the necessary overlap between government and the criminal. And as James says, that incident could have been staged to achieve a number of things: to make it look as if she was managed by gangsters, to induce fear or a sense of protection in the headmaster, or even just to give her orders. The FSB exploit people too. Irina Demidova might not have a choice in the matter. They could be threatening her family. She obviously has the necessary attractions

197

of a honey trap and then there's the encumberance of a child to be fed and educated. She looks like a strong candidate for exploitation and, if this is an FSB operation made to look like a kidnap gang, they could be expanding her role as the situation develops.'

'It might be more interesting to consider why they had to murder Jeremy Spencer,' said Kidd.

'Presumably to do with the pressure we were applying?' said Mercy. 'Maybe he *had* been giving her information about Sasha, he was feeling guilty and, now that he'd seen what had happened to the boy, was threatening to blow her cover.'

'It concerns me,' said Bobkov, 'that we haven't heard from the kidnappers for so long. They seem to have pulled Demidova and they've terminated Jeremy Spencer. This is beginning to sound like an aborted mission, and that's not good for my Sasha.'

'Let's keep thinking positively,' said Mercy. 'George has established that DLT's driver hasn't used the Mercedes CLS for the last two weeks and he's also revealed that it was fitted with a tracker system in the event of it being stolen. George is working with DLT trying to recover the vehicle now. We've also applied for a search warrant for the house in Ryecroft Street that Demidova was using.'

'Didn't DLT offer to let you search it?' asked Bobkov.

'It's a precaution,' said Mercy. 'I don't think Dudko is being obstructive. He's realised that he'd been set up to take Demidova on last year.'

'How was that?'

'It seems she came with the sweetener of a contract attached. There was some industrial diamond deal that Dudko had been trying to pull off for the previous six months and it was miraculously resolved when he took on Demidova. I suppose the FSB is very strong on satisfying base male needs,' said Mercy. 'Sex and money.'

'Well, we've got the cash lined up if the latter is still in play,' said Bobkov.

A text came through from Papadopoulos.

'They've found the Mercedes,' said Mercy.

*

Boxer went to his mother's flat, used a set of keys from her effects to let himself in. He wandered around Esme's home, stopping at the photos of his mother and Amy that Papadopooulos had left out on the desk the night before. He could see from the shots why his mother had taken such drastic action, found his arms squeezing his ribcage to keep the expanding darkness in his own chest under control. It came to him, one of the constant refrains of Betty Kirkwood, his mother's old work friend, who for years after the death of Esme's business partner and the disappearance of her husband kept saying, 'Your mother really needs to find a man.'

'Why?' he'd asked her one day.

'Because she's going to get lonely,' said Betty. 'Not for a while yet, but when she quits this business ... It's one of those industries that drops you like a stone. One minute you're connected and experienced, and the next the fashion's changed and the show moves on.'

And here was the new love of her life – not a man but Amy.

Why had Amy never spoken about her relationship with Esme? Too private, too intimate? They did things together like cooking, which Amy had rarely done with her own mother, not even when she was a child and Mercy had made the occasional cake.

A message came through from Zorrita in Madrid: 'We need to talk about the second bag. Call me at 17.00 Spanish time. I will have the translator here in case we have a problem.'

He checked his watch, half an hour to go. He went through the shots again, nodding at the two faces he knew so well but which he'd never seen so infused with affection.

He called Isabel, told her he was back and that he'd been to see his mother in intensive care. He was shocked to find it was news to her. Talking to her calmed him. The call filled most of the half-hour wait for Zorrita. He hung up and immediately the intercom phone rang. Someone at the door outside. He went to the kitchen, picked up the phone, said hello. No answer. He looked up at the screen to see who was on camera. Someone slipped out of frame. A shoulder was there and then gone. Kids?

Time to call Zorrita.

'You found another bag,' he said.

'Just north of the site where we found the first bag. Same type, weighed down with an identical five-kilo weight,' said Zorrita. 'Had any luck with the DNA?'

'I've arranged a private analysis as well as giving it to the police lab here in London,' said Boxer. 'Why?'

'And how quickly do you expect to get the results?'

'The private lab said later today.'

'OK, that's good.'

'Any reason for these questions, Luís?'

'No, no, it's nothing. It's just if there was a delay.'

'What have you found?'

'A distinguishing mark,' said Zorrita. 'I've spoken to the authorities and explained our time problem with the DNA testing, and they've agreed that if you were able to tell us about the mark they would be prepared to release the body under the special circumstances. But, look, if you're going to get the result in an hour's time or so, then that would be better.'

'A mark, like a birthmark?'

'Yes, but it's not a birthmark.'

'A mole?'

'No.'

'In fact, she has no birthmarks and no moles,' said Boxer. 'Do you mean a tattoo?'

'Yes.'

'I don't know. I've never seen one, but that doesn't mean anything,' said Boxer. 'I know she doesn't have one on her arms, legs or back, but I haven't seen her naked since she was a child.'

'This was on the left buttock.'

'I'll ask her mother.'

'If the DNA results come through, that won't be necessary. It was only if you were going to have to wait a week or more for the analysis.'

'That's very good of you, Luís.'

'We're operating on two sites now. I pushed for another team of divers because there are so many crossing points over tributaries to the Manzanares. We'll find ... everything, Charles. Don't worry, I won't stop until she is returned to you. You have my word on that.'

Boxer was moved, squeezed his eyes shut. Held himself across the chest.

'You're a good man, Luís,' he said. 'I couldn't have asked for more. How … how's the investigation going?'

'It was lucky that we knew she was staying in the Hotel Moderno so we can trace her movements. She spoke to the concierge about clubs, and we'll start by checking those and getting her face around the Puerta del Sol. It might take time, but someone will have seen her. We'll get our break, have no fear.'

Boxer's hands went clammy at the thought of David Álvarez. He thanked Zorrita, hung up and sat back, stunned, as his mind pursued the consequences of the homicide squad connecting with Álvarez. His mobile vibrated. The screen told him it was Dr Perkins from DNA Solutions.

The sweat came up again. The moment of truth. The irrefutable evidence. Was he a father? Did it matter? He took the call.

'Mr Boxer, I have your results for you,' said Perkins, who paused as if he wasn't quite sure how to proceed with this.

'Is there a problem?'

'Are you certain that these slides contain tissue taken from your daughter?'

'The Madrid homicide chief has assured me that is the case.'

'Well, she's *not* your daughter, Mr Boxer.'

He felt a little faint with shock, had to breathe in gulps as if there wasn't enough oxygen in the air. Perkins kept going.

'And nor is she the daughter of Mercy Danquah,' he said. 'The DNA from these tissue slides matches neither of you. Do you understand me, Mr Boxer?'

19

This was not something to be talked about on the phone; this had to be done in person. Boxer sent Mercy a text asking where she was. Still in the Netherhall Gardens house, half a mile away.

Now he was running down Holly Hill through the cold, grey late afternoon, past houses whose front rooms were lit, showing scenes of blissful normality. He hit the junction with Hampstead High Street. The schools were out and the streets full of uniformed kids, as if time had gone back to another era of simplicity and order. He flashed past a group considering the evening showing of a movie at the Everyman and nearly knocked over a *Big Issue* seller outside Tesco Express. He sprinted down Fitzjohn's Avenue and turned the corner into Netherhall Gardens and saw Mercy standing in the street, hands in her pockets. She was looking at him with wild white edges around her eyes, as of a startled horse. He ran down the road to meet her, grabbed her by the shoulders, held her tight at arm's length, told her breathlessly what he'd done with the tissue samples when he'd flown into Heathrow.

Mercy broke down. She hung on to his wrists with both hands, dropped her head and wept.

'I'm sorry, Charlie. I'm so sorry.'

'Listen to me.'

'I should have told you.'

'Just be quiet and listen to me.'

She looked up; their eyes met. She saw what was in his and it wasn't anything she'd expected to see. It was joy.

'The DNA derived from the tissue samples from the body part in Madrid does not match *either* of ours. The body they have found is *not* Amy's.'

It was too big for her to grasp. The emotional volte-face demanded was too extreme. She stared at him, still hanging on to his wrists, as he nodded the new truth into her.

'Amy is *not dead*.'

'But I saw her at Heathrow ... on CCTV. Her passport ...'

'You remember what you said right at the beginning, about Amy putting up a smokescreen? The strange feeling we got reading her note that this was *her* challenging *us*. "You will never find me." She fooled us. She knew our emotional involvement would distort our vision. She sent us on a wild goose chase.'

'But you said that everybody saw her in the hotel in Madrid. You showed them the photo.'

'They just saw a pretty black face under lots of dark ringlets with blonde highlights. You know what people are like, especially with different ethnic groups. They just see a black face, an Asian face. They don't see features, eye colour – difference.'

'I want to believe it, Charlie. I really do. But I just can't quite bring myself to. I don't know why. I'm afraid. I've put everything in one emotional basket and now I've got to take it all out and I can't do it. Not in one go. The disappointment would be too horrible. It would be tragic if—'

'The detective on the case called me, said they'd found another body part and it had a distinguishing mark on the left buttock. A tattoo.'

'Amy hates tattoos,' said Mercy, hope registering in her voice. 'She despises them. Karen is always trying to get her to have one done.'

'When did you last see her left buttock?'

'I haven't ... for years. She locks the bathroom door. You know what she's like.'

'Call Karen. They shared a room in Tenerife. She must have seen her bum, for Christ's sake. They went to the beach.'

Mercy called Karen, asked the ridiculous question, got silence in return.

'You're kidding, right, Mrs Danquah?'

'No, it's very important. We need to know.'

'There's nothing would make Amy have a tattoo,' said Karen. 'She hates them. Hates mine. And doesn't mind telling me.'

'But did you see her left buttock?'

'Left, right, the whole show, Mrs Danquah. We all went skinny-dipping in the hotel pool. She didn't have a tattoo, I'm telling you. What's this all about?'

'Nothing, Karen. We're just trying to help with an enquiry from Spain.'

She hung up, didn't want to get into dead bodies with Karen. She nearly smiled. Boxer grabbed hold of her, hugged her fiercely, buried his face in her neck.

Mercy whispered in his ear, 'I should have told you.'

'That you weren't sure I was her father?'

'I should have told you.'

'It doesn't matter.'

'I *wanted* you to be her father.'

'It doesn't matter,' said Boxer. 'And you know why? Because when I found out that the dead body wasn't Amy's, that she hadn't been murdered, I was so elated. I felt whole again, and I knew that with or without my DNA, she was mine.'

Mercy hugged him to her, wouldn't let him go. The truth was out. A truth that had been stuck in her like a piece of shrapnel that the body had grown around but with an odd movement could still hurt. Every time she'd seen Charlie and Amy together it skewered her, not just with doubt but with guilt at the omission. She'd done it because she loved him, and yet what a thing to do to the one you loved. It had been one of those four-o'clock-in-the-morning torments for the last seventeen years and now it was gone. And what a way for it to have come out. With so little damage. In fact, the opposite. Joy.

And just as she reached the point where she thought she might allow herself some joy something terrible occurred to her.

'If that body wasn't Amy's ...'

'I've got to call Luís in Madrid,' said Boxer.

'Are you listening to me?'

'I've got to tell the homicide chief.'

'Amy found a double. She asked someone to impersonate her. To fool us. And now that girl is dead. Murdered. Cut into pieces because Amy decided she wanted to show her parents how clever she was. She's got to know how much her little prank has cost. It's a whole life that's gone because—'

'It wasn't part of the plan,' said Boxer. 'She didn't mean for it to turn out like that. It was just bad luck. That poor girl met the wrong guy at—'

'You don't know how it was. You don't know the circumstances. All you know is that this girl went to the Hotel Moderno. You don't know Amy's responsibility. What *I* know is that if Amy hadn't wanted to stick one to her parents that girl would still be alive. She'd never have gone to Madrid.'

Boxer got through to Zorrita, gave him the news. There was a long silence.

'Do you understand me, Luís?'

'I understand you,' he said. 'I just don't understand how a girl can end up wearing your daughter's clothes with your daughter's passport and not be your daughter.'

Boxer did his best to explain, said he'd put it all in an email and the translator could talk him through it. They hung up. He turned to Mercy, saw her anger.

'Come on, Mercy.'

'Amy's little game has cost a girl's life, made your mother want to kill herself and has caused us so much *pain* … For what?'

'Amy's still a kid, which means she's at her most selfish. The world revolves around her. Only *Amy* really understand things. She wasn't thinking about history or consequences. Life's a game to be played.'

'One dead girl, an attempted suicide …'

'Did you tell your family?'

'No.'

'No?'

'Uncle David's funeral started today. I couldn't face telling them about Amy when they were about to start mourning somebody else. It would have … Just imagine if I had.'

'Better the way it's turned out,' said Boxer.

'How *is* Esme?'

'Functioning but on life support. There's brain activity, so they're hopeful.'

'This case I'm working on,' said Mercy, gesturing at the house behind her. 'The boy who's been kidnbapped. A ten-year-old. Looks after his alcoholic mother, doesn't tell anyone. Hides it because he knows how much it means to her to have him near her. He has to get himself up, make his own breakfast, entertain himself. Probably has to scrape her off the floor, get her into bed, then run off to school. Then come back to that sort of crap every afternoon. All weekend. And Amy thinks she has a hard life. What did Esme call it? A deficit of love. I think that was it.'

'Steady on, Mercy. You've given yourself half a second of joy and you already want to strangle her.'

She cried. She grabbed hold of the lapel of his jacket and wept into his chest. He stroked the back of her head, kissed her close-cropped hair.

'The main thing is that she's alive,' he said, and the word caught in the back of his throat.

After some minutes Mercy pushed herself away, dug out a tissue, wiped her face.

'Sorry,' she said, looking at the house. 'I'd better get back in there. We're coming up to forty-eight hours with no word from the kidnappers.'

'We've got to find Amy,' said Boxer, not listening, galvanised now by a new fear: the look he'd seen from the Colombian coming down the length of the baseball bat at him. The intent. He would have a name by now. It would be in the newspapers; some journo would have latched on to an ugly murder like that. And there was the Hotel Moderno – he'd given that to El Osito. If his name wasn't out there yet, then the hotel would supply it. Too many people knew.

And then there was that order El Osito had roared several times: 'Don't shoot!' He's mine, leave him for me. And what would be the best way to get to him? He'd work it all out, El Osito, Boxer was sure of that. This was a man who had been brought up on revenge.

*

206

The first one had poked him in the chest, the second had put a gun in his mouth, and the third had beaten him up for trying to find a window in the toilet, the fourth had smacked him round the head for catching him cheating at chess. Now Sasha was with a fifth guard.

He'd noticed that they didn't always come and sit with him in the room. Sometimes the new guard would come in, there'd be an exchange in Russian, some of which he understood, then they'd handcuff him to the slatted bench and both go out. That was worst because it would mean hours on his own, lying down getting uncomfortable and bored.

This time there'd been the usual handover but the guard had stayed in the room and said hello. None of them said hello. He'd uncuffed him even though it wasn't eating time. Sasha could tell from the atmospheric pressure in the confined space of the room that this guard was more friendly. He thought maybe he had a son like him.

'I'm very worried about my mother,' said Sasha, head down, palms on his knees, legs dangling off the bench, feet not reaching the floor.

'I can understand that,' said the man. 'She's not well.'

'She drinks,' said Sasha.

'I know,' said the man.

'It's not really her fault.'

'It never is.'

'She's unhappy.'

'A lot of people are,' said the man. 'It's called life. You don't understand it yet.'

'How do you know?'

'You're a kid. Life is simple when you're a kid.'

'Is it?'

No answer.

'She'll be really, really worried by now,' said Sasha.

'She's being looked after.'

The emotion welled up and, although Sasha didn't want to, he couldn't help himself. He sobbed, felt the tears wetting the material of his mask. The guard sat next to him, put an arm around his shoulders, hugged him into his chest. Sasha got himself under control.

'Nobody talks to me,' said Sasha. 'You're the first one. Why doesn't anybody talk to me?'

No answer. The man knew perfectly well why nobody talked to the boy. They knew to keep their distance from someone they would have to ... deal with. But he was different. He cared.

He rested a hand on the Sasha's thigh, squeezed it reassuringly and his little finger tickled the boy's groin.

Sasha's spine turned to ice.

Jesús and Jaime were sitting in a bar drinking beer with a copy of *El Mundo* open between them. There was a small article on page 6 about an unnamed girl who had been murdered and a part of her body recovered from a bag found under a motorway bridge near Perales del Rio. All their contacts in the Madrid police force were in the drug squad and had no information about homicide cases unrelated to drug dealing or trafficking. El Osito had told them to drop the police, stick to the journalist, which was why they were waiting for Raul Brito from the weekly *Interviú* to turn up. The only break they'd had was at the Hotel Moderno, where they'd found some leaflets on reception with a photo of the girl as they'd seen her on Saturday night and beneath, in Spanish, 'Have you seen this girl? Her name is Amy.' This was followed by a Spanish mobile number, which they'd already tried and found to be dead.

'What do you think about all this?' asked Jesús, broaching the subject he really wanted to talk about but until now hadn't quite dared.

'El Osito did it,' said Jaime. 'No question about it. We're not running around like this for fun.'

'And the English guy?'

'I don't know. If El Osito knows he's not telling us.'

'So we got to be careful. Don't want to end up—'

'Look, before El Osito came out here Vicente told me everything I needed to know. Warned me. This has been coming for a long time. We're lucky we haven't been clearing up a mess like this every week.'

'Why didn't you tell *me*?'

'I did. I just didn't give you any details because I know you can't keep your mouth shut. The one thing Vicente warned me about was not to cross El Osito. You give him the wrong look and he'll blind you, you tread on his toe and he'll take your leg off.'

'I remember that bit.'

'I'm glad it stuck. I can see you shitting in your pants every time he talks to you.'

'This thing he's got about black girls ...'

'It's a bad thing. That's all you need to know.'

'Did Vicente tell you why?'

'There doesn't have to be a why. The wiring's all fucked up in his head. That's the why. Too much snow. That's the why. He's a nut job.'

'But did he tell you?'

'He told me that El Osito's father was shot dead in a hotel in Cartagena de las Indias. It was a gang war thing. They used a black girl to get him into the hotel. Shot her too. He was fucking her at the time.'

'Long hair? Ringlets?'

'You want her shoe size as well?'

'OK, here comes Brito.'

The journalist took a seat, pulling the chair up to the table using a hand between his legs. He had soft brown eyes in a shrewd, pouchy face and hair whose shape, colour and thickness could survive doomsday. He looked from Jaime to Jesús and down at the newspaper.

'*El Mundo?*' he said, as if he'd caught them reading Descartes.

'Beer?' asked Jaime, which seemed to be the only possible retort.

Brito nodded. They called the waiter, ordered three beers.

'What's going on?' asked Brito. 'This about the Russians?'

Jaime turned the newspaper round for him, pointed at the article. Brito read it, nodding.

'We've been talking about that in the office today,' he said. 'One of the young guys wanted to run with it, but we had no photo.'

'Why don't they give her name?'

'They only found a body part and a passport so there's been no formal identification,' said Brito. 'They're running some DNA tests, but the backlog with the cuts ...'

'DNA tests?'

'You know, Jaime, they extract DNA from a tissue sample—'

'Don't fuck with me, Raul,' said Jaime, setting the tone. 'What are they comparing the sample to? You have to have verified DNA from a victim or her parents to confirm ID.'

'She was a runaway. The father came looking for her. So I imagine they're comparing her DNA with a cheek swab from him.'

'So you've done some work on this?'

'Not me. It was talked about in an editorial meeting last night. It was put on the "possible" list if the journalist can find a photo and an angle.'

'Have you got a name?'

'Not yet, and we've only got about a quarter of the story,' said Brito, tapping the newspaper, 'which is why this article is only five centimetres long and on page 6. An ugly crime, but not quite interesting enough … yet.'

'You remember that information we gave you about the Russians on the Costa del Sol. You ran that piece about local government corruption, the girl trafficking …'

'I remember,' said Brito. 'I also remember it solved some of your problems when the police launched Operation Scorpion and there was quite a bit of, what shall we call it, ethnic cleansing? A scouring of the Slavs.'

Jaime looked at him steadily, letting him know that he'd just overstepped the mark: turning what should be his gratitude into doing them a favour was not how it was supposed to work.

'What's *your* interest in this case?' asked Brito, leaning forward. 'Did one of your boys get a bit out of control?'

'Not one of *our* boys,' said Jaime, touching himself on the chest.

'Is this the Russians again? Is this a girl-trafficking thing?'

'We don't know. We just don't like this kind of thing happening without us knowing about it. So we want you to get us all the information you can. All the names. But you don't run with any story. That could be dangerous for you. We don't know who you're dealing with. You print something, they might come after you.'

'This is beginning to sound *very* interesting,' said Brito.

'Here's a start,' said Jaime, pulling out the leaflet. 'The girl was staying at the Hotel Moderno. Her father put out this photo of

210

her. The mobile number is dead. We want full names and any-thing you can find out behind the names. You do that, we'll be very happy and we'll show our gratitude.'

Brito folded the leaflet into his pocket, made some notes, fin-ished his beer and left.

'I don't know what's harder,' said Jaime, wiping his hand down his face: 'dealing with journalists or the police.'

Sasha shrugged himself out from under the man's arm. The man grabbed at him, got him by the collar of his shirt, hauled him back. Sasha didn't even have time to try to rip his mask off; he just lashed out, kicking, punching and screaming. The man took the blows, silent with the effort and concentration on what he wanted. He grabbed Sasha's arms, pinned them to the sides of his body and tucked him under his arms, holding him firmly around the waist. The man rolled and slammed him face down on the slatted bench, tore at the waistband of the boy's trousers. Sasha was momentarily stunned and winded from the impact with the bench. He went limp, blinked behind his mask.

The man had released his arms and Sasha's fingers gripped the wooden slats. He whimpered as he tried to pull himself to-gether for a last monumental effort, knew he would only have one chance. The man stood back. Sasha heard the unbuckling of a belt, turned and kicked out with both feet, and made perfect contact with the man's groin. He went down with a low, guttural groan and slumped against the wall.

Sasha rolled away, scrabbled across the floor holding his trousers around his waist as the door flew open and savage Russian shout-ing exploded into the room. There was a fight, tremendous blows were exchanged, and Sasha sensed that his attacker had taken the worst of it. He heard him being dragged out of the room. There was a furious argument in the doorway. Sasha tried to get his face mask off, desperate to see what was going on. He couldn't work out the clasp at the back and he felt the material cutting into his nose as tried to yank it off. He was hit hard on the side of the head and knocked into the panelled wall.

'Stop it,' roared the Russian. 'Leave it alone.'

Sasha lay stunned on the floor. He recognised this voice and the hand that had hit him. It was the bad loser at chess. The two Russians continued their argument, then the door shut and there was silence in the insulated room, just the panting of his own breath in his ears and his heart banging around in his chest. He did his trousers up as best he could.

Somebody came in. Sasha winced, expecting another blow, but all he did was lift him up onto the bench, cuff his hands behind his back and leave.

The adrenaline backed down and Sasha started to assemble the Russian he'd heard exchanged between the two men.

The fear was racing through him and he trembled uncontrollably as he pieced together the line from the man who'd assaulted him. He was hoping he'd got it wrong, but somehow he didn't think so.

Boxer left Mercy, walked to his flat nearby in Belsize Park. He called Isabel on the way, gave her the almost unbelievable news about Amy. They laughed at the absurdity of having to confirm the butterfly tattoo with Karen. Isabel was desperate to see him. He said there was still a lot to do and he'd call later. They hung up as he reached his flat.

Boxer took the gun out of the safe, put it in the false bottom of a holdall with some cash and packed clothes on top. He dropped the bag off at his mother's flat. He'd decided he'd be better off away from his own place from now on if El Osito was hunting him down.

As he walked to the Royal Free he put in a call to Glider, the small-time gang boss who Amy had slept with on the cigarette jaunt to the Canaries.

'I haven't heard from you,' said Boxer.

'That's cos I got nothing to report,' said Glider, as if that would be obvious to anybody but a moron.

'All right. Tell me what you've done so far.'

'Like you said, I put out all my feelers and I got nothing back,' he said. 'Mind you, the club scene doesn't really take off until tonight and over the weekend.'

'Do you know anybody who *looks* like Amy? Same size, same height, same skin colour, same hair. Bit of a coke head?'

'What sort of a question is that?' said Glider, incredulous. 'Do I know anybody who *looks* like Amy? What the fuck is this? You one crazy mofo, you know that?'

'Mofo?' said Boxer. 'That's the kind of word that really annoys me, Glider. Maybe you and I need a bit more face to face.'

'Look,' said Glider, backing down. 'I'm just saying that's a weird thing to ask. I didn't know Amy at all until ten days ago. I spent a weekend with her and now I wish I bloody hadn't – the grief I'm getting. And you start asking—'

'She used a double to fool us, to make it look like she'd gone abroad. If I can find out who that is then I might be able to find her.'

'A name would help.'

'I haven't got one,' said Boxer. 'I'm asking you because I know you like black girls. You know where they hang out. If you liked Amy maybe it was because she reminded you of someone else – I don't know. Would you like me to send you a photo of her?'

'That would help,' said Glider. 'So, now I'm not sure who I'm looking for. Amy or her double?'

'You're not looking for her double because that girl was murdered in Madrid on Saturday night,' said Boxer.

'Fuck me,' said Glider. 'I can't believe th—'

'Shut up and listen,' said Boxer. 'You're still looking for Amy and, failing that, you're trying to find the name and address of someone who looks like her and who's now gone missing.'

He hung up, sent him the photo of Amy. He called Roy Chapel of the LOST Foundation, realising he hadn't been keeping him in the loop. He told him the full story. Chapel was appalled.

'I'm sending you the photo of how Amy looked on Saturday night,' said Boxer. 'I want you to look through the latest crop of missing persons and see if you can find a match – someone she could have used as a double and who's now been reported missing.'

'If she's a drug user ... people like that don't get reported missing unless she had someone close.'

'Like Amy, you mean?'

'It's a thought,' said Chapel. 'Depends how far out of the woodwork she's prepared to come.'

'I'm sorry, Roy. I know I should have kept you better informed, asked you to stand down when I thought she'd been murdered, but as it turns out you've been doing the right thing. How's it been going digging up leads on Amy?'

'I interviewed her friend Karen and a couple of other girls they hang out with. I've got all the names of the clubs they went to. I've also got a timeline of those nights they went out with each other and looked at the times when Amy split from the group and how long they were apart. And there was one occasion when Amy disappeared completely, never came home.'

'That came out when we first reported her missing to the police,' said Boxer.

'There's not much I've been able to find out about that night,' said Chapel. 'What I have done is drawn up a maximum radius of operation given the timings. I've also analysed musical tastes, see if Amy differed from the others. She was more into electronic trance music. Take a few pills, disappear into the sound. Don't come out of it for hours. Absorb the music rather than listen to it.'

'I didn't know that. Mercy's never mentioned it,' said Boxer. 'You might want to look at comedy clubs doing stand-up, too. Open-mike nights when newcomers can get an airing.'

'All right, that's good. Interesting to know she was into that.'

'She did a schools' night at the Comedy Store and it went down well apparently. Once you've felt that kind of attention as a kid, it can be addictive. This is the first weekend since she disappeared.'

'She's thought this out, Charlie. If she's sensible she'll keep a low profile for longer than a week.'

'Unless she thinks we're still looking for her in Madrid.'

'By the way, I'm not going to go round these clubs myself. No one's going to talk to a fifty-five-year-old ex-copper.'

'So who've you got in mind?'

'My son, Tony. He's twenty-four. Unemployed. Needs the money. And he knows the scene. You met him the other day helping me pack up the office.'

'What do you want to pay him?'

'He'll be happy with fifty quid a night plus expenses,' said Chapel. 'It's not like he won't be enjoying himself.'

Boxer hung up as he arrived at the Royal Free Hospital, found his way to ICU.

Through the glass he could see that Esme was breathing on her own. The nurse came alongside and explained that the brain scan had gone well and they'd taken her off the ventilator at around two o'clock, a couple of hours after the dialysis finished. From now on she was under observation. It was just a question of getting her to regain consciousness.

Boxer went into the unit, sat by her bedside, took her hand. He told her the whole story in all its detail. As he drew near to the end he bent down and put his lips close to her ear.

'I know you love her, Esme. I know it's been your little secret, that you've hidden from me just how much you love her. She's part of you, isn't she, Esme? So I just want you to know I've had the results of the DNA test on the tissue samples that were taken from the body part. They couldn't match her to me or to Mercy. You know what that means? It means that Amy is not dead. The body found with her clothes and passport did not belong to her. She's alive. Did you get that, Esme? Amy is alive.'

There was a fluttering as of an insect on Boxer's cheek. A little wetness. He pulled back to see that her eyes were open. He looked into them. The same green as his own.

'Welcome back,' he said.

20

'It's going to cost a little more,' said the concierge from the Hotel Moderno, sitting opposite Raul Brito, beers between them.

'Like what?'

'A hundred.'

'This crisis, you know, it's getting me down,' said Brito. 'It's like every word costs money these days.'

'They're taxing gossip now,' said the concierge, 'on advice from the Troika. They know the Spanish can't live without it.'

'You know, if I wasn't such an arsehole I'd believe you.'

Raul Brito was not like the young journalists at *Interviú*; he was an old-fashioned newshound. He used his computer only to file his stories and read match reports about his beloved Real Madrid, although he actually preferred to sit in a café with his copy of *Marca* and join in the endless speculation.

'So what's the extra I'm paying for?'

'The father stayed at the hotel too. I got copies of both their passports.'

Inside the envelope the concierge had photocopies of Amy and Charles Boxer's passports, their registration forms, their home addresses and signatures. Brito handed over two fifties, no further questions.

'We've got something,' shouted the diver, breaking the surface, tearing out his mouthpiece.

Inspector Jefe Luís Zorrita raised his arms, saluted the teams. It had been a long, hard and fruitless day. After yesterday's gruesome find of a bag containing the girl's thighs and buttocks under a bridge north of Perales del Río near Villaverde, they'd gone further north to a major junction with four crossing points, where a team of divers had spent most of the day and found nothing. The other team went south of Perales del Río on the M301 with instructions to search the river wherever the road crossed water. Four separate dives failed to produce anything. The two teams reached San Martín de la Vega in the late afternoon with nothing to show.

It was a long way south to the next crossing point. Zorrita and the divers hovered over the map and decided to head north to Vallequillas Norte, check those two crossing points and call it a day. The first point seemed the most likely dropping zone and they made a dive there. There were no forensic teams with them so they carried large plastic evidence boxes in their vehicles.

Finally they'd got lucky.

The diver brought the bag to the riverbank and put it straight into an evidence box. Zorrita put on a pair of latex gloves and undid the knot at the neck of the bin liner. The light was fading and he asked one of the divers to hold a torch.

'This is it,' he said. 'The one we've been waiting for. The girl's head and there's a handbag in here too. Send it back to the lab straight away.'

His sub-inspector sealed the box and carried it away. From the car he called the forensic team and asked them to wait in the lab.

It was nearly an hour's drive to the Unidad Policía Científica on Calle Julián Gonzalez Segador, which meant all members of the forensic team were suited up and ready to go. They opened the box and laid out the contents of the bin liner. A female head with hair roughly chopped off. Two upper arms, elbow to shoulder, a pair of black shoes and a small black handbag.

'There's something weird about the eyes, don't you think?' said Carmen, one of the female technicians. 'They shouldn't be as bright as that. The cornea should be cloudy by now.'

The senior forensic scientist took a closer look with some magnifying specs.

'Coloured contact lenses,' he said, 'to make the eyes look light green.'

'Do you mind if we take a quick look at the contents of the handbag?' said Zorrita.

The forensics emptied it out. One compact. One lipstick. One fold-up hairbrush. Three condoms.

'What were you hoping for?' asked the forensic.

'Some form of identity.'

'What about the passport we found on Wednesday morning?'

'The tissue sample from the leg didn't match either parents' DNA,' said Zorrita. 'She was carrying the girl's passport, but it wasn't hers. As you can tell from those contact lenses, she was pretending to be someone else: a girl called Amy Boxer, who had green eyes. Now we've got to find out who she really is.'

'There's probably an internal zip compartment in the handbag,' said Carmen.

The forensic scientist went back to the bag, found the zip and retrieved a UK passport.

'Chantrelle Taleisha Grant,' he said.

Zorrita asked him to spell it, read out the number and issue date, which he took down in his notebook. He held up a shot of Amy Boxer alongside the undamaged photo of Chantrelle Grant to compare. There was a likeness, not startling but enough.

'Imagine those eyes as light green,' said Zorrita. 'Let's compare Chantrelle's passport photo to the head we've just found.'

The features of the severed head had not decomposed, but the skin colour and texture was like grey putty. For the passport photo her hair had been tied back away from her face.

'There's a similarity in face shape,' said the forensic scientist. 'The ears match and eyebrow to hairline is the same. No distinguishing marks in the photo, though. I wouldn't like to commit myself given the history of this case.'

'That damage to her face …?' said Zorrita.

'The coroner needs to take a look at that, but it doesn't look like the cause of death to me.'

'Any signs of other damage?'

'Not on the skull. I wouldn't say the cause of death was a traumatic blow to the head, but you never know.'

The forensic scientist was turning the head around in his hands.

He was experienced, had spent thirty years looking at these sorts of things.

'We're going to have to wait until morning now, aren't we?'

'For the coroner to do an autopsy? Yes. He'd probably want to see a torso, too. Internal organs. Look at this on the neck,' he said, pointing out two nicks on either side over the carotid arteries. 'Just as we thought: the killer bled the body out before he cut it up and dumped it.'

Zorrita walked the length of the table looking at the remains of a life. 'What about the arms?' he said. 'Any distinguishing marks on them?'

'There's a vaccination mark, and we have a tattoo on the outside of the ... left arm. A red and black five-pointed star. If you can match that to the butterfly we found on the buttock yesterday ...'

'In the back of a British passport there's an emergencies page,' said the sub-inspector, looking at his smartphone. 'There should be the names and addresses of two relatives.'

The forensic flicked through to the back page.

'Alice Grant, and there's a London address.'

Any self-respecting journalist had direct contacts in the homicide squad of the Cuerpo Nacional de Policía and Raul Brito was no exception. But he also knew that wasn't enough, that there were lots of groups handling many different cases, and that to really develop a breaking story he needed to know what was happening before most people knew it had happened. This meant he had a network that spread through communications centres, suburban police stations, forensic teams and coroners, as well as the justice system.

One of the linchpins of this network was his niece Luz, who worked in the main Madrid police communications centre, which handled requests from all the patrol cars in the city and surroundings. She was one of the first people Brito contacted after his meeting with Jaime and Jesús, while waiting for the concierge from the Hotel Moderno to turn up. Luz knew about the first body part found near Perales del Rio as she'd been on the early shift on Wednesday 21st March, and by the time her uncle called she was even able to tell him about the second bag and the extra team of divers who'd been assigned and where they were working. All Brito had to do was ask her to call him when she heard if any of the diving teams found anything else and where they were going to take it, with as much detail as possible. To Luz and her colleagues this was a harmless game which made them feel a little important – that they were somehow involved in breaking news stories.

At around seven o'clock Brito got the call from Luz, who was off work and at home but had left instructions with her colleagues to keep her informed. This meant that Raul Brito was the first outsider to know that a third bag had been found, that it contained a girl's head and a handbag, that it was being taken to the forensic lab on Calle Julián Gonzalez Segador in a car containing Inspector Jefe Luís Zorrita, his sub-inspector, and even who the driver was. Unfortunately he knew none of these officers, but within half an hour he managed to find out all the names of the people on the forensics team. And one of them, Carmen, he did know.

'The Mercedes CLS was found in Cromwell Avenue, a residential street in Highgate,' said Mercy to the assembled Crisis Management Committee in Netherhall Gardens. 'DS Papadopoulos has done a door-to-door on all the houses with a sightline of the car and has two witnesses who saw a large lone male getting out of the car wearing a black overcoat, black gloves, grey trousers and a grey tweed trilby pulled down low over his forehead. He locked the car and walked off in the direction of Highgate Hill. The car has now been removed and is undergoing forensic examination. We've taken samples of Sasha's fingerprints from this house and we'll see if we get a match with any in the car.'

'What about Jeremy Spencer?' asked Kidd. 'Any news on his murder?'

'They haven't found anybody who saw or heard anything yet. All we know is that last night Spencer did erg training with a friend at the Imperial College boathouse gym on the Embankment at Putney. He left there at 10.15 p.m. and would have been home within five minutes. There's no sign of forced entry so either he knew his assailants and let them in, or they already had keys made, possibly with the assistance of Irina Demidova. Given that he died from drowning and was probably in the bath after his workout, it would suggest the latter scenario is more likely.'

'I thought you said he was a big guy?' said Butler.

'He was, but, as I understand it, being upended in a full bath is a very difficult situation to get out of even if you're his size.'

The phone rang, cutting Mercy dead. She stared at it. They all stared at it thinking, is this it? Chris Sexton cued Bobkov's lawyer, Butler. Kidd leaned over and pressed the speaker button, which started the recording and also triggered the triangulation equipment in the kidnap unit's Vauxhall HQ, which would locate the mobile being used.

'Give me Bobkov,' said a voice.

'I'm his lawyer. My name is Howard Butler.'

'We will only talk to Bobkov.'

'He isn't here. He's out raising the money. We need a proof of life before we can proceed with these talks. Can you put Sasha on the line, please?'

'No. You ask your question. We get an answer. We call back later.'

'What is Sasha's favourite book?'

The phone went dead. Sexton looked at the screen of his mobile.

'King's Cross,' he said. 'Disposable phone.'

Two minutes. No talking. Everybody waiting to see if this could possibly develop into the first negotiation of the kidnap or another long, fruitless wait.

The phone rang again. Kidd pressed the button.

'*How to Play Chess Openings* by Znosko-Borovsky,' said the voice, different this time.

Bobkov nodded. Sexton held up a finger, made the call sign.

'We're just calling Bobkov to get confirmation.'

The phone went dead again.

'That one came from Hyde Park,' said Sexton.

Two more minutes ticked past. Silence. They all looked at the phone, willing it to ring. Fed up with being endlessly sweated by the gang, not getting anywhere with them. Not enough contact.

Three more minutes.

The phone rang again. Kidd let it go for three rings. Pressed the button. Silence.

'Hello,' said Butler.

'Can I speak to Tracey, please?'

'Who is this?'

'Ali, from Tesco.'

'You should be ashamed of yourselves,' said Butler. 'She's in hospital.'

Kidd rang off.

'Bloody Tesco,' said Bobkov.

The phone rang again. Kidd pressed the button. Another voice.

'You bring seven hundred and fifty thousand euros, denomination fifty or less, instructions to follow.'

'Wait a minute,' said Butler. 'What's this for? We haven't discussed anything.'

'No discussion. This is about trust. First we have to see if we can trust you. Instructions to follow.'

The phone went dead.

'Canary Wharf,' said Sexton, looking at his screen.

'I'll organise the money,' said Bobkov. 'We have to be prepared.'

'I'll walk with you,' said Brito, who'd been standing outside the main gates to the Unidad Científica, waiting for Carmen. 'Which way are you going?'

'To the Pinar del Rey Metro, but I'm not going to tell you anything, Raul.'

'Why not?'

'Because I don't want to be one of your sources. There's not enough people involved in this investigation for me to get lost.'

'I can guarantee anonymity.'

'From your end maybe, but not from mine.'

'I can guarantee it from all ends because I'm not doing this for a story.'

Carmen stopped in the street, looked him in the eye.

'Don't bullshit me, Raul. When have you ever done anything that's not for a story ... apart from watch Real Madrid?'

'OK, there is a story involved, but it's not this one.'

'Now you're not even making sense.'

'It's easy. If I deliver information on this story, I get a bigger story in return.'

'Who are you delivering this story to?'

'I can't tell you that.'

'How did you know there were only six people in that room tonight?' said Carmen. 'How did you know the names of the two police officers involved? How did you know out of the four of us on the forensic team to come to me?'

'You're the only one I know.'

'That's not true.'

'OK. I read in the newspapers that your pay scale in the Cuerpo Nacional de Policía had just had the equivalent of a 40 per cent cut,' said Brito. 'And *you* told *me* just before Christmas that you have a little girl and you split up with your husband at the beginning of last year.'

'Right, so you came to me because you know I'm desperate.'

'I don't like saying that kind of thing to people,' said Brito. 'It's not your fault; it's just the way life's going at the moment. I'll give you two hundred euros.'

'We've found three bags so far,' said Carmen. 'The first one had a lower leg with foot attached and some clothes with a British passport belonging to a girl called Amy Boxer. We thought—'

'I know what you thought – that the body was hers.'

'The second had two thighs with buttocks attached.'

'Gruesome.'

'Yes, it was. You try not to imagine the guy who's doing this or finding yourself anywhere near him ... like on the Metro,' said Carmen. 'The worst of it is we reckon there's expertise. We can tell from markings on the ankle and two nicks into the carotid arteries that the body was hung upside down and bled out.'

'You mean he's done this before?' asked Brito. 'I don't remember anything like it, not in the last ten years.'

'He could be a butcher,' said Carmen, 'or someone who cuts up animals, like an abattoir worker, a farmer or a hunter.'

'And the third bag?'

'I haven't finished. The left buttock had a butterfly tattoo on it.'

'How do you do this work, Carmen?'

'It feeds me and my little girl.'

'So ... the third bag.'

'The third bag had the head in it, two upper arms, a pair of shoes and a handbag with another passport in the name of Chantrelle Grant.'

'Chantrelle? With an "r"?' said Brito, making notes.

'Yes, her middle name was odd, too. Taleisha or something like that. The sub-inspector was on his smartphone all the time and told us they were Jamaican names.'

'Did the severed head match the passport photo?'

'We think so, but the boss wasn't prepared to commit himself.'

'So what's the story?' said Brito. 'I hear the first girl, Amy Boxer, is a runaway.'

'The cops told us that the runaway had given her passport to Chantrelle so that it would look like she'd gone to Madrid. Her parents are cops or something like that so she knows she has to be clever, send them off on the wrong trail.'

'Who?'

'Keep up, Raul. Amy Boxer.'

'So she's still alive in London, while the double, impersonating her, was killed in Madrid by some maniac,' said Brito. 'Now that *is* a good story.'

'Changing your mind now?' said Carmen. 'Just keep me out of it. Don't even use the word "forensic".'

'You must have filed a report on the police computer by now. Anybody could have seen it.'

'Not anybody and not yet,' said Carmen. 'I shouldn't think there's more than ten people with access to it.'

They arrived at the entrance to the Pinar del Rey Metro. Brito took out four fifty-euro notes he'd already prepared, added another fifty.

'Don't make me look like a whore,' said Carmen.

'There's fifty extra. Get something nice for your little girl,' said Brito, slipping the rolled notes into her hand.

'A couple of other things,' said Carmen. 'The police are working an angle. All the bags were weighed down so they wouldn't float to the surface. The killer used five-kilo weights in each bag. You know, the circular ones you see in gyms.'

'I'm not a gym kind of person, Carmen – as you can see.'

'Weightlifters use them: discs of metal with a hole in the middle. These were painted blue with 5kg written in white,' she said. 'I can't believe some of the knowledge blanks you have.'

'You get to my age and there's only a certain amount of RAM available,' said Brito. 'And the other thing?'

'Her mother's name and address were in the back of her passport,' said Carmen.

'You didn't happen to remember what they were?'

She wrote them down for him.

'Were you going to tell me those last two things?'

'Only if you were a nice guy,' she said and disappeared into the Metro station.

The bell rang at the front door. Bobkov, who was still arguing with Sexton about strategy, veered off to open it. Kidd intercepted him.

'I'll take it,' he said, and checked the peephole.

A man in a black hat and mac was holding up a card: BOBKOV CHEMITRADE LTD. Kidd opened the door. The man raised his hat.

'Only Mr Bobkov can receive this,' he said.

He had a small case chained to his wrist.

Bobkov stepped forward with a key to the handcuff, which he unlocked. He signed for the case, which had barrel combination locks. The man raised his hat again and withdrew to his car. They took the case inside and Bobkov opened the combination locks. They checked the money.

'It's all here.'

'There's no guarantee this money is going to bring you any return,' said Sexton. 'There've been no negotiations to establish what you're going to get. Normally, in a kidnap situation, we demand a demonstration of trust from *them*, not the other way round.'

'Look, Chris. You said in your introduction to this process that the idea was to get them talking, to involve them, embroil them, but they haven't given us a chance,' said Bobkov. 'Contact has been minimal. They've made a serious threat to Sasha. I don't want them sending me bits of my son because I wouldn't come up with some stupid money. I don't care who they are. If they're mafia or FSB they're capable of extreme violence, even to a small, defenceless boy.'

'We've got to secure some sort of return or this could happen again and again.'

'But if they won't talk,' said Kidd, 'what can you do?'

'If they call again with the instructions *I'll* speak to them,' said Bobkov. 'I understand your strategy of putting someone between me and them, but in this case it hasn't worked. They want to talk to me direct. So I will speak to them.'

Another knock on the front door. Kidd left the room, looked through the peephole.

'Tesco,' he said.

He opened the door to a young Asian guy in a Tesco coat.

'Delivery, sir.'

At his feet on a trolley were two boxes of Harvey's Bristol Cream.

'We didn't order this,' said Kidd. 'Somebody called and we told them that Tracey Dunsdon was in hospital.'

'We have a record of that, but the order was later reinstated by Mr Alexander Bobkov.'

'Bring it in,' said Bobkov, appearing at the door.

The young guy wheeled the boxes in, unloaded them. Bobkov signed the order.

Sexton slit open one of the boxes. There was what looked like an order stuffed into one of the bottle compartments. He pulled it out.

'Instructions,' he said.

21

Bar El Rocio, Puerta del Sol, Madrid

'This story's a lot more interesting than I first thought,' said Brito, sitting at a small table in a cramped bar with Jaime and Jesús on either side of him. He ran them through the conversation he'd just had with Carmen, leaving her out of it as she'd asked and making it sound like his own brilliant research.

'So how do you know the parents of this runaway girl, Amy Boxer, are in the police?' asked Jaime.

'I don't. I said "something like the police". I heard the homicide cops talking about them. So, I've been checking it out. I went to the missing persons websites and I found posts about the girl with photos, but they keep it anonymous. You can't contact the family direct. You have to go through the website's helpline.'

'And the father?' said Jaime anxiously, wanting all the information now, immediately. 'You said you had a name for the father.'

'I got that from the Hotel Moderno. He stayed there in the same room as his daughter, or the girl he thought was his daughter. I looked him up on Linkedin. He used to be in the army, then he was a homicide cop in London before he became a kidnap consultant.'

'What's one of those?' asked Jesús.

They ignored him.

'He's white,' said Jaime, 'so it's the mother who's black, and she must be the cop. Why isn't she using the surname Boxer as well? Didn't they get married?'

'I'll work on it,' said Brito. 'Don't you worry. I'll get there.'

'The girl that was killed and hacked up ...'

'Chantrelle Taleisha Grant,' said Brito. 'I've got the name and address in London of her mother too.'

'Have they got any suspects for the killing?'

'No, but they've got a lead,' said Brito and told them about the weights in the bags.

Jaime and Jesús just about managed not to look at each other, but Brito picked up on the tension bristling between them as they stared back at him without moving a facial muscle. The two had bought the weightlifting equipment for El Osito before he arrived, using cash in a sports store called Decathlon. Jaime couldn't remember if he'd ever talked about the Colombian's obsession in front of Raul Brito.

'We're going to need all the documents,' said Jaime.

'I'm going to need some money,' said Brito. 'The expenses have been heavy and ...'

'And what?'

'I'm a newspaper man,' said Brito. 'This is a good story. Runaway girl sends double to Madrid to fool cop parents and the unfortunate double gets killed and cut up. I'd like to run it.'

'We told you,' said Jaime a little too quickly. 'We don't know who we're dealing with yet. It could be dangerous for you – you could get killed.'

'That's what I'm saying,' said Brito.

'What do you mean?' asked Jesús.

Jaime shut him up with a look that took half his face away.

'How much are we talking about?'

'Thirty-five thousand euros.'

'You've got to be fucking kidding,' said Jesús.

Another look that locked the words up in Jesús's throat as if he'd been stabbed.

Jaime sat back, looking at Brito carefully. How much did he know?

'That Russian story. What did they pay you for that?' said Jaime. 'And don't tell me it was anything like thirty-five thousand.'

'This isn't the Russian story. That was a long-term investigation. You wanted instant information. I don't know why, but you did. I got it for you. Along the way I found the real story hidden inside. This one's got legs: intrigue, emotion, tragedy and ... evil. And it's not over yet.'

'Seven thousand,' said Jaime.

'Thirty ... two,' said Brito.

'Ten.'

'Thirty.'

Jesús watched them like it was a tennis game.

'Meet you in the middle,' said Jaime. 'No more.'

'Twenty it is,' said Brito. 'When and where shall we meet?'

'Here in fifteen.'

The brothers left, headed up the street to Sol.

'Are you fucking crazy?' said Jesús in a savage whisper over his brother's shoulder. 'Twenty grand for that? El Osito will kill us.'

'So *you* know how much Brito knows, do you?'

'No.'

'Well, shut the fuck up then. You think El Osito wants any attention from the cops with this deal he's trying to do with the English coming up? You think Vicente wants this new market to be destroyed even before it's got started? You think Vicente wants the cops anywhere near the guy who's supposed to be running his European operation?'

'No, no, you're right.'

'El Osito won't know anything about the money.'

'You mean *we* pay for the story?' said Jesús. 'El Osito told us if it cost money ...'

'I know he did. But we're paying just to keep everything quiet. That way El Osito stays calm,' said Jaime. 'We go to him and ask for twenty thousand, you don't know what he'll say. He might shrug his shoulders. He might tell us to kill Raul Brito. We do that and somebody somewhere will put us and him together.'

INSTRUCTIONS

Mr Bobkov will use his own car, the BMW. We will accept one
  female driver in the car with him.

No mobile phones are permitted in the car.

He will go from the house in Netherhall Gardens to Denmark
  Street near Tottenham Court Road Tube station.

He will go to an Internet café above a shop called Wunjo Guitars, where he will ask for a package left for Mr Bobkov. He will have to show some ID.

From there the driver will take him to Whitechapel Road, where he will receive more instructions.

There must be no tracker system in the car.

The money must be with Mr Bobkov at all times except when he goes into the Internet café.

If the car is followed or any of these instructions are not obeyed the deal is off and Sasha will be killed and you will not hear from us again.

The phone rang. Kidd hit the button. Bobkov held up his hand.

'This is Bobkov.'

Silence for a moment.

'Finally, I wondered how long it would take,' said the voice. 'Just for security: what did you give Sasha for his last birthday?'

'Nike JR Mercurial Victory 111 Turf boys' football boots, in orange.'

'You have the instructions?'

'Yes.'

'Everything is clear?'

'No.'

'What's the problem?'

'There are no timings. When is this supposed to happen?'

'You will be told that later.'

'What do I get in return for this money.'

'Nothing. It is purely to establish trust. To see if we can work with each other.'

'No. I have to have something more tangible than that for seven hundred and fifty thousand.'

'How about Sasha's right leg from the knee down?'

The phone went dead.

The door opened with such force that it cracked back against the wall. Sasha started. No words. They grabbed him, one around the arms and shoulders, the other around the legs, and held him steady.

'What's your favourite foot with the ball?'

Sasha was too terrified to speak. A third man leaned over and smacked him around the head.

'Which foot?'

'Right,' whispered Sasha.

The man took off the shoe and sock from Sasha's right foot. Sasha felt something sharp and metallic around his big toe.

'What are you doing?' he whimpered.

'Shut up, and when I tell you to, scream as loud as you can.'

'What?'

'Scream!'

The bolt cutters tightened around his toe and Sasha screamed. He felt the warmth of his own bood trickling between his toes. He screamed even louder.

'These people,' said Bobkov, furious. 'It's not about the money. I know what this is.'

Nobody said anything.

'They know all about the technology. They refuse to talk. They won't negotiate. They make threats. They offer nothing. They demand trust,' said Bobkov. 'Trust from *me*. Those fucking bastards.'

'You have to keep calm, Andrei,' said Kidd. 'This is part of the plan. They know you're a cool customer. They know they have to take you to the edge and hang you over it to get what they want.'

'It's not about the money now,' he said. 'It's not even about Alexander Tereshchenko. This is about control. This is about powerlessness. This is about insignificance.'

'Let's just play it out,' said Kidd.

'If it's the FSB what do they want with money?' said Bobkov, unable to let go of the rant. 'It's nothing to them. They're not doing this for the money. Seven hundred and fifty fucking thousand.'

'This trust that they want,' said Mercy.

Bobkov wheeled round on her.

'They don't know the meaning of the word,' he said, pointing out the window as if they were right there. 'Trust to them could just as easily mean suspicion or doubt. You don't know what it's like. The world thinks we've moved on, that the USSR

231

is no longer with us, that the communists have disappeared. They haven't. They've just scratched out the title of their party. It's all still there. The apparatus is still in place. Even the aim is the same. It's just more openly criminal, that's all.'

'Do you think this trust they're asking for is more a demand for you to close down your investigation into the Tereshchenko killing?' said Mercy.

'They're working on that,' said Bobkov. 'That you can believe. Irina Demidova being planted at DLT for instance.'

Mercy's mobile vibrated. Papadopoulos.

'We've got a fingerprint match with Sasha,' he said. 'That was the car they used to kidnap the boy.'

'OK, so what are you going to do now?'

'I'm doing what you ordered me to do,' said Papadopoulos. 'I'm meeting Olga for a drink.'

'That's a subtle shift of responsibility,' said Mercy. 'Don't blame me if you don't make it home.'

'You sound different.'

'It's complicated … but the short of it is that Amy's alive. We don't know where. All we know is that she wasn't killed in Madrid.'

Bobkov's mobile rang. He tore it out of his pocket. Hit the receive button twice by accident and the loudspeaker was activated. The video played out with Sasha's screams resonating tinnily around the room. Bobkov dropped the phone as if it had gone suddenly live.

The fixed-line phone rang in the room. Mercy hung up. Kidd hit the button.

'Are you ready now?' asked the voice.

'I want to speak to my son,' roared Bobkov.

'The technology you're using makes that impossible,' said the voice.

'You want to find out if I can be trusted, but I have to be able to trust you,' said Bobkov. 'And what do you do. You send me a piece of shit. You torture my son and send it to me. You offer me nothing. Where is the trust?'

'No, that's true. You give us trust and we make you fear. That is how it works,' said the voice. 'Now we stop with the talk and

232

proceed with the action. Once we see you're prepared to act in a certain way then you will see the same from us. If you don't then all your fears will be realised. Do you have a driver?'

'Yes.'

'Name?'

'Mercy.'

'Is she the black policewoman?'

'That's right,' said Bobkov, raising an eyebrow.

'Good. You're learning, Mr Bobkov. You will leave now for Denmark Street. Remember, no mobile phones. No tracker system.'

'Do you always take your suspects out to dinner?' asked Olga.

'Yeah, I'm the good cop,' said Papadopoulos. 'Since when did you become a suspect?'

'So Mercy's the bad cop?'

'You don't want to get on the wrong side of Mercy,' said Papadopoulos. 'There's Mercy-ful and Mercy-less. I've seen them both and I know which one I prefer.'

The waitress brought a meze platter for them to share. Papadopoulos was drinking beer; Olga was halfway down a glass of white wine. They were sitting in the Beehive on Crawford Street and Papadopoulos was hoping he could count this as an expense while another part of his brain was thinking up a strategy for explaining the amount on his credit card bill when his girlfriend did the monthly accounts. *They* didn't go out to the Beehive on a Thursday evening, not on the combined salaries of a detective sergeant and a social worker saving for a deposit on a London flat.

'Did Mercy-ful put you up to this?' asked Olga.

'I don't think she had dining with the witness in mind,' said Papadopoulos. 'Then again, I told her you were way out of my league.'

Olga laughed. She liked that. Didn't mind this good-looking, self-deprecating Greek. Good men were thin on the ground, even in London.

'So what do you want to know?' asked Olga. 'Now that you've got me under interrogation.'

'I was wondering how I was going to work you round to that.'

'Nobody works me round to anything, George.'

'No, I don't think they do,' he said. 'Not even Mr Dudko.'

'Not even? Not ever. Dudko's a dud. He's got all the connections but they're just not working too well in his brain.'

'He made out it was a joint decision of his partners to take on Irina – Zlata Yankov.'

'See what I mean? Can't even admit to his own crap decisions. I know for certain that Igor Tipalov wasn't even consulted,' said Olga, stuffing pitta bread piled with hummus into her beautiful, lipsticked mouth. 'I need some more wine before I get started on Zlata.'

George told the waiter to bring the bottle and leave it, poured her a hefty glass.

'This is my version of waterboarding,' said Papadopoulos. 'Two bottles and people tell me everything.'

'So what do you do, you and Mercy?' asked Olga. 'I mean I know you're cops, but there's bobbies, pigs, filth and heat … Where are you on the scale?'

'Heat,' said Papadopoulos without hesitation. 'We're in the Met's Kidnap and Special Investigations Team.'

Mercy had been right. Olga was impressed.

'So this isn't about killing anybody?'

'That might be part of it. Do you think Zlata Yankov's capable of that?'

Olga stopped, looked at him seriously.

'I wouldn't put it past her,' she said. 'She's one of those women who always gets what she wants and seems game for any strategy. She was all over Dudko like a rash. With someone who could see through her better, she might well resort to murder. She struck me as amoral.'

'That's pretty strong.'

'To call her immoral would imply that she knew what morals were.'

'I can see I've got you started now.'

'So who "might" have been killed?'

'Zlata was having an affair with someone who was found dead in his bath this morning.'

He looked up. She was shocked. The babaganoush wasn't making it to her mouth. She hadn't expected it to get this real.

'Have you ever heard of a guy called Andrei Bobkov?' asked Papadopoulos, thinking of a likely connection.

'Yes,' she said. 'It's not him, is it?'

'No. How do you know him?'

'He's one of Mr Tipalov's clients,' said Olga. 'Mr Tipalov is our energy specialist, which includes by-products of oil and gas production. Mr Bobkov trades in chemical gases.'

'Just before I met you this evening I had it confirmed to me that DLT Consultants' Mercedes CLS was used in the kidnap of Andrei Bobkov's son Sasha.'

Olga slapped the edge of the table with both hands. There was a hard *crack* from the multiple rings on her fingers, which startled people at the other tables even in the crowded roar of a London gastropub.

'I know Sasha,' she said in a ripping whisper, eyes wide open. 'He's a lovely little boy. Probably not so little now. Is that what this is all about?'

'There's another level of complication that we're trying to disentangle,' said Papadopoulos, 'but I have to be able to trust you to keep your mouth shut about this. You can't talk to anyone at DLT, or anyone anywhere, in fact.'

'That's why I'm employed by DLT. I know how to keep my mouth shut. That's why Zlata was such a problem for me. Always asking questions. I had to keep changing the password on my computer with her around.'

'Bobkov was making himself unpopular with the FSB by investigating something they didn't want him to,' said Papadopoulos. 'That's all I'm going to say.'

'And you think Zlata might have been planted by the FSB?'

'Or a criminal gang.'

'You'll never be able to disentangle that; the two are so enmeshed,' said Olga, driving her fingers into a tight clasp. 'You remember that MI6 guy found dead in a dodgy position in the wardrobe in his flat? Made to look like some kinky sex game gone wrong? All the Russian expats here knew it was the mafia. But, you see, the mafia employ a lot of old KGB people who still maintain their friends in the FSB. They found out that this guy had been developing some software for tracking mafia money laundering in

London. Their FSB friends find out who he is, where he lives and the mafia go in there and kill him. Now what would you call that? Criminal gang or FSB?'

'If you were changing the password on your computer, that sounds like you suspected Zlata ... or had someone told you to suspect her?'

Olga sat back, drank some more wine. The waiter took away the meze platter and brought a steak for Papadopoulos and chicken for Olga. He opened a bottle of Malbec. The two didn't take their eyes off each other. Papadopoulos stretched his neck, his collar getting tight, couldn't ignore the stirring in his trousers.

'When I told Mr Tipalov that Mr Dudko had taken her on he was OK to start with,' said Olga. 'It was only when he heard about the diamond contract going through that he told me to keep an eye on Zlata.'

'The diamond contract?'

'Too long and boring to go into. It was a running joke. Dudko was always talking about it in meetings, saying it was nearly, nearly there. He was just about to bring it in. Land the big fish. Then suddenly it happened, and nobody was more surprised than Mr Tipalov.'

'So he put Zlata Yankov and the diamond deal going through together and decided it was suspicious enough for you to watch her.'

'I wish I'd had the steak now,' she said, nodding.

Papadopoulos cut off a piece, forked it over to her with some Béarnaise sauce.

'He told me to start following her and to draw up a list of all the places she was going to outside the office, which was OK when Dudko was out, but impossible when he's in, because then he likes me to be his personal assistant – it makes him feel all important.'

'What was she doing outside the office so much?'

'She said she was going to meetings but most of the time she was looking at property, as far as I could see.'

'To buy?'

'Rent.'

'But she was living in low-rent DLT accommodation.'

'*And* she never talked to me about it,' said Olga. 'If you're in an office and you're looking for property that's all you ever talk about. And Zlata didn't say a word, but almost every day she went out to look at something.'

'And when you reported this to Mr Tipalov what did he make of it?'

'Nothing. He wasn't interested. What he wanted to know was if she went to see people. I think he was more worried that she would steal our clients, that she was involved in some sort of industrial espionage.'

'And you?'

'She was definitely snooping. She was always interested to know where everybody was. Where's Tipalov today? What's Luski doing? Has Dudko come back from Paris? More than once I found her at my computer, which was why I changed the passwords so she couldn't get into my email accounts.'

'How did Tipalov react to that?'

'He told me to misinform – not just her, but everybody. He didn't even want Dudko to know where he was going.'

'So when you told us he was in Siberia ...'

'As far as I know he's been in Moscow all the time and taking the occasional flight out to places not so far away, like Kursk and Leningrad.'

'Anything to link those places?'

'I don't know. Maybe clients. I don't know the ins and outs of his work.'

'When did you last hear from Mr Tipalov?'

'This morning, eight o'clock. He called me at home before I left for work.'

'Where was he?'

'He'd just landed in Smolensk.'

'What time was it there?'

'Eleven a.m.'

'What about all the property Zlata was looking at. Did you see any of that?'

'Not everything,' she said. 'But I did find out the spec.'

'How?'

'A girlfriend worked in one of the estate agents Zlata went to. She asked her colleague, although in fact he gave it over to her because Zlata wanted just a three-month let, which wasn't his speciality.'

'So what was the spec?'

'A detached house in its own grounds, secure all around with CCTV and electric gates. A garage attached to the house. A basement. A separate kitchen, dining room, living room and at least three bedrooms.'

'Budget?

'Up to twenty thousand a month for the three months.'

'Twenty grand a *month*!' said Papadopoulos. 'Jesus.'

'Some people are living in a totally different world,' said Olga.

'Did you know when she found the property she was looking for?'

'She started at the beginning of February and it was all over by the middle of March.'

'What about the estate agents she went to?'

'I know the ones I saw her go to, but I can't guarantee that's all of them,' she said. 'I'd really love some more of that steak, you know.'

Papadopoulos loaded his fork, held it out to her. She took hold of his wrist and pulled the meat off with her teeth, maintaining eye contact throughout.

'Where did you keep your notes on Zlata?' he asked, swallowing hard.

'On my home computer,' she said. 'I'd write them up on the office computer, save them onto a pen drive and wipe the file clean in case she managed to crack my password. Then I'd transfer it to my home computer.'

'Have you got that pen drive with you?'

'What if I said it was at home?'

'I'd probably ask for the bill,' said Papadopoulos, holding up his hand.

'So what do you think the property thing was all about?' she asked.

'It could be she was looking for a suitable place to hide Sasha Bobkov,' said Papadopoulos. 'It's the single most difficult thing in a London kidnap: where to keep your hostage where nobody else can see him.'

'I want to write a letter to my mum and dad,' said Sasha.

He was in a strange hiatus. His shoe and sock were still off. The big toe was bandaged and hurting, but they hadn't cut it off. Now he was in this uneasy lull. One of the Russians had stayed behind to play chess with him. He was unnerved by the switch from extreme brutality to near humanity.

'Why?' asked the voice.

'I don't know whether I'm going to see them again.'

'What makes you think that?'

'You were going to cut off my big toe.'

'But we didn't. It was just to show your father that he has to take us seriously.'

'The man who touched me. He said ... that you were going to kill me.'

'What did he say? Your Russian's not so good. Maybe you didn't hear him right.'

'I heard him all right,' said Sasha, and repeated the line in Russian.

'He doesn't know what he's talking about. He was angry,' said the man. 'Let's just play the game.'

The man gave him his latest move.

Sasha shook his head. 'I thought all Russians knew how to play chess.'

'I'm out of practice.'

'Do any of you know how to play?'

'One of us does. You haven't met him yet. He's out.'

'Can't you see what's going to happen to you?' asked Sasha, almost sad for his opponent.

The man looked at the board for a long time. Sasha gave him his move. The Russian positioned the piece.

'Do you see it now?' asked Sasha. 'It doesn't matter what you do, you're dead in three.'

'Your mother's in hospital,' said the man suddenly.

'Is she all right?' asked Sasha, listening hard, blinking behind his mask.

'She's OK but she's in intensive care. Why do you care about her so much? She's a drunk. She hasn't looked after you in years.'

'No, but I look after her and she does her best for me,' said Sasha. 'She's lonely, you know. And I know what that is. It's horrible.'

The Russian told him the move he'd just made. Sasha instantly gave him his in return.

'I see it now,' said the man and knocked over his king.

'Why are you going to kill me?' asked Sasha, legs swinging.

'We're not going to kill you,' said the man, gently now, knowing that he shouldn't have said anything but unable to stop himself from getting involved. 'Your father's going to pay us some money and we're going to let you go. Don't take any notice of what the other guy said. Let's play another game.'

Sasha's masked face stared into the man with the blank intensity of a disbelieving prisoner.

'I'd still like to write the letter.'

22

'Where the hell did we go last Saturday night?' asked Jaime. 'We started with drinks at Le Cock,' said Jesús. 'After that ... it would be the usual places. Charada. Joy. Kapital ... maybe the Palacio de Gáviria too.'

'Right, where do we start?'

'Maybe we should call El Osito first? Tell him what we got,' said Jesús. 'That's the important stuff.'

'It might be to you and me, but I know El Osito, and what's more important is how the Englishman found him, because if Charles Boxer could find him anybody can,' said Jaime. 'The answer is in these clubs somewhere. Somebody told him they saw his daughter with El Osito. And we've got to find the guy before the police do.'

'But the police already know Charles Boxer; they can ask him.'

'Jesús.'

'What?'

'You think Boxer is going to tell them anything after what he did to El Osito?' said Jaime. 'Boxer went in there to kill him. The only reason he didn't was because El Osito hit the panic button.'

'You know, we—'

'Don't say it,' said Jaime. 'I know. We should have ignored the call. It would have saved us all this shit and we'd have got rid of El Osito.'

The brothers walked into Puerta del Sol. The square was quiet because it was cold and spitting rain.

'Well, seeing as we're here, we might as well start at the Palacio de Gáviria and Joy in the Calle del Arenal.'

The Mexicans knew almost all the doormen at every club. They tipped them heavily so their dealers could get in easily to sell product. They were careful. First they asked the doorman which nights he'd been on. The guy at the Palacio was new, so they moved straight on to Joy. The doorman there had been on duty the whole of last weekend and was one of their regulars. Jesús stood in for him while he took Jaime inside to a room behind the old theatre box office where he kept his clothes. He looked at the passport photocopy of Boxer, nodded.

'He came in here on Tuesday night asking for one of the DJs, David Álvarez. David warned me he was going to show so I called one of the girls and she took him up there. Don't know what it was about.'

'Is David working here?'

'Not tonight. I don't know where he is. Hold on.'

The doorman took out his phone went onto Twitter and checked out Álvarez's tweets.

'He's doing the first set at Kapital, starting at eleven o'clock.'

'Do you know where he was on Saturday night?'

The doorman scrolled down on his mobile. Nothing. He called someone on the internal phone, waited, asked the question.

'Friday and Saturday he does a set from one until three at the Charada on Calle de la Bola.'

Jaime shook hands with the doorman, clapped him on the back.

'So what's it all about with David?' asked the doorman.

'We're going to have a party,' said Jaime. 'We need a DJ. We like David's music but, you know, we're looking at others too, so don't talk to him.'

'He's great. Very nice guy,' said the doorman.

Jaime held the doorman by the biceps and looked him in the eye to make sure he knew what he meant: if David disappears we know who to come looking for, and if things turn out badly for David you can always persuade yourself it was nothing to do with you.

Jaime let him go, went out onto the street, pulled Jesús away with him, told him what he'd found out as they moved off. The doorman came out onto the pavement, watched the two Mexicans walk away, let his eyes fall back onto the young hopefuls in the queue, shook his head.

Jaime and Jesús trudged up Arenal in silence, turned right past the Opera Metro station and headed towards the Plaze de Oriente. They were both thinking the same thing. They were brothers and this was a tendency. What they were doing now was not work. All they were doing was controlling the risk to which El Osito had exposed their operation: tying up loose ends. And in Jaime's experience that was a never-ending process. Loose ends had split ends.

'You thinking what I'm thinking?' asked Jesús.

'Only I'm three steps ahead.'

'So what are you going to do about it, before it all gets out of control?'

'You ask me that when we've only just found out what the fuck we're dealing with? Give me a break, Jesús.'

'You the one who's three steps ahead.'

'The police are on to it and they've got the five-kilo weights to think about,' said Jaime.

They were walking past the Opera Gym.

'It's lucky we're in Madrid,' said Jesús. 'Full of arseholes trying to keep fit. There's probably a few thousand five-kilo weights just here in the city centre.'

'They'll know the weights don't come from a gym.'

'You got to talk to Vicente,' said Jesús.

'I've been talking to him every day for months. Whenever I mention the problems El Osito has with black girls, he tells me to shut up.'

'Maybe now he's killed one he'll start listening.'

'Slow down, Jesús,' said Jaime. 'We've got to clear everything up first; only then do I go to Vicente. If I go to him with shit still down my front you know what he'll say.'

It was quiet in the Charada. They went through to the bar and sat on stools, ordered two shots of mescal *reserva*. The barman poured, stood in front of them as there was nothing else going on. He knew who the brothers were. He was a user. He took every opportunity to be nice to them. He left the bottle on the counter, didn't ask for any money.

'You were here last Saturday night?' asked Jesús. 'You remember us?'

'Sure,' said the barman, shrugging his shoulders, smiling.

'You remember our group?'

'You were with the tall girl, Conchita – long legs, long dark hair, great dancer – and El Osito was with a *mulata*, but I didn't know her. She was a foreigner.'

'How do you know she was a foreigner?'

'She came to the bar, didn't speak any Spanish. One of the DJs sent her a note written in English, asked me to give it to her.'

'Did you read it?'

'My English is not so good and he was probably asking the same thing all the guys ask.'

'What did she do with the note?'

'She read it and dropped it on the floor,' said the barman. 'I mean, she was with you guys, what does she want with some DJ? Watch him play music all night? You got to be in love for that.'

'What was the name of the DJ?'

'It was David … David Álvarez. Nice guy. Good music. He's not on tonight.'

Mercy's phone rang at the Netherhall Gardens house. Chris Sexton picked it up and explained the situation to Papadopoulos.

'So something's going to happen tonight … finally?'

'Difficult to say with these guys. There's been so little contact we haven't been able to get a hold on them,' said Sexton. 'We're not even sure what will happen if there's a satisfactory show of trust. Bobkov and Kidd have effectively taken it out of my hands.'

'What did the DCS have to say about that?'

'He said they're spooks and they think they know more than anybody else about everything. He's cleared it with the Home Office.'

'Is there a tracker on the car?'

'No, we're concerned that they're FSB. They seem to know about our phone triangulation technology so we reckon they'll be able to detect a tracker. We're using CCTV to keep an eye on their progress.'

'I've got a list of estate agents that Irina Demidova, aka Zlata

Yankov, visited looking for a property to rent with a spec that sounds like a place you'd want to keep a hostage. But I'm having trouble tracking down numbers. I doubt I'll get news on any of this until tomorrow morning.'

'And we can't stop what's happening now,' said Sexton.

'Have you spoken to Tereshchenko's widow about what's happened to Sasha?' asked Mercy, pulling away from the traffic lights.

'Of course,' said Bobkov, staring out of the window, Regent's Park flashing past on the right-hand side. 'She thinks they're FSB. She would. She's completely paranoid, with good reason. She just told me to do anything and everything to get Sasha back.'

'Does that include breaking your promise to her about finding the perpetrators of the polonium 210 poisoning.'

'She loves Sasha. She wouldn't hold me to that,' said Bobkov. 'I told her about this — what we're doing now, this bizarre process where I have to show them that I'm trustworthy. Me? They steal my son off the street, torture him and *I* have to show *them*. This is what she thinks is classic FSB behaviour. I am somehow in the wrong. They now expect me to show my allegiance. This was why Tereshchenko and I left the FSB in the first place. We got out before we had to do something that we really couldn't live with.'

'So you agree with her? This is an FSB operation?'

'Almost everything points to it: the president getting back into power, the inquest into the poisoning coming up here in London in the autumn and next year, and I admit I've been stepping up my investigations. Only James knows this, but I even managed to recruit a Russian nuclear scientist to our cause. He was so disgusted by what had happened he promised to help in whatever way he could.'

'And the British government? How do they feel about it? I mean it's good that they've given you James Kidd, but then again that keeps them in the loop.'

'Now the pressure is really coming down on the British government, who, of course, would like good relations with Russia, but cannot accept executions using nuclear material by a foreign power on their soil. I think there are a lot of people who would like this unfortunate problem to disappear. One man's death is standing in the way of an awful lot. Morality often goes out of the window when the economy is in trouble.'

'So you think Sasha's kidnap is part of the process to get people to shut up about Tereshchenko?'

'Not just me, but his wife as well. She has an eighteen-year-old son. Something else is always implicit in these actions,' said Bobkov. 'On the other hand we always have to be aware of, and wary of, paranoia. Russia is not a normal country. A literary agent asked me to write a non-fiction book about the Tereshchenko case. I said I wouldn't do it but I'd be happy to write fiction. I've always admired John le Carré. The agent wasn't interested. He said there were three places in the world where he thought crime fiction didn't work: Africa, South America and Russia. When I asked him why, he said that they were all too surreal; nobody would be able to suspend their disbelief.'

'And what does James Kidd think?'

'He hasn't made up his mind. He's like that. He only operates on what he knows, which is that Sasha has been taken and, thanks to your investigation, how it was done,' said Bobkov. 'He's unnerved by Irina Demidova and the murder of Jeremy Spencer. He hopes that this next stage of the process will reveal more to us.'

Mercy pulled up outside Wunjo Guitars on Denmark Street. Bobkov went up the stairs to the side of the shop window. The Internet café was on the first floor behind a flimsy door. A couple of people were working online behind some rows of monitors while a gothic-looking girl sat behind a Formica counter.

Bobkov asked for his package, produced his ID. She gave him a Jiffy bag. He took it back down to the car and opened it. It contained a mobile phone, a coil of rope about seven millimetres thick and a printed page in Russian.

This phone can only receive calls. You will tell your driver to take you to Tower Hill Tube station and drop you there. She is not to follow you. We will be behind you and if she interferes she will get hurt. You will bring the case of money with you and the rope. You will be instructed by phone what to do with it. If all goes well you will be rewarded. If there's any outside interference Sasha will be killed.

Bobkov translated for Mercy, who started the car, drove down to the Embankment and past Blackfriars, Southwark and London Bridges. She dropped Bobkov off at the Tower.

He crossed the street, case in one hand, phone to his ear, shoulders hunched over, the desperation growing inside.

'This is very good,' said El Osito, lying in bed, both legs slightly raised, leafing through Raul Brito's research and the documents. 'How much did it cost you?'

'Nothing much. We paid for it out of our own pockets.'

'That's not an answer.'

'I commissioned it. I paid for it. It's not a legitimate expense.'

'A very careful response.'

'Vicente is even more careful,' said Jaime. 'I assume you don't want to have to explain all this to him. You know what he's like about risk.'

'That's good. I'm glad you understand how things are, Jaime,' said El Osito. 'I've already spoken to Vicente.'

He registered the surprise in Jaime's face.

'You think I can operate like this for two months without Vicente knowing?'

Now Jaime wondered what he'd told Vicente. El Osito had already confused him by calling Dennis Chilcott as soon as he'd finished reading Brito's report and telling him to come to room 401 in the clinic. Why was El Osito involving the British in their domestic business?

'What about the other problem?' asked El Osito.

'The Englishman found out about you from one of the DJs in the clubs,' said Jaime, who told him what they'd discovered from the doorman at Joy and the barman of the Charada. El Osito remained calm, hands folded across his flat stomach, the morphine drip maintaining a steady near-euphoric state.

'You know what to do,' said El Osito.

'I've sent Jesús to Kapital. We'll take the DJ to La Escuela after he's finished his set.'

'When is that?' asked El Osito.

'One o'clock.'

'You cover every exit,' said El Osito. 'If he gets away that will represent this "risk" that you and Vicente worry about so much.'

'It's already done.'

A knock at the door. A nurse showed Dennis Chilcott into the room. He looked as bewildered as a tourist who'd found himself yanked out of a holiday and into real life. He was flat-footed and overweight, with his trousers belted under his gut and hanging off his arse. His rumpled roll-neck sweater seemed to be choking him. A brand new Burberry trenchcoat mac was the only thing holding him together.

Dennis Chilcott hated hospitals. Even from the outside. He would do anything not to go in one. The only reason he hadn't cut up rough over the phone was that El Osito had called it a clinic, but as soon as the cab pulled up outside he knew. He steeled himself as he entered the glass doors, saw the blank walls beyond the reception, the people in white suspended in the sterilised interior.

It was better than the NHS hospitals back home. The antiseptic smell was not quite so pervasive and there were no bleeding hooligans or raving drunks ricocheting off the walls. He put on his mental blinkers, joined a gaping-mouthed man on a trolley in the lift and stared at a nurse's calves to distract himself from the horror.

Now he was in room 401 and so appalled by El Osito's damaged legs that he could barely contain himself.

'Jesus Christ,' he said in a voice that came up from the basement of his own nightmares, 'what the hell happened to you?'

'I had a car accident,' said El Osito. 'My legs took the full impact. I'm OK but it will be two months before I can walk again.'

Dennis allowed a wondrous delusion of relief to spread through him. He was still nauseated at the idea of injury, but at least it wasn't a punishment attack or a gang-war wound. No sooner had he thought this than he revised his idea. Was he kidding himself? He knew about the brutality of Vicente's competitor, El Chapo. The media was full of it, and he had the global reach to pull it off.

'I can see you're concerned,' said El Osito. 'Don't be. Tell me.'

'Your competitors, have they …?'

'This is nothing to do with the competition,' said El Osito. 'That all happens back in Cuidad Juarez. This was a car accident. Unfortunate. Nothing more.'

Jaime looked to see if Dennis believed it. He seemed to have suspended judgement for the moment, but he wasn't happy. He was looking at those broken legs as if they were a pair of battered wives insisting that they'd had a fall. The Mexican wished his English was better. He had enough to grasp that El Osito was passing his injuries off as a car accident, something he might well have spun around Vicente too. What concerned Jaime more was that he probably wouldn't be able to understand why El Osito had called Dennis to his bedside. He was maintaining the blankest possible expression in the hope that El Osito wouldn't send him out of the room.

'I want you to do something for me in London,' said El Osito.

'I'll do my best,' said Dennis.

'You have a good network of dealers,' said El Osito. 'How many?'

'Maybe fifty,' said Dennis, not wanting to reveal too much of his operation.

'All over London?'

'We've got it covered, yes.'

'And you have a lot of safe places?' said El Osito. 'Places where you can keep product for distribution and money for collection?'

'I've got a chain of hardware stores and timber yards and, yes, other commercial property where I can store things.'

'I want you to find somebody for me.'

'You know, when I tell people I live in London they always ask me whether I know so-and-so,' said Dennis. 'They don't understand how big London is, how ... different it is now. You can live there for years without meeting your neighbour. I assume, from the way you've just asked me, that you have a name but no address, and I'm telling you it's not going to be easy. Allow plenty of time.'

'I have a name *and* an address, but I know you won't find him there. You can try but my instinct tells me you won't have any luck. But what I can do is tell you how you're going to find this person for me.'

Dennis didn't like the assumption in El Osito's voice. In fact, he didn't like the way this conversation was proceeding at all. It seemed to him that the Colombian's request was not unconnected to the state of the man's legs, and he felt distinctly herded, even if it was by a cripple.

Despite this unease, his finely honed business instincts were intact and telling him to hear the man out, just to see if there were any opportunities on the way.

'You understand that finding people is outside my field of expertise,' said Dennis, 'but I know people who can do that sort of thing.'

'This must be done by you or your organisation,' said El Osito. 'This is no ordinary piece of business. This is not work for a private investigator.'

'I'll do what I can,' said Dennis, 'but in return we'd appreciate a demonstration of your goodwill in terms of what we discussed the other night. Supply and price. If we can agree on that I'm sure we can help each other.'

'Always the businessman, Dennis.'

'That's why we're here,' said Dennis, who, if he hadn't been standing by a hospital bed, would have been enjoying this little reversal of power.

'The man I want you to find could have an impact on our business. He is English, he has police connections and he has infiltrated some of our command structure.'

Jaime was lost, while Dennis's ears were ringing, as they always did when his systolic blood pressure went over 180, which was what happened when he heard the words 'police' and 'infiltrated' in the same sentence.

'So what's his game?'

'His game is that he thought his daughter had run away from home to be with me, but he was mistaken. I picked up a girl in a club in Madrid who *looked* like his daughter. We had sex and that was the end of it,' said El Osito. 'The next thing, he comes to my flat demanding to know where his daughter is. I tell him I don't know. He says I was seen with her and that she's now been found murdered and I am responsible. We had a disagreement and he left. We have discovered how he found me here in Madrid and we are clearing that up. What we need now is for you to find the Englishman in London.'

He handed over Charles Boxer's passport photocopy which

Brito had got from the concierge from the Hotel Moderno.

'The way you're going to do this,' said El Osito, 'is to find his runaway daughter.'

He handed over Amy Boxer's passport photo.

'And why should it be any easier for me to find her if her own father can't track her down?'

'His daughter is clever. She doesn't want to be found by him. The father abused her ... sexually.'

'Wha-a-at?' said Dennis, instantly furious. 'His own daughter?'

El Osito was surprised but delighted to have stumbled across this unexpected outrage. It was as if he'd told the man that Boxer had abused Chilcott's daughter.

'It must have been going on for a long time for this girl to go to such lengths,' said El Osito. 'She found someone who looked like her, gave this girl her passport just to fool her father into believing that she'd run away to Madrid.'

'Tell me how we're going to do it,' said Dennis, his face expressionless with subterranean fury.

23

'Go to Tower Gateway DLR, take a train direction Greenwich,' said the voice. 'No need to work out if you're being followed – you are. Don't do anything other than what you're told to do.'

The train was waiting on the platform with one or two people in each carriage. Rush hour had long gone. Bobkov went to the centre of the train and sat with the briefcase of money between his feet and checked the people in the carriage with him: a commuter in her thirties, trouser suit, dark mac, red scarf. A man in his twenties, laptop bag slung over his shoulder, resting on his thighs, buds in, feet tapping to the music, hands playing on the edge of his laptop case. Neither paid any attention to him. A big man got on, sat almost opposite him, heavy dark wool coat, grey trilby, dark-rimmed glasses, grey trousers, scuffed black shoes, gloves, which he occasionally thumped together as if driving the fingers up to the ends. He looked like the man Mercy had described leaving the Mercedes CLS in Cromwell Avenue.

The doors closed, the train pulled away. Bobkov had always found something eerie about driverless trains, especially ones taking lighted carriages out from the safety of stations into the darkest night. He felt exposed, as if his back was in the cross hairs of a distant sniper. A great sense of loneliness settled over him despite his travel companions.

He thought of his ex-wife lying in a hospital bed under the eerie glow of the intensive care machinery, her face, devastated by alcohol, now strangely slackened by the stroke. A figure so distant from the woman he'd met and fallen in love with, she felt like someone from another life.

They'd been so happy when Sasha was born. But that had been the trigger. She gave up work, stayed at home, lost touch with people. He was travelling all over the world, doing business, networking, then politicking, until finally he went back to the parallel world he had begun to miss. This meant that he could no longer tell the whole truth, and Tracey knew that something had shifted but mistakenly thought it was away from her. She couldn't have been further from the mark.

The train stopped at three stations with nobody getting on or off. The woman took a call on her mobile phone. She smiled and spoke a language he thought was probably Georgian. She had the black hair and dark beauty of the women from that country. At West India Quay station his phone rang.

'Leave the train at Heron Quays,' said the voice. 'Go to the front carriage, wait outside and reboard at the last moment. Sit as near to the front as possible.'

Bobkov did as he was told. As the doors closed on the lead carriage, he looked back at his erstwhile companions. The woman had gone, leaving the young man and the big fellow in the trilby. His new carriage was empty. He sat at the front window, self-conscious, with the briefcase on the seat beside him and the unseen cross hairs wavering over his forehead.

He swallowed hard to control the emotion in his throat as his mind veered away from the professional and out into the deeper darkness of a world with no Sasha in it. That would be true loneliness. The gap left by a dead child was unfillable. He had to pinch the bridge of his nose to squeeze the tears back in. He took a deep breath and sat back to watch his reflection in the window as if he was endlessly journeying towards himself while remaining tantalisingly out of reach.

As the train pulled into Crossharbour station another call told him to get off the train and make his way across the bridge over Millwall Inner Dock. The voice took him along streets in which he encountered no people, over which towered high-rise blocks of glittering apartments. At one point the landmark of One Canada

Square appeared briefly between other office buildings and disappeared as he turned down Byng Street and made his way past the silent North Pole Pub and more apartment blocks towards Cuba Street and the river.

At the end of Cuba Street was an old Riverbus boarding point, now closed. There was a barred gate across the entrance with rubbish and untamed shrubbery beyond. The voice told him that the padlock to the gate had been sheared and that he could go through and onto the West India Pier.

Inside the dark and derelict Riverbus terminal he was told to tie one end of the rope to the handle of the briefcase, using the torch on the mobile to see.

'Now go to the end of the pier.'

He had to fight his way past the thick branches which had grown up in the old terminal to get to the edge of the river. There the covered walkway for access to the boats started on a concrete platform and ended on two wooden piles driven into the riverbed five metres out.

It was difficult to judge the solidity of the floor of the walkway so he held on to the handrail and shuffled along, testing it for strength as he went. At the end of the pier was the slurping darkness of the river. A metal bar had been secured across the exit. The voice told him to tie the other end of the rope to the bar.

'Make sure you tie a good knot,' said the voice. 'We don't want that slipping into the water. And check the knot on the handle of the case.'

'It's all secure,' said Bobkov.

'Now pay out the rope until the case is hanging above the water. The rope should be exactly the right length.'

'OK. It's tight.'

'Now leave. Go back the way you came. Turn left onto Westferry Road and take a right onto Heron Quay. That will take you to Heron Quays DLR station. This time you take the train to Stratford and from there you go by Overground to Finchley and Frognal.'

'What about my reward?' said Bobkov. 'You said there would be a reward.'

'As soon as we've checked the money you get your reward.'

'And when do I get my son back? I've shown that you can trust me. Everything has happened as you asked.'

'If that is the case then you have nothing to fear,' said the voice. 'You will get your instructions for the second payment—'

'The second payment?' said Bobkov. 'I've just cleared my personal and my company accounts in order to raise that seven hundred and fifty thousand. You never said anything about a second payment.'

He had stopped halfway up the covered walkway. The Thames gurgled and lapped beneath him. An engine approached, a boat on the river. Through the windows of the walkway a white light in the middle of the intense darkness kept coming.

'A second payment was implied. The first was to prove that you could be trusted not to involve the authorities. The second is for the safe return of your son,' said the voice. 'Now leave the pier. I want you away from the river. Now!'

'Tell me about this second payment because I don't know where it's going to come from.'

'We're not being greedy. We know we asked you for five million. With no negotiation we're accepting the same again, another seven hundred and fifty thousand. One and a half million for the safe return of Sasha, your only son. Now leave the pier, Mr Bobkov.'

He took two steps and his foot went through the floor. He gasped with the shock and the pain as his leg was scraped up to the knee. The phone skittered away from him and slipped through the gap between the floor and wall of the walkway. Bobkov eased his leg out, felt the skin and trouser material tearing against the ragged edge of the hole. He crawled back to the end of the pier.

The noise of the approaching boat eased as it arrived at the end of the pier. It was a rigid inflatable speedboat with a light mounted on a structure over the engine. There were just two men in the boat. On the inflatable flanks of the boat was written CW BOAT HIRE. The rubber squeaked against the wooden piles as the boat glided under the walkway. Bobkov peered over the edge, lying flat. Both men were in hooded waterproofs. One of them cut the rope and retrieved the briefcase. The boat pulled away and headed back in the direction of Greenwich.

Bobkov crawled back up the walkway, feeling with his hands for the phone. A glimmer of light to his left about halfway up told him that the torch was still on. The phone had landed on one of the steel girders supporting the walkway. He reached through the gap and grabbed the phone, clasped it to his face.

'Hello?' he said.

'What the hell happened?' said the voice.

'My foot went through the floor. It's rotten. I dropped the phone.'

'All right, all right. We've got the money. I'm going to hang up now and you'll get another call in a minute.'

Bobkov crawled off the walkway back into the terminal building. The blood was running warmly down his leg, soaking into his sock. He was shocked to find how physically soft he'd become. It had been fifteen years since he'd left the FSB. Fifteen years of sitting at desks, eating lunches and dinners. He'd grown flabby and pathetic.

This time the thick, stubborn branches growing in the terminal building seemed to grab him, snarling around his ankle. As he left the building, he tripped and fell with his foot trapped in the terminal while the rest of him lay outside, face up to the clouds scudding across the starlit sky. The phone rang.

'Yes,' he said.

'Hello, Daddy. It's me.'

'Oh my God, Sasha,' he said, but the boy's unbroken treble voice had already pierced him, and he had to cough against the emotion and the tears to show his son that he was still strong.

'Let's just get this straight in our heads,' said Darren. 'El Osito wants us to go and see this girl Chantrelle's mother.'

'Her name is Alice Grant. She lives on an estate in north London,' said Dennis. 'You make contact with her and do one of two things: find out where her daughter was living, because that's where Amy Boxer will be going every day to check whether she's come back with her passport, or get the mother to call Amy and tell her to come to her flat to pick up something from Chantrelle. The point being that once we've got Amy Boxer, then we can reel the father in. By all accounts the father is not to be messed with.'

'So it's the father who's the problem?'

'The one who's been abusing his own daughter,' said Dennis. 'We've got a name and address for him. We can check that, but El Osito doesn't think he'll be there. He'll know we're on to him.'

'Look, Dad, we all hate child abuse,' said Darren, 'but what exactly has Boxer done that means we've got to fuck around finding him rather than getting on with what we're supposed to be doing, which is run our business?'

'He has police connections. We think Amy's mother is a copper, and we know that Charles Boxer was in the army and in a homicide squad in the Met. And not only that,' said Dennis, holding up his finger at his prowling son, 'he can identify El Osito, and you know what these blokes are like about that.'

'And why would Boxer tell anybody?'

'His connections. There's an element of risk attached to him.'

'You know what I think?' said Darren. 'And I'm surprised you don't see this yourself, Dad. I think El Osito is shifting the risk he's exposed *his* organisation to … to *ours*. We're going to expose ourselves to Alice Grant for a kick-off. What do we know about her? She might be a cop for all we know.'

'She lives on the Andover Estate in Islington, which, as far as I know, has had its fair share of crack problems, so I doubt it.'

'I don't like it, Dad. The whole thing stinks to me.'

'Nobody *likes* it, but the shit's on our doorstep,' said Dennis savagely. '*And* we don't want that girl exposed to her father's … attentions any longer, right? We're doing ourselves a favour and doing a bit of good on the side.'

'Look, I know you've always had a problem with that kind of thing. Me too, don't get me wrong. But this is business,' said Darren. 'We get the girl, Amy. We reel in the father. What then?'

'El Osito says *he* will deal with the father.'

'And the girl?' said Darren. 'And Alice Grant? They'll know who *we* are. Are we going to let them go? Let them run to the cops? No, so they're going to have to be dealt with 'n' all. It's going to be a right bleedin' mess of killing, all because of El O-*fucking*-sito. And then you won't have rescued her from her father, will you? Out of the frying pan – that what it's going to be for her.'

Silence from Dennis.

'I renegotiated the deal,' he said finally.

'What?'

' I reneg—'

'I heard you, Dad. I just can't believe that's the most important thing running through your head right now,' said Darren. 'Our whole organisation's at stake because of this fuckin' Colombian. And I don't believe a word about his legs getting done in a car accident, neither. There's a lot missing out of this. A lot of shit. What happened to this girl Chantrelle, for instance? Do we know?'

Dennis had to stop and think. Reimagined himself at El Osito's bedside to bring all the detail back to him.

'Yes, he said something about ... he heard later, from Charles Boxer, that she'd been found murdered. Yes, that's right, that's why Boxer had come to see him, because he was the last person—'

'You're really confusing me now, Dad. I just don't get it any more.'

'Look, we know what's got to be done,' said Dennis. 'There's no getting away from it. El Osito has Vicente's blessing. We have to do everything we can for him. What we've got to decide now is who's going to do it, because it's not going to be either of us, is it? We're here and it's got to be done tonight or first thing in the morning. This Boxer fella is in with the Madrid homicide squad. He's getting information from them. He's already on to it.'

'Well,' said Darren, 'if you ask me, it's got to be someone who's got his head screwed on tight and ... we don't mind losing. Because that's going to be the upshot, innit?'

'So who'd be up for it and who owes us?'

Miles Lomax was a thirty-two-year-old Scot with an English accent because he'd been to a public school where anything regional had been ironed out. He'd gone to Durham University to read history and had been all set for a first when he ran into the druggy crowd. He'd left with a 2.2 and had headed straight for London and a life of as little work as possible with as many drugs as he could take.

The first thing to crash was the state of his finances. The next was his innocence, when he lost his girlfriend, Tanya, to an overdose: he woke up with her next to him, blue-skinned, very cold and dead. He'd left her there in her flat, all alone. Finally he started dealing, small scale, and earned himself a criminal record. The only reason he didn't do jail time was that he was nicely spoken and was caught with slightly less than a gram.

Only then, after all that damage, did he get sensible. Not sensible enough to leave drugs behind, but intelligent enough to realise that taking them was dumb and dealing them was the best way of making money without going to an office every day. He started working for the Chilcotts and was their main conduit for cocaine to the upper middle classes and City slickers.

He was not happy with the job he'd been given tonight, but that's what happened when you fell in love. Arabella Risley-Banks had reminded him of the girl he'd lost. She had the same long dark hair and aquamarine eyes and the same inclination to take too many drugs. He'd made the mistake of giving her credit and Arabella had taken to cooking up speedballs. She'd got herself into such a state that her parents had flown her to a rehab clinic in Switzerland, leaving Miles Lomax with a shortfall of twenty-eight grand and a blank space in his heart.

Never again. How many times had he said that to himself?

Now he was heading north from his comfortable modern two-bedroomed flat in a dreary 1970s block in Elm Park Gardens in Chelsea to an infamous estate in some godforsaken corner near Seven Sisters, N bloody 7. The only time he'd been up this way was to visit Tanya, who'd done six months in HMP Holloway for her umpteenth shoplifting offence.

The story Darren Chilcott had spun around the scenario he was heading into had him shaking his head. None of it fitted, gaps everywhere. His reluctance must have fitted itself down the phone line to Madrid and burst into Darren's head because he'd volunteered some muscle to help him out and Lomax had just picked up Tel and Vlad, as they were known, outside Tufnell Park Tube station.

Tel sat up front while Vlad, big and eager, hovered between them like a Labrador who didn't want to miss any of the jokes. Given the cock-up they were heading into, jokes were thin on the ground, although Vlad had as much chance of understanding them as a pooch anyway.

'So what's the job?' asked Tel. 'Darren said you'd need some help, but he wouldn't tell me nothing about the job.'

Vlad's grey eyes bored into the side of Lomax's neck, making him itch.

'The job requires us to think on our feet,' said Lomax, trying to be inclusive.

Vlad's eyes swerved away, looking to Tel for a translation.

'Does he speak English?' asked Lomax.

'Not a lot,' said Tel, 'but he's got hands of iron.'

Vlad stuck his hands forward between the seats, proud of his gnarled and battered lumps of fist.

'What's going to happen,' said Lomax, taking a deep breath, 'is that I'll go up and talk to this woman, find out where the girl is we're suppose to be bringing in.'

'You've lost me,' said Tel.

'The less you know the better,' said Lomax. 'I barely understand it myself. The only time I'm going to need your help is when we abduct the girl.'

'What's abduct?'

'Kidnap.'

'Oh yeah, we done a bit of that before, haven't we, Vlad?' said Tel. 'A girl ran away from Vlad's mate's knocking shop in Forest Gate. We had to bring her back.'

'How did that go?'

'Finding her was the hard bit,' said Tel. 'Then we just tonked her on the head, stuck her in the boot and drove her back.'

'Well, there'll be no *tonking* on the head this time,' said Lomax. 'That's how you end up with dead people on your hands, especially girls. They have thinner skulls.'

'You got a better idea?'

What Lomax had access to were drugs: roofies, special K and G, otherwise known as Rohypnol, ketamine and gamma-hydroxy-butyric acid. The only difficulty was getting it inside the girl. They all had to be ingested to work. This, Darren had said, was why he'd been specially selected for the work.

He parked up on a road in the middle of the Andover Estate. He told Vlad to stick with the car while he and Tel went up and found the block where Alice Grant lived. Lomax, as always, was wearing a suit with an open-necked white shirt and, against the cold, a dark blue overcoat with a scarf. He believed in always look-ing like anybody but a drug dealer. He went up to the fifth floor of the block and saw that there was still a light on in Alice Grant's flat. He took Tel back to the lifts, got his mobile number.

'I'm only going to need you when the girl gets here,' said Lomax, 'so I'll send you a text when she's on her way and you come up to the fourth floor. You got that? That's the *fourth* floor, not this floor, the one below. You wait down there. When she arrives I'll send another text, and then you just come up to the front door of the flat and wait. You don't do anything. Right?'

'What about Vlad?'

'We don't involve him. He's too much trouble without the language. If we need some heavy lifting then he can come in, otherwise he stays with the car. We'll use him at the other end.'

'At the other end?'

'Where we're taking her.'

'Oh, right. Didn't know how many ends there were to a girl.'

'Thanks, Tel.'

Lomax went back to the flat, rang the bell.

The door opened on a chain. Three things hit him straight away. The first was that she was white, the second that she had faded blue eyes and the third that she was a user. He'd seen that ravaged look too many times: forty but looked fifty-five. She was smoking, and at the end of the drag the creases around her lips did not disappear. He felt his job get just that little bit easier.

'Are you Chantrelle Grant's mum?'

'What's it to you?' she said, looking him up and down.

'I owe her some money,' said Lomax, getting that in as soon as he could. 'I'm having trouble tracking her down.'

'She went away,' said Alice, fixing him in the eye. 'She's still away ... far as I know.'

'In Madrid, right?' said Lomax. 'The only thing is I'm leaving for the States tomorrow, first thing in the morning, for a couple of months, and I wanted to give her this money.'

'You'd better come in,' said Alice, unhooking the chain.

He came into the corridor, stood by her while she closed the door, waiting to be invited in, being polite not pushy.

'Cup of tea?' she asked.

She brought him into the living room, sat him down at the dining table and went into the galley kitchen to make the tea. She came back with a tray: tea, biscuits, cigarettes, an ashtray.

'She also asked me to give a package to a friend of hers,' said Lomax, 'but that's a bit more complicated.'

'Why's that?'

'I have to give it to her in person, but Chantrelle didn't know where she's living at the moment and she didn't have a phone number. So I'm a bit stuck with that one. But the money ... I can leave the money with you, can't I? Or would you rather not take the responsibility?'

'No, no, that's all right,' said Alice, keen to be of help. 'What's this friend's name?'

'Amy Boxer.'

'Oh, I *know* her – she's been calling me every day, asking after Chantrelle,' said Alice. 'She came round only yesterday. Left her phone number. Said that as soon as I heard from Chantrelle to call her.'

'So Chantrelle's being a bit mysterious, is she?' said Lomax. 'Now, look, you wouldn't do me a favour, would you? Give Amy a call while I get Chantrelle's money ready for her and tell her to come round here as soon as she can so that I can give her the package?'

Alice picked up her mobile, made the call, stayed at the table counting out the money with Lomax, wanting to know how much it was.

'Oh, Amy. Hello love, this is Alice Grant, Chantrelle's mum. Now look, good news ...'

Pause.

'No, she's not back yet, but Chantrelle's sent this very nice man with a package for you. Chantrelle said he was only to give it to you in person.'

Pause.

'Madrid.'

Pause.

'What's your name, love?'

'Jake,' said Lomax.

'Jake met her in Madrid and gave him this package for you.'

Pause.

'Can't you just leave it and she'll pick it up in the morning?'

'I promised Chantrelle,' said Lomax. 'The money and personal delivery of the package.'

'You're only in Old Street, aren't you, love? It won't take you long to get yourself up to Archway, will it?'

24

'That was my reward,' said Bobkov. 'Three minutes' talk with Sasha. Even at two hundred and fifty thousand euros a minute it was worth every cent. He sounded very fine. He said they hadn't hurt him and they played chess with him, but none of them were any good. His ... his voice ...'

Bobkov was in an armchair with his foot up on a stool. Mercy was cleaning the deep scratches to his leg with antiseptic wipes. She looked up to see the emotion struggling in a face not used to dealing with such extremes of love.

'What about his voice?' asked Mercy.

'It was beautiful,' he said. 'I'd never thought about it before. It's so clear and innocent. You forget ... what it was like to be so sweet.'

Kidd was carrying out the debrief. MI5 had positioned someone in the carriage, the young guy with the laptop pretending to listen to music, but they hadn't tailed Bobkov from Crossharbour DLR station. There were too few people on the street and it had been considered too risky.

They'd discussed an investigation of CW Boat Hire and decided against it, reasoning that it would get back to the gang too quickly. They were better off working the estate agents on Olga's list in the morning.

'If it was the FSB, wouldn't they have access to safe houses where they could keep a hostage pretty much indefinitely?' said Mercy.

264

'Of course they would,' said Bobkov.

'But they've learned their lesson from the polonium 210 debacle,' said Kidd. 'That pointed the finger too obviously at a state-run act of terror. Now they're determined to make it look criminal by not using state security forces or their facilities.'

'So we have to find where they're holding Sasha,' said Mercy.

'That's the good news,' said Kidd, 'because if they were using FSB safe houses in London we wouldn't have a chance.'

'Tea's all right,' said Lomax, 'but there comes a time of night when there's nothing better than a little drink. How about you, Alice?'

They were sitting waiting for Amy. They knew they had at least thirty minutes before she'd show.

'Oh, I don't keep any drink in the house, Jake,' said Alice. 'Far too tempting.'

'Trying to keep yourself on the straight and narrow?'

'I like a smoke and an occasional drink, just don't want alcohol in the house, that's all. Been a source of too much trouble, know what I mean?'

'Totally,' said Lomax, thinking Alice was just the sort to get clouted around the joint after a few bevvies. 'I've got a bottle in the car, mind. I could bring it up, we could have ourselves a little glass and as soon I've handed over the package to Amy I'll take it away again. No harm done.'

She didn't have to say anything; the gleam was in her eye. She'd have killed for a shot. Lomax went down to the car, tapped on the window.

'Are we on yet?' asked Tel.

'Nearly,' said Lomax. 'She's on her way. You come with me now.'

Lomax went to the boot, where he kept a box of assorted booze for when he went on sales trips. Nothing like a shot of vodka over a coke deal. He took a bottle of Stolly and a couple of cans of Coca-Cola. He'd need the Coca-Cola to mask the slight saltiness of the GHB. Not that Alice would notice a damn thing.

On the way back up Lomax stationed Tel on the fourth floor.

'When I text you, come to the door. Don't knock. Just wait outside. If the girl gets spooked she might make a run for it, and

I want you there when she opens the door,' said Lomax. 'And no tonking her on the head.'

'Right,' said Tel. 'No tonking.'

Lomax went back up to Alice Grant's flat. She had three glasses laid out with some ice ready in a bowl. He poured the drinks in front of her. They sat with their vodka and Cokes.

'So where's Mr Grant?' asked Lomax.

'Oh, he's long gone,' said Alice. 'I think I was lucky he hung around until Chantrelle was born.'

'She never mentioned her dad,' said Lomax.

'She never knew him,' said Alice. 'Just as well. Bit of a bad boy. That's why he skipped off. Used to run crack on the estate. Then the cops got heavy on it and that was the end of him.'

'To become a guest of Her Majesty's Prison Service?' asked Lomax.

He'd been right about her. She had the look of a crack hag.

'Don't think so,' said Alice. 'I think he might have been ... done away with. He had a bit of a mouth on him and quite a temper. Not a good combo when you see the company he was keeping.'

'Chantrelle's a bit of a tearaway, I have to say,' said Lomax, taking a measured guess.

'It's not been easy for her,' said Alice. 'I've had my problems, it has to be said. Not always been there for her.'

'Problems?' asked Lomax.

'You know,' she said, wiggling her wrist.

'Drink?' said Lomax, then nodded. 'Ah yes, Mr Grant. Crack?'

'How did you meet Chantrelle?' she asked, as if changing the subject, but not.

'We ran into each other in a club in Madrid. You know, English people together. She was with some foreigners all yabbering away in Spanish so we got talking,' said Lomax. 'My God, she can dance, that girl. You must have done something right, Alice.'

'She's a devil of a dancer,' said Alice. 'That's how she got started, I reckon. Had to keep going ... all night.'

Rather than having a crack-head mum who probably didn't stop during the pregnancy, thought Lomax.

'She was definitely partial to a little snort,' said Lomax. 'Yes, we had a very nice time together and she introduced me to some great people. Real snow kings.'

He could see her sneaking looks at him, sizing him up, working out where he was coming from. She had all the slyness of the user who could smell drugs on someone through four lanes of London traffic.

'Let's raise a glass to Chantrelle,' said Lomax, chinking glasses with Alice, looking her in the eye. 'I was going to leave her a little present, but seeing as you're being so nice ...'

He handed her a little baggie with six rocks in it. She was out of her chair and into the bedroom in a flash. He heard the bubble of her pipe and a huge sigh, as if all her cares had been lifted from her shoulders. Lomax took a plastic phial of liquid GHB from his pocket and gave Alice's half-finished vodka and Coke a heavy squirt. When she came back in her eyes were bright, she was smiling and there was a little shimmy in her hips.

'Chantrelle's not the only one who knows how to dance,' she said.

The doorbell rang. Alice veered away from Lomax and down the corridor to the front door.

'Amy!'

'Hello, Alice.'

'You're just in time for the party.'

Lomax squirted a more carefully judged shot of GHB into an empty glass and slammed some ice on top of it. He picked up the glass as Amy walked into the room, held it up and gave her a small measure of vodka, which he topped up with Coca-Cola.

'Have a drink, Amy,' he said. 'I'm Jake, Chantrelle's friend.'

He handed Alice her glass and picked up his own.

'Here's to Chantrelle,' he said, and they all chinked glasses and drank.

Alice socked back the rest of her drink in one go and slammed the glass down on the table.

'I'll have another one of them please, barman,' she said. 'Let's have some music.'

She threw out both arms to Amy, hugged her and let her go.

'Go on, have a drink, love. Get it down yer,' she said.

Amy took another inch as Lomax poured Alice a careful

measure of vodka. Amy was checking him out. She was young but not completely green.

'You didn't see Amy with all her hair,' said Alice, knocking back half her drink in one go. 'They could have been sisters, her and Chantrelle, couldn't you, love?'

Amy smiled. Lomax guessed she'd seen this state before. He gave her an encouraging look, a little shrug.

'Jake met her in Madrid, didn't you? They had a lovely time together.'

She swerved away and went to the old CD player, turned it on, hit play and danced away from it without caring what was on. Lomax sent Tel the pre-prepared text as Amy Winehouse's 'Rehab' boomed out. Alice, who'd picked up her drink and knocked back the remainder, wheeled round to give the CD player a murderous look.

'We're not having that, are we?' she said.

Lomax gave Amy a small cheers, sipped his drink; she took another half-inch of hers.

'Alice said you have a package for me.'

'It's in the car,' he said. 'We'll pick it up on the way out. I'll give you a lift if you want. The Tube's going to close in a bit. I'll whip you down to Old Street in no time.'

'This package ...?'

'Chantrelle didn't tell me anything about it. She was having a great time, hanging with a crowd. She told me she'd ring you and that I had to give it to you in person. She just forgot to give me your mobile number and address.'

'That's because I didn't give them to her,' said Amy. 'She should have been back here on Monday. That was the idea.'

'You ever been to Madrid?' asked Lomax. 'It's an addictive scene down there. You hit with the right crowd and you could lose two months of your life. That's a place that knows how to party. What was she doing down there? I mean, I asked her, but she was very coy.'

They were alone in the room now. Alice had used the distraction of the music to slip into the bedroom to smoke another rock.

'I'm lucky she didn't sell it,' said Amy. 'My passport.'

'She didn't need to,' said Lomax, feeling her starting to trust him now. 'The guy she was with had plenty. What was she doing with your passport? I wouldn't give mine to anybody. Fancy a top-up?'

Lomax was pouring himself another, not too generous.

'I'm OK with this,' she said, taking another inch. He didn't push it. He wasn't a creep trying to get her drunk.

'Smoke?' he asked, handing her one of Alice's cigarettes. 'I'm sure she won't mind.'

Amy took one. Lit up. She told him why she'd given Chantrelle her passport. Wanted to impress him.

'That's a pretty fucking elaborate way to leave home,' said Lomax. 'All I did was go to uni and hightail it to London straight after.'

'My mother's a cop and my father's a—'

'Don't tell me.'

'You'll never guess.'

'A professional hit man.'

'No,' said Amy, 'although …'

Lomax laughed. Amy did too. Just over ten minutes in and the drug was loosening her off. The inhibitions were falling away.

'He's in the firearms unit … SCO19?' said Lomax, deadpan.

'No, but he does have a gun.'

'Legal?'

'No.'

A little sweat came up on Lomax.

'Your parents still married?' he asked.

'Separated. Divorced. Ages ago,' said Amy, smoking, taking another drink. 'Where the hell's Alice gone?'

'Yes, where *has* she gone?' said Lomax. 'This is supposed to be her party.'

He went to the bedroom door, gave it a little knock, opened it a crack.

'Alice?'

He opened the door more. Alice was on the bed convulsing, her muscles in spasm. She was unconscious. *Shit*. Had he been a bit too heavy with the GHB and the first shot of vodka?

'Is she all right?' asked Amy.

'Just crashed out, that's all,' he said, going into the room, pushing the door shut behind him. He rolled Alice over, got her into the recovery position.

Amy pushed open the door behind him, saw Alice's state.

'Christ,' she said, pulling out her mobile. 'We'd better get an ambulance.'

Lomax turned and slapped it out of her hand. She looked at him in shock. He smiled a little sadly and it instantly dawned on her: the strangeness of the situation, the way she'd started to feel. She turned and made a run for the front door but nothing would quite work properly. It all seemed too slow, as if she was in wellies full of water.

She reached the front door, wrenched it open. There was a man standing there. She had to blink to see him straight. She felt dizzy. He put his hand on her sternum and gave her the gentlest of shoves backwards, and she fell on her bum like a toddler. Tel stepped into the flat, closed the door behind him, saw Lomax in the living room in a hyperactive state.

'What's up?' said Tel.

Amy was struggling to get to her feet like a child in a bath full of water.

'Shut the door, keep an eye on her.'

Lomax was working at maniacal speed. He'd found the rocks of crack in the bedroom, pocketed them. He turned the music off using the remote, tossed it onto the sofa. He had his coat on, the bottle of vodka in one pocket, the Coke cans in the other. The money he'd been going to give to Alice he stuck in an inside pocket. He found some kitchen roll and wiped down the table. The glass he'd been using he emptied in the sink and stuffed that in with the vodka.

'How's she doing?' he asked.

'She's out,' said Tel. 'What the fuck is this?'

Lomax looked around the room. 'Let's get out of here,' he said.

'I don't know whether this is going to be any use to you, but I've found a couple of girls who know Amy,' said Glider, on the phone to Boxer. 'That photo you sent me, I put that around all the girls I know and they forwarded it. We've had a couple of replies. Girls who saw Amy on Saturday night in Camden at a club called KOKO right next to Mornington Crescent Tube.'

'That's a start,' said Boxer. 'How do I get in touch with them?'

'I'll text you their mobile numbers.'

This was a job for Roy Chapel's son Tony. Boxer forwarded the text to him, asked him to follow it up. He sat back thinking, if Glider had come up with those girls on Monday he'd have saved us a lot of trouble. It was the photo: everybody looks at a photo; nobody reads words any more.

A text from Tony. He'd made contact. The girls were in a club in Shoreditch called Sy-Lo. He'd be with them in ten. Boxer thought of the club DJ David Álvarez. What had he said when he'd been thinking about how to contact El Osito? The Spanish market was dead. They were looking north and to London in particular. El Osito must have people here ready to act for him.

Two more thoughts came to him as he sat in the darkened room. He must warn David Álvarez. El Osito would know that Boxer had got to him somehow. They'd work it out. His visit to Álvarez in the Joy club had been no secret, what with the door-man and the girl taking him up to the DJ's zone.

As he sent a text to Álvarez, he worked on his second thought: only what was known in the Jefatura could be leaked to the outside world. It would be in some report or other, filed by the homicide squad: the body wasn't Amy Boxer's, the left buttock tattoo wasn't hers. Only if Zorrita had found another bag with something more revealing could that leak out into the world and expose him to danger. But Boxer was no longer in the loop. Zorrita had no reason to call him now. He was not an interested party any more. He checked his watch, midnight, one in the morning in Madrid. He called Zorrita.

'I'm sorry, Luís.'

'No need to be sorry, Charles. Just let me get out of bed. My wife hates to be disturbed by my work.'

The rustle of bedclothes, the pad of feet, the flap of some clothing, the pulling out of a chair.

'Tell me, Charles.'

'I just need to know if you found anything else today. I mean, something that would help you identify the dismembered body. If

271

I knew the identity of her double in Madrid it would improve my chances of finding Amy.'

'We found another bag on the last dive of the day with the girl's head and passport,' said Zorrita. 'But, as I'm sure you're aware, there's a procedure. I can't reveal anything until the next of kin have been informed.'

'So what's happened so far?' asked Boxer. 'If it was on the last dive have you processed your findings in any way?'

Zorrita told him what they'd found and how the preliminary forensic examination had gone but gave him no detail beyond the head, the passport, the upper arms, the handbag and the weight.

'We filed a report, and a copy was sent to the British consulate, but not until around 10.30 this evening. The consulate won't do anything until tomorrow.'

'And what will they do?'

'They'll contact London and send a police officer to visit the next of kin,' said Zorrita. 'And, Charles, I can't reveal that name to you, so don't ask me. I know you want to find Amy, but you have to put yourself in the other person's place. Her daughter has died and she must be the first person to be told.'

Boxer knew that Luís Zorrita was not a man who was going to bend, relax or ignore this very specific protocol. It would come back on him too easily. They exchanged some final words and hung up.

He sent his text to David Álvarez, his thumbs flashing over the tiny keys: 'This is urgent. You are in danger. Do not ignore this message. You must stop what you are doing and leave immediately. Get out of the city and go into hiding. Do not go back to your flat. Do not go to a relative or friend's house. You must disappear as if you never existed. They know about us. Tell me when you are safe. Un abrazo, Charles.'

By one o'clock Kapital was getting up to full swing. Álvarez had brought the audience to fever pitch. The music was in the floor and walls, shooting up the dancers' legs, pulsing through their vital organs. He didn't want it to end. They were all in a state of ecstatic exuberance, with no past and no future, and as Álvarez

272

merged them into his final track of the night, the next DJ tapped him on the shoulder.

He tore off his headphones. They embraced. Álvarez was wired, more alive than he'd been in months. He decided to stay the rest of the night, wouldn't leave until closing. This was going to be a great, great night.

He went to his changing room, stripped off his sweat-wet shirt, put on a new one, and that was when he received Boxer's text. He read the terrible message, went cold all over.

The one thing Álvarez had on his side was that he knew Kapital inside out. He went straight to the security office on the third floor where they monitered all the CCTV cameras in and outside the building. The security officer was watching three big screens in front of him and had twenty smaller ones off to the side from which he could draw output.

Kapital was a seven-storey building on the corner of Calle de Atocha and a narrow alley called Calle del Cenicero. All the emergency exits came out into that alley. A car was parked about fifty metres up and, leaning against the driver's door, smoking, was a Mexican-looking guy keeping an eye on all the exits.

The security officer pulled up the CCTV feeds from the front of the building, which showed the outside area in Calle de Atocha. Two Mexicans in identical black leather jackets were staring at the front doors. One of them had a view down Calle del Cenicero to his companion by the car.

Álvarez asked the security officer to put the internal cameras up onto the big screens. That was when he saw one of El Osito's freaks, one of the guys who'd been in the Charada that Saturday night.

'Which floor is this on?' asked Álvarez.

'Ours.'

'But where?'

'Down the end of the hallway.'

'Say nothing,' said Álvarez and stepped back behind the door.

They watched the screen. The Mexican looked in all the doors as he worked his way down the corridor. Their door opened. The man saw the screens but not himself, only the empty corridor. The security officer turned in his chair. Álvarez put a trembling finger to his lips.

'You're not allowed in here,' said the security officer.

The Mexican backed out, closed the door.

They watched him on the screen. He went to the end of the corridor, came back past the door, disappeared until he reappeared on another screen going upstairs to the fourth floor.

Álvarez went back down to the changing room on the second floor and fitted everything he could into his trouser pockets. He looked at his coat. He'd need it, but he shouldn't be seen wearing it, so he left it behind.

He tore up the copy of *El País* he'd brought with him and dropped it in a metal bin from under the table. He lit two cigarettes, had another thought, picked up his wet shirt, slung it over his shoulder.

He put the two cigarettes under the paper at the bottom of the bin and left the changing room. In the corridor he found the heat sensor and held the bin up to it. In seconds all the music in the club shut down and was replaced by alarm bells.

Álvarez dropped the bin, threw his wet shirt on top and ran down the stairs to the ground floor, where he joined the melee of people pouring towards the emergency exits, which had automatically sprung open.

They ran out into the cold night. Girls screamed. He joined a group of about twenty people who'd all come out dancing together. They crossed to the other side of Calle de Atocha, stood on the pavement and looked back expecting to see flames. Álvarez carried on up the street and slipped down an alleyway past the Madrid Royal Conservatory. Only at that point did he start jogging and then running and finally sprinting with relief into his new life.

25

They were heading for the disused Rowland Estate in Bermond-sey, which Dennis Chilcott had bought from the local council to redevelop into a mixture of luxury flats and affordable housing with his cocaine trafficking profits. Dennis's little joke was that he was creating his future customer base: cocaine for the luxury flats and crack for the affordable housing.

The housing estate backed on to a disused warehouse, which Chilcott also owned and in which he had installed old shipping containers. Some of these had been used for cocaine transportation and were now let for temporary storage. The warehouse fronted on to Neckinger, but access was from the rear of the building through a pair of padlocked barred gates which gave on to a large yard. Trucks could reverse into the warehouse through massive doors where the containers were then unloaded by forklifts.

Lomax was sitting in the back of his car with Amy's head in his lap, making sure she was breathing properly. Tel was driving. Vlad, who'd been keen to involve himself in some way, was sitting braced in the passenger seat as if they were about to be side-rammed.

'Just tell him to relax, Tel?' asked Lomax. 'I feel as if we're about to crash-land.'

'Vlad?' said Tel.

'*Da?*' said Vlad.

'*Fucking* calm down,' said Tel viciously.

Vlad unhooked himself from the overhead handle, sat squarely in his seat, his horrible hands folded in his lap. The outline of his head appeared enormous, as if electronic impulses might take days to trek across it.

'Does he understand any English?'

'It's more the tone,' said Tel.

Lomax sent a cryptic text to Darren: 'The angel is with us, we seek only to please the Lord.' He sat back, absent-mindedly stroking Amy's neck. He appeared calm but was nervous at what he'd left behind in the Andover Estate. Alice convulsing on the bed had brought back some horrors. Now he was replaying the scene in his head, trying to remember what he'd touched.

The phone rang in the girl's pocket and he dug it out, looked at the screen: 'Josh'. He let it ring out, turned it off.

Tel reached the City on the New North Road, doing as he was told by Lomax, driving like his old nan. It was quiet at this time of night so he cracked on straight through the middle: Moorgate, London Wall, Bishopsgate and over London Bridge. In ten minutes they were outside the barred gates on Neckinger. Lomax gave Vlad the keys. He unlocked the padlock, unthreaded the chain, opened the gates and Tel drove into the yard. Vlad re-padlocked the gates and unlocked the big warehouse doors. Tel reversed in and shut off the engine. Vlad pulled the doors to.

They got the girl out of the car, Tel on the legs while Vlad tucked her shoulders under one arm. They followed Lomax to the far end of the warehouse, where he unlocked a door that led into a narrow alleyway at the back of the derelict estate. Along the alley were some steps off to the right. Lomax went down them and opened the door to a basement storage area consisting of six windowless rooms off a central corridor.

Dennis Chilcott had bought the estate in 2004, and it was a testament to the complexities of local government planning regulations that nothing had happened to it in eight years, apart from further degradation.

To the Chilcotts' gang members these basement rooms had become known as Abu Ghraib, after the Iraqi prison abuse by the US military came to light. The debtors and recalcitrants they brought here wished never to return. Two of the rooms had been soundproofed so that their screams did not disturb the neighbours.

The room they entered contained the now infamous metal bed known as the Griddle because it could be plugged into the wall.

Lomax unrolled a piece of foam rubber lying in a corner and laid it over the chain-link base of the bed. Tel and Vlad dropped the girl on it.

'Dead to the world that one,' said Tel. 'What's she on?'

'GHB,' said Lomax.

'So we could give her one and she wouldn't know anything about it?'

'But *I* would,' said Lomax. 'And I'd have to tell Darren, and he'd have you riding the Griddle for a week, so don't even think about it.'

'Now what?'

'You go back to the warehouse, take my car out, park it legally in the street and give me the keys. By then I'll have her sorted out and I'll see you off the premises.'

'What about our money?'

'You'll get that too.'

They left. Lomax put Amy into the recovery position and went to check the other rooms. He found an ugly collection of tools: pickaxe handles, pliers, mallets, claw hammers, rolls of electrical wire, duct tape, meat hooks, lengths of frayed cable. He shuddered at it all. A box contained plastic cuffs, sleeping masks, hoods and gaffer tape.

Back with Amy, he put a sleeping mask over her eyes and cuffed her wrists and ankles to the four corners of the bed. He checked her breathing, obsessed with it.

Jesús was telling El Osito how carefully he'd planned the operation to capture David Álvarez in the Kapital nightclub. El Osito was listening patiently on the assumption that it had been successful, and Jesús was spinning it out in the hope of getting a medal. It was only as Jesús reported that, as he was moving from floor to floor, the fire alarm had gone off and the whole club had been evacuated that El Osito's face changed to the sick colour of a storm-laden sky. Jaime stepped in to divert attention from his brother.

'You know what this means?' said Jaime, drawing El Osito's psychopathic glare from Jesús.

'Tell me,' said El Osito, as if this was going to be a miraculous revelation.

'Álvarez was warned,' said Jaime.

'But we were the only people to know about the operation,' said El Osito.

'What about Charles Boxer?' said Jaime. 'He's the only possible connection.'

'You *have* to find that DJ,' said El Osito. 'You have to find out where he lives, or his girlfriend, or his parents. You have to find him.'

'I don't think so,' said Jaime. 'We'll have to take some defensive action in case the DJ goes to the police and tells them you were seen with the girl in the Charada. There'll be some awkward questions and they'll want to see your apartment.'

'So what are you suggesting?'

El Osito's mobile signalled a message. He read the text from Dennis.

'They've got the girl in London,' he said. 'Charles Boxer's daughter.'

'Then that is how we deal with this situation,' said Jaime. 'We tell Charles Boxer we're holding his daughter and that he must warn Álvarez not to talk to the police. In the meantime we have to get you out of Madrid as quickly as possible. We have to clear your flat, remove all the weights and sterilise the place.'

'I will go to London,' said El Osito. 'Book me on the first flight out of here. You will come with me, Jaime. Jesús will stay here and sort out this mess.'

'How are you going to talk to Charles Boxer?' asked Jesús, trying to salvage some respect.

'Let's hope his daughter knows his mobile number,' said Jaime. 'You'd better ask Dennis to get that as quickly as possible. Jesús, you come with me.'

The Mexicans left the room, pounded down the clinic's sterilised corridors.

'What are you doing?' asked Jesús.

'Getting you out of there before he has you killed,' said Jaime. 'Now you go to the flat and clean it out. Everything. Clothes, the lot. I don't want a trace of El Osito in there.'

278

'That's it?'

'I'll speak to Vicente.'

'I talked to the two girls,' said Tony, who was calling Boxer from outside the club Sy-Lo. 'They were *with* Amy on Saturday night. One of them even had a shot on her phone of her friend and Amy dancing together. I'll send it. You might not recognise her. She's had all her hair cut off.'

'Had they ever seen her with someone who looked like her when she had long hair?' asked Boxer.

'Yeah. They called them the twins. Said it was a bit freaky. They had the same hair and had it highlighted blonde in the exact same way. They even wore each other's clothes. But they also said that if they were twins they were not born from the same egg. Chantrelle was really wild, into drugs in a big way.'

'Is that her name? Chanterelle? Like the mushroom?'

'Like the mushroom?' said Tony.

Education, thought Boxer. Kids know everything and nothing these days. He asked Tony to spell the name out.

'And a surname?'

'No surname. That's not how people introduce themselves. It's not a job interview.'

'I need a surname and an address, Tony.'

'They said she lived in social housing somewhere off the Holloway Road. Her mother was a crack head and her father a crack dealer, and Chantrelle had been in and out of care before the council set her up in her own flat.'

'That's great, Tony, but I need you to keep working at it,' said Boxer. 'Those girls must know other people who knew Amy and Chantrelle. I have to have a surname and an address. It's critical now. I have to move as fast as possible.'

There was no signal in the basement so every half-hour Lomax had to go outside to check his messages. The last one had been from Darren: 'We need her dad's mobile number like *now*!'

Lomax called him. 'She's still out,' he said. 'Will be for another hour or more. I gave her GHB, tried not to give her too much, but you know how it is, not an exact science when you're trying to spike a girl's drink before she comes through the door.'

'She got a phone with her?'

'Sure.'

'Go through the contacts list and see if there's a Charles Boxer.'

'You think I'm an idiot, Darren?' said Lomax. 'I've been through it already. There's no Charles and no Dad. The only Boxer in her list is called Esme. Two numbers – one mobile, one fixed.'

'Esme?' said Darren. 'Does that sound like a black woman's name?'

'Could be. It sounds old-fashioned,' said Lomax.

'Do you think Esme is the girl's mother?'

'Well, Darren, she's got the same surname so she'll have a better chance of knowing where Charles Boxer is than anybody else you know.'

'Thanks for pointing that out, Miles,' said Darren. 'How are you getting on finding that twenty-eight grand you owe me? Now text me the fucking numbers.'

'You might want a photo of the girl too. Show that we've got her.'

'Yeah, do that 'n' all.'

'The only problem is I don't have today's newspaper.'

'What the fuck?'

'Traditionally, Darren, you show a photo of the hostage with the day's newspaper, so they know it's not some shot taken after a party three years ago.'

'You always knew too much for your own good, Miles.'

Tony again.

'Now I *have* got lucky,' he said. 'I went back into Sy-Lo and those two girls had tracked down someone who actually knows Chantrelle. From school. Her name is Chantrelle Taleisha Grant. She lives at 10 Hornsey Street, not far from the Emirates Stadium. Flat 203. Her mother, Alice, is the crack head. This girl's never met her but she knows she doesn't live far away on the Andover Estate, but no address.'

'Good work, Tony.'

'She's even sent me a photo of Chantrelle with Amy taken about three weeks ago.'

'She knew Amy as well?'

'They spent a couple of evenings together, that's all.'

'Send me the shot.'

Boxer hung up, waited for the message, looked at the shot of the two girls. They weren't so similar that he couldn't tell which was Amy, but he could see, smiling as they were under their great swags of hair, how they could be confused in a quick passport check late at night at Barajas Airport.

He sent a text to Mercy with all the information Tony had gathered. Told her this was urgent, first-thing-in-the-morning stuff, that he'd go to Chantrelle's flat, but it would be a good idea to have her mother's address too. Amy would probably know them both, and when Chantrelle didn't return with her passport, would have started to get worried. He sent the photo too, and the other shot the girls had taken on Saturday night of Amy with all her hair cut off and sown in corn rows.

Mercy bought some beer and wine to drink with the goat curry and jerk chicken she'd just picked up from the Blessed West Indian Takeaway on Coldharbour Lane, which in her mind no longer seemed to be a place of last resort.

They'd eaten the meal, and Alleyne had started to roll a joint, and she'd asked him to hold back while she told him the full story. He sat with his hands resting on his thighs listening, not saying a word. She could tell her story was having a profound effect on him, not only because of its disturbing content but also because, for the first time, she was being intimate with him. At the end of it he reached across the table and held her hand and for the first time she was drawn to him, not physically, but for his silent empathy.

He didn't roll the joint. They drank the wine, went to bed and made love. It was different. He was tender. He held her to his chest as they fell asleep. The messaging signal woke her.

She rolled over and read the message from Boxer, looked at the photo. She rubbed her thumb over Amy's face. She'd been missing her so badly since this afternoon's news. She needed to hold her, wanted to show Amy how much she was loved. Then she could go off and do what the hell she liked.

The murdered girl also smiled from the screen. What a waste. Mercy couldn't help but feel angry at her daughter's stupid determination to prove herself.

'What's up?' asked Alleyne, still drugged with sleep.

Mercy showed him the picture.

'This the other girl?' he asked.

'Chantrelle Grant,' said Mercy.

'That's a very sad thing,' said Alleyne, 'which is why you shouldn't pick up messages in the night.'

He dropped it on the floor, pulled Mercy to him.

Boxer hadn't moved. He was still on the sofa in Esme's darkened sitting room. All he'd done was shift himself into the lying position with a couple of cushions under his head, his mobile on his chest. He'd gone looking for whisky, but Esme was a Grey Goose girl. So he was lying there, sober, and thinking that only two things needed to happen to put his world back into kilter. He needed Amy here, with him, in the room. And he wanted to know what had happened to David Álvarez. If they had got to Álvarez it would tell him something. It would tell him that El Osito was hard at work closing down all possible openings. It would put pressure on the London end of things.

He started as his mobile let out a message signal. He tilted the screen towards his face. David Álvarez: 'I got out. It was close. Am in a cheap hotel. I leave on the first bus in the morning. Thanks.'

'It was close' did not make him rest any easier. He toyed with the idea of asking Álvarez to do one more thing for him: talk to Inspector Jefe Luís Zorrita. Tell him, anonymously, everything he knew about El Osito. Forensics would go into that flat, and even if they'd cleared out all the weights they would never be able to totally remove the evidence of the dismemberment. Was that too much to ask of him? That tweet Álvarez had answered must have been the biggest regret of his life.

The fixed-line phone rang in the other room. He rolled off the sofa and lurched into his mother's office, threw himself into the chair, picked up the phone.

'Hello,' he said.

Silence. He knew someone was there.

'Talk to me,' he said.

'I want to speak to Charles Boxer,' said the voice, a Londoner.

'That's me. Who are you?'

'We'll get to that in a minute. How do I know you're Charles Boxer?'

'You were the one who called this number.'

'I was expecting to speak to Esme.'

'That's my mother – she lives here, but she's in hospital.'

'I'm going to ask you some questions just to make sure I'm talking to the right person.'

'You're going to have to tell me who you are first or I don't answer anything.'

'If you answer the questions correctly you'll know who I am,' said the voice. 'Where were you on Tuesday night?'

'Madrid.'

'Which room did you take at the Hotel Moderno?'

That question made him go very still.

'Room 407.'

'You took 407 because your daughter, Amy, had used that same room,' said the voice. 'What were you doing in Madrid?'

'I was trying to find her. She'd run away from home.'

'You were contacted by a homicide detective called Luís Zorrita. What did he tell you?'

'That a body part had been found with some clothes and my daughter's passport.'

'And you assumed she'd been murdered.'

'That's right.'

'And you thought you knew who'd killed her,' said the voice. 'How was that?'

'Because somebody told me.'

'Was that somebody called David Álvarez?'

Boxer hesitated. But Álvarez was safe now.

'Yes. He told me he'd seen her on Saturday night with a man who had a reputation for violence against women.'

'And what was his name?'

'I only know him as El Osito.'

'You've done very well, Mr Boxer, and I think you know who we are now.'

'Not really.'

'But you know you're talking to the right people.'

'If that's how you want to put it.'

'So how did you find out your daughter wasn't dead?'

'The DNA from the body part didn't match mine or her mother's.'

'So whose body was it?'

'I don't know,' said Boxer, thinking carefully now. 'The last time I spoke to the detective was about the DNA results. We haven't spoken since then. No reason to.'

'Keep it like that,' said the Londoner. 'You'd better give us your mobile number.'

'Why?'

'We're going to be in touch.'

'About what?'

'You're going to tell David Álvarez not to go to the police,' said the voice. 'That if he goes anywhere near the police we will hunt him down, but only after we've dealt with his mum and dad and two sisters. You got that?'

'I understand what you're saying. I'm just not quite sure what's in it for me?'

'The other thing is *you* don't talk to the police either. Not in Madrid and not in London. Right?'

'Like I said, I've got a good understanding of English. I'm just not quite sure why the *fuck* I should listen to you.'

'I was waiting for that,' said the voice. 'See a bit of your anger. El Osito said you were the angriest man he'd ever seen outside Mexico.'

'Angry?'

'Yeah. I think that's what he must have seen before you smashed his legs to pieces.'

'I'm sure, in my place, you'd have done exactly the same thing to your daughter's murderer.'

'Because you couldn't fuck her any more?'

'What?' said Boxer, incredulous. 'Now that's the first thing you've said that doesn't make any sense. Did El Osito feed you that line?'

Silence.

'Why did she run away from home?' asked the Londoner.

'She lives with her mother. It hasn't been going well between them for quite some time.'

'All right. You know what we're going to do?' said the voice. 'We're going to ask Amy ... just as soon as she comes round.'

The fear sliced through him but his professionalism held firm.

'You'll have to do better than that if you want me to believe you.'

'That's why we need your mobile number,' said the voice. 'Can't send pictures down these lines, can you?'

He gave it to him. A few moments later he heard the message signal and opened the photo of Amy. Her hair in corn rows confirmed that it was recent. He couldn't believe they'd got to her so quickly.

'How did you find her?' he said, thinking out loud, rather than asking a serious question.

'Superior intelligence,' said the Londoner, back on the phone again. 'Now you understand why you're going to contact David Álvarez and tell him to keep his mouth shut. And why you're going to promise, on your daughter's life, that you are not going to go to the Met in any way, shape or form. Not even to the girl's mother. Right? If you do go to the Met and they track us down, the one thing I can assure you is that, whatever happens, if we're all surrounded and there's no way out, your daughter will not survive.'

'So what do you want for her safe return?'

'You.'

26

Amy came to. A strange awakening into the dark. The first thing was the smell. Whatever she was lying on had the stink of rancid human about it, a sharp penetrating odour that touched off some atavistic alarm. The next thing was that she couldn't move her arms or feet. She was lying on her back. Her wrists and ankles had been secured to the four corners of the bed. Panic fluttered in her throat. Her head felt as if it had been split in two and inexpertly put back together with low-grade glue. She felt nauseous and dizzy. She couldn't seem to think straight for longer than two seconds and had no memory, certainly no memory of how she'd ended up in this strange state. And she had to go to the toilet.

'Morning. Thought you were never going to come round.'

The voice made her start, which had a terrible effect on her head, a blinding light followed by searing pain, as if someone had driven a screwdriver into her left eye socket and out through the back of her skull. She moaned against it, thought she was going to be sick. She squeezed her muscles together to stop from peeing herself.

'Best thing is you lie still. If you have to move, move very slowly as if your whole body is made from the finest Chinese porcelain. All right?'

'OK.'

'There's no need to be frightened.'

'There isn't?'

'Nobody's going to hurt you,' said Lomax. 'I'm not going to hurt you and I'm the only one here at the moment.'

'What happened?'

'You were drunk and drugged and you passed out. I brought you here.'

'Where is here?'

'Somewhere in London.'

'That's ... precise,' she said, having to work hard to find that word.

'It's the best I can do.'

'I don't remember what happened.'

'That's normal.'

'So what am I doing here?'

'You've been kidnapped.'

She blinked behind her mask, trying to think why she should have been kidnapped. Was she a rich man's daughter? No.

'Why?' she asked.

'Can't tell you. I've got no idea. I was just told to bring you here.'

'I've got to go to the toilet.'

'Bloody hell,' said Lomax.

'It's just a pee.'

'There are no facilities.'

'I have to go.'

'Hold on,' he said and left the room.

There was nothing in the tool room, he knew that. He checked the other rooms. All empty except the last one, which had two big bottles of water, a half roll of toilet paper and a bucket.

How the hell was he going to do this? He needed Tel and Vlad for this game. Should have kept them on. Then again they were a liability. Too thick and too desperate.

He picked up the bucket and loo roll, went back to the room. He jammed the bucket in the corner, put the loo roll on the floor. He made sure the main door to the basement was locked. From the tool room he took some gaffer tape, some new plastic cuffs and a pickaxe handle.

Kneeling on the bed, he wrapped the gaffer tape around her head securing the sleeping mask to her face. He didn't want her seeing him because now she *would* remember and blindfolded he'd have the advantage if she tried anything.

He told her how it was going to be. Then he touched her on the head with the pickaxe handle.

'Any trouble and I'll brain you.'

'I just want to go for a pee, for Christ's sake.'

'That's what they all say.'

He cut the leg cuffs and then freed her wrists. He told her to sit up slowly and stand. She sat on the edge of the bed, but struggled to stand. He had to help her to her feet. She was still all over the shop from the drug and disorientated by never having seen the room. He put her hand on the wall and told her there was a bucket in the corner. When she got there he put the loo roll in her hand.

'Do it.'

'With you here … watching?' she said.

'You'll get used to it and I've seen it all before. I'm no perve.'

She dropped her jeans and pants, slid down the wall to the bucket, peed. She was still groggy, her legs weak and her head pounding, but her thinking went on for a bit longer before breaking up. She knew what she had to do, remembered it from all those endless boring conversations between her parents about kidnap victims and the best way to behave.

Disparate things came back to her. Long-buried words of advice. Her father holding her by the shoulders, looking into her eyes before a judo fight. Telling her before she went onto the mat: look at your opponent, learn about her, how she sits beforehand, how she walks, how she bows. It's all telling you something. Everything helps you decide what you're going to do.

Lomax watched her like a hawk, the pickaxe handle in both hands, feeling ridiculous hovering over her. She tried to stand up, couldn't make it.

'You're going to have to help me. My legs don't work properly.'

He leaned the pickaxe handle against the wall, stood in front of her, hooked his hands under her armpits and pulled her up to her feet. She yanked her jeans up as she stood and leaned into him. He held her by the shoulders and eased her down onto the bed. She was still in poor shape. He got her to lie down, legs together, cuffed them again and secured them to the bed.

288

'Do you have to tie my wrists?'

'For the moment.'

She put a wrist to each corner. He cuffed them and stood back. She knew now that he was definitely operating alone and there could be opportunities when she was feeling stronger and needed to go to the toilet again. Mercy's words came to her: gather your information gradually; don't try to rush it – people will be suspicious. Everything you do should have the aim of improving your situation, your physical and mental state.

Where did that come from? Was it a seminar she was about to give? Something else: make your captor care for you. The more they care the less likely they are to hurt you.

'I'm thirsty,' she said.

He picked up the bucket, left the room. She listened. He didn't go far. He was back in a moment. He cradled her head in one hand. She felt the rim of the bottle on her lips, drank the water down, thanked him. He pulled up a chair, sat by the bed.

'There's no need to be scared,' he said.

She wasn't. She had been scared when she first woke up, but now she knew a little she was more solid. She felt sick and weak but that was the drug. Something else had kicked in.

'I'm going to ask you some questions. I want you to tell me the truth. It's very easy to check your answers, and if we find you've been lying you'll be punished. And you don't want to find out what those punishments are.'

The questions were about her parents: their names, where they lived, what they did. She could sense his interest when she told him about her father. She embellished it by saying how much time he spent out of the country, all the jobs he'd done in South and Central America, Pakistan and the Far East. How she didn't see much of him. She was aware of making it sound as if she was telling him a lot but she was withholding as much as she could. It was more difficult with Mercy.

'She's a copper?' said Lomax.

'Yeah, I know,' said Amy, empathising.

'What sort of copper?'

'A detective inspector.'

'Fuck me.'

'She's tough too. Made me stand to attention by my bed before lights out.'

'Get away.'

'That's why I ran away from home.'

'Is it? I thought it was because your father was messing about with you.'

'Messing about?'

'Sex. Fucking you. Incest.'

'Are you soaked or what?'

'That's what it says here. "Did her dad force himself on her?"'

'Who's asking these stupid questions?'

'Fuck knows, but did he?'

'No way,' she said, disgusted at the idea of it. 'I lived with my mother. I told you, my father was never around. In my whole life I've probably only spent about three nights at his place. So I've no idea when this was supposed to have happened.'

'So you ran away from home because your mum was giving you a hard time?'

'I was bored,' said Amy because what he'd said sounded too pathetic. 'I was bored by school, bored by rules, bored by the future.'

'Yeah,' said Lomax, as if this was obvious. 'It's like that for everybody, but you only run away if somebody's sticking it to you: beating you up or sexually abusing you. Otherwise you just get on with it. It's part of the job of being a kid.'

Nobody had ever put it to her like that.

'Everybody thinks it must be great to be in a band, for example,' said Lomax. 'But it's just another job, except the job is to sing in front of large crowds of screaming people. But it's still work. They live in shit accommodation, eat crap food, travel all day, work all night and take drugs to keep going. I know. I supplied the drugs.'

'So what's it like being a drug dealer?'

'Long hours. You take a lot of crap from all sides,' he said. 'Your suppliers want you to sell more, the customers don't want to pay. You've got to keep your runners in line or they'll cheat your arse. It's dangerous ... from the cops and other gangs, even your *own* gang sometimes.'

'And the good things?'

'You make money,' said Lomax. 'You don't have to get up in the morning and go to an office. That's about it. It's like any job. A lot of shit for some financial reward.'

'Is that why you moved into kidnapping?'

'Good to hear your voice, David,' said Boxer.

'I'd like to be able to say the same,' said Álvarez.

'I'm sorry,' said Boxer. 'I've just got one more thing to ask of you.'

'Whatever it is, the answer is no.'

'You mustn't go to the police,' said Boxer. 'That's all I'm asking.'

'You think I'd go to the police after what I've been through?'

'Some people might.'

'I'm finished with it. I'm not going to talk to anybody about it. I know this is El Osito.'

'That's good, because they told me if you did, they'd come after you but only once they'd dealt with your parents and your two sisters.'

'They said *that* to you?' said Álvarez. 'My two sisters? How do they know about them? They don't even live in Madrid.'

'That's what they told me.'

Silence.

'They've got something on you, haven't they?' said Álvarez. 'You wouldn't be talking to me unless they'd scared you into it. What do these *cabrones* want now?'

'It's OK, David. They're getting what they want. You just have to forget everything now. I mean it. Forget I ever came into your life. Don't talk to anyone about this. You break that and they'll kill you and your family.'

'I'm feeling bad now.'

'Don't. You did a very fine thing. You sent a girl a note to warn her. A lot of other people wouldn't have dared to do even that. You do anything else and it'll turn out very badly for you and for me. So promise me.'

'OK, I promise you.'

Boxer hung up, took a deep breath. That had been harder than he was expecting. He called the number he'd been given, told them that he'd guaranteed Álvarez's silence.

'So you're a kidnap consultant?' said the voice. 'This'll be a first for you, to be the ransom in your own negotiation. Got a nice little something to it, hasn't it?'

'Irony?'

'Yeah, maybe that's the word,' said the voice. 'We done a bit more research on you now that Amy's given us the basics. Bit of a poker player, aren't you?'

'It has been known.'

'Now look. We've incurred some expenses having to deal with your bloody nonsense. So when you hand yourself in we want you to bring a hundred grand with you. Pounds. That should cover it.'

'I can lay my hands on twenty grand today. The rest will take until next week, and that's if the bank'll let me remortgage.'

'I know poker players, and they've always got funds for a game,' said the voice. 'It's what they live for.'

'You'll be talking about really good poker players who don't blow their winnings on the horses.'

'Bring fifty and we won't say anything more about it.'

'Like I said, I can bring you twenty today. The other thirty will take some time. I could probably raise that by Saturday evening.'

'Bring thirty and don't give me any more shit.'

'I'll see what I can do,' said Boxer. 'Let's just get this straight now: I'm the ransom, plus thirty grand?'

'You've got it.'

'So I hand myself in with the money and you will release my daughter?'

'That's it in one.'

'Tell me how that's going to work.'

'We'll think of a way to pick you up some time later this afternoon, and as soon as we've got you in hand we'll release the girl.'

'My problem is not with you. It's with El Osito. What guarantee do I have that you'll release her?'

'*I'll* guarantee that. I'll make sure she's with me when you hand yourself in. I'll be the one who releases her.'

'What time is it?' asked Amy.

'Six thirty.'

'What day are we on?'

'Friday.'

'How long will you keep me here?'

'I don't know.'

'What's the ransom going to be?'

'Don't know that either.'

'So you're doing this for somebody else?'

'I don't like it, but I have to.'

'Why?'

'I owe them money.'

'And you sell drugs for these people?'

'Yep,' said Lomax. 'Which is why I do as I'm told and there's no argument.'

'And they'll cancel your debt in return – is that it?'

'I doubt it.'

'Why not?'

'Because it's twenty-eight grand and I was reminded of that fact tonight when I told them I'd got you,' said Lomax. 'The best I can hope for is they'll cancel the vig.'

'The vig?'

'The vigorish.'

'Still don't know what you're on about.'

'They don't teach anything at school these days,' said Lomax, lamenting. 'It's Yiddish, probably Russian originally.'

'My boyfriend's a Russian Jew.'

'Is that Josh?'

'How do you know his name?'

'He called you,' said Lomax. 'I didn't take it. Didn't want him getting jealous.'

Silence. It made her a bit sad that he probably wouldn't get jealous.

'Why didn't you bring Josh with you last night?' asked Lomax, thinking that would have been awkward.

'He wasn't there,' said Amy. 'He likes to go out.'

'On his own?'

'Tell me about the vigorish,' she said, almost childlike, squirming into the mattress, wanting to be told a story.

'It used to be the percentage taken from a gambler's winnings

293

by the people who'd set up the game,' said Lomax. 'Now it just means a fucking excessive rate of interest. I call it the invigorator.'

'Like how much is it?'

'Two per cent.'

'That doesn't sound too bad.'

'A day?' said Lomax. 'Five hundred and sixty quid *a day*.'

'So your debt doubles every two months?'

'Thanks for reminding me,' said Lomax. 'And that's if you *pay* the vig. If you don't, you get *compound* vig, and I don't want to talk about that.'

'Why don't you just ... run away.'

'That's your solution to everything,' said Lomax. 'You don't know these people. They've got reach.'

'Well, I wasn't suggesting you just ran away to Cardiff.'

'Cardiff? I wouldn't go to Cardiff if you paid me,' said Lomax. 'Maybe Cardiff's not such a bad idea. They'd never look for me in Cardiff.'

'I meant Argentina, somewhere like that.'

'And one day I'd be trudging up the stairs to my shitty little apartment in Buenos Aires, and I'd fit the key into the lock and *thuff*,' said Lomax, putting his fingers to her head. 'The last thing I'd see is my brains all over the door I was just trying to open.'

'You've got far too much imagination.'

'And I don't speak Spanish ... apart from: *Yo tengo un lapiz castaño*.'

'I've got a brown pencil?' said Amy. 'Is that supposed to be dirty?'

'No. It's all I remember from my Spanish classes at school.'

'I can tell you're educated.'

'Not in languages.'

'So you went to uni.'

'A lifetime ago.'

'What did you do?'

'History,' said Lomax. 'And like every politician in the world I learned nothing from it. I went in there with a scholarship. I got a first in my first-year exams. Then I discovered drugs. Here I am. A success story. You?'

'I'm not going,' she said. 'Can I have some more water?'

He knelt down, cradled her head again, let her drink to the end of the bottle.

'I'm hungry,' she said.

'Live with it. There's nothing until I'm relieved.'

'When's that?'

'Fuck knows.'

'What sort of a blind date *is* this?'

He laughed. He liked her. Even fancied her a bit. Pity she was so young.

'What are you thinking?'

'Nothing.'

'Liar.'

'I was thinking you're all right, if you have to know.'

'Is that one of your more successful chat-up lines?'

'I have to admit that one's been around the block a few times.'

'So you haven't got a girlfriend?'

'It's one of the drawbacks of being a coke dealer.'

'Why?'

'You suddenly find there are lots of girls who want to go to bed with you but ... it's not because of your gorgeous looks and scintil-lating conversation,' said Lomax. 'And there's nothing worse than spending your life with a coke head. They think they're brilliant, entertaining and wonderful, whereas ... they're dull, repetitive and complete whores.'

'Is that bitter experience talking?'

'How old are you?'

'Seventeen.'

'Jesus.'

'What?'

'You're a child,' said Lomax. 'I'm thirty-two.'

'Then fuck off, Pops,' she said.

They both laughed.

'You know what?' said Amy. 'I've got to go to the toilet again.'

'You're drinking too much.'

'It must be something to do with whatever you gave me.'

'GHB.'

'Did you tell me that before?'

'I don't think so.'

'Where was I?'

'Can't say.'

'Who was I with?'

'You were on your own.'

She didn't remember a thing about it.

'Get the bucket,' she said.

He played it the same way: checked the door to the basement, put the bucket in the corner, pickaxe handle against the wall, cut the cuffs around her ankles and wrists, told her to sit up slowly and tapped her on the head with the pickaxe handle.

She was feeling a lot better, but sat up very gingerly.

'Christ,' she said. 'How much GHB did you give me?'

'A squirt,' he said, thinking about Alice convulsing, wiping it from his mind. 'Probably too much.'

'I still feel like shit.'

'OK, stand up, put your right hand out to the wall.'

She stood as if she was still very shaky and worked her way along the wall until her foot hit the bucket. She gave a little swoon.

'You OK?' he asked.

'Dizzy, that's all.'

She straddled the bucket, undid her jeans, pulled them down, squatted. She peed lengthily.

'What are you doing?' she asked.

'I'm standing here with a pickaxe handle in my hands.'

She tried to push up with her legs, but collapsed back onto the bucket.

'You're going to have to help me again,' she said. 'My legs won't work properly. Is that normal?'

'GHB affects motor coordination,' said Lomax, leaning the pickaxe handle against the wall. This time she put out her hands. He took them in his and she lunged forward and drove her head into his solar plexus. She heard the wind shoot out of him as she rammed him back onto the bed and pulled up her jeans. He fell back, cracking his head against the wall.

Amy tore at the tape and mask over her face, pushed it all up to her forehead, saw Lomax slumped on the bed, reached for the pickaxe handle but could see that he was already out.

She ripped open the door, ran down the corridor, wrenched

at the door to the basement, realised it was locked. Pulled at it again. It was solid. She ran back to the room, saw him still out on the bed, knew he must have the keys, saw them sticking up in his pocket on his thigh. She picked up the pickaxe handle and walked towards him very slowly. His face was slack. His eyes quivered a little under his lids. She put the pickaxe handle down and rammed her hand into his trouser pocket.

27

Boxer couldn't sleep. He was walking down Rosslyn Hill to the Royal Free Hospital with his holdall. There were people he was going to have to see today. People he had to say goodbye to without saying goodbye. And he had to go to his flat and pick up the money.

He'd thought it through. The obvious thing was to tell Mercy what had happened, but she, unlike him, was not a lone operator. She worked within a team. It would be impossible for her to act without alerting the rest of the kidnap unit to Amy's situation. Once they knew about it, Mercy would lose control. She would not be allowed to act in the case of a family member as it would compromise her decision-making. She would become the victim's mother and be kept at a distance from the negotiations. Amy's survival would be in the hands of others. If there was any suspicion of police involvement it would mean the end for Amy. El Osito had effectively killed her once and he'd have no problem killing her again.

The safest solution, as Boxer saw it, was to hand himself in to the kidnappers. The Londoner he'd been speaking to knew this was between El Osito and himself. There was no such thing as a guarantee in that criminal world. Even in a normal kidnap there was always a moment when the gang had everything: the hostage and the money. Only the relationship built through the negotiation process could guarantee a safe passage for the hostage. Boxer had taken the decision, based on his conversations with the Londoner, that he could trust him to release Amy. In fact, if anything, he'd sensed in him a distrust of El Osito over the incest allegations, that the Londoner now felt he'd been played. It meant that Boxer could rely on him to make sure Amy was safe and gave him greater confidence in this scenario than one with the kidnap unit's involvement. There were the same unknowns in both, but should El Osito discover police involvement there was the absolute certainty that it would be all over for Amy. The only thing that mattered to Boxer was her survival.

He found his way to the ICU and spoke to the nurse. Esme was comfortable. All vital signs were normal. She'd responded to and spoken to the consultant last night and was sleeping well. They were due to wake her to give her some breakfast.

Boxer went in, sat down by the bed and held her hand.

'Is that you, Charlie?' she said to the ceiling, eyes still closed.

'It's me,' he said and leaned over her.

She opened her eyes, nodded at him.

'What are you doing here?'

'I came to see me old mum,' he said.

'Not that old, mate,' she said. 'Have you found Amy yet?'

'I'm getting there,' he said. 'I'm hoping that by the end of today she'll be back. She hasn't made it easy for us.'

'It's my fault, you know … this whole thing,' said Esme.

'I doubt it,' said Boxer. 'Something like this had been brewing for a long time.'

'She'd been driving me crazy all that week she stayed with me while you and Mercy were working, going on and on about how unhappy she was at home. Mercy does this, Mercy did that, Mercy never does the other. And one night I just cracked, told her if she felt that strongly she should just get out. Run away. You'd done it. Mercy had done it. Why shouldn't she do it?'

'She'd been planning it for longer than that.'

'Yes, you're right,' said Esme. 'But she was looking for my approval. She knew I adored her and she wanted my blessing. I didn't want to give it. I didn't think it would solve anything. I just thought it was a matter of time. But she drove me into a corner and forced my hand.'

'She's good at that. She does it to Mercy all the time.'

'I tried to withdraw what I'd said, but I could see her mind was made up so I made her promise that whatever happened she would always keep in touch with me. I told her then that I couldn't bear to lose her. So when you called that night from Madrid and told me she'd been killed on her first night of freedom, I thought ... I took full responsibility for it.'

'I didn't know the two of you were so close.'

'Mercy knew and she couldn't stand it. Hated me for it. I couldn't resist it, Charlie. It's been the only thing that's kept me going all these years. I never expected it. It just came out of the blue. I saw her as a baby, looked into her eyes and thought, you're mine.'

'You never told me and Mercy never let on.'

'It's been a silent battle with Mercy. I've had to play a careful game to make sure I could keep seeing Amy, especially when her Ghanaian family came over. I thought Mercy might turn off the tap at any moment.'

'Mercy's hard, you know, but not cruel,' said Boxer. 'And she's not that hard either. It's just something she keeps in place for old times' sake.'

'You'll have to tell her,' said Esme. 'You'll have to tell her and I'll have to pray she'll let me back.'

'Why don't *you* tell her?'

Amy ripped open Lomax's pocket, jammed her hand in and yanked out the keys. Her concentration was so intense she didn't even see it coming. At the last moment she flinched at the shadow in the corner of her eye. Her head kicked sideways and she felt something crack in her neck and the room turned over. Her cheek hit the floor and she had a millisecond's view of what life was like under the bed before she blacked out.

She couldn't have been out for long, but he already had her up on the bed, blindfolded with tape over another sleeping mask and cuffed to the four corners of the bed. Her face hurt on both sides. Her jaw felt huge; the inside of her cheek was ripped and there was the taste of metal in her mouth. She licked her lips.

'You're a *fucking* idiot,' he said. 'What you have to go and pull a stunt like that for? Was I hurting you? Was I scaring you? Fuck, no. I was being civilised, completely bloody civilised.'

'You call this civilised?' said Amy, screeching with fear now. 'Keeping me tied to the bed. Is that your idea of civilisation? I don't know what your game is or what the people you're doing this for have in mind. For all I know it might be gang rape and murder. Course I'm going to try to escape. I'd be an idiot not to. Or did you really think I was going to lie here nice and quiet until the real nutters turn up?'

'They're not nutters,' said Lomax, quietening. 'Well, one of them can be a bit, but only with idiots who try to fuck him over. Never with women. No, that's not true either. I've seen him slap some crack whores around the place. But that's all you can do with them. They're beyond seeing sense.'

'Listen to yourself,' said Amy. 'He sounds like the blind date from hell.'

'They're not unreasonable,' said Lomax. 'If I'd let a customer run up twenty-eight grand in credit with some of the other bastards out there I'd be hobbling around on no kneecaps.'

'Just think about it for two seconds,' said Amy. 'I'm not one of your crack whores. I don't snort coke. I've got nothing to do with your business. I'm not a buyer and I'm not a competitor.'

'So?'

'So what the hell am I doing here tied to the bed?' she said, roaring at him now, head off the pillow, terrified.

'Just calm the fuck down,' said Lomax.

'Tell me and I might,' she said.

'I don't know. I've asked them, and they just told me to mind my own business,' said Lomax. 'I'm only doing this because I have to. You think I get a kick out of kidnapping kids?'

'Don't call me a kid,' she said.

'You know why I'm really mad at you?'

'Mad at *me*?'

'You've just given me a huge bloody problem.'

'I'm crying for you now.'

'Up until five minutes ago I could have persuaded them that the GHB had taken out your whole memory of last night.'

'It has. I don't remember a thing.'

'But now you've seen my face, and because of the business I'm in, I've got to tell them that. And you know what that means for you?'

The shops were opening as Boxer walked back from the Royal Free to his flat. He'd bought some Jiffy bags. In his flat he lifted the painting of the Italian businessman off the wall and opened the safe. He counted out thirty thousand pounds and left the remainder of the currency in the safe, relocked it. He took the handgun out of the holdall and put it in its usual place under the floorboards in the kitchen.

He sat down and wrote two letters, one to Mercy, the other to Amy. He was surprised at how emotional he became as he set down words to the woman he'd known best in his life and the daughter he'd wished he'd known better. At one point he had to sit back from the table, take a break from it.

It had been a long time since he'd consciously examined himself to find true and unsentimental words. Before, he'd only ever become aware of his inner state as a result of some subconscious welling. When he'd thought that Amy was dead, the dark hole widened inside him, incomprehensible and beyond his control. He was driven by it. And yet now it had gone. No black hole. No hurt. In fact the opposite: a fullness. These two women were a part of him. Even that last conversation with his mother had contributed to this state. His self-sacrifice was bringing him back to the world. He was puzzled by it.

A preliminary examination of the head and neck by the coroner late last night had shown that Chantrelle Grant had probably not died from a blow to the skull nor been strangled; he would need to see the torso to give a definitive cause of death.

Zorrita was up early with the two diving teams. He'd had the sudden inspiration during the night to search north-east of the site where they'd found the girl's head, where the A3 motorway crossed the river before heading to Valencia.

In the light rain that was falling he re-examined the road map and reasoned that the bag would have been dumped on the west side of the motorway bridge. The bag, like all the others, would be weighted, so he had the two diving teams working their way towards each other.

Within the first hour they'd found the bin liner and brought it to the surface. It was big. Zorrita knew that the killer had decided to keep the torso intact to save himself from the horrific mess of innards everywhere. It was too big for any of their boxes, so they wrapped it in a plastic sheet and took it straight to the lab.

Mercy had assigned three people to help George Papadopoulos work the list of estate agents he'd been given by Olga. She couldn't resist following up Boxer's text request for Alice Grant's address from last night because it was their best chance of finding Amy. She'd asked the IT department to run a check on Alice Grant from the Andover Estate and they'd come back with a full address and a messy record of petty crime, drug possession and a marriage with a renowned crack dealer called Jevaughn Grant which had resulted in a daughter, Chantrelle Taleisha, born 22 January 1991.

It was 10.30 a.m. by the time she parked on the Andover Estate. It took some time to find Alice Grant's flat. She rang the doorbell, which did not appear to work. She hammered on the woodwork. No answer. She tried the neighbour, who came to the door in her dressing gown, bleached-blonde hair all over the place, and looked at her warrant card.

'Detective inspector?' she said, arms crossed under her bosom. 'A police constable was round here earlier asking after her. I told him, I know she's in there because she was having herself a little party last night. Music and stuff. And knowing her as I do, she doesn't get out of bed much before midday, so what with a bit of booze inside her—'

'What did the constable want?'

'I don't know. He said it was important, that he had to talk to her as soon as possible. I told him to go down to the estate office.'

'What will they do in there?'

'They've got her mobile number and, failing that, a master key.'

A mobile phone started ringing in the flat. It rang out and started ringing again.

'Dead to the world,' said the neighbour, eyebrows raised.

'How many people were at this party?'

'Just a few,' said the woman. 'Her front door was knocked on three times. I heard a male voice and a couple of women's voices. Bit of Amy Winehouse on the sound system. That's all I can tell you.'

A young police constable came from the lifts and stairwell area, followed by an older guy with a tagged set of keys. Mercy showed her warrant card, told them her business and that they'd heard the mobile ringing in the flat.

'We got a fax this morning from the British consulate in Madrid,' said the constable. 'It's not good news for her, I'm afraid.'

The door was open by now. The constable went in, calling Alice Grant's name. Mercy followed.

The kitchen was empty, as was the darkened living room. The standby light glowed on the sound system. The bedroom door was ajar but dark with light only at the edges of the blackout blinds.

The policeman continued to call her name and rapped at the bedroom door. He turned on the light.

'Oh Christ,' he said.

Mercy looked past him, saw Alice Grant lying on her back. Not far from her outflung arm was a green crack pipe. There were flecks of vomit on her face and down her front. The pallor of her face and stiffness of her body gave no doubt that Alice Grant was dead and had been for a number of hours.

'Don't touch anything,' said Mercy, backing away, pulling the constable with her. 'We need a homicide squad for this.'

Dennis and Darren Chilcott travelled on an easyJet flight out of Madrid to Gatwick, while Jaime and El Osito took British Airways business class to Heathrow. Jesús had stayed behind to clear El Osito's flat and scour the bathroom floor and the shower with hydrochloric acid before spraying bleach on everything to destroy any possibility of DNA testing.

El Osito was taken to the plane in a wheelchair. It wasn't a pain-free flight as business-class seats were no different to economy, but they were given a meal. He was in an ugly frame of mind when he arrived in London. A limousine took them to the Pestana Chelsea Bridge Hotel and Jaime arranged for a private doctor to visit with a shot of morphine. By midday El Osito was installed and asleep. Jaime fingered his mobile as he looked out over the railway tracks towards Battersea Power Station and sent a cryptic message to Vicente letting him know they'd arrived. The reply gave him a phone number to call. Soon after he left the hotel heading for a Colombian restaurant in the Elephant and Castle shopping centre.

The Chilcotts arrived at Gatwick a little after one o'clock. They took the train to Clapham Junction and from there a cab to Dennis's six-bedroomed house in Camberwell Grove. They dropped off their bags, picked up Dennis's Range Rover and drove to the warehouse on Neckinger.

'I can't believe the shit we're going through for this guy,' said Darren. 'Since we've met him we've spent about forty minutes discussing business and the rest of the time arm-wrestling, club-bing and now sorting out his girl problem. Are you sure Vicente's the right person to be doing business with?'

'He's the one supplier who's really taken on the problem of UK delivery,' said Dennis. 'You don't remember what it was like before. Going over to Mexico and buying half a ton here and half a ton there and then relying on some hare-brained public schoolboy to bring it over in Daddy's yacht. Those days are over and thank Christ for that. But now we're in the hands of an organisation there's politics and relationships to consider. Vicente needs the Colombians to supply him. They can switch to El Chapo in a blink. He has to keep them sweet. And that means you can't tell El Osito to get lost. We're just playing our part in maintaining the relationship and Vicente will remember us for that. This is how they work. Loyalty still counts for something in this world.'

'So what are you going to do?' asked Amy, now that they'd calmed down, taken a break from each other. 'You ever been in this position before?'

'What position?' said Lomax, irritable.

'Holding someone's life in the palm of your hand,' said Amy, who still couldn't quite believe what was happening.

Lomax looked at her. Blind and trussed, she'd become animal to him. He was distancing himself.

'It happens,' he said. 'Drug runners try to fuck me over. I spend my day weighing and checking purity so that they know not to take the piss. But there's always one. If the measures are out or the purity's dropped, I isolate the bastard. He gets dealt with. The boss sends a hitter round with a baseball bat. Bones get broken. Interfering fingers get crushed. You can't be seen as a soft touch in this game.'

'So how did you run up a twenty-eight-grand debt?'

'You know something?' said Lomax. 'You got to think before you speak. Kids and old people are the same. No filters. Something occurs to them and comes straight out with no thought attached.'

'But it's true, isn't it?'

'There you go again,' said Lomax. 'It's more important for you to be right than anything else. You have to prove your superiority. Well, here's your first lesson.'

He lashed her across the face with the back of his hand. The pain ricocheted around her head; tears sprang into her sleeping mask.

'What did you do that for?'

'Think about it.'

For the first time in years she thought, I want my mother.

'I know kids like you,' said Lomax. 'I used to be one myself until I had some sense knocked into me. Want me to talk you through it?'

Her mouth was crumpling. She was scared. She nodded.

'Why is it a bad idea to remind people of their mistakes?' he said.

'Because it makes them annoyed.'

'Yes, but why's that?'

'People don't want to be thought of as dumb.'

'Nearly,' said Lomax. 'You've just got to get the other half.'

'The other half?'

'You. You're the other half,' said Lomax. 'What gives you the right to tell me I'm stupid when you haven't got the first idea of the circumstances. So this is your first lesson in life: you haven't got a clue. Say it.'

'I haven't got a clue.'

'How do you get a clue?' asked Lomax. 'I'll tell you, because you'll never guess. You shut the fuck up. You find people who know what they're on about and listen to them. Shit. I don't know why I'm bothering.'

'Why are you?'

He knew the truth of it and it made him sad. He'd told her already, but she hadn't listened or maybe she had and hadn't believed it. He wasn't going to tell her again. She was a danger to him. She wasn't going to come out of this alive now. But Lomax, unlike Amy, had learned a few things in his time: don't tell anyone a truth they won't be able to take.

'I've never known anybody under the age of twenty able to listen,' said Lomax.

There was a knock at the door outside. Amy's body stiffened.

'What's that?'

'Your new blind date.'

28

Alice Grant's flat, Andover Estate, London

'There are only two glasses here,' said Mercy, pointing to the living-room table with a latex-gloved hand. 'Her next-door neighbour said there was a party and she heard three voices – two female, one male. There's a glass missing.'

'Unless one wasn't drinking,' said DI Max Hope from the homicide squad.

'There's no alcohol in the flat. There's no Coca-Cola in the flat. There are no Coke tins in the rubbish,' said Mercy, ignoring his comment. 'I think you'll find there's alcohol in the half-finished glass and something else.'

'Like what?'

'I don't think she would vomit from just smoking crack. She's ingested something with alcohol that's made her sick,' said Mercy. 'She had the music on, her neighbour said. You might want to check the remote for fingerprints, because I don't think it was Alice who turned it off.'

The forensics were in the room now that the police photographer had left. They were nodding along with her. The remote went into an evidence bag. The liquid from the glass went into a bottle, the dregs from the other glass too. The glasses found their way into bags as well.

'And what were you and the constable doing here?' asked Hope.

'I was hoping to trace my daughter, Amy, who's gone missing,' said Mercy. 'The constable was going to tell Alice that her daughter, Chantrelle, had been killed in Madrid. Amy and Chantrelle were friends. It's a long story, but I'd like you to compare any fingerprints you find in this flat to these.'

She gave Hope the card with Amy's prints on that she'd lifted from the mirror in her room the night she'd disappeared.

'You keep your daughter's prints with you?' asked Hope.

'It was the only thing left of hers in the house when she ran away. She'd tried to erase herself from my life. I had an old fingerprint kit with me from a course.'

'That's not going to stand up in court.'

'It doesn't have to. I just want to know if she was here.'

'Somebody's wiped half this table down,' said the forensic. 'The other half where the two glasses were hasn't been touched. You can still see the circles of Coke where the two cans were.'

'The neighbour says the party ended abruptly just after midnight,' said Mercy. 'The first person turned up at about eleven. Someone left and came back a few minutes later around ten past. There was another knock a little after eleven thirty.'

The forensics were working around them so Hope and Mercy left the room, went outside the flat and stood in the taped-off corridor.

'I don't mean to tell you how to do your job,' said Mercy. 'I'm only doing this because I'm anxious about my daughter. My instinct's telling me to get some quick answers about what happened here. I'm scared for her.'

'You've given me a good start,' said Hope, who hadn't taken her interference badly.

They exchanged numbers.

'The neighbour said that Alice had been trying to stay off the crack. Hadn't had any since the new year. The only time she left the house was to get her money, go to her NA meetings and do some shopping. It sounds to me like the party came from the outside, and there had to be a reason for it.'

'We need to talk,' said Lomax, nodding the Chilcotts back up the steps into the alleyway, 'out of her hearing. I've no idea what your plans are for her, but it's best to keep your hostage in the dark about your intentions. Know what I mean?'

Dennis and Darren exchanged glances, not quite sure what

he was on about. Lomax seemed to have thought himself into a position well beyond them.

'Everything all right?' asked Dennis, going for upbeat.

'Depends what you mean by "all right",' said Lomax. 'She's in there, if that's all that concerns you.'

'What else?'

'There are no facilities and I've been on my own here for twelve hours.'

'What happened to Tel and Vlad?'

'I sent them home, didn't want them to mess the situation up.'

'How would they do that?' asked Darren. 'They're just go-fetch boys – that was the idea.'

'They couldn't be trusted to keep their dicks in their trousers.'

'Why? She tasty or what?'

'She's female, which is all they care about,' said Lomax. 'But it's not the point.'

'Why bring it up then?'

'It had an impact on the situation.'

'You know I always told Dad, that Miles Lomax bloke, he's too fucking brainy for his own good,' said Darren. 'Read too many books, ain't yer?'

'I seem to remember, Darren, you chose me for this job for precisely that reason,' said Lomax.

'Faith that was well placed, I'd say,' said Dennis, trying to keep it calm.

'So what have you got planned for the girl?'

'We're exchanging her for somebody else plus thirty grand.'

'Was that to cover my twenty-eight-grand debt?'

'No,' said Darren brutally.

'So you're exchanging her for someone who's prepared to be a hostage in her place?'

'That's about it.'

'That sounds like a very strange kidnap arrangement to me.'

'It doesn't matter what it sounds like to you,' said Darren.

'So the girl goes free and you get a replacement plus thirty grand?'

'That's it,' said Dennis.

'Then we have a problem,' said Lomax.

'What went wrong?' asked Darren.

'She was weak after the drug I gave her. I had to help her up off the bucket she was using for the toilet. She jumped me, tore off her mask and saw my face before I got her back under control.'

'She'd already seen your face last night,' said Darren.

'One of these days I'll give you some GHB, Darren,' said Lomax. 'You'll find it'll take you a few days to remember where your arse is, let alone scratch it. GHB erases memory.'

'So now you're saying she's seen your face when she's in a fit state to remember it.'

'You're quicker than I thought, Darren,' said Lomax.

Boxer left the letters to Mercy and Amy on the dining table. The one to Mercy included instructions about things like the safe and the gun. She already had a set of keys to his flat. She was the only person he trusted to mind her own business.

He still had until evening before he had to hand himself over, so now he was on his way, with the thirty grand, to what he realised was going to be a very strange final meeting with Isabel, the woman who could have been the one, but now he would never know.

As he sat on the Tube his father came to mind, and he imagined it must have been a similar experience for him when he set about leaving his life in the space of twenty-four hours. Except that he'd just walked away. There were no goodbyes. Not even any final cryptic meetings or messages. Why hadn't he at least written a letter of explanation for his son to open in later life?

It was cold but sunny as he walked up the hill to Isabel's house. He felt remarkably cheerful and free of care. It was, he thought, perhaps how martyrs feel once they've embarked on their sacrificial mission.

Isabel was not expecting him. He hadn't called her because he knew she worked from home on Fridays, which she set aside for reading manuscripts away from the constant demands of the office.

'Why didn't you call?' she said. 'We could have done something.'

'I don't want to do anything,' he said. 'I'm waiting for a call to

311

send me somewhere for work and I wanted to spend the time I had left with you.'

'You look happy.'

'I am.'

'Does this mean you've found Amy? Are we celebrating?'

'Not quite, but she'll be back with us soon … I'm pretty sure.'

'That's very cryptic of you.'

'You know what it's like when you've got to extricate yourself from the wrong choice. It takes time for a seventeen-year-old to swallow her pride.'

They went to the kitchen. She poured him a beer, gave herself a glass of white wine. She was in jeans, which was surprising, because she normally dressed for maximum feminine impact. She even apologised for being caught in her 'sitting around reading' clothes. He told her she looked great – even younger.

'I just wanted to thank you for looking after Mercy that night,' said Boxer. 'You were the only person who could have done that.'

'We covered a lot of ground,' she said.

'About what?'

'Amy, inevitably, and … you.'

'Did you get anywhere with the latter?'

'We talked about when you were married.'

'Not our finest hour.'

'No. She said as much.'

'I'm not sure I'm the marrying type,' said Boxer.

'Why not?'

'Too secretive,' said Boxer. 'And I can't take the pressure of my secrets under the relentless observation of a marriage.'

'Have you lived with anybody else since you split from Mercy?'

'Not for any length of time. I'm more of a staying-over kind of person.'

Isabel wanted to ask about those secrets, but she also didn't want any answers. This was her ideal state: to be in the presence of someone substantial who only gave her glimpses of himself. It was her own, very personal definition of love.

'Mercy told me you that you were a good father to Amy when she was small, but how your work interfered and gradually you grew distant.'

'Did she admit to you there was some question mark about Amy's paternity?'

'Yes, she did,' said Isabel, hesitant, a little astonished.

'We all have our secrets,' said Boxer. 'Some bigger than others. Even between two people as close as Mercy and me. That can be difficult in marriage.'

'And how do you feel about that?' asked Isabel.

'It doesn't matter to me. I'm beyond genetics. It comes down to what I feel for Amy. I've always considered her my daughter and even more so this past week. If a lab tech says I'm not her father it makes no difference. I'm both deserving and undeserving. When I found that the body part did not belong to her I was so relieved … elated, even though I haven't always been there for her.'

'A lot of men would find it hard to deal with a revelation like that.'

'You mean Mercy's deceit?' said Boxer. 'That's what you really mean. And you're right. Men have killed for a lot less. Paternity reaches down to their core. But I'm not that kind of guy.'

'How do you know?'

'You can't kill someone, even if it is in the heat of battle, and hope to remain the same. Once you've felt that kind of savagery and done that kind of damage to a fellow human you can never re-enter the world of men. You're always going to be separate, an outsider. Some can live with it, others can't. It was why Mercy, and then Amy, became very important to me.'

The truth was flowing out of him, but even in this new heightened state he could still feel the checks, small dams arresting the flow, never allowing himself to reveal everything. It wasn't easy to overcome a lifetime's withholding in a few hours.

Isabel sensed there was something different about him and imagined that, at this dramatic point in his life, he'd decided to draw her further in. She went to him, sat on his lap and kissed him, running her fingers up the back of his neck into his hair. Within minutes she was bent over the kitchen table with her jeans around her knees, her pants stretched between her thighs while he drove into her from behind with a passion and a need that had her hanging on to the edges of the table, as their empty glasses slid around and fell over.

313

Once that first crazy desire was over they went upstairs, took off their clothes and made love again, slowly, until the afternoon light started fading and Isabel drifted into sleep.

Boxer lay there with his arm around her, staring out of the window for a long hour. He whispered, 'I love you,' to her, even though he knew she couldn't hear him. He was trying it out, seeing if he believed it, seeing if it hurt. Then he quickly got up, took his clothes downstairs, dressed and left the house.

As he came out of the gardens in front of the development, his mobile rang. It was the Londoner.

'Go to an Internet café and phone store on the Finchley Road called Hari's. It's between the Tube station and the O2 Centre. You ask for Ali. You'll get your instructions there.'

Zorrita was sitting in the coroner's office, watching him put the final touches to his report after his full examination of all Chantrelle Grant's body parts.

'The interesting thing,' said the coroner, 'is that I could find no evidence of violence sufficient to have caused death. The forehead bruise was consistent with bumping into a door or something like it and there was no evidence of haemorrhaging. The facial wounds were nasty but superficial, probably from a belt buckle. She hadn't been strangled, stabbed or shot. All her arteries were intact. None of the important organs showed any sign of damage. She'd had sex so I sent a sperm sample to the lab, so we'll get some DNA from that ... eventually.'

'Are you saying you don't know?' asked Zorrita.

'No. It's just surprising, that's all,' said the coroner. 'Given that the body was found in this state, we had expectations.'

'That she was murdered.'

'Exactly,' he said, nodding. 'I managed to extract a blood sample large enough to reveal a high level of alcohol and cocaine, so I checked her liver and found it contained cocaethylene. That led me to look at her heart, because that combination can produce a metabolite which induces marked coronary arterial vasoconstriction, leading to myocardial ischaemia, infarction and sudden death, which is what had happened.'

'So you're saying that *technically* she wasn't murdered?'

'The way I see it, she was obviously out partying with someone. I think he got her back to his apartment. There was clearly some violence and some sex, but there doesn't seem to have been any sexual violence.'

'Could she have been dead by the time the sex took place?'

'Quite possibly,' said the coroner. 'It takes between six and twelve hours for the cocaethylene to be produced.'

'And time of death was ... ?'

'Around six in the morning,' said the coroner. 'If the man had been consuming alcohol and cocaine to the same level as the girl it's more than likely that he would have passed out and woken up hours later to find a dead body on his hands. He probably panicked when he saw the marks on her face, thought he'd killed her and decided that the best way to get her out of his apartment was to cut her up.'

'You'd only do that if you had good reason to believe you were guilty or you didn't want to be investigated by the police,' said Zorrita. 'I mean, some student wouldn't take a girl home, pass out and wake up in the morning thinking his only way out was to cut her up and dispose of her. The killer bled her too. He'd thought about it. Knew how he was going to control the potential mess.'

'Pig farmer?' said the coroner, shrugging.

'I think we're still talking about someone with a criminal mind,' said Zorrita. 'Not a total innocent.'

'How's it going with your list of estate agents?' asked Mercy, on the phone to George.

'No luck so far, and we've seen everybody on Olga's list,' said Papadopoulos. 'Our problem now is coverage. We can't rely on just phoning around and asking if they've handled an enquiry from Irina Demidova or Zlata Yankov because firstly, we don't know what name she's been using. If she's got two names on the go she probably has more. And secondly, there are all sorts of people in these offices, and not everybody knows who the other agents' clients are.'

'So you need to visit each one and show the photo,' said Mercy.

'And hope that the agent who was dealing with her is in the

office at the time,' said Papadopoulos. 'There are still agents on that list that we have to revisit because of that.'

'What about entering the spec for the house on one of those property sites, like Primelocation, and seeing what it throws up? Maybe some of these rentals don't get removed very quickly, and if it was for a short let they might not even bother to take it off the market.'

She hung up and went into the Netherhall Gardens house.

'Where's Bobkov and Kidd?' she asked.

'Bobkov was called to the Royal Free Hospital about forty-five minutes ago. Kidd went with him,' said Sexton.

They heard the front door open. Someone went into the kitchen and Kidd joined them in the living room. He was sombre.

'What happened?' asked Mercy.

Kidd thought about it, searched for better words, gave up, shook his head.

'Tracey died,' he said.

'I thought she was in ICU.'

'They'd taken her out. She was no longer considered critical,' said Kidd. 'There was a major pile-up at this end of the M1 and they needed the places. She was doing fine, but had a heart attack and they couldn't get her going again. Andrei's doubly broken up.'

'What else?'

'When you told us that Irina Demidova/Zlata Yankov had infiltrated DLT Consultants we sent a coded message to Igor Tipalov, telling him to stop all extra-curricular research and to get out of Russia as fast as possible,' said Kidd.

'He was acting for me,' said Bobkov, pushing past Kidd into the room, 'on the basis of information we'd been given by the nuclear scientist Professor Mikhail Statnik about the polonium 210 production of certain RBMK reactors. The first bad news we received this morning was that Professor Statnik was found dead in his apartment in Moscow. An hour later we heard that Tipalov had been found shot in his car on the road between Roslavi and the RBMK reactor just outside Desnogorsk, near Smolensk.'

'And what is the feeling about the impact of those deaths on our situation here?' asked Mercy.

'We've faced up to the worst possible scenario,' said Kidd.

'Which is what?'

'You have to remember that we are not dealing with a state here,' said Bobkov, the desperation now visible in his face. 'We are dealing with a man. There's an important distinction. If you cross a state, the impact is minimal. It whisks you away like a fly. However, once the state has become synonymous with a man and you cross a man of such power then that slight becomes personal. Criticise me and I will have you shot. Hold me to ransom and I will sacrifice the hostages. Oppose me when I've bestowed great wealth on you and I will impoverish and imprison you. Marshal foreign opposition against me and I will have you poisoned in a way that the world will never forget. Try to humiliate me by proving my involvement in such an act and I will kidnap your son, strip you of your wealth, murder your supporters, bring you to your knees to beg me for mercy and ... and I will show you none.'

'Look, Andrei, we're not going to give up on Sasha,' said Mercy firmly. 'We're going to find out where they're holding him and—'

'Sometimes I think that's what he wants: to bring you to that point of hope where your faith has been re-established only then to show you how pointless your efforts have been. So that once again it will leak out to the world that this is a man you should never cross, because there is no moral boundary he won't overstep.'

Mercy delivered her findings from the estate agents but stopped when the phone rang. Bobkov limped across the room, pressed the button.

'This is Bobkov,' he said.

'Have you prepared the next instalment?'

'Yes,' said Bobkov. 'What is to be my reward this time?'

'You will be reunited with your son.'

'I have a question for Sasha. A proof-of-life question,' said Bobkov. 'I want you to ask him, "When is a man truly free?"'

'What?'

'Only he will know the answer, out of all of you.'

Bobkov cut the line, limped back to his chair, slumped into it and sat there with his hands steepled, gnawing at the tips of his forefingers to stop the tears from coming.

*

317

On the way to Notting Hill Gate Tube station Boxer listened to his phone messages. There was a long one from Mercy detailing what she'd found in Alice Grant's flat. Nothing she said made him think he should change his course of action. The least dangerous path for rescuing Amy was to keep the Met out of it. He deleted the message.

He came out of Finchley Road Tube station and headed north to the O2 Centre with four lanes of traffic crashing beside him. He was oblivious to the noise. He went into Hari's phone store and asked for Ali. A young Asian guy beckoned him into the back room. He opened a Jiffy bag and asked Boxer for his phone. He gave Boxer a new phone, switched it on for him. He took him further out the back, through a storeroom to an outside metal staircase. They went down into a yard at the bottom. He pointed him towards a red car waiting in the road, told him the driver knew where to take him.

29

'I'll give it to you in order of appearance,' said DI Max Hope, the officer who was investigating Alice Grant's death, calling Mercy. 'The first thing back from the lab was the composition of the drinks on the table. Both glasses contained a combination of Coca-Cola, vodka and GHB. If full, the GHB element of the half-full glass would have been just over a gram, which, combined with alcohol, would have been enough to knock anyone flat. The GHB content was lower in the almost-empty glass and we're assuming it was refilled after a much higher dose had been consumed because, in the absence of an autopsy report, that's the only explanation we've got for Alice Grant's seizure.'

'What about fingerprints?' said Mercy, anxious.

'The ones you gave me on the card matched those on the half-full glass. Alice Grant's were on the almost-empty glass.'

'Were there any others?'

'We got an almost full set from the underside of the music centre remote and they matched some partials we found on both the drinking glasses but they didn't belong to Alice Grant. We've found a match on our database to one Miles Lomax.'

'How did he end up on your database?'

'In 2003 he was caught in possession of just over one gram of cocaine. He was lucky. No record. No track as a dealer. He got off with two hundred hours of community service,' said Hope. 'I've since spoken to a project team within the Serious and Organised Crime Command who tell me they've had their eye on him for a

319

while. They're sure he's dealing and using an elaborate system of runners to deliver his gear, but they don't want to arrest him until they've found his supplier.'

'Have you got an address?'

'The project team have him at a flat in 5 Elm Park Gardens in Chelsea, but we're not getting any answer from it,' said Hope. 'There's one other player involved. One set of prints we found on the inside of the front door of Alice Grant's flat belonged to Terence Mumby. He has a record as long as your arm, the most serious of which is GBH. He's done jail time and we've got a current address for him in Tufnell Park.'

'If you're going to pick up Mumby you don't want to spook Miles Lomax, who sounds like the major player in this,' said Mercy. 'How's it gone with the door-to-door?'

'We've had one sighting of Terence Mumby in the stairwell of Alice Grant's block just before midnight,' said Hope. 'And we've had a sighting of a strange threesome just after midnight: two men with someone smaller in between them who looked as if he/she was being carried. They went to a car parked in the Andover Estate, which was thought to be a silver Golf or an Audi, but no registration number was seen. The smaller person was put in the back with one of the men, the other got into the driver's side with someone else in the passenger seat.'

'When do you expect to get the autopsy results on Alice Grant?'

'Tuesday,' said Hope. 'The interesting thing is Lomax and Mumby. There's no discernible link. Lomax is university educated, living in Chelsea; Mumby left school at sixteen with no qualifications and lives in north London. The one thing missing from his record is drug offences.'

'Somebody put them together to do this job?'

'But what's the job?'

'I'd be interested to listen in when you question Miles Lomax.'

The red car was a minicab driven by a Bangladeshi. He took Boxer through Belsize Park, past the Royal Free Hospital and dropped him at Hampstead Heath Overground station.

'Ten pound, please,' said the driver.

'What?' asked Boxer, incredulous.

320

'Ten pound.'

'They said six on the phone.'

'All right, six,' said the driver, depressed.

Boxer only had a ten-pound note.

'No change,' said the driver, pleased.

'Where now?' asked Boxer.

The Bangladeshi gave him a strange look and pulled away.

Boxer waited, looked at the cheap mobile phone he'd been given. It rang. Private number.

'Get on the Overground in the direction of Stratford. Come off at Caledonian Road and Barnsbury. Cross over the tracks and take the Offord Road exit. We'll be in touch.'

He sat among Polish workmen in paint-spattered overalls who muttered into their mobile phones. He left the train following two Somali girls, their oval faces encased in colourful hijabs and wearing long brightly coloured skirts, each with a black biker jacket on top.

Another call came through while he hung about on the Offord Road. The voice took him through empty residential streets full of silent Georgian houses, past Barnsbury Square and the Albion pub, where smokers sat out in the cold. He turned left at the Crown, past the Celestial Church of Christ on Cloudesley Square and into Liverpool Road. A single person followed him on the other side of the road and only left him when he walked into the Angel Tube station.

'I've come to say goodbye,' said Lomax.

'What do you mean?' said Amy, her legs starting as if ready to run.

'No, no, don't worry. Stay calm,' he said and added in a low voice, 'I didn't tell them anything. You're going to be OK. You're going to get out of this.'

'But what's it all about?' said Amy. 'Why did you kidnap me?'

'I still don't know. All I do know is that you're going to be released. There've been some negotiations and you're going to be exchanged for somebody else. All you've got to do is stay calm and everything will ... unfold. OK?'

She nodded.

'Two guys are taking over from me. One of them is going to come and sit with you now. They're good guys and they won't hurt you.'

Lomax leaned over and took her hand, whispered in her ear, 'Promise me one thing: that you'll forget I ever existed.'

'I promise.'

'See you in Cardiff,' he said and kissed her on the cheek.

It made her emotional. She'd never cried over anybody leaving her before, but when Lomax went it was like losing a lover. The tears welled.

Lomax went back outside.

'She's all yours,' he said.

Dennis and Darren nodded, looked at him in unison as if measuring him so that he knew if he hadn't been the subject of their talk for the last five minutes, he would be for the next.

'Good job,' said Dennis.

'Let's talk tomorrow,' said Darren. 'Dad and I'll have a chat about the money you owe. We'll sort something out, right?'

Lomax nodded, walked down the alleyway, feeling their eyes on his back.

Dennis waited until he heard the door to the warehouse shut.

'What do you think?' said Darren.

'I get the feeling he didn't tell us everything,' said Dennis. 'He told us about the girl, but there's something even bigger he's left out.'

'He's a risk, you ask me,' said Darren. 'If he's picked up we're done for, and what with El Osito here, it could blow the whole operation.'

'It'll send a message too. Everybody knows he's into us for twenty-eight K,' said Dennis. 'We have him done and it'll make everybody sit up. They'll know we haven't gone soft.'

'You want me to call the Wolf?'

Dennis nodded, put his hands in his trouser pockets and trotted down the basement steps and into the room where Amy was tied to the bed.

'Hello, love,' he said.

She knew immediately from his voice that he was older, probably older than her dad, maybe fifty or more.

322

'We're going to get you some food,' said Dennis. 'What would you like? Just don't make it complicated. We're talking sandwiches here, not coq au vin.'

'Moroccan falafel salad on granary,' said Amy.

Dennis laughed until he saw she was serious.

'I said don't make it complicated.'

'That's my favourite at Pret.'

'We're talking greasy spoon here, love. Bacon or sausage sarnie, fried egg if you're lucky.'

'Whatever,' said Amy. 'But no white bread.'

'You're a health-conscious little filly, aren't you?'

Dennis went out into the alley. Darren was giving more instructions to Boxer over his mobile. He held up a finger. Finished.

'How's it going?' asked Dennis.

'His passport photo's out to the network. They're passing him on to each other. He's clean. No tail from the off.'

'Do you believe that?' said Dennis. 'Ex-army, ex-Met, kidnap consultant. They're all mercenaries, those bastards. He's got to be connected to something.'

'Don't know about that,' said Darren. 'Think you'd go and smash someone like El Osito's legs up if you were connected? I think he's a loner.'

'Keep him on the move until after dark, and then we'll bring him in from that greasy spoon in West Ham.'

'And what are we going to do about little Missy?' said Darren. 'You thought about that?'

'We're going to leave all that to El Osito,' said Dennis. 'He wanted this. He deals with it.'

'We've found the estate agents,' said Papadopoulos. 'It was a short let for three months so they never took the house off the market, just as you reckoned. We input the spec and there were only three possibilities for a detached house with an adjoining garage, a basement and good security system.'

'Where is it?' asked Mercy.

'Chiswick. Milnthorpe Road. Seven bedrooms, off-street parking, fences all round, swimming pool at the back, CCTV cameras front and back linked to screens in a study on the ground floor at the front. Basement with wine cellar, sauna, utility room and cinema,' said Papadopoulos. 'Irina Demidova passed herself off as Galina Zonov – passport, everything. They have a photocopy. She paid fifty grand up front from a Cypriot bank account in that name.'

'Who's the owner?'

'A South African called Jeremy Doveton, who's in Jo'burg as we speak,' said Papadopoulos. 'We have his phone number.'

'I want you to put a report together for DCS Makepeace with everything you know about the house and the names, addresses and phone numbers of the neighbours on either side, the house directly opposite and the one at the back. Let's get two surveillance teams in front and behind as soon as possible.'

'The estate agents have a full set of spare keys and interestingly the house is due for a security system inspection by Barrier Alarms. The tenants were warned before they took the house on and agreed to allow access.'

'Well done, George,' said Mercy. 'Put it all in the report.'

She hung up, called Makepeace, filled him in.

'Still no contact from the kidnappers?'

'One call at 1.26 p.m.,' said Mercy. 'They asked if the next instalment was ready. Bobkov was in a bad state after the news of his ex-wife's death and the killings of Tipalov and the nuclear scientist. He gave them a strange proof-of-life question and they haven't come back. That call came from Twickenham.'

'How many people have made calls?'

'In the run-up to the ransom delivery yesterday Chris Sexton took three calls within about five minutes, all from disposable phones from all over town. So three out and about and at least one at base. The gang is minimum four people.'

'And when they took the ransom?'

'One talking Bobkov down on the phone, two in the boat, although one of those was probably from CW Boat Hire.'

'So they seem to be most vulnerable at base when most of them are out in the field during the set-up phase,' said Makepeace.

'Bobkov is definitely cracking up now. He's losing his cool with the gang. Quick action is what we're looking for here.'

The phone rang in the living room. Mercy went in to listen. Bobkov took the call.

'Your son gave this answer to your question,' said the voice. 'A man is only truly free when you have taken everything from him.'

'He doesn't just have a good memory,' said Bobkov, 'he understands things too. Do you?'

'You'll get your instructions within the hour,' said the voice.

Terence Mumby was sitting alone at a table in the Fortess Café on the Fortess Road in Tufnell Park. He was drinking sweet tea, which he blew on before bringing it to his lips. There was an empty plate in front of him which looked as if it had been licked clean by a dog. The window next to him was fogged to just above his head so he was only aware of blurred figures as they passed by.

A police constable looked through the clearer glass at eye level and spotted the back of Tel's head. He nodded at the men in the unmarked car. One of them got out and went into the decor of despair that was the hallmark of the Fortess Café and Restaurant.

'Hello, Tel,' said the detective, slapping him on the back so that the tea slopped onto his plate. 'Let's you and me go and have a little chat.'

The detective showed his warrant card and took the mug of tea from Tel's mitt, helped him to his feet and walked him to the door.

'Oi,' said the man behind the counter. 'That's three pound fifty.'

'I'll be back,' said the detective.

Tel found himself in the back of a hot car sandwiched between two detectives who both smiled at him. He knew he was in big trouble.

'Where were you last night, Tel?'

'Tucked up in bed.'

'At midnight? All nicely tucked in?'

'Nice and toasty,' said Tel.

'That's odd,' said the detective, 'because somebody saw you at the same time on the Andover Estate.'

'Never been there in my life.'

The Wolf was sitting in a car on Elm Park Gardens about ten metres up the road from the entrance to number 5, which itself was only twenty metres from the Fulham Road. He had a photo of Miles Lomax on his mobile, which was resting on the steering wheel. He'd had to drive like a maniac to get here in time because Darren had told him that Lomax was bound to go straight home for a bath and some kip having been up all night. Well, he hadn't so far.

The Wolf had already gained access to Lomax's apartment building by following another tenant in. He'd seen that there was a lift and a staircase. Lomax's flat was on the fifth floor so he was bound to use the lift. There was another flat on the same floor and the Wolf had looked through the keyhole and found it to be in darkness and no response when he knocked. He decided that this was how he was going to do it: wait in the stairwell and as Lomax unlocked his door, push him in, shoot him in the back of the head and leave him dead in his flat. He went down to the basement where they kept the bins, wedged the door open so he had easy access from the street and went back to his car. Now all he needed was for Lomax to come home.

He was getting uncomfortable with the Ruger Mark 1 KJW resting in the special pocket he'd had made for it in his leather bomber jacket. The dashboard clock told him it was 5.45 p.m. He got out of his car and walked up the street to stretch his legs. After about fifty metres a VW Golf drifted past with a driver looking for parking spaces and – what do you know – it was Miles Lomax. The Wolf looked up the street. No spaces. He watched the car turn the corner, knowing that the road went round in a horseshoe back to the Fulham Road.

He was in two minds whether to follow it or not. He jogged up the road and turned the corner in time to see Lomax parking his car. The Wolf sprinted back the way he'd come and went down into the basement of the apartment building just as Lomax was walking up from the Fulham Road. He ran up the stairs to the fifth floor and waited, hanging back in the stairwell.

As Lomax was sorting through his keys outside the front door, two men came from across the road and stood on either side of him.

'Hello there,' said the first man. 'You look as if you've been up all night.'

Lomax ignored him, assumed he was addressing someone else, found the right key.

'Hey, you!' said the second man.

'You talking to me?' asked Lomax, turning to him.

'Just want to have a little get-together, don't we?' said the first man.

'What?' said Lomax, annoyed. 'Is this some sort of scam? You want some advice: don't scam a scamster. Now fuck off.'

'Don't be like that, Miles,' said the second man, his face close up now.

The use of his Christian name made Lomax go very still.

'Thought you'd like to come down to Holloway with us,' said the first man. 'Tell us what you were doing on the Andover Estate last night.'

Not even the cool Miles Lomax could stop the streak of terror leaping through his guts and up into his face. Their warrant cards were out now. He walked slowly to their car and got into the back seat with them. They drove around the horseshoe of Elm Park Gardens with one of the detectives calling DI Hope to say they were bringing in Lomax who had now sunk between them. The three detectives then proceeded to have an animated discussion about Arsène Wenger which was so unrelenting in its tedium that Lomax would have caught up on his kip if he hadn't been so terrified.

The Wolf waited, his gun hanging from his hand by his right leg. Five minutes went past. The lift came up and stopped at the fifth floor. The Wolf took a deep breath. The doors opened and a woman in high heels crossed the floor to the flat opposite Lomax's. The Wolf frowned and sank back down the stairs as she let herself in. He trotted down to the basement and out into the street. No sign of Lomax. He walked up and down the Fulham Road and then checked Lomax's car. He sighed. Lomax must have changed his mind and joined the rest of London for a Friday night in the pub. He hoped it would just be a pint and not dinner as well. He went back to his own car to wait. Knew the Chilcotts wouldn't want to hear anything else other than the words: job done.

As they neared the police station on Hornsey Road one of the detectives sent a text. They parked in the yard behind the station and brought Lomax through to reception. They passed one of the interview rooms on the way, whose door had been purposely left open. When Lomax and Mumby caught sight of each other they both knew what they were in for. That was also the moment when Lomax remembered what he still had in his pockets.

The estate agents called the tenants of Milnthorpe Road at just after four thirty to tell them that the owner had been in touch with his insurance company about another matter, and they'd advised Jeremy Doveton that he would have to have his security system checked before midnight tonight if he wanted his policy to remain valid. The agents said they'd contacted Barrier Alarms, and they had a technician in the area who could drop by in the evening to check the system.

'Would that be all right?' asked the receptionist.

'Wait,' said the voice.

The twenty-four-year-old receptionist, selected for having the sweetest phone voice, heard an animated discussion in a foreign language.

'What do they want to do?' asked the voice.

'They just want to check all the windows and doors to the outside, make sure the alarm system is still working and take a look at the CCTV cameras. The alarm system will have to go off but only for a few seconds. The whole thing should take about half an hour.'

More discussion. The receptionist inspected the latest work she'd had done on her fingernails.

'Can you come tomorrow?' said the voice.

'Well, the owner would obviously rather it was done this evening so that the building and contents insurance is still valid. Barrier Alarms say they aren't able to send someone else until after the weekend and the owner doesn't want to take that risk.'

'All right, all right,' said the voice. 'Tell him to call before he comes.'

'He should be with you some time between now and eight o'clock. OK?'

The phone was slammed down in her ear. Papadopoulos gave her the thumbs-up. She smiled and rested her forehead on the desk with the stress.

30

At 6.00 Mercy got a call from DI Max Hope telling her he'd just taken delivery of Terence Mumby and that Miles Lomax was on his way.

'I can't get there just yet,' said Mercy. 'I'm right in the middle of something. When are you going to start the interview?'

'Don't worry, we won't get going on Lomax for another couple of hours,' said Hope. 'First of all we want to get a search warrant for his car and second we want to extract as much from Tel as possible before we get started on Lomax. The good news is that Lomax still had a phial of GHB on him when we arrested him. We'll leave him to sweat. The boys who picked him up said he looked terrified. I think he knows he's killed Alice Grant.'

While Mercy was taking this call two dozen top-quality roses were delivered to the house on Netherhall Gardens. The card stuck among them had the same instructions as the last time, except that the Internet café was on Lavender Hill, near Clapham Junction and was called Wireless Up the Junction. Mercy was to drive Bobkov there, with no mobile phones, drop him off and immediately leave the area.

Mercy gave Papadopoulos her mobile phone and told him to take it to Baron's Court Tube station and wait for her there.

James Kidd, who'd only just returned after spending most of the afternoon in meetings at MI5's headquarters in Thames House, discussing the deaths of Professor Mikhail Statnik and Igor Tipalov, was now in conference in the dining room with Bobkov,

Chris Sexton and DCS Makepeace, who was on the phone.

'We can no longer discount the possibility that Andrei Bobkov himself is a target,' said Kidd. 'I've just had a long meeting with my boss about what Andrei has been put through and our concern now is to avoid another Russian state killing on British soil.'

'Our concern is for the boy,' said Makepeace. 'That has been the focus of our team, and it's not going to change now. I already have a police firearms unit in Eastbourne Road behind the house in readiness for an assault. I've just had a call from your boss at MI5, James, offering the services of one of your operatives to go in as the Barrier Alarms service engineer. I'm told he will prepare the ground for the firearms unit to perform the rescue operation.'

'As soon as we know where they're taking Bobkov we'll organise a tailing operation. Their intention will be to bring him into the drop zone clean. We're going to have to hope it's not such a deserted area as the Docklands were last night.'

'It's a question of timing,' said Makepeace. 'Once we've secured Sasha, you can pull Bobkov from the danger zone.'

'We're going to be a little more ambitious than that,' said Kidd. 'We want to bring as many of these FSB boys in as we possibly can. Andrei has agreed to our plan, which is that we will continue with the ransom drop as if nothing has happened.'

'It's just about the only thing left that I can do for my friend,' said Bobkov. 'My intelligence operation in Russia is finished. If we can prove their intentions against me then that is something else we can bring to the Tershchenko inquest next year.'

'Rather you than me,' said Makepeace.

Mercy put her head in the room and told them the instructions had arrived. Kidd made his call.

Mercy drove Bobkov south of the river to the Internet café in Clapham Junction. He was silent, completely lost in thought, staring out the window at London life drifting past.

'I'm very sorry about Tracey,' said Mercy.

'Thank you,' he said. 'I'm sorry too. She deserved a better life than the one I gave her.'

Mercy dropped him off just after 18.30 and headed straight out to Chiswick, picked up Papadopoulos from Baron's Court on the way.

'Any news?' she asked.

'Nobody's left the house yet. We're not to go anywhere near it until the operation is under way.'

Over a period of two hours the police surveillance teams, now installed at the front and rear of the house on Milnthorpe Road, confirmed the presence of six men inside, one of whom was almost permanently stationed in front of the CCTV monitors in the study. They took it in turns, rotating between playing cards in the dining room, sitting in front of the screens and going down to the basement.

One of the surveillance team had firearms experience and was relaying information about the house to the team waiting in their van on Eastbourne Road. The biggest problem was a line of sight for a sniper to the person manning the CCTV screens. His seat was in the corner of the room and the only possible angle was from the neighbour's garden over a high fence. To make it more difficult, there were trees and a bush in front of the crucial window. The MI5 operative posing as the house alarm service engineer was going to have his work cut out.

At 18.50 three men left the house on Milnthorpe Road and headed for Chiswick railway station. There were already two MI5 agents in position on the platform: a woman with a child in a buggy and a punk rocker. The train arrived and they all boarded.

At 18.55 the MI5 operative posing as the Barrier Alarms service engineer telephoned the Milnthorpe Road house, introducing himself as Tom Brewer. He said he would be there in around fifteen minutes.

Two of the three men who'd boarded the train in Chiswick got off at Wandsworth Town, while the third stayed another stop and got out at Clapham Junction. The punk rocker remained on the train. The woman with the buggy got off and watched the Russian walk up the hill in the direction of Wireless Up the Junction. She split away and went into a department store.

Meanwhile the police firearms unit van moved up Eastbourne Road in Chiswick and repositioned itself on Milnthorpe Road, where it parked thirty metres up from the house.

At 19.07 a Barrier Alarms van pulled up outside the electric gates of the house on Milnthorpe Road. The MI5 operative got out and rang the bell, showed his face to the camera set into the gatepost and gave his name. The gates opened. He got back into his van and drove into the off-street parking area, which triggered lights on the front of the house on either side of a large arched window above the front door. The door remained closed until he approached it with his case of tools.

A well-built man who spoke English with a thick Russian accent brought him into the hall, which had a magnificent sweeping wooden staircase to the left with some colossal artworks hanging on the wall going up the stairs. A triple-level chandelier, reflecting light off the white walls and white marble floor, lit the hall to a surgical brightness. The keypad to the alarm system was to the right of the front door. Tom Brewer inspected and memorised all its features. He asked the Russian for a quick tour of the house before he got down to testing the system.

The Russian started with the study next to the hall, where the screens were housed in a large open wall cabinet. There was a desk and chair in front of them and an empty cup of tea next to a full ashtray. There was a door to the stairway down to the basement in the far corner of the room. Across a corridor was the kitchen, where another man in his early thirties, who looked as fit as the Russian who'd opened the door, was making a pot of tea. He nodded but said nothing. The rest of the ground floor was empty. The dining room showed evidence of a card game, with decks of cards, score pads, ashtrays and cups of tea and coffee.

'I'll start at the top of the house and work my way down,' said Brewer. 'I'll leave the alarm test until last, if that's OK?'

The Russian nodded and joined him as he started up the stairs. He watched as Brewer checked all the contact plates on the bed-room and bathroom windows on the second floor.

They went through the same process on the first floor. There was a room off the master bedroom, which was only accessible through double doors in the west wall. It was a walk-in wardrobe and dressing room with access to a large bathroom. Brewer noticed how carefully he was being watched and how the Russian made sure that he never got behind him.

As he checked the bathroom window he noticed that the Russian was standing in the double doors between the bedroom and dressing room and that he was getting bored. He yawned and stretched and put his hands behind his head and twisted from side to side. As Brewer finished checking the dressing-room window the Russian turned without thinking.

That was when Brewer hit him.

The Russian was sharp and was able to make a significant move by the time the first blow landed on his neck so that Brewer missed the carotid. The Russian turned. Brewer aimed a punch to his throat. The Russian fell back, bounced back up off the bed and drove his fist into the side of the MI5 man's head. Brewer went down, lashing out with his foot, sideswiping the Russian, who collapsed onto the carpet. He drove the heel of his boot into the Russian's face, whose head kicked back and hit the wooden frame of the bed. Brewer saw that he was stunned, got to his feet and drove his heel twice more into the Russian's head, knocking him unconscious. He dragged him into the dressing room, cuffed his hands and feet with plastic ties from the tool case and stuck tape over his mouth.

The door to the master bedroom overlooked the staircase and hall below. Brewer glanced down, saw nobody. He trotted down the stairs, looking over the bannister to make sure there was no one underneath. He opened the front door, stuck two fingers in the air and headed for the study and the monitors connected to the CCTV cameras. Nobody there. As he cut across the corridor to the kitchen he heard the toilet flush to his left. He waited in the doorway of the kitchen. The toilet door opened, feet came up the corridor. He stepped out of the kitchen and chopped the Russian beneath the ear on the jawline with the edge of his hand. The Russian went down hard and fast on the marble tiles.

Brewer ran to the front door, hit the button to open the electric gates and opened the rear doors of the Barrier Alarms van. Two helmeted firearms officers got out and another three came in from the van outside the gates.

'Dressing room,' he whispered, pointing upstairs.

Two officers ran up the stairs.

'Corridor,' he said, and two officers dragged the other Russian into the reception room on the far side of the hall and closed the door.

Brewer took the remaining officer to the door in the study which led down stairs to the basement.

The firearms officer handed Brewer a Glock 17 pistol, opened the door and followed him. There were two closed doors in the area at the bottom, one leading to the sauna and utility room and the other to the cinema. The wine cellar was only accessible from the cinema.

Brewer pointed the firearms officer into the cinema. The padded doors opened noiselessly. It was dark and he turned on a helmet light. The cinema was empty. He moved up through the seating to the wine cellar, which was locked as the owner said it would be. He came back, signed this to Brewer.

They turned to the final door. Brewer crouched down and opened it. The utility room was in semi-darkness, the only light coming from a large glass panel set into the door of the sauna. With the light on inside, the occupants couldn't see out. Brewer looked through the glass across a small anteroom to another door with an identical glass panel. Through it he could see a man in shirtsleeves wearing an empty shoulder holster and sitting on a towel on a wooden slatted bench. The boy was lying next to him on another slatted bench. He was blindfolded and had his hands cuffed behind his back.

Brewer looked for the gun. Couldn't see it.

Brewer rearranged the grip on his Glock, nodded to his partner. He was going to go for it. He opened the door and slipped into the anteroom, where the heat and steam was generated for the sauna. He tried the next door, but it wouldn't budge. This was the one door in the house that the owner had assured him could not be locked from the inside. The Russian must have wedged it shut. He looked through the window and saw that the Russian now had Sasha in his lap and his gun to the boy's head. Brewer spotted a broom in the anteroom, jammed it against the window panel frame and pushed hard, feeling the obstruction slide back. Two bullets came through the half-open door and embedded themselves in the wall.

334

The Russian was standing now, holding Sasha, who was rigid with fear, the gun at the boy's head.

'Put your gun down,' he said.

Brewer put the Glock on the floor and backed away from it.

'Tell your friend to do the same.'

The policeman obeyed.

'Hands on heads,' said the Russian. 'You both walk in front of me.'

They shuffled into the area at the foot of the stairs.

'How many upstairs?'

'Two in the reception room,' said Brewer.

'How many outside?'

'Two.'

'Snipers?'

'One.'

They went up the stairs came out into the study.

'Tell everybody to stand down, drop their weapons, leave the building inside and out.'

The firearms officer spoke into his cheek mike.

'What transport have you got?'

'A van.'

'Where?'

'Outside the front door.'

'We take the van. You drive,' he said to Brewer. 'You stay. Tell them to move all the vehicles apart from the van away from the house.'

As they came into the hall the firearms officer spoke into his cheek mike again. The front door was open, the forecourt lit by automatic lighting sensors. Vehicles started backing out and driving away.

'We get to the front door, you stop. I want you close in front of me when we go out.'

The two officers in the reception room had left but the two upstairs had stayed. They looked down through the bannisters and saw the procession moving towards the front door. As the four made their way through the hall a clear metre opened up between the Russian and the two other men. The Russian was carrying Sasha on his left hip while his gun was pointed at Brewer's back.

The shot was unsilenced and very loud.

It hit the Russian in the back of the neck.

The boy fell from his paralysed arm, the gun clattered to the floor and the Russian's legs crumpled beneath him.

Mercy waited for the all clear and moved into the house. Sasha Bobkov was on his feet and the firearms officer was cutting through his plastic cuffs. She put her arms around the boy, partly to comfort him but also to stop him removing his blindfold.

'I'm Mercy,' she said. 'You have to keep the blindfold on for the moment. We've got to get your eyes used to the light gradually, OK?'

'Where's Daddy? Is he here?'

'He's coming, don't worry,' said Mercy, taking him by the hand. 'We're going outside now and I'm going to take you to an ambulance, and they'll give you a check-up. Are you feeling all right?'

'I'm OK. I just want my dad, that's all. I really want to see him.'

'He's not far away. He just had to make it look as if he was delivering the ransom to the kidnappers while we got you out of the house. He'll be coming soon.'

'And where's my mum? Is she here?'

'Let's just get you to the ambulance,' said Mercy, hugging Sasha to her, who put his arm around her waist. 'You've been a very brave boy, you know that, don't you?'

'I don't think so,' he said. 'What's wrong with my mum? There's something wrong with her. I know. They told me she was in hospital.'

She took him up the steps into the ambulance, where they laid him down. The paramedics cut away the material around the clasp at the back of the mask, turned the lights down, told him to close his eyes, pulled it off and fitted the boy with a pair of dark goggles.

'Will you stay with me?' asked Sasha, reaching for Mercy's hand. 'I like your voice.'

She couldn't stop herself, leaned forward and kissed him on the head. He wanted her to hold his hand while they gave him a check-up. He looked at her intensely, as if she was his guardian angel.

'Thank you,' he said. 'Thank you for saving me.'

He said it so sweetly and earnestly she nearly broke down and wept.

'You don't know it,' said Mercy, 'but you've been a big help to me.'

'Tell me what happened to my mum?' he asked. 'I know she'll have been worried and she probably had to have a drink to help her cope. Was that why she had to go to hospital?'

'I think she was very upset when the school called to say you hadn't arrived and she started drinking. When they came to speak to her they couldn't get in and your father was called because he had keys to the house,' said Mercy. 'Your mum wasn't in a good state. I don't think she'd been eating properly, she was dehydrated, and they thought the best thing was to take her to hospital.'

One of the paramedics tapped her on the shoulder.

'We're going to have to get going now.'

'I'll go with you.'

'That's not going to be possible,' said the paramedic.

'He's under sixteen and I haven't finished talking to him.'

The paramedic shrugged.

A text came in on her phone: DI Hope telling her he would start interviewing Lomax in about half an hour.

'Where are we going?'

'Charing Cross Hospital,' said the paramedic, closing the door.

Mercy called Papadopoulos and told him to follow the ambulance in her car. She put the phone away, stroked Sasha's forehead, squeezed his hand. The ambulance set off with a whoop from its siren.

'I know you don't want to tell me,' he said.

'She had a stroke in hospital,' said Mercy. 'You know what that is?'

'It's a blood clot in the brain,' said Sasha. 'People die from that.'

'They moved her into intensive care and she was stable,' said Mercy. 'Then there was a big car crash on the motorway and they needed places in the unit so, because she was stable, they moved her out.'

Sasha looked up to the ceiling and nodded.

'I know what you're going to say now,' he said.

'She had a heart attack and they couldn't revive her,' said Mercy. 'I'm really sorry, Sasha.'

'Was my dad there when she died?'

Mercy shook her head. Sasha sobbed so violently that his shoulders came off the trolley. She hugged him to her and he cried into her neck until he fell back exhausted.

'She always said she didn't want to die alone,' said Sasha, quietly. 'And I promised her she wouldn't.'

Bobkov picked up the phone in Wireless Up the Junction and waited there for nearly half an hour until a call told him to head down the hill to Clapham Junction and take a bus towards Wandsworth. He boarded a 156 but was told to get off at the first stop on St John's Hill. It was getting dark as they took him through the streets onto Battersea Rise and then alongside Wandsworth Common. Fortunately MI5 had included a dog walker among their agents so that when Bobkov took one of the paths that headed into the darkness of the common they could bring him in without raising any suspicion.

At 19.35 Makepeace got the full report of what had happened in the house on Milnthorpe Road and called James Kidd to tell him that Sasha was now safe, that they had two men in custody and one dead. Kidd thanked him for the update.

'It means you can abort your operation,' said Makepeace. 'We have two people for you to interrogate. You don't have to put Bobkov in danger's way.'

'The operation is already under way. We have no way of communicating with Bobkov,' said Kidd. 'Where's the boy?'

'He's been taken to Charing Cross Hospital,' said Makepeace. 'Why can't you send in one of your agents and tell him it's all over?'

'Thanks for keeping me informed,' said Kidd. 'Much appreciated.'

'You do realise that if anybody calls Milnthorpe Road now, they will no longer get a reply. That could put Bobkov in serious danger.'

'Has anybody called any of the phones you've recovered from the scene?'

'Not yet,' said Makepeace. 'We're not getting anything from the captured Russians. Not a word.'

'They won't say anything,' said Kidd. 'Let me know if anybody calls those mobiles you've taken. It will have an impact on the operation.'

Bobkov had walked past the tennis courts and was then instructed to go to the middle of the cricket ground. It was dark now and felt darker out on the expanse of open field, with only the lights and traffic of Trinity Road some way off. Bobkov was nervous. The hand carrying the case was sweating. The heat from his body was rising from the front of his coat into his face and he could smell his own fear. He knew what was coming. He was on his own now. None of the agents had dared come with him. The dog walker had kept to the lighted path in front of some houses overlooking the common. The dog was off the lead but didn't fancy it out in the distant dark. Bobkov felt the profound loneliness of his situation, as if he was enduring a metaphor of the last ten years.

The Russian captives remained silent. At 19.47 one of the mobiles recovered from the house on Milnthorpe Road rang. An MI5 agent answered it but said nothing. A voice asked for Evgeny. The agent said that Evgeny wasn't available. The phone went dead. The agent called Kidd and Makepeace immediately.

Bobkov came back into the light. The first glow of the ugly orange street lamps on Trinity Road almost warmed him. He stepped onto the pavement and was instructed to cross the four lanes of heavy traffic. He thought this could be the perfectly absurd ending to an unreal existence – flattened by a truck mid-operation.

He was directed away from the blast of the traffic and past Wandsworth Prison before being sent down a maze of residential streets to Garratt Lane. They were reeling him in. He felt he was close to the end now as they sent him up towards Wandsworth High Street, past the supermarket and across the road into the Southside shopping centre.

Bobkov had always hated shopping centres, but this one seemed to have a particular ruthlessness to it, with no attempt made by the architects to ease the experience of financial stripping. He walked the glassy surface of the polished floor wincing at the neon. He was sent up the escalator to the food court and the cinema complex.

There was a vast throng of people queuing to see the latest blockbusters including a young Asian contingent after tickets for a Bollywood romantic comedy. Yes, he wouldn't have minded a bit of love and laughter himself.

The crowd engulfed him, the roar of London chat, the smell of food wafting in from the fried chicken joints, and the phone went suddenly dead. He stopped to look at it. There was still battery power. The screen was functioning. He raised his head in time to see the crowd parting, as if something biblical was in train, and a man in jeans, a navy-blue zip-up jacket and a Knicks cap closed on him. His arm came up. Bobkov dropped the briefcase as two colossal hammer blows smacked into his chest, and he was falling backwards and the London chat had turned to screams, and where before space had seemed impossible now there was half an acre around him and the smell of popcorn was strong in his nostrils until it wasn't.

31

Boxer was in a greasy spoon in West Ham. The place was now empty. He'd been there for more than an hour. He went to the toilet at the back of the café. As he relieved himself two men came in, stood behind him and told him to keep looking at the wall. He finished, zipped up and one of the men put a mask over his eyes and wound gaffer tape twice around his head. He told Boxer to put his hands behind his back and the other cuffed him. They searched him, found the money and took it. They walked him out of the toilet and further into the back of the café and then out into the open air. They told him to get into the boot of a car.

After an hour the car pulled up. A chain was unthreaded from a metal gate. The car moved forward before reversing, and the roar of the metropolis receded. The boot opened. Two men pulled him out and walked him down the length of a building to a door at the end, which they unlocked. They pushed him through and he hit the wall of an alleyway that was too narrow for both men to walk either side of him. They took him down some steps and into a narrow corridor. They pushed him to the end into a small room on his left.

'Who's that?' asked Amy.

'It's me, Amy,' said Boxer.

'Dad?' she said, which was the first time in years she'd called him that.

Dennis pushed past him into the room.

'Your dad, he's doing a very fine thing for you, little girl.'

341

'I'm not a little girl,' she said without conviction.

'I'll leave you alone. Please don't try anything stupid. It'll just mean you both get killed.'

'Wait,' said Boxer. 'You and I had an agreement. I said I would hand myself in with thirty grand, and you promised me that my daughter would be released. You gave me your word.'

'I did. And that is what is going to happen, but only after we've concluded our business here. If I release her now she can go straight to the police – her mother, for instance.'

'She shouldn't be anywhere near here when … *he* arrives,' said Boxer. 'You know what he's like.'

'There's nowhere else for her to go. She stays here. We'll put her in another room.'

'He shouldn't even see her. He shouldn't know about her,' said Boxer.

'She'll be fine. I'll make sure of it,' said Dennis. 'Now take some time together.'

He closed the door.

'I'm blindfolded,' he said.

'Me too,' said Amy. 'I'm on the bed, tied to it.'

He edged forward, hit the metal frame with his knee. He sat down, hands still behind his back and gave her leg an affectionate squeeze.

'Give us a kiss, Dad. I need a kiss.'

He knelt down, shuffled forward, leaned over, found her cheek and kissed her. He rested his face against hers.

'You're going to be all right,' he said.

'What's going on?' she whispered in his ear.

'It's complicated,' said Boxer, 'and it's best you don't mess your head up with it. All you need to know is that I offended a Colombian gangster in Madrid. He wants revenge and he's reeled me in by kidnapping you. As the bloke said, you're going to be released.'

'And what's going to happen to you?'

'We'll see.'

'Listen to me,' she said, and he put his ear close to her lips, felt the terror in her body. 'I tried to escape when there was just one guy looking after me. He uncuffed me so I could go to the loo and I hit him, tore off my mask and saw his face.'

'And he knows you saw it?'

'Yes, he's one of their drug dealers,' said Amy. 'He came to see me before he left and said he hadn't told them, but I don't know. I think he'd have had to. Couldn't risk it. And if he did tell them, they won't let me go and they'll ... they'll ...'

'Don't worry. Keep calm,' he said, kissed her on the cheek again and forced himself to say, 'Everything is going to be fine.'

The paramedics had told Mercy she couldn't come into A & E with them. They'd dropped her outside the front of the hospital. After an emotional goodbye she'd felt an almost maternal wrench as she left Sasha in the back of the ambulance.

She'd then had to drive at speed, with a blue flashing light on the roof, all the way across London to get to Holloway police station in time for the start of DI Max Hope's interview. She tried calling Boxer on the way, but his phone was switched off.

The preliminaries were just winding up as she was shown into the observation room. She wasn't sure if she was going to be able to stand watching someone else interview a suspect whose information she needed so desperately. She stood with her face up close to the window and observed Lomax, tried to work him out. He wasn't looking good. He was unshaven and clearly hadn't slept. But there was intelligence in his eyes and a belligerence in his manner. This might be a tough nut to crack.

'Now, you can lie to me about the contents of this little plastic bottle,' said DI Hope, holding up the evidence bag with the phial of liquid GHB found in Lomax's coat pocket, 'but it won't help you. We'll do the analysis and we'll find out the contents. The same applies to this little bag of white rocks.'

'GHB and crack,' said Lomax. 'I use them when I go clubbing.'

'What's the GHB for? To spike girls' drinks?'

'I'm not a creep,' said Lomax. 'I use it to get high.'

'Where were you last night?'

'Out.'

'At the Andover Estate?'

'I've never been to the Andover Estate in my life.'

'Never?'

'Never. Not my part of town.'

'Which part of town is that?'

'I don't know because I've never been there.'

'But you know it's not your part of town so you must know where it is.'

'No. I only know where it isn't.'

'Tel says he was with you at the Andover Estate last night.'

'Who's Tel?'

'Terence Mumby. Your partner in crime last night.'

'Never heard of him, so he must be lying.'

'The two of you were seen carrying a girl between you and putting her into a car which we've since found out was a silver VW Golf GTI registration LG 59 KFC.'

'What time?'

'Just after midnight.'

'In the dark?' said Lomax. 'Somebody's identified us in the dead of night on the Andover Estate? They're all crack heads in there. You got some of them to buy themselves a future by agreeing to your version of things?'

'I thought you'd never been to the Andover Estate?'

'It's notorious,' said Lomax. 'So notorious you'd make sure you never went there.'

'We have another witness who saw you in the stairwell of Danbury House on the Andover Estate at around 11.25 on Friday night, smartly dressed, this woman said, in a blue coat and an open-necked white shirt, and then again a bit later, at 11.40, with a bottle of vodka and two cans of Coke. We have another witness who saw Tel hanging around in the same stairwell on the fourth floor of Danbury House at 11.55 p.m. That's a hell of a lot of sightings of two people who say they've never been to the Andover Estate in their lives, Mr Lomax.'

Nothing back from him.

'Do you know Alice Grant?'

'No.'

'Did you visit Alice Grant in her flat, number 504 Danbury House on the Andover Estate, on Friday night at around 11.25?'

'No.'

'You're absolutely certain you don't know her, never met her and never been to her flat?'

'Yes.'

'Can you repeat that for me saying the words very clearly.'

Lomax did as he was asked.

'You know what the problem is here, Miles?'

'Mistaken identity.'

'No, the problem here is that someone's died,' said DI Hope. 'Alice Grant *died* last night.'

'I'm sorry to hear that.'

'She drank vodka and Coke with a very high concentration of GHB in it and she smoked crack on top. She choked on her own vomit. Now, we've found GHB and crack cocaine in your possession. That taken in conjunction with all the sightings of you on the Andover Estate is making it hard for us to ignore your involvement in Alice Grant's demise. And there's one other thing ...'

'What?' said Lomax, exhausted, his defences already starting to break down.

'Aren't you wondering what you're doing here?'

'The police move in mysterious ways,' said Lomax.

'Why were two officers waiting for you when you finally came back to your flat in Elm Park Gardens in your silver Golf GTI registration LG 59 KFC?'

'Whim?'

'Which we've since discovered contains a bottle of vodka and some cans of Coke.'

'That's a crime now, is it?'

'How well do you know Terence Mumby aka Tel?'

'Not at all well, because I've never met him before in my life.'

'So what was he doing driving your vehicle away from the Andover Estate last night?'

'I can't think what you're talking about.'

'His fingerprints are all over the front of the car, inside and out, all over the leather steering wheel and the leather gear stick,' said Hope. 'I wouldn't let Terence Mumby anywhere near my car, even if I knew him ... especially if I knew him.'

'You're probably a very sensible man.'

'Think about it,' said Hope. 'Go over in your mind what you did last night that meant that two police officers were waiting for you when you came home.'

He had thought about it while he'd been sweating it out in the cells. He remembered holding the glasses and filling them with drinks. He'd taken his own and left the other two, but he was pretty sure they wouldn't get much in the way of fingerprints from them.

'I've already thought about it,' said Lomax, 'and decided that their presence must have been delirium-induced.'

'You're a clever boy, aren't you, Miles? You're educated,' said Hope. 'You're playing this game because you know what you're looking at here, don't you? Murder and kidnap.'

'Kidnap?'

'You were seen with Tel, carrying someone to your car,' said Hope. 'She's been identified as a seventeen-year-old girl called Amy Boxer.'

He pushed the photograph Mercy had sent him across the table. Lomax, who was still trying to maintain his crumbling facade by sitting sideways and cross-legged, glanced over his shoulder at the shot.

'Tel says she doesn't look like that now. The long hair's gone and it's in corn rows, but that was the only shot her mother had of her.'

Lomax blinked, said nothing, but the sight of Amy had restarted something in his mind.

'I can see she's ringing bells with you, Miles,' said Hope. 'Feeling a bit guilty about something, are we?'

Lomax felt himself pitchforked into a corner now, with this DI lunging at him at will. He didn't know Tel well enough. He could be blabbing away, trying to save himself from a kidnap charge. What was the sentence for that? He had no idea. What did they have on him that placed him at the scene? Or did they have the idiot Tel's word and bugger all else?

As he thought this he realised his brain had embarked on a little diversion to stop him thinking about what was really bothering him. Ever since he'd left Amy in the company of Dennis and Darren, ever since he'd whispered, 'See you in Cardiff,' in her ear, he'd been thinking about her. He'd thought he was hard. He'd walked away from people many times before, people he could have saved from some very bad treatment, figured they would

346

learn from it. But Amy was different. She wasn't part of the scene and this wasn't a question of a punishment beating. They couldn't rely on her to keep her mouth shut. The only sure way was to ... He couldn't even say it to himself. He'd walked away from her, thinking he could do what he'd always done, but it had played on his mind and he'd found himself writhing in his seat at traffic lights, hands clenched on the steering wheel.

'Glad to see you're thinking now,' said Hope. 'Want a clue as to why we came knocking at your particular door?'

Lomax stared at him with 'Go on then' eyes.

'The neighbour said there was a party going on at Alice Grant's. She heard music. Amy Winehouse. Then it was turned off,' said Hope, and held up the evidence bag with the little remote in it. 'This, I'm afraid, along with all the witness statements, and Tel's desperate blabbing, puts you at the scene.'

Lomax's face drained as he remembered. His panic at seeing Alice Grant convulsing on the bed. His attempt to put her into the recovery position. Amy coming in and seeing the state of her. The girl's instinct to call for an ambulance. Slapping the phone out of her hands. Her rush for the door. He'd picked up the remote, turned off the music, thrown it on the sofa. Dumb.

'Now look, Miles. I know it's not your normal line of work, kidnapping,' said Hope, gentle now. 'We know you're a drug dealer, which is why your prints are on our database. And this means we're inclined to believe that you're not doing this off your own bat, but because you have to. You owe someone. Is that right?'

Lomax gave him the long, hard 'Go on' look that didn't concede anything until he knew what he could get in return.

'We might be able to look at Alice Grant's death as manslaughter rather than murder, but only if you come completely clean about what you were doing with Amy Boxer. Where did you take her? Who were you taking her to? Unlike Alice Grant, Amy's is a life we can still save, and if we succeed in doing that then we can talk to the CPS on your behalf. I'm not going to lie to you and tell you that you'll get off scot-free, but I'll make sure you don't go down for two life terms.'

A long silence followed in which trains of thought left and returned to the same undeniable terminus: the choice between two life terms or being hounded to death by the Chilcotts. But there were also a couple of deciding factors: the way the Chilcotts had looked at him, measuring him up for a coffin, and Amy. He had to admit it to himself: he liked her.

'We took her to the derelict Rowland Estate at the back of a warehouse on Neckinger in Bermondsey,' he said.

Mercy, whose face was right up close to the viewing panel, dropped her forehead against the glass, closed her eyes and breathed out a long emotional sigh.

'We're holding Charles Boxer,' said Dennis. 'He's ready for you.'

Jaime told him that El Osito was still sleeping after his morphine jab in the afternoon.

'I'll wake him up at eleven,' he said. 'Send a car for us then.'

Jaime sat on his hotel bed in the dark, looking out over the lights of the city, the bridges across the river, the traffic on the Embankment. He had a Walther PPK in his hand, which had been handed over to him in the Colombian restaurant in the Elephant and Castle shopping centre. It was a small gun, no larger than his hand, its metal warm from being close to his body. He aimed it out of the window at the intermittent flashes of the warning lights on the four towers of Battersea Power Station. Then he put it next to him on the bed, stared between his feet.

A while later he took another call, this time from the journalist Raul Brito in Spain, who gave him the latest developments in the case of the dismembered girl.

At 11.00 p.m. he shrugged into a leather jacket, slipped the Walther PPK into an inside pocket, crossed the corridor to El Osito's room and let himself in. El Osito was still sleeping. He turned on a bedside lamp and took out a small bag of cocaine. On the glass surface of the bedside table he prepared two lines and nudged El Osito awake. He surfaced with a huge intake of breath through his nose and stared silently at Jaime with shining black eyes.

'What's going on?'

'They have the Englishman. They're sending a car now.'

'What time is it?'

'Just after 11.00 p.m. local time,' said Jaime and handed him a rolled twenty.

El Osito, still fully clothed, leaned over and snorted the two prepared lines and lay back on the bed, staring at the ceiling. Jaime positioned the wheelchair next to the bed and dragged El Osito into the seat.

'I want to change my shirt,' said El Osito. 'I stink.'

Jaime found him a new shirt. El Osito peeled off the old one. He dressed and Jaime put a jacket over his shoulders. They went down to the reception area, where one of Dennis's drivers was waiting with a VW Caravelle parked outside. They got El Osito into the back and locked off his wheelchair. Jaime sat with him, told him the latest news that Raul Brito had given him over the phone. El Osito laughed in a way that was so mirthless it sounded like the barking of a savage dog. He stopped as suddenly as he'd started and began doing some stretching exercises, twisting in his chair and then lifting himself with his powerful arms as if in readiness for what was to come.

Jaime leaned his head against the window and wondered with what horrific mental gymnastics El Osito had trained his mind in preparation for this event. Vicente had said that El Osito's torture sessions were the stuff of legend, but these were punishments meted out to wrongdoers as a warning to others. There was no precedent for anybody who'd done the sort of damage to him that Charles Boxer had. Jaime didn't want to think about it. He knew that violence was a necessary part of their business, but he'd never had the appetite for the excesses of some of his associates. Perhaps the heavy use of drugs had dehumanised and deranged them so that they saw others like animals. But that didn't really explain it.

He hoped the girl wouldn't be there. He wished he could speak English better, to impress on Dennis how important it was that El Osito shouldn't know about the girl. That was a scenario he dreaded. Vicente had told him that El Osito's torture sessions had been based on extensive reading about the Chilean DINA's methods, under Pinochet in the 1970s. He had been particularly fascinated by the activities in a torture centre in Santiago that was known by two names: the Discotheque and La Venda Sexy. Jaime hadn't wanted to know any more than that.

349

32

Mercy was on the phone to Makepeace giving him a recap of the Lomax interview.

'And you've tried calling Charles?'

'His mobile's turned off,' said Mercy. 'The last I heard from him was the text message he sent early this morning, which started me off on this investigation. I've contacted the hospital where his mother is being treated and they said he went to see her this morning, early. I've also spoken to his girlfriend, and she says she saw him at lunchtime and he left abruptly in the late afternoon having behaved quite ... strangely. Since then, nothing.'

'So, given Lomax's testimony, you think Charles has handed himself over in return for Amy's release and that what he's been doing today is ... clearing the decks, as it were?' said Makepeace, finishing awkwardly.

'Saying his goodbyes is what it feels like to me,' said Mercy. 'My concern is that Lomax doesn't know what it's really about. They wouldn't tell him anything beyond that it was a hostage exchange.'

'An exchange?'

'That was the original intention.'

'And what changed?'

'Amy tried to escape and saw Lomax's face in the process. He had to report that to his bosses because it presents a risk of exposure to the whole organisation,' said Mercy. 'So it seems likely they're going to renege on their deal to release Amy.'

'What do we know about Dennis and Darren Chilcott?'

'Surprisingly little. I contacted the project team in the Special and Organised Crime Command who've been tracking Lomax and they're very excited about it. This is the supplier they've been looking for. The Chilcotts were completely under their radar.'

'This place, the Rowland Estate, do we have access?'

'Lomax has said he will cooperate fully.'

'How many people does Lomax think will be involved?'

'He reckons there'll be at least one person in the warehouse, possibly two. There'll be another person outside the basement where they're keeping the hostages because there's no phone signal inside and they can't hear what's going on outside, especially in the two soundproofed rooms.'

'Any CCTV?'

'There's none in Neckinger itself, except on some council buildings, but there's two in the yard outside the Chilcotts' warehouse, but Lomax will help us get around that.'

'So a four-man firearms unit should be enough for the job,' said Makepeace. 'I'll make my way to Bermondsey with them now. Let's meet at the Neckinger end of Grange Walk. You bring Lomax and an accurate set of plans and we'll mount the assault from there.'

The VW Caravelle pulled into the yard from Neckinger and reversed into the warehouse. The driver and Jaime lifted El Osito out in his wheelchair. He propelled himself down the warehouse towards Dennis Chilcott, who was walking up to meet him.

'We have a small problem,' said Dennis.

'Tell me,' said El Osito, used to problems, relaxed about them now.

'I agreed to release the girl if Charles Boxer handed himself over,' said Dennis, 'but the girl tried to escape and in the process saw one of my dealer's faces. I've arranged to have the dealer terminated, but we don't know if that's been successful yet. If we let her go, she can compromise our whole operation.'

'That is not a problem,' said El Osito. 'I will deal with them both, personally.'

Dennis glanced at Jaime, who sent his eyebrows over a low jump.

'Follow me,' said Dennis.

El Osito had to restrain himself, constantly braking to stop from running into the back of Dennis's legs. They reached the steps to the basement. Dennis trotted ahead and opened the door, looked down the corridor, beckoned to Darren.

'Where's the girl?' he said quietly.

'She's in a separate room,' said Darren, pointing to a closed door.

'You wait outside. I'm going to try and keep this under control,' said Dennis. 'Help Jaime bring him down the stairs in his wheelchair.'

El Osito was teetering at the top of the steps, couldn't wait to get on with things.

'Good to see you, Darren,' he said. 'We need a strong boy like you.'

Jaime tilted back the wheelchair, Darren grabbed the front and they lifted him down, eased him around the corner and sent him along the corridor to Dennis at the end.

Dennis pointed him into the room. El Osito swivelled round, drove himself into the room, nearly rammed the bed, hadn't expected it to be so small.

'Cut away his blindfold,' said El Osito, getting straight down to business. 'We have to see each other's eyes. Get rid of the mattress.'

Jaime stepped forward, pulled the mattress out from underneath Boxer, who was cuffed to the four corners of the bed. He was now lying directly on the wire mesh stretched over the metal frame. Jaime cut away the tape over the sleeping mask and stripped it off his face. Boxer squinted against the neon in the room.

'Cut away his clothes,' said El Osito. 'He should be naked ... just as I was when he came to me.'

El Osito had already seen the wires attached to the bed, which passed through a small box for controlling the current. He was pleased. The Chilean DINA had used this sort of thing, but it was not what he had in mind for Boxer. He had something far more psychologically excruciating for him. The man had inflicted terrible injuries on his legs and would probably be expecting the same from El Osito, but he'd decided to be much more imaginative than that. This was not going to be tit for tat. His intention was to utterly debase Charles Boxer before he sent him into the ultimate darkness.

Jaime cut away Boxer's shirt, trousers and underpants. He stepped back with the shredded clothes, leaving him naked. Boxer looked at El Osito calmly as Jaime plugged in the bed and placed the control box in his boss's lap.

'And so, *mi compañero*,' said El Osito.

'What is it about me, El Osito, that makes you think I'm your *compañero*?'

'I use that word just to remind you,' he said, 'that you and I are the same. Maybe you think we are different, that you are good and I am bad. Perhaps you see yourself as some avenging *hidalgo* … what is *hidalgo* in English?'

'A knight.'

'Like *noche*? That is good. The dark night.'

'There's a "k" at the beginning, which is silent,' said Boxer.

'The silent dark knight,' said El Osito, nodding.

'Maybe "nobleman" is more accurate.'

'You know what I found out today?' said El Osito. 'The autopsy they did on the girl you thought was your daughter? It showed that she was not murdered. She had a heart attack from a toxic mixture of alcohol and cocaine. It happens. Just bad luck. Funny, don't you think, after all we've gone through?'

'More ironic than funny,' said Boxer.

'You know, maybe you are too relaxed. Maybe I have to bring some, how you say … tension into the game,' said El Osito, switching on the current.

Boxer's body spasmed as the electricity spiked into him, tried to arch away from it, but it was all over the bed frame. El Osito turned it up some more so that Boxer started to convulse, had to work hard to stop himself from biting his tongue. His body jerked wildly as the pain shot into his head from his feet and out to his hands, his muscles contracting and contorting against the powerful impulses. El Osito looked at him calmly until Boxer finally shouted out in agony. Only then did he ease back the current.

'Now we bring in the girl,' said El Osito.

'Not the girl,' said Jaime in Spanish. 'She's nothing to do with this.'

'You bring the girl,' roared El Osito. 'Now!'

'He want you to bring the girl,' said Jaime, looking down the corridor.

'No,' said Dennis. 'That's not going to happen. She's not involved.'

El Osito put down the control box, reversed into the corridor.

'What you say, Dennis?'

'The girl is off limits.'

'I'm sorry, Dennis. I don't understand. You tell me you want me to deal with the girl. I say, no problem. Now you tell me the girl is off limits. What is this off limits? This makes no sense to me.'

'You do whatever you have to do to him in there,' said Dennis. 'He smashed up your legs. I can understand that. But the girl's got nothing to do with it. You leave her out of it.'

'But you still want me to kill her?' said El Osito. 'That's what you say to me. The girl has seen one of your *compañero*'s faces. She has to die.'

'Yes, but you don't involve her in what you're doing to him.'

'But she is the reason he is here. Without her being so stupid none of this would have happened. She too has a price to pay.'

'And she will pay it, but it will be clean.'

'Now, I think, if I'm not mistaken, that we're talking about money again, aren't we, Dennis?' said El Osito. 'How much is it worth to you? I know you. You always thinking about the business. So how much do you want?'

'This has got nothing to do with business.'

'I don't agree,' said El Osito. 'Let me see now. I give you two months' free product. How about that? Five hundred kilos ... free.'

'Look, Osito. This isn't anything to—'

'Three months? How about four? By then you taking the three hundred kilos. So that make eleven hundred kilos free,' said El Osito. 'The girl, she is going to die anyway.'

Dennis pushed open the door to his left. Amy was lying trussed up on the floor like a small goat he'd once seen in Mexico waiting to be slaughtered for a lunch party. 'She is going to die anyway' resounded through his head as he calculated the street value of the product El Osito was offering. Sixty million pounds. It was

354

too much. El Osito had found his price. Everybody had one. He backed off down the corridor with Jaime's ferocious eyes on him and left the basement.

'Now, bring the girl, Jaime,' said El Osito quietly.

They were sitting in the back of an unmarked van on Grange Walk: Makepeace, Mercy, Lomax and the four men from the Metropolitan Police Firearms Unit. They had gone over the plan several times and were just taking one last look at the map of the warehouse and estate and how they were connected.

Makepeace stayed in the van while Lomax led the firearms unit and Mercy up Grange Walk and into Neckinger. They kept close to the wall of the warehouse. The lead officer of the firearms unit opened the padlock and silently unthreaded the chain. Another officer squirted lubricant onto the gates' hinges so they didn't squeak. Lomax went in. The four officers hugged the warehouse wall, weapons ready: Heckler and Koch MP5SF semi-automatic carbines and Glock 17 pistols.

Lomax slid the key into the lock of the small door within the two big wooden gates of the main warehouse and let himself in, flipping the lock onto the latch as he stepped inside. Dennis was sitting in a cheap white plastic chair with his head in his hands while the driver of the VW Caravelle stood over him looking hopeless. The screens showing the output of the CCTV cameras were unmanned.

'It's only me, Den,' said Lomax, seeing the shock on Chilcott's face.

'What the fuck are you doing here?' he said.

'I just couldn't take it,' said Lomax. 'From the moment I left you, I haven't been able to get the girl out of my head. I've been driving around all over London. Don't know what to do with myself. I'm desperate, man.'

'You and him, both,' said the driver.

'So what's going on?' asked Lomax.

'You don't want to know,' said the driver. 'She's in there with the Colombian nutter.'

'Nobody moves,' said a voice from the door. 'Not a finger. Hands on heads the lot of you.'

'Oh, my fucking Christ,' said the driver as the firearms unit came in one after the other, spreading into the room. 'What the fuck have you gone and done now?'

'Shut it,' said one of the officers. 'The three of you stand in line. That's it. Drop to your knees. Now face down, hands on the back of your heads where we can see them.'

Two officers went over and frisked all three men, before pulling Lomax to his feet. They marched him down the warehouse, leaving Dennis and the driver with the remaining two officers, who taped their mouths shut and cuffed their hands behind their backs. One officer stayed behind while the other called Mercy in before jogging down the length of the warehouse.

Lomax opened the door, went into the alleyway.

'Hey, Darren, come here. Den wants a word,' he said.

'What the fuck are *you* doing here?'

'I came back because of the girl. Den wants to talk to you about her. Can't forgive himself. We're going to get her out.'

Darren walked up the alley, a puzzled look all over his face. He turned into the warehouse, walked straight into a Glock 17 at eye height and stopped dead.

'The door to the basement, Darren, is it locked?' asked the firearms officer.

'You fuck ...' said Darren, staring into Lomax with lacerating hatred.

'Yeah, all right, Darren,' said the officer. 'Answer the question or you're looking at kidnap *and* accessory to murder.'

'It's open,' he said. 'They haven't locked it.'

'How many in there?'

'Two. The Colombian in the wheelchair and Jaime the Mexican.'

'Are they armed?'

'I don't know. I doubt it unless they've managed to buy some guns since they arrived from Madrid.'

'Not a word now, Darren,' said the officer, who walked him back to join Dennis and the driver on the floor. He beckoned to Mercy, pointed her to the doorway to the alley.

The two other officers marched down the alley and trotted down the steps to the door to the basement. The lead officer eased the handle down.

Jaime cut the plastic cuffs around Amy's ankles, got her to her feet. She was trembling, barely able to stand. She'd heard the entire exchange between El Osito and Dennis. Jaime put an arm around her shoulder to support her and brought her into the room where El Osito was watching Boxer. He put her in the corner. She was whimpering like a hurt animal.

'Cut her hands free and take her mask off,' said El Osito.

'What's going on?' said Boxer. 'I had a deal with Dennis and this was not part of it. He said she would not be involved and he would let her go. This is between you and me.'

'Not any more, *mi compañero,*' said El Osito. 'Dennis just sold me the rights to do what I want. You, take off your clothes.'

'Come on, Carlos, for God's sake,' said Jaime. 'This isn't right...'

'Shut up, Jaime,' roared El Osito. 'You don't tell me what is right. Give me a hit.'

Jaime handed him the bag of cocaine. El Osito took two pinches from it, one for each nostril.

'You strip naked,' he said to Amy, pointing a thick powdery finger into her face, which had no mask now and revealed the full terror streaming from her eyes. Her lips quivered as the diamond points in his black eyes drilled into her.

'Don't do it,' said Boxer.

El Osito picked up the box, turned on the current so that Boxer started to writhe and buck on the bed.

'I only stop when you take your clothes off,' said El Osito. 'Every second you delay the current goes up.'

'I don't know what to do.' she cried.

'You do what I tell you,' said El Osito, easing up the dial so that Boxer started to shout and scream.

She couldn't bear it any longer. In seconds she stripped to her underwear.

'Naked,' said El Osito.

Jaime stepped back into the corridor, couldn't bear to watch this any more, the girl's terror was too degrading. He gripped his face in his hands, trying to force out this new range of horror images.

Amy was naked. She squatted in the corner trying to hide

herself from the monster in the wheelchair. She was crying un-controllably. El Osito turned the current to the bed off. Boxer's body flattened on the bed and twitched. He was bleeding from the mouth. There was the smell of singed hair in the room. He stared at El Osito, his heart racing, the blood pinging in his throat.

'Now you see,' said El Osito, eyes locking onto his. 'There are far worse things than some broken knees.'

Boxer realised that nothing was going to stop this now. The monster was out of his cage, no physical or mental restraints. Pure evil inhabited the room. So powerful was its presence that even Boxer couldn't stop himself from trembling as the Colombian snorted more coke and his face darkened, losing all expression so that anyone who looked into it would know that an appeal for humanity was wasted breath. The Colombian's lightless eyes fell on the naked and trembling figure in the corner of the room, as she desperately tried to make herself a part of the wall.

'Now you,' said El Osito, 'get on top of your father.'

Boxer, his face contorted with pain and shock, jerked his head off the bed and, straining against his cuffs, roared at the Colombian. What part of this monster's mind had been so ruined that he could bring such a hideous image to mind? It seemed too terrible for this to be any ordinary hatred, but was rather some dark, ancient, atavistic horror which had been released to take its revenge on humanity.

'I can't take this any more,' roared Jaime in Spanish.

He ripped out the Walther PPK from inside his jacket. Vicente had told him to wait until El Osito had killed the Englishman, but this was too much. He aimed at the back of El Osito's head, pulled the trigger. The noise was so loud in the hard confines of the room that for a while nobody could hear anything except the high-pitched whine of evil receding.

Mercy was sprinting down the length of the warehouse. She swung round the door jamb at the end, ricocheted off the walls of the alleyway and, as she reached the top step going down into the basement, heard the gunshot. It was as if she herself had been hit. Her body stiffened, her eyes widened, her mouth opened but no scream came out.

The firearms officer had put down his carbine and drawn his Glock 17. He pulled open the door and threw himself forward low down. At the end of the corridor he saw the Mexican with a gun in his hand, smoke still coming from the barrel.

That was when Jaime really wished he had better English. He turned, raising his arms without dropping the weapon, but holding it up in the flat of his hand. The firearms officer took no chances and shot him twice in the chest. In seconds he was on him, checking the room, saw a man in a wheelchair slumped forward, blood on the wall beyond. He had his gun out in front of him as he came through the door and beyond the hard edge of his sight saw another man, naked, tied to a bed frame, and a girl, naked and foetal, lying on the floor, shivering as if freezing cold.

'Cut me loose,' said Boxer, hoarse from screaming.

The firearms officer pulled a Bowie knife from its thigh holster and cut the four plastic cuffs. Boxer tried to stand, found he had nothing in his legs and fell on his knees. He crawled on all fours to his daughter, held her, kissed her shoulder.

'We're OK,' he whispered in her ear. 'We made it.'

Mercy burst into the room, saw Boxer's naked back covered in burn marks and realised that he was bent over Amy on the floor.

'Is she all right?' she said, panic-stricken, dropping to her knees.

She touched her daughter's face. Amy was nodding and crying. In one hand she held her father's fingers, in the other she gripped her mother's hand, wasn't going to let go, ever.

33

Mercy was sitting in Makepeace's office in the same black leather chair she'd occupied just over a week ago, when she'd been told that her daughter had been murdered. She could barely believe her emotional transformation: one moment facing a lifetime of loss and devastation, the next miraculously happy.

Makepeace was on the double sofa. Between them was an empty armchair waiting to be filled by James Kidd, who was coming to give them 'a full explanation' of what had happened last Friday.

'How's Amy?' asked Makepeace.

'Getting better,' said Mercy. 'She couldn't bear to be alone for the first three or four days, had to sleep in my bed. If I left her even for a minute she'd come and find me, even if she was deeply asleep and I'd just gone to the bathroom. Completely traumatised. She reverted to childlike behaviour. I got a psychologist involved from the start and she's coming round now. And she's ... she's been ...'

Makepeace reached for his coffee, nodded her on.

'She's been incredibly loving too,' said Mercy, struggling with the emotion rising in her chest at the thought of how her little girl had been returned to her. 'To both of us. Charlie's been very good with her. She wriggles under his arm on the sofa and puts her head on his chest as if he's the pillar in her life. They talk ... endlessly, as if they've never talked before. As if the whole thing has started again from scratch.'

'That's very ... gratifying,' said Makepeace, unable to find a bigger word for the experience.

'Amy's biggest problem is guilt. It's going to be a while before she can forgive herself. She can't bear to think of what happened to Chantrelle. Even though the autopsy revealed she hadn't actually been murdered, she knows the terror she must have gone through. The dismemberment has caused a lot of trouble too. The psychologist is trying to unpick the confusion over her responsibility for that, which she's stitched into her own mind.'

'And what about Chantrelle's mother?'

'She didn't know her so well and there was a long history of trouble between Chantrelle and Alice, so the relationship wasn't there. She's appalled at how Alice died and again feels guilty because it's as a consequence of her behaviour, but it's not with the same intensity as for Chantrelle,' said Mercy. 'Did I tell you that she wants to do weekend work at Charlie's LOST Foundation? I think that would good for the guilt, you know, helping to find other kids who've lost their way.'

'And what about her grandmother?'

'She could hardly bear to face her. We took her to the Royal Free and had to practically drag her into Esme's room. If Esme had died I think Amy would have been suicidal.'

'I'm surprised that in running away she was prepared to leave Esme.'

'That was interesting or, rather, frustrating,' said Mercy. 'Amy did go back at one point to ask her advice, but Esme was already in hospital by then, and when she heard Charlie's voice on the video intercom she ducked away from the camera. If she'd stayed we'd have all been saved a lot of trauma.'

'And how is Esme?'

'She was discharged Thursday morning. Charlie and Amy went up there to settle her back in and Amy stayed the night. The first time she's been away from me. The psychologist says it's a good development.'

'It's been a journey,' said Makepeace.

'Not quite the one any of us expected,' said Mercy. 'But strangely the rewards have been amazing. I wouldn't want to go through it again, but ... well, my mother would have made it out to be something religious. You know, human suffering and faith resulting in greater self-knowledge.'

'And you?'

'It's been a lesson in consequences,' said Mercy. 'And what resulted from those consequences gave us the ability to show the people we really are.'

'And what about Charlie?' asked Makepeace. 'Has he been to the psychologist?

'You've got to be joking,' said Mercy. 'This is why he got into the kidnap game. He has to be where it all matters. He loves it.'

'You know what I mean, Mercy,' said Makepeace. 'How did he get himself into that situation? That was a big lesson in consequences, if ever I heard one.'

'He did what he thought was going to be best for Amy and he was prepared to sacrifice himself to achieve it.'

'I read the transcript of the interview with Dennis Chilcott,' said Makepeace. 'It was very revealing about Charlie, as I'm sure you know.'

'Then why ask me?'

'Because I wanted to know if Charlie explained his behaviour in Madrid to you,' said Makepeace. 'He smashed a man's legs up with a baseball bat.'

'He said he lost it, out there on his own, when he saw that Colombian drug baron strutting his stuff around the place, having murdered our daughter, cut her up, thrown her away. Then taking another girl back to his apartment to do exactly same thing. He wanted to punish him. Make him understand the pain he'd caused.'

'Is that it?'

'That's what he told me,' said Mercy, holding up her hands in surrender.

Makepeace nodded, drank some coffee, offered more to Mercy, poured some for himself too.

'You mentioned Chilcott,' said Mercy. 'What's been the fallout from taking those two into custody?'

'Well, on that particular score the kidnap unit has come out very well,' said Makepeace. 'The project team in the Special and Organised Crime Command have earned themselves some international recognition for closing down the Chilcotts, who they knew nothing about until the Lomax interview. These guys were bringing in two and a half tons of cocaine a year and half of it was being made into crack. They were just about to step up their imports to three and a half tons, arriving in containers at Liverpool docks, with the help of El Osito. The Madrid drug squad are happy because they've picked up Jaime's brother and closed down Vicente Carrillo Fuentes's container business into Algeciras. We've definitely come out smelling of roses on that one. It's our own backyard that's been left stinking.'

'Talking about stinking backyards. What about Lomax?' said Mercy.

'That was an embarrassment,' said Makepeace.

'He wouldn't have gone back through the warehouse,' said Mercy. 'When the shooting started, he was in the alleyway. I saw him there. He'd just brought Darren Chilcott into the warehouse. Two of the firearms officers were at the bottom of the basement steps and the other two were in the warehouse guarding the Chilcotts and their driver. When I went down into the basement he was left on his own in the alleyway. He must have disappeared into the Rowland Estate and found another exit.'

'Well, he hasn't showed up on any CCTV in the area so far.'

'Oddly enough, Amy got quite fond of him.'

'Fond?'

'Bit of a crush. They hit it off in a Stockholm syndrome kind of way,' said Mercy, shrugging. 'She said she learned a lot from him.'

'From a drug dealer?' said Makepeace.

'Even drug dealers have to have ... interpersonal skills,' said Mercy.

Makepeace checked his watch and ate a biscuit, as if thinking of better things.

'So what are we expecting to get out of this meeting with James Kidd?' asked Mercy.

'Your guess is as good as mine,' said Makepeace. 'We're owed an explanation and no lesser person than the home secretary called me to say that Mr Kidd was coming here in the "spirit of openness", which I have to say sounds a bit diaphanous for my taste. I'd rather he came with some solid facts, along the lines of why the *fuck* he dumped my department so massively in the shit.'

Mercy wasn't sure whether she'd ever heard the DCS swear

before. She started looking forward to the meeting, had imagined it as some dull post-mortem, with MI5 playing their cards close to their chests, but it looked like the boss was going for the jugular.

James Kidd was shown in, hands were shaken, more coffee distributed.

'The home secretary called to say you were going to reveal all,' said Makepeace.

Kidd went very still as if this was not in his script.

'As you're aware, we agreed to your presence in the negotiating phase of the kidnap because we hoped for an insight into the nature of the gang we were dealing with: criminal or FSB-inspired,' said Makepeace. 'We also gave your operative the ultimate responsibility for bringing the boy's kidnap to a safe conclusion because of the unarmed combat expertise required. You agreed to look after Bobkov in the endgame and we supplied you with all the information necessary to bring that about.

'I certainly don't like the way things *did* turn out. But what really enrages me, Mr Kidd, is that the people in my department have somehow been blamed, in the massive media coverage of this event, for a "botched kidnap negotiation".'

'They weren't quoting me,' said Kidd.

'Somebody told them that something went wrong in the negotiating process, which resulted in Sasha being fatally wounded in the house and Bobkov senior being shot as he was handing over the ransom.'

'We don't talk to the media.'

'Now let's get things straight, Mr Kidd. First of all, we *know* Sasha survived the rescue. The police marksmen saw to that. Mercy escorted him out of the house, spoke to Sasha in the ambulance while they checked him out and travelled with him to Charing Cross Hospital explaining to the poor kid how his mother had died. By the time Mercy got out of the ambulance in front of the hospital he wasn't in any physical distress at all. However, when we called to get an update on his condition later that night, we were told that he was dead on arrival and none of the paramedics responsible for his welfare during the ambulance journey can be traced.'

'Shock can have a devastating and delayed effect on the system,' said Kidd. 'Also the kidnappers had been using drugs to keep him sedated, and these can have a catastrophic effect on blood pressure and heart rate.'

'At least you admit he wasn't fatally wounded,' said Makepeace.

'Sasha was in perfectly good shape when I left him,' said Mercy.

'Secondly,' said Makepeace, on a roll, 'Bobkov senior was *your* responsibility, Mr Kidd. You made the cockeyed decision to carry on with the drop when it was completely unnecessary. I, personally, called you to let you know that we had suspects for interrogation ...'

Kidd held up both hands to halt the tsunami of accusations. The DCS eased up, sat back on the sofa.

'I couldn't pull Bobkov senior for operational reasons,' said Kidd.

'That doesn't mean anything,' said Makepeace. 'You're going to have to do a lot better than that.'

'All right, let's go back a few days,' said Kidd, taking control. 'The real game-changer for us was when Mercy revealed that Irina Demidova had penetrated the offices of DLT Consultants, as Zlata Yankov,' said Kidd. 'As soon as we heard that we knew this was an FSB operation, which meant it became an MI5 operation and that meant certain operational developments could not be discussed openly with you.'

'As your partners in the negotiating process, it would have been polite to have told us that you were taking this to a different operational level,' said Makepeace.

'Except that we wanted you to continue to perform exactly as if it were a normal kidnap, which was why we didn't tell you, for instance, that the DCRI, the French interior intelligence services, found Irina Demidova and her son Valery dead in a house in a small village outside Fontainebleau,' said Kidd. 'To have given you the bigger picture then could have compromised our plan.'

'Which was?' said Mercy, rattled by Kidd's latest disclosure.

'I can't reveal that to you.'

'Not acceptable,' said Makepeace. 'The home secretary gave me guarantees.'

'Let me put it this way,' said Kidd. 'Once we were given the news about Professor Statnik and Igor Tipalov being killed in

Russia, we had to accept that our intelligence cell's cover had been blown and that Andrei Bobkov would now become a target himself. We therefore decided on a course of preventative action.'

Silence. Mercy and Makepeace exchanged looks.

'So Bobkov was working for British intelligence,' said Makepeace, 'rather than under his own steam?'

Nothing from Kidd. Silence, punctuated only by the tapping of his fingers on the leather arms of his chair.

'The fact that you wanted us to continue to perform normally, as the Met kidnap unit,' said Mercy slowly, thinking out loud, 'does that mean you *intended* it to look like a botched negotiation?'

Still nothing from Kidd.

'Was it important for their future safety that the outside world believed that Bobkov senior was shot and Sasha was fatally wounded and DOA at Charing Cross?'

'I am unable to reveal any MI5 operational detail,' said Kidd, looking her directly in the eye, expressionless.

She smiled at him. He winked, but she wasn't quite sure whether it was that tic of his or if he was confirming her suspicions.

34

It was early afternoon and it still hadn't rained. Boxer and Mercy had been banished to the sitting room by Isabel, who had never mastered the ability to cook and talk at the same time. The television was on, as it was in most UK households during the Olympics. Sweden was playing Argentina at handball, an unlikely attraction, but there was always someone riveted at some point. Three bottles of wine stood on the table, two red and one white, all of which had been opened. Boxer was drinking a beer and Mercy was on her first glass of Rioja.

'So, you and Isabel,' said Mercy. 'Four months. That's a record, isn't it?'

'In the post-Mercy era, yes, it is,' said Boxer. 'How are you getting on with young Marcus?'

'No need to make him sound like a schoolboy, just because he's younger than me.'

'So when do you think you'll be able to take him to SCD 7's Christmas party?' asked Boxer. 'I can just see him offering the DCS a toke ...'

'Don't go there, Charlie,' said Mercy, smiling.

'You know what I'm saying,' said Boxer. 'He's a nice guy and he's been good for you, but I know what you're like, and this isn't a career move.'

'I thought we were having a nice little family gathering where we didn't talk about things like ... guns under the floorboards, baseball bats and—'

Mercy shut up as Isabel came in with a tray of canapés, told them not to eat them all. The doorbell rang and she asked Boxer to deal with it.

It was Esme. Despite the sun breaking through the clouds, she was wearing a red mac with a matching umbrella.

'Lost your confidence?' said Boxer.

'I've tried and been soaked too often this summer,' said Esme, kissing him, handing over two bottles of white Montrachet with a look that told Boxer they were not for sharing.

He opened one and poured her a glass. She went into the kitchen, kissed Isabel and walked straight back out again without offering to help. They went into the sitting room.

The doorbell rang again. Mercy let in Marcus Alleyne. They kissed and hugged each other for a while because Mercy had been away on a course all week and hadn't seen him. He gave her two bottles of red, both 1999 *grand cru* burgundies.

'Where did these come from?' asked Mercy.

'Well, they didn't fall off the back of a lorry,' said Alleyne. 'I just put the word out that I wanted to take something special to a party and this is what came back. Don't know anything about it.'

'What if I told you a hundred and fifty quid a bottle?'

'I'd say, let's put them by the front door and take them home with us.'

She took him to the kitchen and introduced Isabel, who despite never having met him, kissed him on both cheeks.

'I'm half-Portuguese,' she said. 'If you're a friend of my friends you get kissed.'

'You hear me complaining?' said Alleyne.

They went in to the sitting room, where Mercy gave Boxer the two bottles of wine with a raised eyebrow.

'Bloody hell,' he said, looking at the labels.

Mercy introduced Esme. Alleyne shook her hand with a quick bow and a grin.

'You're the fence from Brixton, aren't you?' asked Esme.

'Me?' said Alleyne, innocent as the day.

'I was just wondering if you could get me a decent pair of trainers. Size six. Nikes?'

'Would that be for running, gym or tennis?'

'I didn't realise it would be *that* complicated,' said Esme. 'Can we smoke in here?'

'No,' said Boxer. 'There's a patio out the back, through the dining room.'

Isabel brought in more canapés and a bottle of champagne.

Her daughter, Alyshia, and her boyfriend, Deepak, arrived as if they'd come straight off a Bollywood movie set. There were more introductions.

'Is she part Portuguese 'n' all?' asked Alleyne, mesmerised by Alyshia's beauty.

Kisses were exchanged, glasses filled. Isabel came in to drink some champagne. They were waiting for Amy now. Esme headed for the garden. Alleyne joined her. Isabel went back to the kitchen. The smell of weed drifted into the sitting room from outside. Mercy rapped on the French windows.

'Come on, Marcus,' she said.

'Don't be such a spoilsport,' said Esme.

Mercy gave her one of her dead-eyed looks and backed away.

The canapés were almost finished when Amy arrived alone. Esme and Alleyne came back into the sitting room, Esme giggling, Alleyne with his beatific Rastafarian grin. Amy was kissed and hugged by everyone and they immediately went in to the dining room to eat. Amy sat next to Mercy, who looked at her questioning.

'I got delayed at LOST,' said Amy. 'You know what it's like.'

'I thought we were going to meet ... Josh?'

'He didn't want to come,' she said, shrugging as if it wasn't her fault.

'You told him it was informal,' said Mercy, 'that we weren't going to measure him up for a morning suit.'

'I told him,' said Amy. 'He's just being Josh. Which means ... complicated.'

They started with clams and mussels in white-wine sauce. Boxer took personal charge of Esme's bottle of Montrachet to ensure her exclusivity. The main course was one of Isabel's Portuguese specialities – *borrego assado* – slow-cooked lamb over roast potatoes. They drank the burgundy, which made everything else taste like rubbish afterwards, and Isabel proposed a toast: 'To families, and to quote Dickens, one of our greatest Londoners, "Accidents can occur in the best-regulated families."'

They finished with home-made almond tart and ice cream, and Isabel produced a decanter of vintage port.

The television was on constantly, sometimes unwatched and then occasionally drawing half the room.

By evening most people had left. Isabel was taking a siesta upstairs while Boxer, Mercy and Alleyne, having cleared away the tea, had cracked open the beers.

'You've got to see this,' said Amy from in front of the television. 'Jessica's running her eight hundred metres now.'

Amy, who had never admitted to admiring anybody, had developed a passion for the British heptathlete Jessica Ennis, not just because of some mixed-race sisterhood, but also because she could see that the success of the London games had fallen squarely on her shoulders. Amy wanted to see Ennis triumph, and when she saw her coming off the final bend and refusing to accept third place, she went delirious.

'You show 'em, sistah!' she yelled, her fists punching the air, jumping up and down, engulfed by the noise of the crowd roaring in the stadium.

She'd barely recovered when it was Mo Farah's turn to run the ten thousand metres against the Kenyans and Ethiopians, to show that the boy from Hounslow, via Mogadishu, had the right stuff. There wasn't a moment in the race when any one of ten men couldn't win it, until the bell for the final lap, when eighty thousand people stood up in the stadium, along with twenty million in their homes, and decided that this was Mo's moment. They turned the sound up for the last lap, and Boxer, Amy, Mercy and Alleyne were screaming and leaping, hollering and roaring at the top of their lungs. GO, MO! GO, MO! GO, MO! They lost themselves in the euphoria of the moment, in a noise so loud they couldn't hear each other shout, the four of them jumping up and down together, in unison with the tumult.

'Did we win something?' asked Isabel, bewildered, stumbling into the room.

ACKNOWLEDGEMENTS

This is not so much an acknowledgement but more an admission of a huge debt and a massive gap in my life. Those of you who notice these things will have seen on the dedication page that my wife of twenty-seven years passed away after a hard-fought and courageous battle against leukemia. This was the last book she worked on. Her first symptoms started the day after we sent *You Will Never Find Me* to Orion.

It's no exaggeration to say that Jane made me into the writer I am today. She helped with research, she was a brilliant sounding board for ideas, and she was my first reader. She taught me how to write female characters, what to cut and what worked, and she told me the brutal truth, but . . . with love. In the long process of writing she always encouraged me and gave me total support. She was an instinctive editor because she was a voracious reader (she'd 'done' the Russians by the age of twelve when I'd barely started on the English) and she had phenomenal judgement. She was also tireless. She read and re-read my work over and over and it didn't leave the house until we were both satisfied.

When asked what on earth she did out in the depths of rural Portugal while I was writing she always replied very modestly: 'I do the stroking.'

I'll miss all that stroking.

She will always be in my heart.

ABOUT THE AUTHOR

Robert Wilson has worked across the world, including spells ship-broking, tourguiding and exporting bathrooms to Nigeria. After escaping car crashes, civil wars and angry baboons, he settled in Portugal. Since then, he's written ten acclaimed crime novels including the CWA Gold Dagger award winner, *A Small Death in Lisbon*, and the CWA shortlisted *Capital Punishment*.